ALIEN™
THE COLD FORGE

THE COMPLETE ALIEN™ LIBRARY FROM TITAN BOOKS
THE OFFICIAL MOVIE NOVELIZATIONS BY ALAN DEAN FOSTER:
ALIEN
ALIENS™
ALIEN: COVENANT
ALIEN: COVENANT ORIGINS

ALIEN: RESURRECTION BY A.C. CRISPIN

ALIEN™: OUT OF THE SHADOWS BY TIM LEBBON
ALIEN: SEA OF SORROWS BY JAMES A. MOORE
ALIEN: RIVER OF PAIN BY CHRISTOPHER GOLDEN
ALIEN: THE COLD FORGE BY ALEX WHITE

THE RAGE WAR BY TIM LEBBON:
PREDATOR™: INCURSION
ALIEN: INVASION
ALIEN VS. PREDATOR™: ARMAGEDDON

THE COMPLETE ALIENS OMNIBUS, VOLUME 1
BY STEVE AND STEPHANI PERRY
THE COMPLETE ALIENS OMNIBUS, VOLUME 2
BY DAVID BISCHOFF AND ROBERT SHECKLEY
THE COMPLETE ALIENS OMNIBUS, VOLUME 3
BY SANDY SCHOFIELD AND S.D. PERRY
THE COMPLETE ALIENS OMNIBUS, VOLUME 4
BY YVONNE NAVARRO AND S.D. PERRY
THE COMPLETE ALIENS OMNIBUS, VOLUME 5
BY MICHAEL JAN FRIEDMAN AND DIANE CAREY

THE COMPLETE ALIENS VS. PREDATOR OMNIBUS
BY STEVE PERRY AND S.D. PERRY

ALIEN: THE ILLUSTRATED STORY
BY ARCHIE GOODWIN AND WALTER SIMONSON
ALIEN: THE ARCHIVE
THE ART OF ALIEN: ISOLATION BY ANDY MCVITTIE
ALIEN: THE SET PHOTOGRAPHY BY SIMON WARD
THE ART AND MAKING OF ALIEN: COVENANT
BY SIMON WARD
**ALIEN: COVENANT, THE OFFICIAL
COLLECTOR'S EDITION**
ALIEN NEXT DOOR BY JOEY SPIOTTO
ALIEN: THE COLORING BOOK

ALIEN™

THE COLD FORGE

A NOVEL BY ALEX WHITE

TITAN BOOKS

ALIEN™: THE COLD FORGE
Print edition ISBN: 9781785651946
E-book edition ISBN: 9781785651953
Published by Titan Books
A division of Titan Publishing Group Ltd
144 Southwark Street, London SE1 0UP

First edition: April 2018
10 9 8 7 6 5 4 3 2 1

A CIP catalogue record for this title is available from the British Library.

Printed and bound in the United States.

Did you enjoy this book?
We love to hear from our readers. Please email us at readerfeedback@
titanemail.com or write to us at Reader Feedback at the above address.

To receive advance information, news, competitions, and exclusive offers online, please sign up for the Titan newsletter on our website
www.titanbooks.com

DEDICATION

To Stephen, Matt, and Kelsey: my Three Musketeers.
I'm not sure which ones of you are which,
though, so don't ask.

1

LINE ITEMS

ENCRYPTED TRANSMISSION
LISTENING POST AED1413-23
DATE: 2179.07.20

(Unspecified A): Have located indigo flag.
(Unspecified B): How close are they?
(Unspecified A): Very.
(Unspecified B): Acknowledged. Execute.

Dorian Sudler knows he shouldn't smoke.

Jana, the shipyard doctor, complains about it every time she sees him. She'll be in to check on him before he goes down into his cryo pod, and he enjoys the look on her face when he does something she hates—pleasure from displeasure.

Maybe he should try to fuck her before going away. She'll probably let him if he says he's depressed about the looming year-long sleep. No, he has work to do before he goes under, and his bosses have expectations. Just as he shouldn't smoke, the director of special resources shouldn't be fraternizing with employees during an audit.

His quarters are nice, even if he hasn't used his bed recreationally on this trip. He's enjoyed painting the Earthrise, viewing it through the station's large panoramic windows, the sharp blue heavy against the gray craters of the moon's surface. It's a lovely view, because it's a reflection of the power and respect he deserves.

Dorian's slender fingers flicker across the keyboard, running a query concerning the Luna shipyard rightsizing. He finds a healthy organization, green with profits and productivity, and he smiles. He's cut off the dead leaves, and now life can grow anew. Weyland-Yutani stock will expand one tenth of a percentage point. If nine other directors do as well as him, trillions of dollars will slosh into Weyland-Yutani coffers.

Scanning through the line items, he looks for any last people on the cusp, people whose performance has been less than stellar. Thirty percent of the way down the page he finds Jana's name, highlighted in yellow on his bowling chart. There were two major insurance claims this past month, and it is her job to head off those sorts of problems—like smoking, for instance. Dorian ticks off her name, running a simulated personnel roster with a fresh doctor, and finds fewer medical claims. He tags her to be fired by email, scheduling it to occur the week after next, once he is long gone. Luna security and human resources can handle the details.

He indicates "poor performance" as the cause.

On the fifty-seventh line he finds Alphonse Kanner, a branch manager in the turbine machining division. Alphonse killed himself last week when he learned of his impending termination at Dorian's hands. The program lists Kanner as a wash, neither profitable nor a loss.

But that's wrong.

Dorian snatches his cigarette out of the ashtray and sucks hard, burning it down to the bitter filter before stubbing it out with trembling hands. Smoke hisses out through his nose as he grits his teeth. The computer is wrong.

Alphonse Kanner has a two-million-dollar company life insurance policy, purchased on his eighteenth birthday. He made the payments and it continued in perpetuity, regardless of employment status. It would cost the banking division significantly more than the average loss of an employee. If he'd died due to an on-station accident, it would've been even worse.

Hands blur across the keyboard again. Dorian finds Kanner's contract, signed and certified by some idiot more than two decades ago. Clicking from one link to the next, he locates the insurance policy, opens it, and rapidly scans the terms. He lets out a shaking breath, because he's right, as always.

Suicide exempts Kanner from the payout. Even better, it came before he ratified the generous severance package they'd offered him. So no, Kanner isn't a wash. He's a two-million-dollar score that Dorian, not banking, brought home.

Muscles tense, Dorian rubs his clenched fists against his suit trousers. The banking operations unit will receive credit for the diminishing trend in payouts, but this is Dorian's win. He considers adding a comment to the line item, perhaps firing off a message to his superiors, but he's here to save billions, not millions. He can't sweat the small stuff.

"Dorian." A voice comes from his open door.

Jana is there, standing ready, clipboard in hand. He smiles, then considers his anger, and introduces a pained quirk to his lips. He needs to blow off some steam.

"You okay, buddy?"

Dorian shuts his computer screen. "Can I be honest for a moment?"

She places her hands on her hips and smirks. "This had better not be a last-minute pass."

He stands, stretches out his arms, and strides over to her, his fine Italian shoes heel-toe clicking. He has an impressive height for such an avian frame. No one expects him to be as large or strong as he is—not when they see him at a distance. Jana ever so slightly draws her arms in close. He has wide shoulders, and when he is two paces away from her he thrusts his hands into his pockets, elbows out, thumbs hooked into his trousers. He wants her to know that he could surround her, devour her.

"I just wanted to talk… to you, specifically." He gives her a practiced, pained smile. "Everyone hates me, doctor—I'm fully aware of it. I spend most of my days on a ship… mostly in cold sleep. Then I come out and rightsize an organization. Then I go back to sleep."

She cocks an eyebrow, but doesn't back away. He's read her correctly.

"Everyone has a job to do," she says.

"All I ever see are people's personal tragedies." Dorian's gaze wanders out the window, as though he can't make himself look her in the eye. He bites his lip. "You can smell it on me."

But she's smelling his something else. Scent is the strongest mnemonic, and he wonders what baggage comes with his.

"Cigarette smoke," she says with a coy smile. "Not personal tragedies. And speaking of cigarettes, do you have another?"

Dorian's eyes lock with hers, and he feigns a grin.

"I thought you didn't smoke, Doctor."

She shrugs and takes a step closer. "Everyone has a job to do. Mine is promoting a 'healthy work environment,' but I'm about to be off the clock."

In all of her cajoling and admonishment, she'd been lying. How could he have missed that? What *else* had slipped past him? There's a flash of heat in his gut—not lust, but anger. Between this and Kanner, the whole damned outpost ought to be scuttled. They're doing things wrong.

"I'm not stupid, you know," she says. The liar steps closer to him and touches the top of his tie. "I know what you want." She hooks her finger into it, gently pulling it loose. "It's obvious, and we're probably never going to see each other again."

The liar slips his tie free. She can't see the fists at Dorian's sides. She's taken the power from him... or at least tried.

"I can settle for the cigarette after," she says, moving in for a kiss. When her lips are almost upon his, he looks down his nose at her.

"You've misread the situation, Doctor," he says. "I only wanted to talk to a friend, and this behavior is highly inappropriate."

Her face flushes as mortification creeps in. She glows with the beauty of someone who has lost all leverage. Dorian feels a powerful urge to bed her in that second, but then she'll assume he was insincere about "wanting to talk." No, he can't ruin this perfection.

She stammers something and turns away. It takes all his control to keep the smile from his face.

"I trust you can be professional about this," he says. "Everyone makes mistakes."

"Okay, yeah," she says. "Yes, of course."

"I'll be in the cryo tube in an hour, and you can forget all about this unfortunate incident."

Maybe Jana will be able to. Maybe he'll remain a minor source of embarrassment for a few days, and then disappear from her mind. In two weeks the factory supervisor will call her into his office and gently break the news that she's been let go.

Stepping through the door, she leaves, and he appends her termination order to state that she made a pass at him, which is inappropriate for a medical professional.

Her termination letter indicates that she is not to collect unemployment insurance, or he will file a sexual harassment charge against her. Weyland-Yutani's margins will improve an infinitesimal fraction of a percentage point.

Dorian checks his itinerary. His next stop is RB-232, his arrival a year from today. Whatever it is, it's classified, and he'll be briefed on site. The cause of his audit: "poor performance." He reads further, and smiles.

There's a problem on RB-232; it's worth billions of dollars.

Closing his eyes, he takes a long breath, stilling his heart. Scientists are fun to fire. They think they're too smart to be disposable. He'll have that place running like oil on water in no time.

The chimpanzee is screaming again. It won't go near the egg.

Blue Marsalis wonders how it knows that death awaits within. Her lab technicians have been so careful not to allow the animals to witness one another's impregnations. Watching from her side of the thick tempered glass, she grows impatient with the beast. There's a schedule to keep.

She would've restrained the chimp, anesthetized it, but in the past the resultant embryos were less than spectacular. She thinks of the old butchers' tales, that a frightened sheep produces sour meat. The face-huggers prefer their meat sour, as do the snatchers that come from them.

"Get in there, you little shit," Kambili Okoro, her regular lab assistant, says. He runs a rough hand over his stubble, pulling at his dark skin—a nervous habit.

"Keep it together," she replies in a male voice not her own. This body doesn't belong to her. "We can't miss the moment."

"Why don't you just man up, go in there, and shove the bastards together?" he asks. "Those things usually leave androids alone."

Blue stands up straighter and gives him a nasty look. This is the fourth time this week her lab tech has told her to "man up." Kambili has been a consistent problem since he came to the Cold Forge, largely because he can't be replaced. There are few Weyland-Yutani geneticists with his classified credentials, and even if there were more, the next crew rotation isn't for another year. She's stuck with him. He knows it.

"That's a panicked chimpanzee," Blue says. "It can apply six hundred kilograms of ripping strength, and do so with ease."

Kambili shrugs, still watching through the sample collection area's window. "So can you."

"Have you ever had your arms ripped off?"

He sighs around his chewing gum. "Obviously not."

"Marcus's body is fully equipped with pain receptors. When that happens, I will feel it."

"Then don't let it happen," he says.

Blue cocks her head and wrinkles her nose. "If I damage this body, I'm not going to be able to get around the station. It's not like we get resupplied every day." She pauses, and then adds, "I'd appreciate it if you'd stop with the 'man up' talk, too. I didn't choose this body. It's the one the Company provided."

"Seems like you're enjoying it," he mumbles.

"What did you say?" she asks, but she heard him perfectly well. Blue's ears pick up the lightest vibrations. She hates him for being right.

He gives her a glance, taking in her light complexion, strong jawline, and male build. She can tell he's appraising her body—known as Marcus—and its many uses. These are things he has no right to consider. She's seen it before from the other station personnel, and she hates him for it. His mouth widens into a grin, and he starts to laugh.

The screaming stops.

They missed the opening of the egg.

The chimp thrashes about on the ground, but already the face-hugger is delivering its lethal payload. The primate wraps a paw around the yellowed tail that encircles its neck, pulling with inhuman strength, but can't budge it at all. Its slapping slows as the creature chokes it out, and it stumbles against the wall, sinking onto its belly.

It happens so fast, within the span of three breaths.

"Fuck!" Kambili says. "Go!" He slams the release button to flash freeze the chimp chamber. Jets of icy liquid nitrogen fill the space, instantly bringing the temperature down as Blue races around the console to get to the telesurgical systems. She sinks her arms into the robotic stirrups and a pair of silvery articulators descend from the ceiling.

Using the surgical arms, she shoves the chimp onto its back. Its hair already is rimed with ice crystals. Deftly switching through the modes, she arrives at the surgical laser and slides the hot point down its stomach, tearing away the skin. Another two tics on the modes brings her the bone saw.

"Time?" she calls out.

"Twelve seconds," Kambili says.

She places the bone saw against the chimp's exposed sternum, but the world lists to one side and clicks into place. At first, Blue thinks her telesurgical system has locked up. It wouldn't be the first time the station has experienced equipment failure in the middle of an important experiment.

But then she has the nauseating sensation of falling upward, while having her head turned against her will. Her hands clench and in response the bone saw impales the ill-fated primate, sending up a spray of blood and bile. It spatters against the metal deck before freezing in place.

"Wha… thfu—man?" Kambili's shout is disjointed and stammering.

The world won't stop spinning. Blue falls to her knees, but the ground beneath her gives her no sense of direction. Gravity still works—all the styluses and pads remain firmly affixed to the lab tables—but the spinning world accelerates.

"Thiiiiiiiiii—nk itsa—" she begins to say, but that's as

much coordination as she can muster. The gaze of one eye drifts toward the ceiling while the other remains in place.

The lab dims out.

Blue comes out of it, and the first thing she detects is the scent of shit. Her lungs don't want to draw air. She goes to grasp the helmet, but her fingers don't want to collaborate. Another jolt sends her forward in the bed, and she retches up bile.

She gasps, drinking in the cold air like pure water on a hot day. Her hoarse, whimpering voice startles her. Trying again to wrap her saliva-slicked fingers around her helmet, this time she pulls it off. It moves with a sucking pop. She can't hold up the six-pound assembly of wires and electrodes, so she hugs it to her so it won't fall onto the floor.

Blue is back in her room, shaking uncontrollably, the brain-direct interface gear resting atop her in a mound of sick. Exhausted, she wipes her mouth with her free hand and lies back in the hospital bed. It's dark, but for a small night-light in the corner. She keeps it that way when she rides inside Marcus, so her real eyes won't try to see.

She hears the banging of distant boots, and it draws nearer, heavy and fast.

"Marcus," she says, but it only comes out in a moaning whisper.

The android rounds the corner in a flash, taking the BDI gear away from her and snatching up a towel to clean her face and neck. He wipes her down, and then places the helmet at her bedside. The rest of her remains spattered with vomit.

"I'm okay," she croaks, but he peers over her, making absolutely sure.

"I'm going to turn on the lights, Blue," he says in a gentle voice. "Are you ready?"

She shuts her eyes and nods. Red light filters in through her eyelids. A warm hand comes to rest on her forehead.

"I'm afraid we have quite a mess," Marcus says. "Can you open your eyes for me?" She does, even though the bright ceiling lights are like glass shards in her brain. Marcus leans across her bed, gazing into her eyes, not remotely concerned about the sticky mess of bodily fluids touching his clothes.

He's beautiful, but not attractive—clear green eyes like emeralds, high cheekbones descending into a stern jawline. Above his perpetually sympathetic brow, wavy blond hair catches the light. She expects to feel his breath on her face as he draws closer, even though she knows he doesn't respire.

"Pupillary response is normal," he says, pressing two fingers into her neck. "Pulse one-twelve."

"Water?" She smacks her lips.

He fills a cup and passes it to her. "It seems we've gotten our exercise today."

She swishes the bitterness from her mouth and swallows, some of the liquid dribbling down the sides of her chin. It doesn't matter. Marcus will have to give her a sponge bath, anyway.

"What happened?"

"Wireless connection loss, possibly from a solar flare," he says. "You were only synchronizing with two of my systems at a time, and that threw our balance by a considerable—"

She shakes her head. "With sample sixty-three… Did Kambili…"

"I'm sorry to say that it was a failure," Marcus says. "We lost the sample."

She shuts her eyes again. "Fuck."

Marcus picks up the interface headset and begins to clean it. He stops short and gazes at her abdomen.

"You've dislodged your pouch," he says. "You may have done it during a seizure, caused by the disconnection."

At least her catheter didn't come out. She remembers a time when she didn't need colostomy bags. She remembers pizza and beer every Friday. She remembers being an avid jogger at Johns Hopkins. She had a life before her diagnosis—a trajectory that should've kept her on Earth.

Blue doesn't look down to see the results. "Clean it up, please."

"Right away," he says, filling a cup with warm water and a few drops of disinfectant. Marcus removes the broken pouch and cleans away the excess. Gently swabbing at the area around her stoma, he makes a pained face.

"What?" she says. He's programmed to make that face when giving bad news.

"I really think you should consider going full NPO regimen, Blue," he says. "I'm concerned about laryngeal spasms."

Nil-per-os. Nothing by mouth. Blue juts out her chin, and she feels something of her own surly grandmother in that gesture. "I'm not giving up my goddamned Jello, Marcus."

"Then consider…" he says, pausing and pretending to think. Marcus already has identified the next thousand branches of the conversation, but she knows he pauses for dramatic effect. "Consider returning to Earth. You could remain in cold sleep, or if that's not appealing, Earth has excellent palliative care. I don't believe it's healthy for a person to spend their waning hours designing weapons."

She grunts as he hits a tender spot. Her stoma has changed shape due to the constant bedrest, and the area around the appliance has gone slightly red. He's right about the NPO, but she won't allow it. Not as close as she is.

"'Waning hours?' God, you sound like one of those old poetry-quoting models. Like a Walter or something. Have you got some William Carlos Williams for me?"

He gives her a bashful look. "That wasn't my intent." Gently peeling her hospital gown off her emaciated arms, he sponges her off. She'd been so proud of her body once. She'd shared it with so many people.

"Besides," she says, "you're Company property, and I'm a major asset. You should be trying to convince me to stay."

He clips another bag onto her abdomen and tightens the connection with a kind smile. Then he replaces her gown with a fresh one. "I'm directed to keep you safe, above all else."

She reaches up and touches his cheek with a quivering hand, its muscles atrophied from her condition. "And what do you do when safety isn't an option?"

"Then I keep you happy."

"I'm a scientist," she says. "I'm the happiest when I'm doing my job." She taps his forehead. "Up here." Her hand comes to rest at her side. "Anyway, there's not a resupply for another six months. How do you expect me to get back?"

"We could freeze you. Await transport. You'd awaken at home as if no time had passed. And you're wrong about the lack of transport. The Commander has authorized me to inform you that an auditor is docking in three weeks."

"What?" Blue would've sat up if her abdominal muscles weren't in such pain.

"I apologize," he says. "I simply wasn't authorized to share that information before now. I'm concerned about the amount of stress this has placed on you."

"Why is an auditor flying out?"

"I haven't been told. I'm sure it's nothing serious, but they could be concerned about the slow progress here at the Cold Forge. Several projects are behind schedule."

"My project."

"And Silversmile," Marcus says. "I'm sure you're not the only—"

Blue shakes her head. "Give me my portable terminal, and get out."

Marcus picks up the terminal, places it in front of her, and takes an unceremonious leave. Blue waits until the door is closed, glaring at the open portal until she's safe. Then she unfolds the keyboard, balances it on her stomach, and logs into the digital drop. She isn't supposed to do it too often—it's dangerous if the station has too many outgoing signals—but something in this auditor's arrival chills her skin.

They can't know what Blue has been doing with the egg samples. Weyland-Yutani hired her to find a way to control the strange beasts, to manipulate their DNA in utero. Back on Earth, she had been one of the planet's leading geneticists. But now, far away in the stars, she has seen the brutal recombinant DNA of the creatures, and feels nothing but hope.

It first became apparent at the moment of impregnation. The fleeting heat of a molecular change within the esophagus of the chimpanzee, not a larva or worm placed into the subject, but a set of complex chemical instructions that went beyond the intricacy of anything humanity had ever seen.

Weyland-Yutani wants the creature, but Blue wants the code. Within it, she's certain she'll find the key to her survival. Yet capturing that injection is like a photographer trying to capture the moment a kingfisher enters the water—twinned beaks meeting across its mirrored surface. She could spend a decade with hundreds of eggs, and still meet with no success.

Blue doesn't have hundreds of eggs. She doesn't have a decade. The last doctor told her she didn't even have a year of life left in her. The last of her muscles will deteriorate. She'll cease to breathe on her own. Her nervous system will be pockmarked with sclerotic tissue. Neuropathy will take her legs.

She shakes the image from her head. Blue doesn't want to be thinking like this, but the auditor's presence has forced new pressures into her mind.

The terminal boots up in her hands, and she types in her password. The phrase isn't as long as she'd like, but her muscle memory simply isn't what it used to be. She's never logged into this terminal while inside of Marcus's body—he would remember. She's never allowed any cameras to capture the password.

Checking her personal inbox, she finds a message from an old high school friend, with a picture of Blue's mother, who passed away ten years prior. In it, Blue wraps her arms around her mother and smiles, and bright green trees wave in the background. A field of grain stretches away to their right.

The friend who sent the photo is an independent contractor, taking orders from an intermediary, taking orders from Elise Coto, one of the one hundred-twelve vice presidents of Weyland-Yutani. If Blue is discovered, she'll be terminated, with no right to passage home. She will be allowed to stow, but will have no access to a cryo pod.

It will kill her.

Blue removes her medical bracelet and snaps open the plate to reveal a micro interface bus connection. She plugs in the bracelet, which functions as a digital one-time pad. This smiling pastoral with her mother is picture A227-B, and hidden inside the picture are pixels that exhibit twenty-seven precise degrees of brightness variance—enough for the alphabet and some spaces. The cipher program maps the eight hundred relevant pixels and translates them.

Blue's heart catches as she reads the message.

```
              NEEDED RESULTS
          CANT PROTECT US ANYMORE
                GOOD LUCK
```

2

ARRIVAL

Electropolarization dims Dorian's window as he watches their approach to RB-232. The station becomes a silhouetted barbell against a sea of fire. His briefing indicates that, at one side of the barbell, are the crew quarters. At the other extreme lies the Sensitive Compartmented Information Facility, or SCIF. The light of Kaufmann, the system's star, gives the station a furious halo, and Dorian's brain quickly draws parallels between the hues of fusing matter and the oils in his easel case.

That halo also provides the perfect camouflage.

Setting aside the classified reports on RB-232, known as "the Cold Forge," he guzzles another bottle of the salty crap he drinks after every cold sleep. He's grown accustomed to the taste, because he loves cryo. With every voyage, he becomes more unstuck from his parents, his childhood friends, his days in Boston. This is his twentieth voyage.

He's killing his past a little bit more with each ticket.

He'd like to paint the transiting station, but it's all so plain—just a shadow on orange. Dorian wonders what it would look like if the heat shield failed, and for a split second the station's corridors and beams were placed into the ultimate radiance. What would that be like inside the station? He spends his next hour sketching, enjoying the stark contrast of black on white that comes from his conté crayons.

"Docking in fifteen, chief," Ken Riley, the *Athenian*'s captain, announces over the loudspeaker in the common area.

Dorian misses his room on Luna. Now *that* was a view. Here, he has only a cryosleep pod and public washing areas. There's no one on this ship Dorian considers fuckable, either. He's the only person who isn't essential to the transport's functioning. Riley flies, Susan Spiteri is the copilot, Montrell Lupia operates comms and navigation. They all act as Dorian's security detail while he executes his audit. He's never had need of their services to stop an insurgency, but he often visits remote locations to deliver very bad news. In his heart of hearts, he hopes to see Spiteri gun someone down one day.

It'd be entertaining, to say the least.

While the crew struggles to prepare the tiny vessel for docking, Dorian skives off in the lounge, pulls out his easel case, and enjoys a stint with his artwork, working his arms and thawing his bones from the long slumber. Sometimes, he wonders if he should've been a painter, but if he'd taken that route, he would have been denied the perk of having his life extended by the constant cold sleep.

According to the reports, there are thirty-two people on board the station, participating in three special projects. Two of them are behind schedule. One of them, "Glitter Edifice," is running out of funding and supplies. He doesn't know what "Glitter Edifice" is or what it does, but it looks like boring genetic work. The documents were heavily redacted.

He's laying the finishing touch on a gesture drawing— the lines of RB-232 pierced by the persistent rays of the sun—when the ship jolts and his grip slips. A hard, scraggly line leers back at him from the surface of the Bristol board. The piece was only a study in shape, but he quite liked it before this imperfection, and a rage swells in his gut. Dorian grits his teeth and scribbles across the surface, decimating the tip of the conté crayon. Then he crumples up the paper and tosses it into the incinerator, along with his now damaged crayon.

It'll be hard to get to an art store ten parsecs from Earth, but he'll figure something out. He still has plenty of tubes of oil paint.

"Airlock secured, sir," Ken says. "We're latched on."

"Smooth landing, Captain," Dorian says.

"Thank you, sir." The captain has missed the sarcasm, and Dorian regrets not injecting more venom into his tone. He goes to the crew baths and washes his hands, then dries them on a white hand towel, smearing charcoal black into its fibers. Walking to his mirror, he fashions a tie into a complex, multi-layered knot that would make

Van Leuwen weep with jealousy. Squaring his shoulders, he regards himself for a long while before re-combing the sides of his hair and slicking them back down with some product. He makes sure the upward curve of his regal cheek flows straight into the lines of his coiffure.

"Sir?" Ken's voice comes over the intercom again. "They're, uh, expecting to meet with us soon."

"They can wait, Captain," he replies, smoothing a single stray hair back into place. "We've been in transit for a year. They'll live another five minutes without us."

"Acknowledged." The most noncommittal response anyone can give on a ship.

Ken, Montrell, and Susan shuffle past the crew baths and into the common area, where they all tell jokes and crack open beers. In spite of Ken's recent failure, Dorian likes them all. They never ask him questions. They keep him informed. They shuttle him to the places that need auditing, and don't try to induct him into their "family." Families are overrated.

As he grooms, he wonders about the last time the crew of RB-232 saw a suit. It had to have been when they left Earth, or at some sort of commissioning party. Their clothes would be five years out of date at a minimum, and Dorian is excited to see what they will make of him. Once he's fully satisfied with his appearance, he joins his crewmates at the airlock.

They're all enthusiastic to get out of the *Athenian* and explore their new—albeit temporary—habitat. He likes that. They'll report back to him with any strange corporate culture entanglements they find, and he can eliminate those responsible.

Klaxons blare. Yellow dome lights flash around the airlock, and the doors open onto a spacious, though empty, docking bay. The meager inhabitants of RB-232 stand before him in the center of the deck, a thin parody of a military unit. They slouch against crates and sit cross-legged on the floor, then scramble to their feet as he enters. His eyes divide them into groups of threes, then he counts the groups: eighteen people. That means four have abstained from attending his boarding. He'll take special care to memorize the faces and names of those who are present.

A set of dim blue blinking LEDs runs along the floor in a train, emerging from his ship's docking clamp and away down the central strut—some kind of wayfinding system, perhaps? Dorian looks left to see if he can spy where they're going, but he can't see the end of the long hallway, so returns his attention to the gathered crew.

At the center of the group are a man and a woman, standing stiff as boards. They're veterans, and he knows what they will say before they speak.

"Welcome to the Cold Forge. I'm Commander Daniel Cardozo, and this is Anne Wexler, my chief of security."

Ex-military always speak first. They love to posture like they're the heart of the operation, but on a day-to-day basis, in the middle of deep space, they're worthless. RB-232 is shrouded in so many cover stories that it's the dark secret of a dark secret. No one will be attacking them. They probably make viruses here, and with a virus there's nothing to shoot.

Cardozo is older, saltier than anyone else there, with skin like tanned leather. Likely he's seen armed conflict, and is enjoying what amounts to retirement. Anne is Dorian's age, smooth and lithe. She might be bored. Dorian hopes she is. Bored people are apt to do stupid things.

"Commander. Anne." Dorian shakes both of their hands in turn.

"Director," Anne begins. "My records may be out of date... Have you received all of the required safety training? Hazmat certs? Materials safety? Escape vehicle orientation and codes?"

I have my own goddamned spaceship, woman. Nothing annoys Dorian more than all of the pointless presentations he has to endure at each new installation. Hours and hours of time thrown away, just so he can memorize some codes he'll never use. "Absolutely," he says. "I'm not sure why the records didn't come across."

Anne nods, but doesn't press the issue. She knows he's too important for such garbage.

"You're familiar with the purpose of this station?" Cardozo asks.

"I've only read a few of the reports. Carter Burke wanted to start a special project, but the Governance Board weren't confident in his ability to see it all the way through. Something about it being too much for a junior executive." He'd read between the lines. "This, then, is a backup to his project?"

"Yes," Daniel says. "I've heard he's pretty far along. Do you know if he's gotten any results?"

"No clue," Dorian says. "Different department."

Cardozo gestures toward three personnel, two men and a woman. "These are our project leads, Blue Marsalis, Josep Janos, and Lucy Biltmore."

Judging from his appearance, Janos works out, and Dorian takes his hand first, shaking firmly, puffing out his chest a bit without making it too obvious. The man has a broom of a mustache, and his clothes are clearly well loved, fraying in places. This will be Dorian's morning workout partner. Perhaps Anne can join them.

Biltmore comes next, shy and uninteresting. Lucy has the sort of homegrown look that Dorian can't stand, and he inwardly hopes she'll need to be shuffled off the station. She looks like a child jammed into an adult-sized flight suit. He gives her a hearty greeting and moves on as soon as is socially acceptable.

When he reaches Marsalis, he stops dead. Wavy blond hair, artificially attractive features. He knows a synthetic when he sees one.

"Aren't you a Marcus?" he asks.

The Marcus's mouth twitches with a socially required smile. This question has produced a fascinating irritation in the synthetic, which Dorian has never experienced. He reminds himself to keep up his friendly, almost boisterous manner with a hearty handshake.

"I get that a lot," Marsalis says, thin-lipped, taking back his hand. "I'm a human, piloting a synthetic. My real body is in my quarters."

"That's incredible." Dorian circles the Marcus, looking

him up and down with a grin, while the android remains unmoving. "Well, Blue, I'm Director Sudler."

"Nice to meet you, Mister Sudler."

So Blue Marsalis will be the piece that doesn't fit into Dorian's machine. "Please, call me Director, at least until we know each other a little better." He quirks his lips.

Marsalis chuckles and looks at Cardozo with a sarcasm Dorian has never seen on a synthetic face.

"I didn't know 'Director' was an honorific on Earth nowadays," Marsalis says, crossing his arms. "You know… Mister, Missus, Mix, Doctor… Director."

Dorian glances about, taking in the reactions of the crew. They're afraid of an auditor, but they're enjoying Marsalis's commentary. Maybe he can make her appear rude. He shakes his head, frowning.

"I'm surprised that bothers you, Mister Marsalis. Or is it Miss Marsalis? Or should I call you Blue?"

"I'm sorry," Marsalis says, offering his hand once more. "You can call me *Doctor* Marsalis… at least until we know each other a little better."

Dorian laughs to cover his annoyance. Marsalis's denigration and blatant disregard for the authority of an auditor is like a needle pressing against soft tissue under his fingernail. If he fires Blue, however, it'll have to be for more than simple revenge, or he'll appear weak.

But he *will* fire Blue.

"I'm sure you'd like to see your quarters, Director Sudler," Cardozo says. "Perhaps you could get settled in and then—"

"Nonsense, Daniel," Dorian says. "Let's dig in. I've been sleeping too long already. Show me your projects."

"Then allow me to show you our operation," Cardozo says, then he speaks to no one in particular. "Navigation, take us to the central SCIF." A short chime fills the corridor. The lights along the floor change direction, running away in a blue stream. Dorian cranes his neck to follow their new pathway.

"That'll help you get around while you're down here, especially in the SCIF," Cardozo says. "You wouldn't believe how twisty it can be. Some of these modules were designed for prisoners."

"Cute," Dorian says. "And do you have any prisoners?"

Cardozo gives him a wry smile. "Yes, we do. Let's go say hello, then."

It strikes Dorian as overkill. The idea of a sensitive, compartmented information facility on a secret space station ten parsecs from Earth. What can they have to hide that isn't already shrouded by the radiation of Kaufmann?

The central strut of the station stretches at least a half of a mile, with sockets for additional prefab modules along the way. It has a pleasing repetition to it, and looking out the windows to his left, Dorian can see the heat shield protecting them from the rays of the dwarf star below. The plates are articulated—was the station designed to be moved? RB-232 was clearly created to be expanded, and yet it sits mostly empty, save for the two ends. It's a waste. The station should be bustling with employees and additional crew quarter modules.

Yet that's not his focus. Auditors get little benefit from identifying lost opportunities. Those could be costly, and his job is to *cut* expenses.

"Why do you call it the Cold Forge?" Dorian asks, walking alongside the three project managers and a few of their personnel. Ken, Susan, and Montrell accompany them.

"Because this entire station is dedicated to the manufacture of adaptive weapons, biological, artificial intelligence and software," Anne replies, her matter-of-fact voice carrying through the cavernous central strut. "Kind of like the forges of old, where they used to make swords. Except we don't make ships, missiles, or pulse rifles here. We win wars."

"I see." Dorian gives her a boyish grin, presenting himself to her as charmed because he doubts she has ever charmed anyone.

"You can see from our superstructure that we have the SCIF on one side and crew quarters on the other," Anne says. "The SCIF is vibration-isolated with full air gaps to all of the networks. No data in, no data out without clearing our official channels. That means we can fully lock it down during resupply missions."

They pass a glass door, and Dorian peers inside to see the blinking lights of server racks. In the center of the round chamber, a console awaits, its screen dim.

"That's Titus," Cardozo says. "He'll be assisting you

during your audit with your classified, non-project data. Have you read the classification guides for RB-232?"

"Yes, Commander," Dorian says, and the man preens slightly. It's been a while since someone called him by rank alone. "But I'll need to run numbers on all three projects here, and I'll want some specifics."

"I'm not sure you'll be able to see all of my project," Marsalis says, his (her?) eyes cast absentmindedly to the ceiling as though counting crossbars. "I'm sure you'll understand. There are several dimensions that aren't available to the operating unit heads, so a regular director—"

Dorian stops and narrows his eyes. "I think you'll find that I'm not a 'regular' director, Doctor Marsalis. I'm here on the full faith and credit of the senior vice president, and while on site I'm cleared at all levels of classification, with all code words." He looks down his nose. "But while we're on the subject, how… *exactly*… do you enter the SCIF to work on your project?"

"I don't follow," Marsalis says.

He strides up to the doctor, his long bird legs closing the distance in just two steps, and then waves his hand over the synthetic's head, and the doctor recoils.

"There are no strings on this puppet," Dorian says. "You're a walking, wireless transmitter." He turns to Anne and grins as though they're sharing a joke, though deep down, Dorian doesn't find it amusing. He already sees the biggest budgetary abuse on RB-232. "So why did we build a multi-billion-dollar SCIF if we're going to put a radio inside of it?"

"My comms are secured," Marsalis says, "and I was given special dispensation by Elise Coto."

"Coto is our VP of Genetic Interests, and she insisted Blue have an assignment here, in spite of her… difficulties," Anne adds with a small defensive note. "Doctor Marsalis is a leading researcher in her field."

Dorian's ears prick up. Behind the perfect synth face of a man, Blue is a woman. A thrill tugs at his heart. He's never met anyone like this doctor. Cardozo is an old jarhead. Anne is a wannabe jarhead. Lucy is a joke. Janos is a geek… but Blue Marsalis is someone new. What does it do to a person to live through a synthetic? When she imagines a mirror, does she imagine Marcus, or her own face? Is she gnarled by illness? He wants to needle her more to see what color blood comes out.

"Then I guess we'll get to see something amazing, since we've made a special exception for you," Dorian says.

"Yes, you will," Cardozo says. "But your crew will have to learn to love the quarters. I didn't get authorization for them, so they'll be staying put." He looks meaningfully at the trio from the *Athenian*. "This stuff is all 'need-to-know.'"

Dorian nods to Ken, who gleefully retreats. The rest follow. Ken doesn't care for this business crap, anyway, and he doesn't even bother to hide it. Dorian has never considered what they do with their copious free time—they can stare at the wall for all he cares. He only ever needs them when he has to be transported, or wants corporate reinforcement.

The crew of the *Athenian* disappears into the bowels of

the station, and Cardozo gestures for some of his own crew to follow, instructing them to show the visitors around.

At the end of the central axis they pass into chain-link caged walls, and the passageway begins a steady incline, ending with a bulkhead door secured with multifactor security: biometric, code, and key. Yellow caution stripes surround the doorframe, and a set of surveillance cameras records them from every possible angle. When Dorian looks back at the corridor beyond the chain-link, he finds glittering black USCM autoturrets trained on his position.

"What are those for?" he asks, nodding to the guns. "Intruders on the station?"

"We call this area the 'killbox,'" Anne says. "Two hundred feet of constricted corridor with radio-transparent chain walls. There's an emergency seal behind us. Anything tries to get out of here, we open fire with caseless ten-twenty-fours."

"'Get out of here?'" Dorian repeats. "So what, are we going to wear IFF tags?"

"No," Blue says. "Those guns are designed not to care if you're friend or foe. If you're in the killbox and they come on, you're dead. We can't risk anyone bringing something out of the labs."

Cardozo turns around, hands clasped behind his back. "Director Sudler, everything you're about to see remains classified under TS/SCI Mountain protocols. You will not be exporting reports from this station without clearing them through myself and Anne as export control. You will not speak of this to anyone else, including those who possess Weyland-Yutani TS/SCI clearances. The penalty for such an action would be breach of paragraph six, subsection B of your employment contract, and would subject you and your estate to both civil and criminal action. Do I make myself clear?"

"That's the same deal I face on every station, Commander," Dorian says. "I think I can handle it."

Daniel gives him a wide grin. "Going to be tougher when you see what we've got inside. Let's open her up, Wexler."

Anne and Daniel enter codes, scan hand and face geometry, and insert a pair of keys, turning them at the same time. With a hiss, the SCIF door slides into its pocket. Daniel beckons them in, and as they step over the threshold, Dorian sees that the bulkhead is nearly a half-yard thick. There can be no breaking it, no ramming it.

The SCIF common area stretches before them, an open structure three stories tall with a glass-enclosed control room at the top. Anne ushers Dorian inside, and the rest of the Cold Forge crew follows.

"The SCIF is one hundred thirty thousand square feet of specialized laboratories, servers, and workstations. It's designed for scientists to work in concert, and all our personnel float between projects. Don't let its compact size fool you—there are a half-mile of corridors connecting a hundred tiny rooms in here."

"Impressive," Dorian says. "Looks like your security folks have your work cut out for you. What's that up there?" He points to the glass control room.

"That's our interface to the AI mainframe, Juno,"

Daniel says. "She'll be assisting you from inside the SCIF. Any SCI queries that you have go through her. Remember, Titus is for 'total station control.' Juno is for 'just the classified stuff.'"

Dorian gives him a crass smirk. "You can't be serious."

Cardozo shrugs. "Stupid enough to remember the difference, right?"

They first take him to "Rose Eagle"—some kind of reactor and focusing array, spearheaded by Josep Janos. They explain that it's a way of disrupting entangled communications networks and injecting information into them. At that, Dorian spaces out. Janos has a way of speaking that makes his technical explanations unbearable, ending every sentence as though it is a question. Every time his voice rises, so do Dorian's hackles.

But Dorian already knows that Rose Eagle doesn't matter. It's on schedule, to be delivered to a bunker in West Virginia during the next crew rotation. Janos is returning home when that occurs, to take R&R for a year and hike the Appalachian Trail. He has no vulnerabilities to exploit, and so Dorian loses all interest. There's nothing more boring than a project running according to plan.

Next is "Silversmile," a neural network virus which began its life as two words. Unlike Rose Eagle and Glitter Edifice, its randomly selected pair of words sounds ominous, like a brand name. Using the printers, Lucy Biltmore has made herself a mission patch and logo which she shares with her laboratory assistants. She's used her custom wordmark throughout the operating system.

There's an irony in the nomenclature of the digraph—
Weyland-Yutani's classification authority selects monikers
designed to discourage mental associations, but Lucy has
embraced them. If she deployed weaponized code at this
moment, adversaries would have little trouble tracing the
project back to RB-232. Dorian watches the skinny woman
with her cartoonishly large eyes and mouth, her messy
pixie cut, and he looks forward to reprimanding her for
this blatant oversight.

Anticipating Dorian's arrival, Lucy has prepared a
show and tell with large, attractive readouts and graphs.
There are many bullet points. She produced a video with
motion graphics depicting the effects of Silversmile on a
computer network. The method is simple. Silversmile uses
whatever comms it can find to infect other machines, then
it lashes together a distributed processing system. The
more computers it can infect, the smarter it becomes. Once
it feels confident, it intuits the most critical infrastructure
and attacks it first. Perhaps a dam turbine, perhaps a life
support system.

"But we're writing it to be restricted to a single location,
because, you know…" Lucy trails off as ANY QUESTIONS?
appears on the screen behind her.

"Enlighten me," Dorian says, and Lucy squirms under
his gaze. She's afraid of losing funding.

"It'd be like the apocalypse." She laughs nervously.
"It'd just spread until it hit a system smarter than it was."

Dorian folds his hands behind his back. "And… at
this point in your project, aren't most systems smarter

than it is? What's the reason for all the delays?"

"Computer science is the process of solving unsolved problems." She holds her hands close to her chest, pulling on her fingers as if she's wringing a washcloth. "So, you know, I don't think it's easy to put an exact delivery date on—" He watches her waffle. Her answers are vague and insipid, and project managers have delivered code for centuries now. Even her growing panic is uninteresting— it's like playing a game without an opponent.

"Are you from the same Biltmores as the North Carolina Biltmores?" he asks, interrupting a string of vocalized pauses. "Like, the big estate there?"

She smiles, overly toothy beneath her swollen lips.

"I… don't know."

Dorian shrugs. "Okay. Just curious."

He turns. "Next project."

3

THE KENNELS

They file through hallways and away from the common area. The safety lighting here is uncomfortably bright, and the floor and walls have been treated with some sort of polymer coating. They reach a bend in the corridor, and a tremendous vault door sprawls before them, covered over in various biohazard warnings.

It takes all of Dorian's composure not to roll his eyes. A genetic weapon is easy to control in space. A virus won't propagate through airless chambers. In the worst-case scenario, everyone on the research facility dies, but the virus is contained. Yet they've locked off Glitter Edifice even from the rest of the SCIF.

Again, multiple keys and multiple codes come out. Blue assists this time, with her own codes and biometrics. A loud klaxon sounds, and a computerized voice fills the intercoms.

"Kennels open. Logged access, Doctor Blue Marsalis."

"Juno keeps an extra special eye on this place," Anne says.

Blazing chartreuse covers the hallways beyond, and where most of the station contains exposed pipes and ductwork, Glitter Edifice has only bare walls with black text signs to direct them. Dorian cocks his head.

"Wouldn't have been my first choice of color."

"Safety measure," Blue says. "Human optical response is strongest between bright yellow-green and black... though we also could've used a light cyan."

"Everything looks purple after you get out of here, though," Josep adds. "Cone strain on your eyes because your green receptors are overworked." The second statement is enough of an explanation that it rises at the end.

"I'll... keep that in mind," Dorian says. "And why do we care about green-black contrast?"

"Survival," Blue says, ushering them in.

The place feels like a bunker. It reminds Dorian of the subfloors of Weyland-Yutani's Tokyo office—impenetrable concrete vaults of records and archived hard drives stored in suspension fluid. It would be easier to rob a bank than to get into the kennels. Here, the corridors are claustrophobic, not the soaring halls of the rest of the Cold Forge, and the lights are even brighter, giving the whole place the feeling of a bad computer rendering.

They pass a wide, tempered-glass window with a break mesh on both sides. Dorian leans in for a closer look and sees a dissection table. Along the back wall, he spots specimen jars the size of human torsos, and distorted, bony hands floating inside—tails where their wrist bones should be, scrotum-like diaphragms at the joining. Inside the room, a young black man in a lab coat looks into a microscope.

Dorian stares at the claws in wide-eyed fascination.

"This way," Blue calls out. The party has already moved beyond him.

Lucy's eyes are even wider here, her large lips pursed and white. She's genuinely afraid of this place.

"Is that some kind of trophy room?" Dorian asks her, whispering.

"More like hell," she replies. "Don't eat any pomegranate seeds while you're down here."

"More of a rare steak man, myself."

"You'll get along just fine then," she says. They round a corner to a tall room, at least the height of the SCIF common area, with a power loader against the far wall. A darkened set of glass panels punctuates one of the walls, and at first, Dorian believes they're black, or perhaps smoked glass. He notices loading clamps at the base of each panel, making them look as though they're stacked like blocks. The panels are each ten feet by ten feet, large enough to fit a truck or docking vessel. As he steps closer, he realizes that the glass panels are clear, and the other side is pitch black.

Blue points to the array of industrial lights high above them. "Special lensing. Sheds light on the cell block, but not the cells. Keeps the disturbances to a minimum."

"Disturbances?"

"They like the dark." She pulls a tablet terminal from the wall and types something into the control keys. Everyone steps away from the windows, backing up to the observation area on the other side of the chamber. "I think you'll be more comfortable over here, Director Sudler."

"Why?"

"The effect can be unsettling." She shrugs. "Don't touch anything."

He shakes his head and steps closer to the windows. "Show me what you're going to show me."

The tap of a key echoes through the chamber, then comes the steaming hiss and the rending of metal. Something is screeching. Dorian flinches, but doesn't move away. He watches the lights flicker on behind the windows, one by one, illuminating the cells in stunning green. He steps closer to the cell nearest him as the last light flickers on.

The creature before him seems to drip from the ceiling before rising slowly to its feet, hateful lips pulled into a sneer around glassy teeth. Its head is a long, smooth shaft of gray like tumbled granite against the oily black of its body. Chitinous protrusions form a brilliant exoskeleton, rippling with muscular potential. Its tail is an array of ever-shrinking bones, tipped by a wicked barb. It is the intent of every murderer, poured into a mold and painted pitch black. It is a symphony of death, a masterpiece of hellish design, raw will.

Blue was right, the effect is unsettling, and he barely notices the yelp that escapes his lips before utter captivation sets in. Dorian walks along the edge of the cell, and the creature stalks along with him, following his movements without eyes. Its posture is sunken, powerful legs bent like coiled springs. Tendrils of sticky drool ooze from its mouth. His heart rises in his chest, and he wants to weep for the beauty of it. Blue is a genius of the highest order.

"Did you… make these?" he asks, his voice almost a whisper.

"No," Blue says, to his relief. "I'm not even authorized to know the origin of the eggs."

"What are they called?"

"I have my own names, but nothing I've submitted, since they're highly classified. One of the Company sourcing guys called them 'Xenomorphs,' but that's kind of a misnomer. Any creature for which we don't know the taxonomy is technically a xenomorph," Blue says. "We've been calling them snatchers, honestly, because they're so goddamned fast."

"And what do we want with them?" Dorian asks, but he's beyond questioning their presence. "Why research them?"

"They have a broad-based, general application," Daniel says. "With appropriate control loops, you're talking about quashing insurgencies, destroying structures, bringing down entire countries. They're the most potent biological weapon of our age, and if they could be turned to our advantage… Do you even remember the last time the United States Colonial Marines purchased a complete threat response system?"

Dorian rests a hand on the glass as though to touch the creature's muzzle and it snaps at him like the arc of an electrical current, leaving a smear of ichor across the glass. A klaxon sounds, and a luminous outline of red appears around the back wall of the featureless cell. The screaming from the other cells stops dead. The creature lashes out again, then scrambles into the corner and cowers, wrapping its tail around its legs.

No domesticated creature ever compares to its natural brethren. If this is an example of a creature, a "snatcher," that's been raised in captivity, what must a Xenomorph be like when encountered in the wild? His mind races, trying to imagine.

"They're remarkably capable of adaptation," Blue says, interrupting his musings. "The first time they hit the glass, we open the heat shield and expose them to the star for five seconds. This marks the first time one has ever taken a second swipe."

4

PLAGIARUS PRAEPOTENS

Blue had hoped to scare off the auditor with her demonstration. It had certainly worked on the last Company clown to tour the Cold Forge. She considers showing him an impregnation, but given his awe-struck response to the full-grown snatcher, it's unlikely to have the desired effect.

She regards him as he strides from one cell to the next, inspecting the aliens as if they were his troops. They respond to him with interest and curiosity, causing her to feel a strange pang of jealousy. Whenever she and Kambili check on the cages, they find the creatures curled into a ball in a state of near torpor.

With his tall, slender limbs and black suit, Sudler and the snatchers seem to be the perfect pairing.

"Well," she says softly, "we've got a fucking freak on our hands."

"I'd consider showing him a little more respect," Daniel whispers.

She chuckles. "Like he does for you, 'Commander?'"

Daniel slicks back his short, gray hair. "Sometimes it's nice for an old vet to be appreciated. It's not easy commanding on a station full of nerds." He regards their visitor and adds, "Besides, he's your gateway to more funding. Look at him. He *loves* this shit."

As if feeling their gaze, Sudler turns away from the snatchers.

"Since I'm going to be conducting my research on the station," he says, "I'll require quarters with the crew."

"I told you," Daniel whispers. "Squeeze him."

Blue forces herself to smile. "You like the kennels that much, do you?"

Sudler's pale blue eyes shine in the lime-tinted light of the cells. "I think it's the future, Doctor Marsalis."

"Well, then," Daniel says, "we'd better get you situated." He gestures toward the door, and Sudler precedes them. Once on the other side Blue heads toward the vivisection lab.

There she finds Kambili sitting at his workstation, head bobbing, chewing gum, earbuds in. She's glad the auditor didn't ask her about alien reproduction, because that would've led to an awkward conversation about the eggs and chimps—and why most of the aliens were terminated before reaching adulthood.

She's been tasked with finding a reliable way to create

and control the snatchers, with an eye toward military deployment. Fifty percent of the way through her funding and eighty percent of the way through her chimps and eggs, she hasn't even started that task. It isn't something she relishes explaining.

Up to now conditions have been perfect. The Cold Forge is remote. Elise Coto, the vice President of Genetic Interests, has been willing to lie for her—provided Blue could get what she wanted from the alien genome before anyone catches on. Then they'd be able to unveil their discovery to great fanfare.

"Was that the auditor?" Kambili asks, startling her. He's taken out one of the earbuds.

"Yeah," she replies.

He smirks. "Did you tell him you're not doing your job?"

"No." Blue scowls, and judging from the look on Kambili's face, it's effectively menacing. "Did you tell your wife back home that you've been fucking Lucy?"

"Listen—"

"No, *you* listen," Blue says, drawing close to him. Marcus is shorter than Kambili, but the android body could break him in half and he knows it. "Stay in your lane, or I will *ruin* you. Are we clear?"

He averts his eyes. "I just want out of this shithole."

"I want you out of here, too, but I need your help for now, so I guess we're both pretty screwed."

"I'm not going down for you."

Blue's nostrils flare. How can he be so brilliant and so thick at the same time?

"I didn't ask you for that. Just… just work until I'm dead, okay? Then you can pin this all on me. Don't get cold feet just because of 'Director Sudler' out there. Either I'm right, and we both get paydays and promotions… or I die, and you can tell everyone how horrible I was. No matter what, you're going home next rotation, so… you know… *man up*." She says this last bit in Marcus's lower register, imitating Kambili's characteristic eye roll.

Kambili juts out his jaw, shaking his head. His muscles are tense and it looks as if he wants to hit her, but that would be a hand-breakingly stupid idea. Blue crosses her arms, waiting to feel the blow, but it never comes. After a pregnant silence, she uncrosses them again.

"Just tell me what other choice I have, Kambili."

"In the last test…" he replies, and Blue perks up. "After you were, uh, logged out of Marcus… I think I saw it on the thermoptics."

Blue inhales slowly, trying to keep her breath from shaking with excitement.

"Saw what, Kambili?"

"I couldn't let Marcus see, or he might tell someone, so I covered my workstation, but by the time I could look again, the fluid had metabolized with the soft tissues of the host."

"What did you see?"

He pulls on his stubbly chin. "I think you're right… *Plagiarus praepotens* is real."

There it is. Her life's work, or the work for her life. The second animal that none of the Company researchers seem to recognize—a bacterial terror that can rewrite DNA orders of magnitude faster than CRISPR technology. Weyland-Yutani thinks the face-huggers are larval snatchers, but they're really hosts for the deadliest pathogen in the universe. And within the genetic code of *praepotens* lies an unlimited potential for a cure for her genetic disorder—for everyone's disorders.

Blue has given the face-huggers a real name, too: *Manumala noxhydria*. The evil hand, the jar of night.

She clenches her fists. "You should've told me."

"Told you what? That I saw it, and we were still too slow?"

"That I was right!" she bellows, though Marcus could get a lot louder. "God *damn* it, Kambili. We should've been setting up the next test immediately!"

"I knew you'd say that!" He wraps up his headphones and tosses them onto the desk. "You keep blowing through the eggs this fast, you're going to get caught! You get fired, then you don't have any medical assistance and—"

She glares at him.

"I've..." he starts, but falters and takes a moment to compose himself. "I gave two years of my family's life to this job. By the time I get back, my kid is going to be five years old, and she won't even know me. If I lose the bonus at the end of this, if I lose my job, my family is fucked. So it's not just your ass on the line here. Keep your head screwed on straight."

Kambili is a cheating piece of shit. He hooked up with Lucy almost the day he arrived and hasn't stopped since.

Maybe he feels some concern for his wife and daughter, but not enough to keep his dick to himself. Blue sees in him what she always sees in distant, unaccountable men—a willingness to break any rule that inconveniences him.

But he's right about the sample speeds.

Elise can cover up project progress, but she can't cover for those missing *noxhydria* egg samples, each of which is classed as individual equipment. The monetary value of the eggs is something like a hundred and fifty thousand dollars apiece, but that's only the cost of acquisition. The Company tracks them as though they were bars of gold, because they're irreplaceable.

Elise's last transmission rings in Blue's head.

NEEDED RESULTS
CANT PROTECT US ANYMORE
GOOD LUCK

What changed? Is it the auditor? If Blue accelerates her plan, will they smoke her out?

"It's been a week," Kambili says. "Maybe we could, like, go back to plan A. Try to find *praepotens* inside the body of the face-hugger. We've got ultrasound and microsurgical—"

Blue shakes her head. "You know that won't work. We melted our extraction tools last time, and we don't have any more spares. Plus, we never found a decent concentration." The pathogen won't concentrate without a live victim. The *noxhydria* has to be aroused, and the greater the fear, the more of the *praepotens* it will pull together for payload injection. She imagines securing one of the chimps over an egg with some mechanism to catch the face-hugger's slithering pharynx and milk it when it attacks. It'd frighten the shit out of the chimp, for sure.

In their own ecosystem, would the adult snatchers try to help face-huggers propagate the pathogen? Blue imagines them restraining the victim somehow, and wishes she had more information on the behavioral patterns of the creatures. She doesn't even know where they're from.

Constructing a milker would take time, and she'd need help from engineering. It would draw Sudler's attention, since both the articulated restraints and the mechanism would be substantial. Some of the machine-learning devs would have to help her with a targeting system, too.

Marcus could do it if Blue wasn't piloting him. He was fast enough to snatch the pharynx, strong enough to wring out its contents, plastic enough that it couldn't infect him. But he'd be obligated by his programming to tell others at the Company what he'd been forced to do.

What if she explained her situation to Marcus? He might deem her safety to be in jeopardy and preserve her confidence. He might also recognize that she's taking dangerous risks and force her into deep freeze for a flight home. Blue wishes she had more training in synth psychology.

"Blue? You still in there?" Kambili says, and she blinks.

"Yeah, sorry."

"I asked you what you wanted to do."

She nods. "Fear," she says. "We've got to find a way to stimulate the chimps and capture the pathogen directly from a surface it won't metabolize…" She needs something antibacterial, or maybe plastic. "Oh, my god… I'm an idiot…"

"What?"

"We put a puncture into the dorsal side of the chimp's esophagus and fuse in a bio plastic lining up to the throat. We can do collection next to the spine. Keep the chimp restrained, but not sedated."

Kambili smiles, not his usual baleful, sarcastic smirk, but the genuine smile of someone witnessing a breakthrough. "Just like a colostomy bag."

"How soon can we set up the next test without breaking cadence?"

"Four days."

"Thaw one of the chimps. Get started on the surgery."

Blue returns to her own body to find it reasonably pleasant. Her guts hurt, but that never changes. Her breath rattles a little when she inhales, the sound of all the fluid aspirations she's had over the years. Her esophageal muscles don't work very well. Her back stings a little from the bedsores as she rolls over.

The Company had agreed to furnish her with a bed that would prevent them, but when she'd first arrived at the station, it wasn't there. It didn't show up in any resupplies since then, either, and she complained to her management once every three months.

Being Marcus tires Blue, not because it takes spectacular activity to pilot him, but because she must eventually return to this room, this body. Sometimes, it seems easier not to be able to escape into the android.

"Lights," she calls, pulling off the headset as the vibrant day cycle fills her room.

She needs to contact Elise back on Earth—get her to stall somehow. Blue doesn't know what pressures her co-conspirator faces, but she needs another month. She knows she can isolate the raw pathogen and start reverse-engineering it from there. When Marcus arrives, he can give her the terminal and some privacy so she can encrypt a message.

Her buzzer rings. "Enter," she says, and it unlocks.

When the door slides open, Dorian Sudler stands on the other side like a knife, perfect, hardened and sharp. Blue's heart freezes over. No longer is she ambulatory, looming over him in a powerful synth body. She's alone in her hospital bed, feeling small and weak.

"I just wanted to meet you in person," he says with a smile, stepping over the threshold. He holds in his right hand a pack of cigarettes and a sterling silver matchbox. It's hard for her to make out any details, but judging from his well-groomed appearance, the matchbox is probably some expensive heirloom. Normal people would use a cheap lighter, but not this clown.

"You can't smoke anywhere near here," she states. He puts his cigarettes and matches down on her nightstand, obnoxiously close to her, and smiles.

"I wouldn't dare," he says, then he gives her a long look. "I didn't expect you to be so…"

Blue waits for him to say "frail."

"Black."

"You said you were with Human Resources?" she asks, looking forward to reporting this conversation.

"Yes, but don't be so sensitive. It's 'Special Resources.' Highly classified assets like yourself, so we can skip all of the typical nonsense training. You know how it is. The regs don't really follow you out this far from Earth." He narrows his eyes. "Sorry, I simply got the wrong impression from that Aryan doll you walk around in."

Blue's breath comes out in an angry hiss. "Okay, well… we've meet in person, Director Sudler," she says, lacking the force of Marcus's voice. "I'm off the clock, so I'll thank you to leave now."

"I have trouble with faces," Dorian says, languidly waving a hand next to his eyes as though there's something physically wrong with them. "Hard to interpret emotions from synthetics. Do you ever have that problem?"

"It doesn't matter if you can't read Marcus's face, Director," Blue says. "Weyland-Yutani pays for my scientific acumen, not my feelings. Please get out."

"All right, all right," he says, raising his hands and starting to back away. "I didn't mean to disturb you. Just so you know, I'm at the end of the hall if you need anything."

"You're in the observation deck? That's not a bedroom."

"Facilities is making a few modifications," he says. "I like the view of the sun."

"Yeah," she replies, remembering the view of the boiling fusion through the panoramic black glass windows. "Everyone does. That's why it's a common area."

"I won't be on the station long," he says. "Like you, I have some unique needs for my quarters, and I need to be able to spread out—get a bunch of archival records in there."

Your "unique needs" are nothing like mine, you prick.

"In case someone misses the view, though," he adds, "I have an open-door policy. Feel free to come in any time and chat or relax. I love company. If you ever need to talk—"

"I won't."

"—about what happened with Miss Coto…" he says, but trails off at her comment. "I'm sorry, you're right. I'll leave."

She reacted. She knows she did. It's not as easy to control her face when she's outside of Marcus. Blue may as well ask. "I'm sorry, what happened to my boss?"

"I just got the news, myself. They sent it to my ship terminal during the demos." Dorian jams his hands into his suit pockets. "Miss Coto has been arrested and placed on administrative leave. They found her accepting payments from an old competitor, in serious breach of contract, and that she'd embezzled from company coffers. Caught with her hand in the till, I'm sad to say."

Blue's lungs become blocks of ice. She covers her panic with a feeble cough.

"That's terrible," she chokes out. And it is. Elise has a family. Blue imagines what that's like for the kids, watching their mother be led away. Elise won't have her fortune to defend herself. She won't land in a minimum-security prison. Her breach of contract and the ensuing civil battle will sap any assets she had. Blue hopes her old boss had a war chest squirreled away for a day like this.

"In the extreme," he agrees. "What a waste."

"Okay, then thank you for passing it along," Blue says. "Letting me know. I need to get some rest, so just… show yourself out."

"As you wish." He turns to go.

"And another thing, Director Sudler," she says, trying to keep her voice steady. He turns back. "I'd appreciate it if you don't ever contact me inside my room."

Sudler hesitates. "What I'd like to know is, why did Coto do it? She had everything: power, influence… Hell, this place basically belonged to her. Didn't she have enough money—without resorting to career-ending thievery?"

He leaves without waiting for an answer.

Blue has her suspicions about Elise's motivations. When Blue was a fellow at Johns Hopkins, she was diagnosed with Bishara's Syndrome, and the irony of the case brought it to media prominence. "Prominent Geneticist Suffers Rare Genetic Disease." There were twelve others diagnosed in the world, all children of lifelong colonists and spacers. She was the subject of numerous puff pieces about taking charge of her destiny, and having access to the greatest medical supplies and minds in the country.

In the beginning, she'd believed the bright side of the story, conducting her research in Earth-borne labs, finding corporate partners, uncovering the mystery and seeking to solve it out of public heroism. But then she grew short on sand in her hourglass, and tried more and more desperate solutions. She began to self-medicate. She lost her fellowship.

Along came Elise Coto saying, "I know where you can find your cure." She flung Blue to the stars, to this pit of hell, nestled in the heavens. Blue remembers the pain of her first days here, the screech of the first snatcher, the horror at the face-hugger, how she'd thought of herself as the heroine of a journey.

If she could only reach the end, she'd be well again.

But the snatcher became a tool, and the journey a job.

They're going to subpoena Elise's records, she realized. *They've probably raided her house.* How long before they find the secret messages passed to Blue? How careful was Elise? Will they only see pictures, or will they find the pair's shared ciphers?

Dorian Sudler is playing some kind of vicious game, she thought, *but what?* When she looks over to her nightstand, she sees his silvered matchbox standing guard by his cigarettes. She picks it up and inspects it—rubies inlaid into an engraved constellation—one she doesn't recognize. She doubts it means much to him, either, considering that the suits are almost never scientifically minded. Pretty boy probably just thought it was a neat design.

Out of spite, she slides it open to look inside: some fragrant, sweet wooden matches and a torn-off piece of striker paper. She removes his striker and most of his matches, leaving just enough for it to rattle when he picks it up. She tucks them into the underside of her mattress and smiles.

"Good luck finding more fancy matches on a space station, fucker," she says, muttering to herself.

An hour later, Dorian returns, apologizing, asking about his cigarettes.

INTERLUDE

JAVIER

Being an IT guy for an air-gapped SCIF isn't the sort of cybersecurity job Javier Paz had hoped it would be. When he'd gone into network security and counterintelligence, he'd expected to be conducting forensic sweeps, locking down nets, and chasing away hackers. The SCIF at the Cold Forge sounded like a dream. But there are no hackers that can cross an air gap.

And so, Javier's job is to flash all the computers after Silversmile has had its way with them. It wreaks hell on the systems, but usually only gets as far as the power supplies. The virus is programmed to notice anything they care about and fuck it up as much as possible. In a lot of ways, Silversmile resembles middle management to Javier.

As he walks down the line, flash tool in hand, wrecking the data on the ICDDs, Silversmile has done another thing it was programmed to do.

It's found another pathway—in the flash tool.

Silversmile latches onto the tool with little difficulty, riding on the bits that confirm the destruction of data, loading itself into the onboard drive image—a pathway that never would've existed without some help. Now, when each drive is imaged, it gets a fresh install of Silversmile. It's a greedy virus—taking control of everything it can. It will proceed to burn out all of the power supplies overnight.

When Javier is done, he locks up the Silversmile lab and heads for Juno's control console. He needs to put the flash tool back on the charger and connect it so Lucy can update the image to whatever she wants next.

The instant Javier connects his flasher to the bus on Juno, the lights in the room go red, a klaxon sounds and the console monitor flashes.

>>SYSTEM BREACH DETECTED<<

5

RESCUE PUPPIES

The first time Blue took Marcus for a sprint down the central strut, it was euphoric. Hurtling forward through the kilometer-long hallway felt like flying, and reminded her of her undergrad days of triathlons and cross country. For the first time since she'd begun to die, she felt alive.

Now that sprint can't end fast enough.

Blue rockets through the halls as fast as her synthetic legs will carry her, past the empty crew modules, past the docking bay and escape pods, past the open sockets for more labs and servers, toward the open door that leads to the SCIF. Daniel waits in the doorway, waving her onward with one hand, a pulse rifle in the other.

She enters to find the SCIF in chaos. Sirens shriek, lights flash, red warning lights pop up, then disappear for no reason.

"Up here!" Anne calls, drawing Blue's attention up to

Juno's server cage. Anne leans out over the catwalk that lines the structure and gestures to a quick-access ladder. Blue takes the ladder two rungs at a time, throwing herself upward with each pull. When she crests the top, she finds a sizable group of her crewmates shouting at one another while Lucy and Javier frantically type away at terminals.

"What the fuck were you thinking, Javier?" one of the lab techs shouts. It's Nick, from Josep's project, a pushy little asshole from Oxford.

"That's how I always charge the tool! It's fucking 'read only'… It can't… You can't write to it without—" Javier protests, his face unnaturally pale. "It's supposed to be read only when you're—"

"Don't bother him right now," Lucy says, her voice uncharacteristically decisive. Blue has never seen her in a crisis, and wonders when she grew a backbone. "We fix the situation first."

"What's going on?" Blue asks Anne, pulling her aside. All of the digital folks are here in Juno's cage. She doesn't see Kambili, and that's a good thing. It probably means the kennels are still in good shape.

"Silversmile crossed the air gap," Anne says, "and it's contaminated Juno. Before you ask, we managed to lock it out of the general quarantine protocols."

"Shit. Did they take Rose Eagle offline? We can't risk the virus getting off the station."

"That was the first thing Josep did. Wreaked havoc on it, though. I don't think it'll be ahead of schedule for much longer."

"Okay." Blue let out a long sigh. "Any other damage?"

"The virus started a fire in its own lab while we were dealing with this. Halon took care of it, and they've still got backups. Right now they're fighting for Josep's Rose Eagle source data. It's all compromised, including the backups. The virus didn't eat them yet, but we can't restore without potentially destroying Juno all over again. Blue, the Glitter Edifice project files... They're—"

"I have my own backups," Blue says quietly, waving off Anne's concern. "They're current to last cycle."

"What? Where?" Anne's eyes narrow, and Blue regrets opening her mouth.

"I've been maintaining a private server in the kennels, just in case something like this happened." Blue glances around, keeping her features neutral. "Looks like I was right." In truth, she didn't want Juno poking around her files. She *certainly* didn't want the other project managers to have access, when she had no intention of filling her Weyland-Yutani project charter.

Anne guides her away from the group, out onto the catwalks.

"An unauthorized server? You know I never would've condoned that! How long has this been going on?"

"Six months."

"You kept this from me... while we were together?" Anne bares her teeth and ruffles her hair. "Jesus Christ... Unbelievable."

"Don't be like that," Blue says, starting to call her "babe," but the word dies in her mouth. Anne had been the one to end it. She enjoyed Marcus's body well enough, but she couldn't stand to be with someone "so close to the end."

"Don't make this about us," Blue corrects herself. "I took precautions to keep my project intact, and they're working."

"Yeah, well I wouldn't be so sure. Silversmile has targeted the control systems for the kennels."

Blue shakes her head. "It can't open the cells. No computer can. Only a human has access to those controls."

Anne laughs bitterly, resting her hands on her hips. "I know that. Not the cell doors—the heat shield. The virus destroys the most expensive and critical systems. It knows how much we value Glitter Edifice. Right now, everyone is busting their asses to save your big bugs. Just be glad Juno doesn't touch the life support systems, or we'd all be dead."

Panic sets its claws into Blue's chest.

She imagines every one of her fully-grown snatchers, burnt to a crisp in seconds—watching them pop like ancient flash bulbs, vaporized in the heat of Kaufmann's radiation. If that happens, the Company will cut its losses and shutter her project.

They'll send her home.

She'll never touch the aliens again.

"Ladies…" They both turn to see Dick Mackie striding toward them down the catwalk. The Australian's ordinarily tanned skin is sallow, probably from a long night of drinking. When he finally reaches them, a wave of body odor washes in their direction. "I see we're having an eventful morning."

Anne snorts. "Glad you could finally join us, Dick. It's been ten minutes since I called."

"Had to freshen up," he says with a grin. Given his appearance, it's a complete fabrication. Blue has known Dick to get all kinds of contraband onto the station, from unlicensed firearms to cocaine, and she imagines him doing a line to get his head screwed on straight. "What's wrong? Don't tell me the puppies are loose."

She hates it when he calls them that. When they were testing his kennels design with one or two specimens, he named one "Heath" and the other "Shrimpy," and moped when Blue had to kill them. In spite of his many eccentricities, he's created a secure work environment.

"No," Blue says, thankful that at least they're not facing a quarantine all-kill. "But Silversmile has control of Juno. It's trying to open the heat shield in the cells."

"Bloody hell," Dick says, pinching his lower lip. "You've got to get out there."

Blue cocks her head. "What?"

"The Turtle! The EVA thingy," Dick says. "Since the repair pod went belly up, it's all we've got. It's not exactly radiation proof, but your kind won't get cancer. You're the only one who can do it," he says. "Well, Marcus is, anyway. I can talk him through it, if you don't want to control him."

Blue looks up to the ceiling. "I'm sick of everybody telling me what to do with this body. It's the only one I have."

"Is this really the time to be complaining?" Anne asks. "Your project is about to go up in smoke."

That isn't true. They still have twenty eggs, and if all the adult creatures are dead, Blue might be able to use it as an excuse to replenish her stock of snatchers. That means accelerated testing for her side project. They could be pulling two embryos a week or more without raising an eyebrow.

"It's not worth the risk," Blue says, and Anne gives her a shocked look. "We still have a small stock of eggs. I don't have a replacement body. You can't do this project without me, and if I can't get around, it's on hold until the resupply."

6

SMOKE & MIRRORS

When Dorian first hears the klaxons, he expects some kind of minor incident. That's how things on space stations work—two hundred warnings for every little thing. "Much ado about nothing."

His bed is comfortable, his eyes heavy. The light of Kaufmann dimly suffuses the observation deck with an evening glow through the electropolarized glass coatings. It's a peaceful place, minimalist surroundings balanced against the raging inferno outside. He could watch the glow of fusing gasses for hours at a time.

But the klaxons won't go away. He hears crew shuffling in the hall, the rapid footsteps receding down the central strut. Muffled shouting echoes into his room.

He harbors the tiniest spark of hope that one of the snatchers has escaped, just because he'd like to see what it would do to a crew member. Would it be swift, or relish the violence? Surely the crew would have it all under control by the time he got there. After all, controlling the creatures is the whole purpose of the station.

He wishes Blue would open up to him more about the animals. He wants to know everything about them. If she has a dead one, he wants to touch it. Somehow the strange claws in the lab vats must be connected to the screeching, chitinous beasts.

His intercom beeps, and Dorian swears.

"Director?" says Commander Cardozo. "Are you awake?"

"I am now," Dorian replies, the words hoarse. He's been in cold sleep for a year, but the first time he tries to bed down for real, he gets interrupted. If this is some sort of routine drill, he's going to kill someone. Or at least see to it that they're terminated.

"We've got a situation at the SCIF. As the station commander, I'm requesting your presence, ASAP."

His heart speeds up. Maybe he was right, and someone *is* dead. He climbs out of bed and pulls on a pair of trousers over his briefs.

"Do I need to alert my crew?" he grunts, rummaging through his baggage for a dress shirt.

"No, they should be fine."

"Is everyone okay?"

"Yes," he says, and Dorian's heart sinks just a little. "… though we've got a tricky operation in the works. As the highest-ranking voice of the Company, we need your input."

"Okay. Be there in ten." Knowing that it isn't a matter of life and death, Dorian takes a little extra time getting dressed.

* * *

When he arrives at the SCIF, his bed head is tamed and shirt sharp. He left off the tie, since he's supposed to appear informal. Daniel is ready for him at the door, failing to hide his displeasure at Dorian's response time.

"The eggheads are busy inside. They'll bring you up to speed."

"And you're just going to stand here and hold the door?"

Daniel shakes his head. "This is an IT and security problem, but if this door closes right now, it might not reopen without some serious mechanical tinkering. No one inside needs my opinion, and they certainly don't need me getting in the way."

"So you might have to take the door off the hinges?"

"Yes, sir, and if that happens, safety protocols dictate that we destroy all of the biological specimens, so we don't want that."

Dorian imagines all those incredible creatures, murdered due to sheer human incompetence.

"No, we don't."

The Commander punches something into the terminal next to him. A set of wayfinding lights clicks on in the floor—bright green with a white flashing runner.

"This'll get you to the war room," Daniel explains. "Please head straight there."

Nodding without reply, Dorian follows the line through the bowels of the SCIF and into one of the many conference rooms. It's clear from the layout and affordances that the facility was designed for three times the number of staff. It could easily have housed three hundred people and fifty projects.

When he arrives, he finds a shouting match between Anne, Blue, and a third person—a tanned man he doesn't recognize. A long edge-lit table runs the room, and screens dot every wall. Blue stands in the back corner, arms crossed, staring daggers at her two colleagues on the opposite end.

"It's perfectly safe! And if it's not, I can repair you!" the tanned fellow shouts at her, so Australian that his "you" stretches on for three syllables. "Come on, dag."

"I don't believe we've met," Dorian says, extending his hand to the new person. "Director Dorian Sudler. I'm here to help, mister…"

"Dick Mackie. Nice suit," he replies, "but as you can see, we're all a little pinned at the moment, so if you could stay out of the way…"

"What seems to be the problem?"

"Director," Blue says, "we're in an emergency, so we don't have time to brief you."

"You want to let them die," Anne says, "so we've got all the time in the world. Director, the Silversmile virus is threatening the cells. We've got people working on flashing Juno, but if we don't lock down the heat shields, it's going to incinerate our cargo. We've got an EVA kit that can be used for repairing the star side of the station, but it takes an android body to survive."

"Perfect," Dorian says with a bright smile. "Let's get this cleared up."

"It's not that simple," Blue says. "If something happens to me, to this body, I won't be able to lead the project. Silversmile has just jeopardized itself and Rose Eagle. Fucking up Marcus will take down Glitter Edifice." She looks to Dorian. "Director, we can make more specimens to train. Egg storage is completely intact."

Dorian is seized by questions about snatcher reproduction, but there's no time to ask them.

"Yeah," Mackie says, "except you haven't had any more reliable births. The past three eggs have been duds. What if something's happened, and you've got only duds in there?"

Blue throws up his... *her* hands in exasperation. "We'll cross that bridge when we come to it."

"You've got sixty-three adult specimens in the cages," Mackie responds, sinking into a chair. "You bloody well better cross it now."

"Status update, guys," someone says, the voice coming over the intercom speaker.

"What is it, Javi?" Anne calls back. It must be Javier Paz, the sysadmin.

"The virus has partitioned itself, and it's doubled down on the kennels. It got one of the shield doors open."

"What are you saying?" Dorian asks, letting an uncomfortable edge sink into his voice.

"We're down one specimen," Paz says. "I'm sorry."

"I have every confidence in our ability to impregnate,"

Blue says. "As strong as your opinion may be, Dick, I'm the ranking scientist and—"

"Go out there and lock down the heat shield," Dorian says. "Now."

"Director, you're not listening—"

"No. I'm not. Either you will go out there and lock down the shields, or Marcus will. If it's Marcus, you're fired. I hope I make myself clear."

Everyone gapes in stunned silence. Anne's mouth hangs open.

"The project won't work without me," Blue says. "I'm the only one with—"

"There are other, smarter people in the galaxy. I'm sure we can find them. Now, I expect you to get out there and do your job." He looks them over, his eyes scouring theirs for any sign of insubordination. No one speaks to him.

No one fights back.

"Good choice," he says, his glare boring into Blue. "I want him suited up and vacuum-packed in five minutes, Anne."

7

WILD DOGS

The "Turtle" fits Marcus's body a little too snugly. It might as well have a sign that says "ultra skinny people only." Blue pulls the five-point restraint into place and does a final system check. All green.

The Turtle isn't much of an EVA suit, just a mirrored shield on the back and plates along all the edge surfaces. A pack stores propellant on her back, the same as the EVA suits of old. Unlike the old spacesuits, however, this one is composed of many of the same highly reflective composites as the Cold Forge itself. So was the defunct repair pod, before Dick Mackie fucked up a docking procedure. Blue will be able to face Kaufmann for two minutes before her android body begins to suffer melting temperatures. It will take her ten minutes to reach a catastrophic failure.

A normal human would be fried, or develop cancer if they were lucky enough to live.

"Okay, mate." Dick's voice is raspy over the radio. "I'm going to close the blast shields inside the kennels now."

In spite of herself, Blue is glad to have him helping. If he didn't close the interior doors, the snatchers might've figured out the heat shields were locked, and charged the glass until they broke through. Blue knows their awareness. She's seen them test the limits of their cages almost every day.

Sitting inside the SCIF airlock, Blue can feel the clanking of the interior doors locking down. Like the composite glass cell doors, the kennel blast doors are manual and air-gapped, requiring human in the loop operation. Silversmile cannot hack them open.

"Interior doors secured," Dick says. "The puppies aren't going anywhere."

"Copy," Blue responds, pressing the button to cycle the airlock. "Heading outside."

Blinding light slices into the chamber as the hatch slides open, revealing the fires of Kaufmann below. Blue grunts and shuts her eyes, hoping she hasn't done any damage to Marcus's optics by looking into the star.

"Remember, Blue, these are just easy games," Dick says. "You've got an extra life."

So says you. Blue positions her back to the star and pushes out of the airlock, dragging her tools with her. She can't look back again, or she might be damaged. Glancing right, she sees the brilliant, golden hull of the SCIF, its latched grid of modular heat shields dotting the decks. The only articulating heat shields are positioned over the kennels cells. It was Blue's behavioral modification routines that created this vulnerability. If she hadn't given her program the authority to access the beasts' heat shields, she wouldn't be doing a spacewalk over a star.

She reminds herself that she isn't really here, that she's resting comfortably back in her room. Whatever occurs, she'll still be alive at the end of all of this, though if she fails... maybe not for very long.

"I'm on the outer hull," she breathes, grabbing onto a handhold, but searing pain forces her to release it. She moans and clutches her hand, spinning slowly backward.

"Talk to me, Blue."

"It's too hot to use the handholds!"

He laughs.

She could kill him for that.

"It's a bleeding star beneath you, you fucking wanker! Of course the oven rack is hot!"

She stabilizes herself with the Turtle's polished boosters. Her silhouette against the hull is like a slithering blob of pitch against a surface of solid gold. Jets of air bring her closer to the hull. The pain in her hand recedes.

"Keep your tools in front of you," Dick says. "It'll keep them cooler."

"Okay." Marcus's husky voice is cracking. She hates how frightened and small he sounds. Compared to everyone else, she's a creature of incomparable grace.

Everyone except the snatchers.

"We've got an ongoing code injection against the kennels," Lucy says. "Juno is trying to close off all of the data ports, but Silversmile keeps opening them."

"Can you flash Juno back to her init state?" Blue asks. "Just restore her to factory?"

"If we do that, Rose Eagle goes down, and you lose your protein folding," Lucy says. "We'll lose all of the SCIF data."

Falling silent, Blue steers her pack toward the nearest heat shield portal and stops in front of it. She clicks the locking wrench into place, positioning it against the bracing bolts, and presses the trigger. The panel secures to the station with a grinding chunk she can feel through her arm.

"Better than losing Juno altogether," Blue says.

"You know what?" Lucy replies, an uncharacteristic edge in her voice. "I'm the genius programmer, and you're the geneticist, so how about we both stick to what we know?"

While Lucy will forfeit her experimental data, at least she has a functioning product that's easy to store. She can simply connect a drive to Juno, and she'll have a working version of Silversmile in captivity. Blue feels badly for Josep, though. He can't possibly be insulated from this failure.

No time for that.

Blue snaps her wrench onto the next panel and ratchets it down. She's burning up in the suit, and all of Marcus's pain receptors are firing signals straight into her brain. She wonders what her real body's heartbeat must be like. When she'd configured the brain-direct interface, she'd told it to keep pain intact, to pass along those critical messages. She thought she'd need pain to stop herself from accidentally cutting off a hand or incinerating her surrogate body.

But with each passing second, her skin grows hotter and her head grows lighter. The stress can't be good for her. She begins to wonder if she might die out here, after all.

"You all right?" Dick asks. "You're breathing pretty hard."

"I'm fine." Blue latches onto the next bolt. Two down, sixty-one to go. "Just hot, is all. I'm not sure I can do all of these." She clicks the button. The locking bolt spins. Her head swims.

"Did I ever tell you about the time I got attacked by wild dogs?"

Blue shakes her head inside her helmet, Marcus's thick blond hair brushing against the sides.

"Attacked... by wild dogs." She has to catch a handhold and sears her glove.

"Yeah, me and my brothers got into a bit of a scrap out on my dad's farm. Let me paint a picture for you. Deep in the Outback, south of Amoonguna, just red dust and hardscrabble. We raised emus on a hundred acres of land. Every day, either you shot something to eat or you ate some fucking emu. We had some chickens and such, but not much in the way of veg."

She spins down another heat shield. "Do you ever get tired of being such a fucking stereotype, Dick? You really expect me to believe you were a subsistence hunter?"

"One of the first Mars colonists was from the Outback—

my great, great, great grandmother. She's buried there. And you know what? Bush Aussies are perfect for space work."

"How do you figure that?" she grunts, working her wrench loose.

"In the Outback, you see the same thing every day. Nothing is easy. Everything is trying to kill you, and everywhere you live has a stupid name," he says. "I don't think I'd ever seen a tree until I went to school in New Zealand. So tell me, how is that different from space life?"

"The sunsets are probably nicer." Blue vectors herself toward the next target.

"Listen, mate, you're above the raw fury of a star. No view on Earth can compare."

"Don't remind me."

The radio crackles for a moment. "So can I finish my story or what?"

When Blue locks to the next door, she feels scratching and scraping through the metal. The creature underneath senses her, and is desperate to get out.

"Yeah... yeah, sure."

"So I was scrapping with my brothers and I threw a knife at Dylan and got him in the arm. He threw it back at me and missed by a mile, but he was crying and madder than a cut snake. Him and my other brother, Dalton, decided to hike back to the ranch without me."

"Your names are Dick, Dylan, and Dalton?"

"Quit interrupting. You've got heaps to do out there." Without waiting for her to reply, he continues. "I wasn't about to go back and get a hiding from my da, so I picked up my knife and went for a walkabout in the other direction. I just headed for the western sun. It was a big property, and you could go for a nice long time without ever seeing anyone."

She tries to imagine the baked clay earth and the drought-starved brush.

"I finally linked up with the highway, and it was getting late, so I figured it was time to head home. The sun started going down, and everything got a little cooler, thank God, and I'd started to enjoy myself when I saw them—a couple of coyotes pawing after me."

"Shit!" Lucy hisses into the mic, and one of the heat shields on the far end of the cell block yawns open.

Blue grabs onto the station instinctively. She feels a pop rumble across the deck as the interior glass gives way. Black smoke pours from the open cell, contaminated air sucked into the void. She stares at the opening, wide eyed, hoping it doesn't come out. Blue can't hear it, but she knows the beast is screaming and shrieking, clawing and biting.

"Lucy, do you have control of Juno, or not?" Blue says, her breath coming too fast.

"We're doing our best here!"

"Your best isn't good enough." Blue nearly drops her locking wrench as she pulls away from the hull. She's hyperventilating. "Oh, Jesus. Okay, Lucy, I expect you to—"

"Oi. You. Stop interrupting," Dick says, his tone authoritative. Her breathing slows. "Now do you want to hear my coyote story or not?"

She catches hold of the wrench and grits her teeth. She still needs to lock down more than fifty cells. She'll be out here for hours at this rate.

"These coyotes aren't like what you Americans have, all scrappy and healthy. Outback coyotes don't turn down a meal, especially when that meal is a little boy all alone."

"Even if that meal tastes like Dick?" Blue asks, voice quavering.

She locks in the wrench.

Another cell down.

"Clever girl." Dick chuckles. "My first thought is to run. That's what any sane person would do. We Aussies aren't known for our sanity."

"You're in the top ten for quality of life and medical care on the planet. You can spare me the tough Aussie routine."

"You're thinking of the cities, dag. Sydney and Brisbane in particular. Not Alice Springs. Certainly not Amoonguna. Those are places nobody wants. Mars is more fucking hospitable than my hometown. If you wanted to eat, you had to kill, and you could just as easily wind up on the menu."

She latches a few more cells as he pontificates about the conditions of the Outback. It's working, keeping her mind off the intense heat and fear of failure, until another shield opens up next to her. This isn't like her behavior mod routine, where it flaps open and closed again. The door comes open slowly, the air inside rising to a thousand degrees Fahrenheit as solar winds buffet its particles.

She vectors backward toward the star, careful not to go

too far. Oily smoke fills the chamber, then erupts outward as the interior glass bursts like a bubble. The snatcher scrabbles out of its cell onto the golden surface of the Cold Forge. This marks the first time Blue has seen one with nothing between them. It doesn't appear to be dying.

"Shit," she says, repeating it over and over into her comm like a prayer. "Shit, shit shit shitshitshit."

"Steady. Steady on, mate," Dick says. "I wasn't going to be some victim. I'd read about the French Foreign Legion."

Smoke wafts from the creature's form like steam as the last air particles trail away. Its lips curl and claws flex. It's getting ready to jump. It shouldn't be functional. The solar loading on its black carapace should be boiling its guts faster than its skin can expand.

To Blue's horror, the other heat shields begin to open. They waft aside like the fronds of a fern in a gentle wind.

"When they're outnumbered," Dick says, voice rising above Blue's swearing, "they fix bayonets and charge."

"Silversmile has control of the shield!" Lucy says, but she's way too late.

The creature explodes, yellow acid blood and shrapnel spraying in every direction. Blue watches the others break free from their cells before a smear of sulfurous yellow smacks against the lens of her helmet. An acrid stench fills her suit. Blue screams as the electropolarized plastic begins to fail, blown glass bubbling away from her.

"Get back to the airlock," Dick says, any pretense of storytelling gone now. She throws one hand against her helmet, scraping the bubble free and fusing her glove to the plastic. It's eating through into her palm. It burns like nothing she's ever felt. She can't see, but she's begun to tumble. The full wrath of Kaufmann's heat bears down in waves.

"Blue… *Blue!*" Dick shouts. "It's not real. You're not dying, but you've got to get out of there."

She tries to steer the Turtle, but it won't listen to her. She can't find a way to right herself. There's a "return-to-home" command on the right side of her pack—accessible via the hand that's melting to her helmet at that very moment. She twists in open space, feeling for it. The other snatchers are going to pop at any second, a barrage of molten grapeshot.

"Okay, Blue, hit the return-to-home, now." Dick's voice is calm and sure.

Low-pressure warnings fill her ears. She's losing oxygen—not that it matters. Marcus doesn't need to breathe, but the thought of not filling her lungs induces more panic. Her visor's protections are failing as acid disrupts the lattice of polarizing nanotubes. The sun blisters her face, and she can't communicate because her microphone has fused with the half-melted visor.

"Fuck, fuck, fuck," she whispers with what air she has left. Her left hand won't reach the control surface. Her visor is either black in the middle or painfully bright at the edges. She's going to lose Marcus out here, spinning in the abyss. She won't be able to work on her project again until the resupply in six months. Sudler will figure out her secrets long before then.

This false death will be the beginning of a much longer real one.

"Fuck, fuck, fuck… fuck it."

Using her left hand, she unbuckles herself from the EVA pack's restraints, careful not to let go of the dangling straps. She spins it upside down, stopping it with the edges of her boots. She leans into it, shielding her face from the sun as best she can, and looks through the edge of her visor. There's the return-to-home button, just next to her left hand. She presses it.

The pack violently pulls away as its thrusters engage, and Blue snatches out at the belts that once held her fast. She barely catches hold of one, but Marcus's arms are strong and solid. He won't let go.

Particles of radiation load the back of her suit, baking her inside. The saving grace is that she continues to spin like a rotisserie, getting an even heat as opposed to being burned to death on one side.

The pack zips through open space, bucking wildly as it compensates for Blue's unstable weight. She catches sight of the hull, but it's a shower of acid blobs and appendages in a haze of dissipating black smoke.

If she takes another hit, she won't make it back.

"Blue! Blue do you copy?" She can't respond with a dead mic. Her legs swing out as the EVA pack pinwheels her toward the ship, and she nearly loses her grip on the strap.

"Come on, baby," she says. "Just a little more, and—"

She slams against the hull like she's just been hit by a transport, and the pack twists loose from her clutching hand. It rockets away from her, but she can't see where. She only knows it went up.

"No!"

Blue flails outward with her free hand, searching for any possible purchase. She finds a thin ledge and digs her fingers into it, pulling her body close. The radiant heat of the station sears her hand and torso where the suit touches, in spite of its substantial protections.

Pulling herself upward, she spots a shadowed opening. The airlock. The pack must've scraped her off while trying to enter. Her foot finds a purchase below her and she kicks, desperate to fill the edges of her vision with the cave-like sanctuary.

She reaches inside and finds the airlock's handhold, pulling herself to safety. Throwing her back to the cold wall, she slams the cycle button to begin repressurization. Back under the sway of artificial gravity, she sinks to her knees, hyperventilating. The fucking Turtle rests against the far wall, having successfully "returned to home."

When enough air fills the chamber, she hears Dick on the loudspeaker, calling for her to give him a status. But she can't speak. She can't stop shaking. She reaches up to unlatch her helmet, and in spite of the oxygen, she still can't breathe. There's a distant, incessant beeping.

Her hands seize up and the world pitches. Something must be wrong with the gravity drive, because a force pulls her hard toward the deck. She doesn't recognize the warning beeps that she's getting. They don't sound like any of the error codes she knows.

As she sinks to her knees, she recognizes the warning from a long-ago hospital stay.

It's her bedside oxygen alarm.

8

TRUTH WILL OUT

"How is she?"

Dorian sort of cares, and sort of doesn't. On the one hand, Blue is the most interesting person on this scrapheap, and on the other, she jeopardized the lives of all his specimens with a few amateurish lines of code. Too many adult snatchers died in the fires of Kaufmann. Each one was priceless, but as a Company line item, they were close to a million dollars each: procurement, housing, power, logistics. Blue's research will have to pay dividends, or her project will be catastrophically in the red.

She could've asked for help from someone more qualified to write the containment code, but she didn't. Why not? Why did she insist on doing everything herself?

"Stable. Dying," Anne says, crossing her arms. "The usual."

"Don't do that," Dorian chides.

Anne stands in his doorway, leaning against the frame.

She came to him to give him an update after Marcus intubated Blue. He'd set up his drawing stool to sketch the starlight filtering into his room, but lost interest. When Anne arrived, he was still sitting at his stool, newsprint firmly mounted in place. He'd started drawing her instead.

"Don't do that," Dorian repeats. "Cross your arms, that is. I had you one way, and you've moved too much."

Anne narrows her eyes. "What? You're drawing me?"

He smiles and inclines his head. "You're a picture. I should absolutely draw you."

She smiles more coyly than he'd expected, as though she'd hoped to hear such a tacky line. Dorian feels attraction to Anne in the same way that he enjoys pornography— prurient, mutable, forgettable. She carries a few of his fetishes: her fitness, her sharp eyes, her potential for violence. He's only ever felt lust, never emotional attachment. Once upon a time he avoided women because they reinforced the fact that something was wrong with him. Now, however, Anne is a distraction, and he needs to be removed from the annoyance percolating in his veins.

He's seen her looking at him, too. Anne is a physical animal, someone who enjoys a workout, someone who likes lean, muscular men. Dorian noticed her looking the same way at Marcus—watched him walking away, glanced down at his chest when he crossed his arms. Dorian's physique will afford him some advantages.

The way he styles his hair, waxes his skin, his speech patterns—Dorian affects a synthetic look. He wonders if Anne likes that, specifically, about him. Does she enjoy all of her men as plastic objects? Does she make Marcus fuck her when Blue isn't in control? Or maybe Blue and Anne have enjoyed each other's company before.

He reaches across to grab his pack of smokes, and finds he's running low on matches. He's even more annoyed because he remembers he still can't find his striker paper. It's not like it matters—he has an electric lighter—but he enjoys the ritual of it all.

"Please don't," Anne says, but she doesn't turn to leave or stop him.

"Smoke?" he asks.

"Draw me. I'm not cooperating with this." But she puts her hands down by her sides, the way they were before. "I haven't showered or anything."

"I think that's beautiful," he lies with a thoughtful smile. "It's a hard day's work, well-earned on your skin." He doesn't like stink. If she takes his bait, he'll insist on fucking her in the shower. "Can I ask you a question?"

"Shoot."

He looks into her eyes from across the room, and imagines how he appears—a lanky, athletic fellow in a suit, dark against the fury of a star. It's a nice composition. She should enjoy it.

"Why are you nice to me when no one else is?"

This is a lie, more or less. Anne isn't any nicer or meaner than any other crew member, except Blue. If he were basing his question on deference, he should be trying to fuck Lucy. If he were basing his question on respect, he'd be trying to fuck Commander Cardozo.

He hopes to cement the idea of a special bond between them. At first, she'll see him as pleasantly misguided by her politeness, but at the crux of his sentence lies another implication. *"You've made me feel less alone."* Because Dorian has been so cold to everyone else, Anne will wonder if she's the only person with the ability to do so.

"What are you talking about? Commander Cardozo is—"

"Doing his job," Dorian says. "He's a military man meeting a superior."

"I was in the Colonial Marines, too," she responds, raising an eyebrow. "Don't you forget it."

"You're more adaptable than that, though. He defines himself by his military career. You seem more like someone who defines herself by... potential."

"Are you bagging on the Marines?"

"I wouldn't dare."

"Goddamned right you won't." She nods at him. "How long do I have to stand here?"

This is tricky. She can't feel trapped or hit on, or it will end abruptly.

"Oh, sorry. I was just kidding around... about the drawing stuff. You don't have to stay if you don't want to."

It's frustrating, having to cloak his intentions behind plausible deniability, constantly having to cover for one physical urge or another. He understands why the Company wouldn't want him sleeping with the subjects of his audits. They think his targets would feel compelled to please him, just to keep their jobs. Yet the sex part is boring. No, for Dorian it's about overcoming the defenses of an enemy. Pulling the levers of power is just cheating. Harassment is a game for the limp-dicked old executives.

Dorian is better than that. He does, however, wish he could let Anne know she's playing against him. It would be fun to see her genuine reaction, if she knew what was at stake.

"Oh, really?" She looks disappointed. "I thought you really were sketching me."

"I was," he says, "but I don't want to hold you up if you have somewhere to be."

She strides inside a few paces. "Security is done for the day. Juno is offline, and Javier's rebuilding her. Dick is making sure the cells will still work. It's all 'hurry up and wait' at this point."

He glances down at the conté on newsprint, rough black streaks of smudged gestures. They look feminine and strong, sharp diagonal cuts of hips and shoulders, in contrast to the vertical framework of the door. To draw for posture is to render someone nude to their bone structure, stripping away poor clothing choices, regrettable pockmarks on skin, and even expressions.

"I didn't have long," he says, "but would you like to see what I got so far?"

She moves to his side and looks over the paper. What does she see in it? She's little more than a stick figure with geometric volumes superimposed over her form. He wipes his hands on a rag.

"Why don't you draw digitally?"

"Because I can't feel it."

This is the truest thing he's said since arriving at the Cold Forge. He cares little for the real people in his life, and recognizes his indifference as one of his great strengths. Stories, however, can make him cry. When he stares into the eyes of a painting, he can connect in a meaningful way, even for the briefest of seconds. For Dorian, portraiture is like the process of archaeology, sweeping away pure white sands to find the figuration hidden underneath. His tools are crayon and charcoal, smudge stick and eraser.

It's a filthy process.

The screen adds a layer of unacceptable sterilization. It removes the essence to which he would connect. Perhaps that's why it's so easy for him to hurt people on a spreadsheet. Figures have no scent, no life, no beauty.

"It's beautiful," she says. It isn't though, any more than a lump of dirt is beautiful pottery. She's lying to him because she thinks he's proud of it. She's interested in his approval.

He waits for her to become awkward enough to take a seat.

"You never answered my question," he says. "Why are you so nice to me?"

"I think you're misunderstood," she replies.

He swerves his expression away from the wan smile he wants to give her. He'd love to tell her about every person who's ever called him a corporate shill, a hatchet man or a heartless son of a bitch, and that they're entirely correct. He loves the interplay of patterns created and broken. He likes to win, and in moments of transcendent blunt honesty, he knows he likes for someone to lose. That's the only way the game can be meaningful.

"How so?" he asks, but he knows her answer before she speaks the words. *It's a tough job. Someone has to do it. It's a company, not a charity.* All of it meaningless because it robs him of his agency in the equation. He loves to shut down projects. He enjoys every minute of it. He brings balance to a great machine by introducing chaos into the component parts.

"Would you mind if I tried again?" he says, gesturing for her to bring her chair closer and sit in front of him.

She does.

He begins with the broad strokes of her face: the brow line, the lips, the way her jaw meets her ear, the shape of her head. He's rushing, though, to get to her eyes—the main event. Once he reaches those glassy blue orbs, he can stare into them for as long as he wants without an excuse.

Dorian asks Anne about her childhood, and hears about life on the flooded Gulf Coast, about all of the hurricanes and tornadoes and tragedies of small-town life. He's an excellent listener, practiced in the art of making someone feel not only heard, but appreciated. He laughs at her jokes, indulges her glances at his body. Looking directly into her eyes as he is, he can follow each and every one of them.

She tells him about her father's suicide when she was in high school, and the reason why she joined the Corps. She tells him of her mother's opiate addiction and her estranged sister who works in a New York advertising firm. She talks about college at Purdue. She talks about briefly dating a pro baller. Lastly, she talks about joining the Corps and being dishonorably discharged for public intoxication during a siege.

She never once asks about Dorian. That would be a warning sign, if she did. No one should notice him—not the real him.

When she's had her fill of his false indulgence, he looks long into her eyes, leans forward and kisses her. She doesn't protest. Quite the contrary. She wants him. She burns for his touch, and he doesn't expect her to be so bold or powerful. She shoves him down and shows him all the wonderful things her body can do, devouring every inch of his flesh. She washes him in her fantasies, wringing every last drop of ecstasy from his bones, and showing him that he's been missing from her station life for far too long.

He is startled.

He is aroused.

He is accepted.

He fights her for dominance, tumbling across the sprawling bed in his quarters, over the dresser, onto the sink. She fights dirty, biting and scratching, and in the end, he recognizes her raw strength. She holds him down and throttles him as they climax one last time.

Anne Wexler has won, and for once, there are no losers.

It's near the end of the night cycle when Dorian awakens, stiff and coated in dried sweat, to find Anne staring at him, her chin propped up by an elbow. At first, he worries that it might be some sort of legitimate affection, like the way lovers watch one another sleep. He's pleased, therefore, when he sees the subtle cues of worry upon her face.

"What's wrong?" he asks.

"This was fun."

He gives her a quizzical look. "Is that the face you make when something is fun?"

"Sorry," she says. "I just know I shouldn't have done it."

Mustering a semblance of sympathy, he says, "You didn't do it alone. I'm not supposed to be fraternizing with the station employees. Could cloud my judgment."

She cuddles into the crook of his arm, which strikes him as completely out of character with her matter-of-factness and animalistic fucking. He hopes he hasn't found some soft core at the heart of her. It would be too disappointing.

He likes Anne, or rather, he enjoys her company. She makes good decisions, and doesn't seem like the type to mourn. If she remained near him, she'd provide a source of reasonable entertainment.

She strokes his chest and sighs, her hand warm on his exposed skin.

"And what is your judgment?" she asks, and kisses the tender flesh of his ribcage.

For her to ask so quickly after sleeping with him exposes her lovey-dovey bullshit for the act that it is. She thinks he's stupid, or at least she hopes he is. An average man, blissed out on post-coital dopamine might choose this moment to share a personal crisis or some vulnerability. Certainly, Dorian's personal walls are the thinnest after sex or a good, hard workout, when lassitude tugs at his guard.

He marvels at her willingness to share her body with him to gain this information, though in his opinion it couldn't have been any real sacrifice. He knew how to please her, understood her needs, pushed the requisite buttons.

What other intrigues does she have around the station?

Dorian has never loved anyone, and he certainly doesn't love Anne. However, this question cements her into a special place in his heart. He, too, has fucked his way through several superiors, to get to where he is today.

"Silversmile's escape yesterday put everyone on thin ice," he says, choosing truth. "In many ways it was a successful test of the project, in others, an abject failure. The evolutionary characteristics Lucy talked about in the outbrief were promising, but a weapon that can't be controlled is only a liability."

"You can say that again," she agrees. "Lucy may have been brilliant back on Earth, but she isn't cut out for the contracts sector. Seems more like the bong-smoking Palo Alto type."

That can't be a simple observation, given Dorian's position within the Company. She's trying to get him to cut Lucy's project. But is it because she hates Lucy, or because she wants to preserve Blue's funding?

It's understandable to take shots at Lucy. She's weak,

and jeopardizes the entire enterprise.

"Doctor Janos's communications array is in shambles, his data and his backups could be lost. He's privately assured me that he can fix everything, but if I'm being blunt, I find that questionable. I'd be surprised if either project survives."

"That's sad," Anne says. "He was essentially done. Years of work just… flushed."

He stops, deliberately leaving out Glitter Edifice. He wants to see how she will interpret his silence. He runs his fingers along her shoulder and down her muscular arm— the arms that overpowered him in bed.

"What about Doctor Marsalis's project?" Her voice is measured, like someone pretending not to care.

"Glitter Edifice is already a money sink, and Doctor Marsalis has been unwilling or unable to produce results. She hasn't been forthcoming about her methods, nor about any discoveries regarding the creatures' biology. On top of all that, she's lost the vast majority of her data to the virus." He shakes his head in disgust. "I'm tempted to seize her project assets, stuff her into cold storage, and place the whole thing under new management."

He knows Blue must've been working with Elise Coto, but he doesn't yet know how. Simply firing her wouldn't be nearly as sweet as exposing her secrets. Dorian glances down at Anne, and he wonders how else he can make her useful.

"Blue, uh— Doctor Marsalis can be difficult, I know," Anne says. "I think a lot of that is the way she presents things. I'm sure she's made more progress than she's telling you about."

"Anne," he says, "I can only measure success by results, not vague assumptions of competence. Her project reports were falsified. Her boss was arrested, and now—conveniently—her local backups are gone."

"What?"

"Yes," he says, sitting up. "Now, I don't doubt that the good doctor has been doing her job, but *what* job, and for whom?"

"Jesus Christ," she mumbles. "Look, I'm not comfortable talking about this when she's fighting for her life in the next room."

"Anne," Dorian continues, making sure to look directly into her eyes, "Blue is on Company medical care. If she loses this job, she won't survive the trip back to Earth. If you know something that will make her valuable to us, now is the time to say so."

Anne recoils slightly, her arm drawing up over her breasts. He finds it a strange gesture, physical vulnerability felt under mental threat. Was it that he referred to Weyland-Yutani as "us?" He'll make amends to her later, when he wants sex. He'll offer up some morsel of usefulness, and she'll try to fuck it out of him. Their relationship is transactional now, and that gives him the greatest possible comfort.

Love is a fool's game.

"Listen…" she says. "Blue had a backup server that she was operating without supervision. I'm sure she found something important, because she never told me about it, not until the Silversmile outbreak."

"Whatever it holds, she needs to share," he says. "The Company isn't her personal piggy bank."

Anne relaxes, her arm falling back to her side.

"Just… don't fire her. She probably did something stupid. I mean, I know she does stupid things from time to time—"

"I'm not going to fire her."

Not until he's secured the server, and is on his way home.

9

ADRENALINE

The central strut is only a little over half a mile, which means Dorian has to jog up and down it twenty times to break a sweat. He huffs along in an oxygen deprivation mask, trying to make his feet heavy and shoulders weak, but his body is far too invigorated by the latest developments.

The ineptitude of the Cold Forge is spectacular. He's going to cycle off all the personnel off all the projects—including Anne, since she's been withholding information about Blue. It's going to be a bloodbath, and when he turns in his quarterlies he'll have eliminated one of the largest cash hemorrhages on the Company books. His annual bonus is typically based on the cost-saving measures he's taken, and this one will be off the charts.

Footsteps sound behind him and he slows up a tick, allowing the newcomer to catch up. When he glances right he finds Josep maintaining a healthy clip, even though the man has circles under his eyes.

"Morning, Doctor Janos."

"Morning, Director." His voice is chipper, even if his face can't follow suit. He's puffy, and shows signs of stress. His greeting doesn't rise at the end, either because he isn't explaining something, or because he feels like a marked man. The two continue together in silence for a while. Dorian likes Josep's form, his athletic prowess, his muscular shoulders and legs, but after two laps, he's already having trouble keeping up. Has he been drinking?

"Director," Josep huffs. "A lot of the crew have been talking, and I want to give you a piece of friendly advice."

"Friendly advice," he repeats. He's heard the phrase before in fiction, but never in person. He knows what inevitably follows—a threat of some kind, typically veiled as a concern. What "friendly advice" could the crew of this abomination offer up?

One of Dorian's feet hits a misstep, and he nearly takes a tumble. Josep catches his arm and steadies him. Beneath his mask, Dorian burns with humiliation.

"You okay, man?" Josep asks as they come clamoring to a halt.

Who is this person, who thinks it's okay to touch his betters? The meters come raining down on Dorian as they stop, and he inwardly curses Janos for the interruption. He'll never get back to where he was—he'll be too spent.

"I'm fine." He pulls back his arm. "I think you had some advice for me?"

"Director, uh—" Janos pauses. He must've envisioned

this going differently. "I just think that… you know, if there are some problems with our funding, you should tell us."

Dorian straightens up, forcing his breathing under control even though it makes him lightheaded. He's going to show Janos how power plays work. He starts by stonewalling.

"Some of us have been on this station for years," the man continues. "We were looking forward to going home triumphant. I don't want you to have a revolt on your hands, you know?"

"You know" is the sort of thing someone says when they're too scared to give their actual opinion. It's a sheep's bleat for the flock to join him.

"Part of the benefit of having three project leads on the Cold Forge is that you can assist each other, right?" Dorian asks.

"Yeah." Janos looks confused. "Look, man, I'm not sure where you're going with this."

"I read your dossier. Didn't you go to Berkeley? Specialized in computer science and cryptography?"

"Yeah. I did." Janos smooths down his massive mustaches. "Undergrad in chemistry from Stanford."

"Which is what enabled you to help with Silversmile."

"Yes."

Dorian sucks in a long breath, holding it even though his lungs beg for him to blast it from his lips. "So if you're so fucking smart, how about you explain why an experimental virus wiped everything you've worked on since arriving here?"

Janos looks at him as though he's been punched.

"Because it would seem to me," Dorian continues, "that you'd have some basic goddamned precautions in place to stop exactly this from happening, Doctor Janos."

"I... I..." he stammers. He's well outside the realm of expectation, and that's something Dorian knows how to manipulate. He raises his eyebrows.

"And since we're offering people friendly advice about how to do their jobs, here's mine. Get your fucking resume up to date, and expect to be on the next long haul home unless you turn all of this around."

Janos's face is priceless. He gapes like a fish, suffocating on the beach after a wave has brought it ashore. In a way, that's what happened to him. A violent force came crashing along and lifted him out of his comfortable little world, depositing him out of reach and out of hope. It wouldn't be the first time Dorian has seen something like this.

"Maybe I phrased that wrong," Dorian says, placing a hand on Josep's shoulder. The man tenses at Dorian's touch. A normal person would fear being struck, but that's what makes the play work so well. Josep won't lash out, but Dorian wants to prove it. He wants to show Josep what cowardice infests his heart.

"You said you wanted to know where you stand," Dorian says, looking into Josep's shrunken irises. "That's where you stand this very second—but it's only because your project is in ruins, and you threatened me with revolt."

"It was a turn of phrase—"

"You understand that it's in your best interest," Dorian

says, raising a finger, "to shut up. Just… listen."

Josep straightens up, and Dorian takes his hand away.

"You don't have to lose your job. The next transport rotation isn't for three months. If you can get Rose Eagle back online by then, hey… no harm, no foul. Or, you can find some other way to make yourself useful. You led your project to great success here, before it all came crashing down." He lets a moment of silence pass between them to punctuate the tragic statement.

Josep's gaze drifts away.

"Maybe you ought to be in charge of Silversmile. Help me understand the reasons that Lucy and Javier fucked this whole place up so badly. I can make the case to Corporate that you're just a bystander in all of this. I can downplay your involvement with the virus, including your mishandling of information security. Would you like to see that happen, Doctor Janos?"

Josep pulls the most pathetic face yet.

"Lucy is my friend, Director."

It takes all of Dorian's control not to laugh. "And what do you think she's going to say to me when I start discussing which projects to cut? Do you think she's going to remind me that you were just collateral damage, and that you don't deserve to be let go? After all, her project still works. Her code is still intact. Where's yours?"

Gritted teeth. He knows Dorian is right. In the end, everyone is willing to turn on their friends to preserve what's theirs. Josep can't afford to go home empty-handed after all of this effort.

"It may not come to that, you know. There's always the chance you could get Rose Eagle back online. And hey, maybe you could help me with data recovery on Glitter Edifice. You're a data genius, right?"

Josep grimaces. "What do you mean? Doctor Marsalis lost her research along with mine."

"Don't be so sure," Dorian says. "It looks like she took all of the precautions you should've, and set up a redundant, air-gapped private server. Of course, she hasn't been forthcoming on the details. I guess it's news to you, too."

He blanches and swallows hard. After the hangover and short jog, Dorian wonders if the man is going to throw up onto the deck.

"I didn't know."

"Well," Dorian says, putting his hands onto his hips and stretching his back, "I've got three people who could lead that recovery effort: the evasive Doctor Blue Marsalis, the destructive Doctor Lucy Biltmore... and you. Any recommendations for how to tackle it? Maybe you could start by helping me locate the fucking thing."

"Sure..." he replies. "Well... as you said, I've got a lot of work to do."

Dorian licks his lips. "I'll let you get to it, sport." Then he continues his jog, leaving Josep behind. As he passes the main station server room, he glances over the racks of Titus, pleased that it wasn't hit by Silversmile. They might've lost life support.

He had worried he wouldn't be able to get back to his run, but the adrenaline of attacking Josep has given his muscles an effervescence they hadn't possessed earlier this morning. A half-hour passes, and he's able to drain away some of his zeal, forcing his body to keep moving. It's going smoothly when heavy, slamming footfalls approach from behind, fast.

Dorian spins on his heel, nearly toppling when he sees Blue closing on him with inhuman speed.

"Jesus Christ," Dorian pants, bending over.

"Apologies, Director Sudler," Blue says. "I thought you would like me to join you running. My name is Marcus. Blue has asked me to inform you that she's feeling better, and should be returning to work tomorrow."

Dorian squints at the artificial being. Marcus is what he would be, were he not saddled with humanity. Lean, lithe, and perfect. Dorian hates that he's been rendered a panting wreck by his exercise routine. He stands up straight, inclining his head toward the synthetic.

"And how is he?" he asks, but Marcus's report reminds him of the frail woman lying in her bed, wasting away. "Uh, she?"

Marcus gives him a pleasant smile. "Recuperating. Muscle relaxants, antibiotics, and painkillers to dull the aches of intubation. I expect her to be out for the remainder of the day."

Dorian frowns. "So she isn't a party to our conversations?"

"No, Director, though I am bound to care for her well-being, so I'll brief her on the contents of our discussion."

Dorian chuckles to himself. There are so many pieces in play now, and he wouldn't have dared try this with

Blue in command of the body. She might recognize it. She might stop him.

"Weyland-Yutani Master Override Alpha One Thirteen Authorization Sudler."

Marcus snaps to attention.

INTERLUDE

DICK

The kennels are quiet. They're always quiet when the blast doors are closed. The creatures only awaken when they sense an opportunity for escape—or when they sense people. Then the snatchers are happy to instill a bit of fear, regardless of whether or not there's anything to gain.

Dick walks the SCIF from room to room, checking for the fiftieth time to make sure that everything's in its place. Without the threat of Kaufmann's light, he's had to rig up a shock system sensitive to sudden movements or loud noises. Move too fast, get a nasty shock. If they bleed, the cell will flood with lye, and if the beasts do anything too stupid, he's happy to purge the entire block into space.

Next, he walks to egg storage, where he spies twenty powered storage cases with meticulous climate control. They're monitored for humidity and temperature, as well as galvanic skin response. They're wired to incinerate and flood with lye as well, on the off chance that one of them opens up inside the box. If one of those skittering bastards were to get loose, Cold Forge would be down a crew member, no question.

The litter of empty cases attests to the lateness of the project.

His power loader exoskeleton stands idle in the back. Dick always dreads strapping into it, since the creatures watch him whenever he carries a storage case to Blue's lab. He can't shake the feeling that they know what he's carrying, even if they can't see it, can't smell it.

Lastly Dick heads to the chimp tank. He looks forward to seeing them every day, even if he's going to kill them. They're the only things on the stupid station that are always nice, even if they don't speak a lick of English. He'll probably take one of the thawed ones, feed him, check him over on the vet table, and put him back. It'll be a lovely diversion from the darkening mood Dorian Sudler has brought with him. Dick knows he shouldn't get attached, but the temptation for animal contact is too great.

And yet, when he draws near, he hears screaming.

They're riled up from something like Dick has never heard before. Carefully he creeps to one of the many armories they've placed throughout the kennel complex and takes a rifle. Sadly, it's not one of the caseless ammo pulse rifles like the Colonial Marines use—that would punch holes in the space station. Dick doubts his gun would be enough if one of the bugs got loose, but the armories are a comfort to the scientists. He throws the bolt to chamber a round and slinks closer, not willing to take the safety off until he understands what's going on.

One of the cages is open, and Kambili Okoro has a beast on its back atop the vet table. Kambili wears a bloodstained surgeon's gown and bonnet, and he's digging around in the poor thing's fucking neck. Fine strands of crimson drip from the table. Some kind of plastic tubing, like a sausage casing, hangs from a rack nearby.

Okoro isn't supposed to be down here. The chimps aren't his department. This isn't his shift, and even if it were, he isn't supposed to harm them in front of the others. They've been careful in the past not to scare the animals. This will make their care and feeding much more difficult.

The chimp moans as its compatriots beat on their glass. It's crying. It's not even well sedated, probably because Kambili lacks Dick's veterinary training.

"Oi!" Dick steps from the corner. "What the bloody hell is this?"

Kambili raises his hands as though the rifle is being pointed at him, a skin-fusing iron in his grip. He doesn't speak, and Dick can't read his expression through the surgical mask.

"Did you fucking hear me, mate?"

The chimp on the operating table languidly raises a hand, questing toward some unseen object in the air. It's not paralyzed.

"Shit," Dick mutters. "Step back!"

Kambili has just long enough to mumble a confused reply before his patient bellows and snatches off half of his face.

In that instant, time slows down. Kambili goes stumbling backward, hands rising, not fully aware of the cause of his newfound pain. The chimp kicks off the table, enraged, and its intestines come spilling out. Dick fires a shot, hitting it squarely in the chest.

It still comes for him, entrails dangling, painting the floor a brilliant red like the stroke of some massive brush. One bullet is never enough when the target is committed. He pops it twice more, and it trips from the blood loss, drugs, and guts, sliding into his feet, and then going still.

Kambili crouches in the corner, his screams merging with those of the chimps.

1 0

SERVICE & SERVERS

The station has a med bay, right outside the crew quarters module, though Blue has rarely had occasion to use it. Her room is equipped with most of the advanced technology she needs for her complex daily care. She hasn't been to a real hospital in years. So it feels strange to her to be standing in the med bay over Kambili's bed, his face so bandaged that only one eye and part of his mouth are visible.

She's fatigued, and the connection to Marcus's body lacks its usual sparkle—her brain can't buy the illusion that she's a healthy, safe person. Phantom pains crisscross her chest, and she finds herself coughing for seemingly no reason at all. Her real body is a dream. Marcus's body is the truth. It has to be, because she refuses to live her final days fading away like a pathetic husk.

Because, looking at Kambili, she knows her work will be put on hold, and she'll soon be fired.

He coughs, and she instinctively reaches out to touch his hand. It's a stupid gesture. Marcus's skin, though warm, feels wrong somehow. No one would take comfort in his touch—no one except Anne, and Blue feels certain that's some kind of fetish.

Glitter Edifice could've been something great. It could've been the cure for all genetic disease. It could've ushered in a new era of medical miracles. It could've been Blue's ticket back to a wonderful life full of press interviews and symposiums. Her intellectual property might've belonged to the Company, but the book deals and film rights would've been worth a fortune. She'd have been set for life—a much longer life. *Plagiarus praepotens* is the ultimate builder, able to rewrite and reconstruct organic matter in seconds. It should've built her a brighter tomorrow.

She'd never bought into the foolish Company vision of a weaponized snatcher. It was as if she'd split the atom, and all they wanted were nuclear bombs.

Kambili stirs beneath her, and his mouth makes a clicking, gurgling noise. It must taste like penny syrup inside there—Blue knows the sensation well. One of his hands rises to point to his half-exposed lips. She leans down so she can hear him better.

"This…" he slurs, his voice hoarse and broken from screaming. "This is your fault."

Blue steps back, eyes wide. "What?"

"Was trying to prep next sample." His voice is barely a whisper, but Marcus's perfect ears hear every detail. "You rushed me. Threatened me. You should've been there."

"I didn't have a choice, Kambili. Sudler is a problem. I needed you to prep the chimp, ASAP."

"Because... you're dying?" He laughs, falling into bitterness. "Now I have no face. Why is your life worth more than mine?"

She frowns. No one has ever said that to her. "This isn't just my life, or your life. If I'm right, this could change the entire shape of genetic research."

"Call it whatever you want, you selfish bitch."

Her sympathy evaporates. "You should've been more careful."

"Get out," he whispers.

"Kambili—"

He tries to sit up, despite the sedatives in his system. "*Get out.*" The words are muffled by the bandages around his mouth, and his voice cracks. He falls back to his gurney, groaning and sobbing.

Blue turns to leave, only to find Lucy in the doorway, staring at her with hollow eyes.

"What the fuck did you say to him?" she asks, but Blue walks past her without answering.

There's no way for that discussion to go well, so she dodges it altogether. She prays she won't see Sudler when she walks into the hall, or Anne, or Dick—or anyone else for that matter. She doesn't have the strength to deal with all of the recriminations.

She's read Dick's report of the incident, filed on the re-imaged SCIF computers. Other than the startup logs, it's the first entry on the new system. She knows how it will look. It's another major accident in two days. They'll send her project into suspension, if they don't shut it down altogether. She's doomed.

Lab techs dodge her in the hall. Dick's facilities guy gives her the stink eye. She passes Josep talking anxiously with his trio of engineers, and he gives her a guilty look, like he's the one with something to hide. Yet he's the only project manager who hasn't royally fucked up.

She needs to get back to her lab, but she has no plan. She'll figure it out when she gets there. Maybe she can access her logs. Maybe she can perform the *noxhydria* experiment by herself. Maybe she should just tell Sudler what she's doing, and hope for the mercy of the Weyland-Yutani Governance Board.

It'll take weeks, though. It could take years.

Blue is almost back to the SCIF when Daniel flags her down. Like everyone, he shows signs of stress, but they're subtle. His easy, commanding smile is a little slower, the creases of his eyes a little more pronounced. He hasn't put his clothes through the ironing machine, and he's the only crew member who cares about that sort of thing.

"The SCIF is closed until further notice," he says. "Before you ask, it's on my authority."

"So I don't need to go kicking Sudler's ass?"

He smirks. "I wouldn't recommend it. Things are tense enough."

She puts her hands on her hips and looks down at the deck with a sigh. "Please, just let me in. I've still got work to do."

Daniel sucks his teeth. "You know I'm charged with everyone's safety. This is a major accident. Sometimes you science types get ahead of yourselves, and it's my job to rein you in. This is for your own good."

She shuts her eyes. "Fuck that, Dan. Please, just let me in. I need to feed the chimps."

He arches an eyebrow. "That's Dick's job... and since the mishandling of those animals is what got us into this situation, I will not authorize that."

She points to her head. "Remember? I've got two faces and the grip strength of a power loader. I can handle myself."

He folds his hands behind and spreads his legs to shoulder width, the classic military "at ease" posture. She won't be passing him.

"I said no, Blue."

"Fine," she says, shaking her head with gritted teeth. "That's just fucking great." Without another word, she heads back to the crew quarters. These bastards are going to kill her.

Reaching the end of the long strut, she enters the corridor with all the crew rooms. At the end of the hall she spies the sign for the observatory, and glares. Nothing had been on schedule, nothing was according to plan, and yet everything seems so much worse now that Dorian Sudler is here. She wishes him a stroke, or an aneurysm. She wishes the glass would fail in his room, sucking him out into the scorching vacuum beyond. She wishes she could trade bodies with him, her failing form his only anchor.

Blue has never hated anyone so much in her whole life, and that's before Anne backs out of his room, pushing disheveled hair back into place.

The physicality of an android body prevents true anger. Marcus has no heart to race, no breath to quicken. His is a cold fury, with calculating eyes and quick synapses. Blue sometimes fears his inhuman strength, and the things she might do with it.

Instead, she stops in her tracks, narrowing her eyes. "Really, Anne? How stupid are you?"

Anne glances back at her and freezes, wounded. She juts out her lower lip, her arms tensing with the muscles Blue had once caressed.

"I don't want to do this with you right now."

Blue gives her a wry grin. "Why would you? You just did it with Dorian."

Anne closes the distance between them with remarkable alacrity and bares her teeth at him.

"You know something, Blue? You need to figure out how to make some friends really fast. I don't fucking belong to you, so don't pull this macho shit on me."

Blue gestures to the door. "But him? What is *wrong* with you?" She watches Anne's jaw muscles work in her slim cheeks, and her irises contract.

"Maybe I just wanted to feel *alive* for once," she hisses.

She storms off, and Blue lets her pass with eyes downcast. For no rhyme or reason, it still hurts. Those nights they'd spent together were her first to feel like a normal human since her diagnosis. Maybe she did love

Anne Wexler. Blue shakes the thought away as soon as it rears its ugly head, because she can't let it be true. She can't let anyone into her heart anymore.

With a bitter flood of emotion, she passes numbly into her quarters to see herself lying on the bed. The brain-direct mask flickers across her eyes, and a glimmering tendril of drool leaks from the side of her mouth. She's so emaciated and pockmarked. She's disgusting. It's like staring into a mirror and finding only a gloomy, malformed reflection of the self.

What if Blue takes Marcus's hands and smashes her skinny little throat? What if she takes the tranquilizers designed to help her sync, and injects twenty cc's of them into her intravenous drip? If she smashed her mirror and took a shard to her wrist, would she feel it, connected as she was to Marcus? She imagines the blazing pain as it slices into her wrists, and watching herself drain out. Would it be any worse than the slow death of Bishara's Syndrome?

Reaching out, she lifts her own hand, dizzied by the sensation of holding her flesh and being held. She shouldn't be here, shouldn't be alive. No one else with the Syndrome made it past age thirty.

Her mobile terminal beeps and she lets go, her wrist flopping to the bed. Blue takes the terminal from its charging station and keys in her password. There's a picture inside her mailbox, and she opens it. It's Silky, her old cat from Earth, the one she gave away at the start of her tenure on the Cold Forge. The address is scrambled.

Marcus is calm, but she hears her body suck in a breath.

She searches out her cipher drive from her mattress and plugs it into the side of the terminal. It references the picture and the one-time pad.

A message appears.

```
ELISE COTO GONE
WE ARE STILL LISTENING
GIVE US YOUR RESEARCH
WE CAN EXTRACT YOU
```

Elise is blown. Her assets will be seized. At this point, it's far more likely that the sender of this message is a Company agent who's gotten control of Elise's side of the one-time pad.

But then, does it matter? What are they going to do, kill her? Blue encrypts a message into a picture of her grinning cousin at the beach.

```
I AM IN
HOW
```

Two difficult days pass, and Blue is a ball of nervous energy. Whoever her mysterious benefactor is, they haven't responded to her question. She imagines the Weyland-Yutani fraud investigators back on Earth, laughing and building a case around her confession. Is there such a thing as entrapment in a situation like this?

It won't matter. Her court hearing will take at least six

months after she arrives home. She'll be dead long before the lawyers can decide what to do with her. Unlike Elise, she has no family, no one to destroy.

Blue needs to get back into the SCIF so she can take the drives out of her server and stash them somewhere, *anywhere*. She has partial genetic sequences of larval snatchers, as well as the *noxhydria* face-huggers. While it's not a clean sample of *Plagiarus praepotens*, the sequences are still valuable to investors.

Do her confederates have eggs?

Can they get a clean sample?

Anne is her best way back into the SCIF. The other project managers won't help her. Daniel has already made his allegiances clear. As much as Blue doesn't want to face her, Anne is the only one who can give her a fighting chance.

It's lunchtime. The crew should be in the lounge, chowing down on the food she'd like to eat. She'd stopped going to the lounge after they'd implanted the G-tube in her stomach, taking the one thing she could eat in her quarters—gelatin. Watching everyone else chew would ignite pangs of longing inside her beyond any unrequited love she'd ever felt. And every time the conversation turned to how shitty the food was, Blue would find herself infuriated with her crewmates. She'd give anything to be like them again, easy and carefree.

Sometimes, she would eat with them as Marcus, but the acute senses that made him so intoxicating with Anne made the food unbearable. Experienced through his senses, her meals were no longer a blend, but sorted into a dozen discrete characteristics, each amplified beyond the capacity for a human brain to process. Sometimes, Blue would take a pinch of sugar into Marcus's mouth, because it was the only thing that translated well.

Perhaps if Marcus's brain-direct interface wasn't a hacked-together solution, she'd be able to taste morsels like the others. Maybe she could be in there bitching with them about the quality.

The thing Blue misses the most about eating, however, is the conversation. Yet she can't simply sit and stare while the others gorge themselves. They become awkward if she watches them. So much of a day, so many worries and hopes, are shared around a meal. She's been excluded from all of that. Maybe that's why no one likes her anymore. She isn't part of the campfire circle that's existed since the dawn of humanity.

Reaching the lounge door, she pauses. They'll assume she's there on business, and be annoyed with her for even showing her face. Maybe she could choke down a meal to get back in the good graces of her crewmates, then see if Anne will speak to her in private. Would that look desperate?

The door opens, and she scans the room, spotting a few of the lab techs, but no project managers. There's a ping-pong table in the back corner where some of the crew congregate, obstructed by the serving buffet. Anne likes it over there. It's one of the only sports where she can beat Blue's synthetic body.

When Blue rounds the corner, she finds Dorian Sudler staring at her, eyes shining, wearing a grin far friendlier than he deserves. He sits holding a pair of chopsticks over a plate of steaming teriyaki noodles, the kind she would kill for if she could still have them.

"Doctor Marsalis," he says. "I didn't expect to see you in the lounge." He gestures to Marcus's body. "I didn't know your type ate… you know, food."

"I can. I don't, though." She returns as much of his smile as is required by decorum. "I was looking for someone."

"Oh. Who is it? Maybe I've seen them?"

"It's fine," she says. "Just Commander Cardozo."

Sudler digs into his noodles, and Marcus's olfactory receptors deliver her the salt, wheat, and umami scents she cannot enjoy. She briefly fantasizes about slamming his head into the plate so hard that the table snaps from its mounting brackets.

Placing a clump of noodles in his mouth he chews with relish, then swallows.

"Sad to say that he's still in the SCIF. Lots of cleanup to do after this past week."

"How long before we can return to work, Director? I was getting somewhere with my project, and—"

"Maybe you'd like to brief me on that?"

She flexes her fingers to avoid making a fist.

"I'd rather have some results before I do."

He picks through the noodles, looking for bits of meat. Finding one, he pops it into his mouth.

"You know, Doctor, *any* progress would be a result for

Glitter Edifice. I can take you over there now, and you can show me what you've learned."

She bites her lip. "I'm not ready yet."

"Okay, well, let me know when you are. Meanwhile, I'm sure you've got a number of tasks outside the SCIF you can attend to."

"Sure." She nods. "Okay."

He regards her for a long moment while he consumes another strand of sticky noodles. She wants to leave, but he looks as if he's going to speak again.

"Can I ask you," he mumbles, taking a swig of water in order to speak more clearly, "what got you into genetics?"

That takes her by surprise, and she casts her thoughts back. Blue's uncle died suddenly when she was only eight years old. One day he was fine, and the next his immune system turned against him, destroying his skin and respiratory system. The medical community had created gene therapies for multiple sclerosis, Tay-Sachs disease, Parkinson's, and numerous others, but those took time. There still was no rapid response system for cases like his, and colonists like him were at particular risk for one-off genetic disorders.

She wanted to help the colonists and stop future cases like her uncle's. But she'll be damned if she shares any emotional memories with Sudler, though.

"I was smart enough to be a doctor," she replies, "and gene sequencing was paying better than it ever had before."

He nods, taking it in. "So when you were in college you didn't, you know, know about your condition?" She hates it when people ask her that. The medical press found it particularly entertaining.

"No."

"That's so amazing. How fortunate that you have that training."

"It's almost as good as being born with a real life expectancy."

"Sorry," he says, that smiling mask never falling from his face. "Didn't mean to hit a nerve."

"It's fine," she lies. "Please let Daniel know I'm looking for him, would you?" Before he can speak again, she turns and leaves.

When she reaches her room, she glances over to his door. He'd only just started eating and won't be back for some time. If he's going to shutter her project, she may as well find out who else is getting the shaft. She taps the open key, and the door slides aside, allowing her passage into the observation room.

"Guess you ought to rethink your 'open door' policy, fucker," she mutters, passing inside.

She had always imagined Sudler to be a meticulously clean man, given his spotless appearance and pressed suits. She finds, instead, two folding easels and a mess of paints, filthy papers and old brushes and palette knives. Against the backdrop of Kaufmann's light, the whole place strikes her as Bohemian.

Coming to one of his canvases, she scowls. It's a pleasing mishmash of angles and geometric shapes—a decent imitation of a Georges Braque. Does he haul this shit all over the galaxy? When he's ruining lives, does he retire for a nice, relaxing painting session?

Clearly, the answer is yes.

Mixed into the shapes, she sees the curve of Anne's body, clearly outlined in burnt umber, shading to orange starlight. Back in her own body Blue wants to throw up, but of course, that could kill her. Instead she turns away and looks for Dorian's personal terminal. It's not hard to find among the clutter of painting supplies. She lifts open the screen and the Weyland-Yutani login shield pops up.

Sudler probably thinks Blue can't code or hack, because of her background as a geneticist. He'd be wrong. She's written thousands of programs, and has set up massive server farms. She wrote the program to open and close the heat shields on the kennels. That was disastrous, but it gave her unique insight into the Cold Forge's IT and devops policies.

Thus she knows all of the exploits for his system, and bypasses the login screen with little trouble, reaching a directory listing of encrypted files. In the event someone dies or quits, the company has to be able to decrypt the contents of their drives. She has the master keys, because she exported them from the SCIF without permission after she wrote the behavioral modification code for the kennels.

Blue grabs copies of the most recent hundred files— all small, so most likely documents or spreadsheets. She drops them onto a portable drive and deposits that in Marcus's pocket, then powers down the system. In and out in under five minutes, and when she leaves, the corridors are empty. She makes it the short distance back to her room with no difficulty, since the bastard decided to be her neighbor. Sometimes, she thinks he intentionally did it to annoy her, though only a creep would do something so ridiculous.

In seconds she's back to her own terminal with the stick plugged in and master decryption cracking open Sudler's files. Some of the filenames are a little scrambled, but she selects the top one, a spreadsheet.

It's a personnel rotation report, and it lists everyone on the station as slated for termination, with a recommendation for fresh blood all around. Blue smiles.

This is her ace in the hole.

Marcus's firm hand presses against her shoulder, gently rousing Blue from slumber. She sucks in a breath and blinks the sleep from her eyes. This past month, her left eyelid has become sluggish and unwilling to respond.

"You have some visitors."

She smacks her lips, her mouth sticky with dried saliva. She checks the time. It's the middle of the night cycle.

"Send them away," she croaks. "I'm not decent."

"I'm afraid they're quite insistent. It's the Commander."

That perks her up. "Okay. Plug me in."

Marcus takes the brain-direct interface from its place at her bedside and gently settles it over her shaved scalp. She can always tell when the connection is successful, because his ears can detect the hiss of her oxygen tanks, while hers cannot.

When she'd first arrived, she insisted on being in her motorized wheelchair to meet visitors. Now, it sits idle in the corner of her room. She spends more time inside Marcus than she does inside herself, and every time she comes back, her world feels a little worse.

She walks to her bedroom door and opens it to find Daniel on the other side, his face grave with concern. She can't read his thinly lidded eyes, but she sees something he's never shown her before—his martial sternness.

"Sorry to wake you," he says, obviously not sorry, "but there's something we need to discuss. Right now." The dim illumination of the night cycle casts the hallways beyond in an eerie red glow. She doesn't bother asking him if it can wait. She knows it can't.

"Sure," she says. "Come on in." She steps aside, but he remains fixed outside her door.

When Blue was in high school in New Jersey, she had an internship at a robotics design firm. She'd gotten interested in creating some hobby projects, and because she couldn't afford the servos, she took five of them from her office. Then one day, a security guard came to her cubicle and stood before her, just like Daniel stands now.

"Fuck," she says.

"Will you come with me to the SCIF, please?"

It certainly doesn't look optional.

Blue steps into the hall, where she sees Anne standing nearby, a dark look on her face. They fall into a small caravan and make their way down the central strut. She passes the infirmary and glimpses Kambili's still body through the window, his vitals a pulsing nightlight in the shadows. When they reach the docking area, Blue spies the crew of the *Athenian*, lurking in the darkness, quietly chatting as they share cigarettes. She wonders what they're up to. Maybe they're prepping to launch. Dorian certainly got what he was after. He has all the information he needs to make a case for cleaning out the Cold Forge.

Escape pods line the walls, capable of taking her back to Earth in a sleepy decade, each pod with space for two people. On her worst days, she's thought about climbing into one and launching, hoping that they'll have a cure for her by the time she arrives. There are very few people with her condition, though, so probably not. Civilization has written her off. She has to save herself.

But she's failed. That's why they're walking to the SCIF in the middle of the night.

She wonders if Sudler will force her off the station and onto the *Athenian* with him, or if she'll have to stay aboard until the next crew rotation, confined to quarters. Maybe he'll trot her before the Governance Board like a prized pig ready to be slaughtered. Maybe she'll choke on her spit and die of pneumonia before then.

When they reach the SCIF entryway, he's waiting there, hands in his suit pockets, a professional smile on his face. He relaxes in the floodlights of the great door like an actor on the stage about to deliver a monologue. Lucy, Javier, Dick, and Josep stand nearby as well, looking considerably less pleased.

Lucy stares daggers at her. Blue knows it's because of Kambili.

"Good evening, Doctor Marsalis," Sudler says. "We have some questions for you." Blue smacks her lips. Her android body feels no fatigue, but freshly awakened, she still stretches his muscles.

"I take it we couldn't wait until the morning?"

Anne and Daniel ascend the ramp to enter their access codes and open the door. Blue feels certain her access codes have been revoked, and so doesn't bother to ask if she should help. The buzzer sounds and the colossal door swings wide as lights flicker to life inside the SCIF.

"Care to tell me what this is about?"

"We'll get to it," Sudler replies, ushering all of them inside. Maybe she should punch him. She could plow her fist into his nose and snap it before her time here is over. He would, of course, sue her earthly estate to pieces, but what does it matter? She tucks that thought away for later. Like a funeral procession, they pass under Juno's glass cage, headed straight for the kennels.

"Miss Wexler tells me you've maintained an unlicensed server," Sudler says, falling in beside her. "And I've been asking around. Seems like no one else has heard of it. Care to render any comments on that?"

She glances over at Anne, who finds somewhere else to look.

"That's my fault," Blue says, careful to keep the edge from her voice. "I told her because I thought it'd make her feel better about the destruction caused by Silversmile."

Sudler nods. "I see. So your research is…"

"Destroyed by Lucy's project, just like everyone else's."

"You lying bitch," Lucy says, shaking her head. "I can't fucking believe you."

A flash pops behind Blue's eyes—it's getting harder to keep her temper in check.

"Yeah? Well where the fuck is it, huh, Lucy? Can you show me, or are you just going to run your goddamned mouth?"

"Ladies," Sudler says, his voice stained with irony as he grins at Blue's body. He winks. "Please. We can be civil about this, can't we?"

"All right, that's it," Blue says. "I'm so tired of your shit, Sudler. You're seriously going to get all cute about my gender now? You think this is funny, asshole?"

Everyone's gaze slews to him, and he shrugs innocently, his shark smile vanishing.

Blue gestures toward him. "This is the guy you decided to sleep with, Anne? Really?"

But Anne doesn't respond. Lucy closes the gap to Blue, filling her view.

"You make it your business to know who everyone is fucking, don't you?" she growls, her big eyes narrowing to slits. "Then you pull your strings and get them hurt." Lucy's eyebrow twitches upward, and she licks her overlarge lips. "I guess it's your turn now."

Instantly the dots connect. Kambili has decided he has nothing less to lose, and told Lucy where the server is. Sudler probably put pressure on Kambili after hearing about the system from Anne. And Josep—he's there to help the others crack it open.

Inside, they'll find years of malfeasance. They'll find her research, her journals, her clear and explicit goals of medical application, transmission logs to Elise Coto, and copies of the cipher used to decrypt Blue's picture messaging. It won't take long before they locate her last received transmission and realize the conspiracy is very much alive. They're going to arrest her for fraud and embezzlement, and she will never see the cure for which she's fought.

"I've seen Sudler's private records," Blue says, her voice shaking and rising out of Marcus's natural range. "He's going to fire all of you. Don't do this for him. Don't—"

"Show some dignity, Doctor Marsalis." Sudler purses his lips.

It's all crashing down. If ever there were a time to break the man's face, it's now. She takes three quick steps toward him.

"Marcus, engage override Epsilon," he says.

Her leg locks in place.

She feels herself say, "Override confirmed. Locking out pilot controls."

Sudler jams his hands into his pockets and saunters over, nose wrinkling in a grin. He clucks his tongue.

"I can't believe you were going to hit me."

"I would never strike a human, sir," Blue says, even as she strains to control the muscles in her throat.

"Of course not," he says, clapping her on the shoulder.

"That's because you're Company property. Now go back to synthetic storage and shut down, if you please. We'll take it from here."

"Yes, sir. Very good."

Dorian sighs. "I've got to say, I like this side of you, Blue."

1 1

VIABLE
COUNTERMEASURES

They found the hidden data port and the server behind the wall panel down one of the utility corridors, just as Kambili said they would. Dorian stares at the set of metal boxes, happier than he's been in a long time.

Companies aren't about providing a service to the people who work there. They aren't about social progress or any of that other bullshit. Companies are about maintaining the balance of profit to expansion, and winning—two things which Dorian has done handily.

"Get the techs from Rose Eagle and Silversmile up here," Dorian says to Anne. "I want her results ready to take back to Earth by tomorrow."

"Tomorrow?" Anne shakes her head. "Do you really think that was an appropriate way to handle her?"

How can she not understand the expert maneuvering that's brought them to this victory? How can she possibly question him, especially at that moment? Dorian glances around the hall and surveys the reaction. To his dismay, Lucy seems to be the only one pleased with the way this is playing out.

Fury grows within him. Anne's words are like grease on a precious diamond. They could be easily wiped away, but he's shocked someone put them there in the first place. His hands shake with disbelief.

"She's a *thief*, you idiot!" he roars, then he pauses, takes a deep breath, and gets his voice under control. "Every single egg sample she misappropriated was worth hundreds of thousands of dollars. Every adult snatcher rotting in a cell is worth a *million*. Glitter Edifice has a net value sixteen times that of Rose Eagle, and a hundred times the price of Silversmile. Doctor Marsalis's kennels are the only reason *any* of these other people are here." He sweeps his hand over the assembled crowd.

"We were very successful," Lucy protests.

"At fucking everything up!" Anger starts to burn again. "And you did a good fucking job!"

"Blue wasn't lying, was she?" Anne asks. "You're going to fire everyone."

"No," Dorian says. "But I *am* making a lot of transfers— starting with you. Just about everyone here is too good for this place. I want to move you to Tokyo, Miss Wexler, where your talents will be better utilized."

As a security member, her talents are basically nonexistent. She's failed to contain any threats, and he has trouble imagining Anne Wexler or Commander Cardozo repelling hostile boarders. At this point, he needs her, however, and the Tokyo office is an effective carrot. He can always betray her after he has what he needs.

"What about us?" Lucy asks.

Dorian pauses to consider his response. The Company will never again require Lucy's services. After the Silversmile debacle, he's going to blacklist her so she can't get as much as an interview. She's through.

"Miss Biltmore, I'm not going to fire any project managers. No doubt you'll fit in at our Berkeley technology incubator. Mister Janos, we've got numerous cryptography postings." Dorian lifts a hand to fend off any questions. "These are details that are better left for later. We all have a job to do, and I want that goddamned research." His voice rises. "Do I make myself clear?"

Before they can respond, he adds, "I presume you all understand that Doctor Blue Marsalis will no longer be employed by the Company. Her clearance is revoked. She is to be prevented from having any further access to vital station assets."

He turns away, indicating that the discussion is at an end. The techs arrive, as do reheated pizza and sodas from the lounge. Whatever they're doing, the various programmers settle in for a hard couple of hours.

A makeshift lab pops up around the wall panel they removed to locate the server, complete with portable terminals, folding tables, and dozens of food wrappers. There are several members of the crew Dorian has never met. They introduce themselves to him as if he should care.

The camaraderie between the low-ranking workers flourishes as they laugh and pore over the problem. Even Blue's low-level techs are in evidence, helping with the effort, expressing shock and dismay, providing insights into their former boss's mindset. What began as a couple of managers standing around a hole in the wall transforms into a war room.

These are people working for the ledgers, and Dorian feels the pendulum swinging away from chaos. Balance will return to the Cold Forge, though he'll be damned if it continues under the same management. With such colossal losses assessed against each project, the place is a gold mine. If his new appointees get the RB-232 back on track, his bonus will be of celestial proportions.

Still, it's hard not to love chaos sometimes. His money results from terrible management and bad decisions, from the failure of others, and he's grateful that his job only sends him to places that are massive blunders. He always longs to be closest to the raging wildfire.

The day cycle wears on into night, and the techs show no signs of a breakthrough. When he asks Lucy about their progress, he gets only noncommittal mumbling and technical jargon. So he asks Josep. Blue's research is carefully locked through quantum cryptography, something Rose Eagle can break, he's assured. They have men and women trying to get the entangler back online.

It's been hours. They don't need him to hover, so

Dorian wanders off into the kennels, toward parts he's never seen before. He visits egg storage, marveling at the robust countermeasures placed on the egg boxes. He commandeers one of the techs to show him video of an early impregnation. All of the later ones are stored on Blue's secret server.

They sit down together at one of the chem lab workstations and the video begins to play. A chimp lies strapped before a stony oval the size of a large garden vase. The egg blooms at the top like a flower, its meaty-white insides almost delicate. A caul pulls aside, and the creature springs forth, almost too fast to see, until it lands a deadly blow.

This is the claw he saw floating in the lab. He leans toward the monitor for a better look, and counts eight fleshy articulating fingers with bony joints like those of an old woman. The whip-like tail lashes out, folding around the anthropoid's neck to choke it out with negligible effort.

The chimp strains against its straps, and falls still.

"How long can those creatures survive outside the eggs?" Dorian asks. The tech shrugs, clearly uncomfortable with being spoken to.

"We've never checked, sir. We, well… wouldn't have wanted to waste one by letting it die."

"How strong are their tail muscles?"

"About as strong as a boa constrictor, I guess."

Dorian scoffs. "Is that what passes for a unit of measurement? What tests have you run?"

"I don't, uh, think," the tech stammers. "I-I don't know."

"And what did you do when you worked on this project?"

"I, uh, made sure the sequencers ran correctly and, uh, logged everything for Doctor Okoro and Doctor Marsalis."

"I see. Show me a video of the birth."

The tech keys in a few codes.

"Do I not work here anymore?" he asks.

Dorian shakes his head. "I guess that depends on whether or not I can get you to show me some simple videos, doesn't it? Birth. *Now*. Get a move on."

The tech quickly finishes his query and brings up footage of the same chimp, strapped to a different table. Its hair is matted at the back where the spider's fingers gripped it hard enough to break skin. Its eyes flutter open, and it looks confused.

"What happened to the claw thing?" Dorian asks.

"The face-hugger? It slips off after a day or so and dies. We find them withered up on their backs."

Abruptly, the chimp cries out onscreen, and Dorian jumps. His full attention returns to the video. The animal shakes and screams, frothy saliva blowing from its throat and covering its face like snowflakes. It struggles against the restraints, terror etched on its face, then freezes as though it's having a grand mal seizure.

A lump rises in the skin of its belly, and Dorian's breath catches.

The lump stretches thin until a phallic protrusion breaks the surface in a spraying gout of blood. The chimp convulses once more, then goes limp. The fleshy, wormlike creature stands upright, its long arms questing into the air as they drip with blood and mucous. Its tiny teeth glisten as though made of metal, and it screams aloud—the sound of steam hissing from a small pipe.

"Oh," the tech says, interrupting Dorian's reverie, "we did, you know, run an autopsy, and find that the hosts were iron deficient, so we think, like maybe... maybe the snatcher scrapes metals from the host bloodstream. We're calling that stage the, uh, chestburster."

"Very literal names you've got here. No poetry."

Footsteps. Dick Mackie steps over the threshold behind them, a beer in each hand.

"That's what came with our source documentation. Shipped with the samples. No species names, no indicated origins. Just 'egg,' 'face-hugger,' 'chestburster...' We had to name the big buggers, ourselves."

"Yeah. 'Snatchers.' Wouldn't have been my first choice."

"You're welcome to come up with something better." Dick passes one of the beers to Dorian and he checks it out. It's a shitty American pilsner, but Dorian hasn't had a beer in ages, so he's grateful. It's unopened, which is a relief. He often wonders if a crew would have the balls to try and do away with him.

Onscreen, the chestburster burrows back into its host, and rivers of blood and bile pour from chimp's open chest cavity. The animal's body jolts as the chestburster gnaws its way upward.

Dick waves away the tech, who seems all too happy to leave.

"Two things about the chestbursters, mate. One, if they can't find a hole in their cages, they dig in and eat for a day. Two, they take on the characteristics of the host. All of the adults in our cages have got chimp proportions, and they favor loping on all fours. They don't look like the file drawings that Weyland-Yutani sent with the egg samples."

"How so?"

Dick takes a long swig of his beer, then winks. "Those drawings had *human* proportions, cobber. Wouldn't want to be the poor sod who discovered these things."

Dorian feels a pang of jealousy toward the chimpanzee. He has no desire to die, but he imagines leaving his genetic legacy to such a worthy beast as the snatcher. He has never wanted a child, but he briefly imagines the creature that might come from his DNA and it gives him chills.

"You seem like a man who appreciates these animals for what they are," Dick observes.

The beer is cool on Dorian's lips, and the sugar and yeast bring him calm after a rough day.

"They're fine art, plain and simple. Predation perfected."

Dick winks. "Thought you might say that." He keys in another code, and the monitors all switch to the live broadcasts from inside the cells. "It's feeding time. Why don't you kick back here while me and the boys handle the rest?"

Pleased with Dick's offer, Dorian puts his feet up on the table and sips his beer, sharp eyes scanning every monitor for signs of activity. Within a few minutes, a small slit opens up on each cell, and chunks of bloody meat pour inside.

Each creature's routine is the same: attack the slit, grab the meat, gorge upon it with jaws distended. Their bloody hands rove their bodies as they eat, covering themselves with gore like birds bathing in a fountain.

He watches them for hours, these marvelous children of the stars. And slowly, Dorian drifts off into a peaceful slumber.

INTERLUDE

LUCY

"Where were you?" the young woman asks as Lucy comes huffing up the stairs into Juno's cage. It's Carrie, one of the Silversmile techs.

"Just, uh—" Lucy stammers, catching her breath. "Just checking on the progress of Blue's server decryption."

Carrie smirks. "Girl, you've really got it in for her."

"Screw her." Lucy takes a sip of diet soda. "This whole station is going to be better after she's gone." She checks her watch again. Everything is taking too long. She's ready to get the fuck out of here.

"I'm just saying we ought to stick together," Carrie says. It shocks Lucy to hear her talking that way. They've been working together for a few years, moving from project to project, and Carrie is always the first to go knives-out.

"That's the problem." Lucy reclines in her chair, tipping the can toward Carrie as though it was a beer. She wished to god it was a whiskey and Coke—she could certainly use one. "We *were* sticking together. She played us all, and now look at us."

Carrie gives her a concerned look. Lucy has been getting too many of those lately.

"You want to change the subject?" Carrie asks. "How is your mom, anyway? Still worried about her?"

"She's fine," Lucy snaps back, because if she talks about her mother after what she's been doing on the Cold Forge, she's going to cry. "Let's just stick to the task at hand."

Juno's server chamber is normally the nicest room in the whole SCIF, and the best place to relax. There are no exterior windows in this part of the station, but Juno's command view over the central area gives it a panoramic feeling. Plus, the chairs are a lot cushier than the ones in the lab. She's caught Javier sleeping here plenty of times.

"Don't you think we're a little to blame for this situation?" Carrie asks, raising an eyebrow. "I wrote the code for the flash tool. Maybe I ought to be fired."

"What? No," Lucy says. "Javier should've checked the tool before plugging it into a main. And you'd better watch what you say. If Director Sudler heard you talk like that…" She runs a thumbnail across her throat like a knife.

"Maybe I *want* to get fired," Carrie persists, standing and moving to the next bank of readouts. She unslings a portable terminal from her shoulder, flips it open, and begins checking numbers. "Or just, you know, laid off. I'm tired of this shithole, Lucy. I want to go home."

But Lucy doesn't agree. She'd broken up with her last boyfriend before taking the assignment. He wanted marriage and a baby. She wanted freedom, and on the Cold

Forge, Lucy met Kambili. The sex was good, consistent, and without obligation, and after a few months of it she'd begun to understand why people wanted children.

On Earth, she'd be nothing to Kambili. Missus Okoro claimed the entire planet—and her husband—for herself. In the light of Kaufmann, Lucy can be anything she wants for him.

His bandaged face springs to her mind. Even with the latest medical science, Kambili will never look the same again. She considers all the long nights they've spent talking, the way he looks at her after they make love, and she knows she will lie with him again after the bandages come off. She loves him, and soon they'll all be going home. A bitter part of Lucy hopes Kambili's wife will cast him aside when they arrive.

"Shit," Carrie says, pulling Lucy back into the present. "Motherfucking *bullshit!*"

"What?"

"How the fuck did it get back out?" Carrie frantically types in queries and checks the results, eyes raking desperately over the display. "All our hard work!"

Lucy sits up, taking her feet off the desk. "How did *what* get out?"

"Silversmile!" Carrie glances over to Lucy. "Juno just lost comms with the kennels!"

Lucy shakes her head. "Got to be a bug with the reinitialization. We scrubbed those drives thoroughly. This is a factory-fresh cloud."

"Well, okay, but that means Javier didn't get the lines

working like he said he did." Her voice is a combination of anger and something else. Fear.

Lucy rolls her eyes. "I double-checked, and Javier can't afford to make any mistakes. I know he did it right."

Carrie puts her terminal down and slides it toward Lucy, where it almost knocks over her soda. Lucy has never seen her tech so worked up, and it's almost comical. She smiles and leans over the terminal, certain that there is a rational explanation.

"The cells aren't wired up," Carrie says, pointing to a row of red "NSC" icons lining the side of the screen. "They're showing 'no status connection' errors."

Lucy blinks at the screen. It's true. The table header indicates the kennel cells—but that *can't* be right. It had better not be right. She types in a query and pings the central cell database gateway. It pongs quickly and reliably. Two of the cells are green with "LKD" icons.

Why would two of the cells be responding correctly if the rest aren't? Her heart freezes in her chest, and her trembling hands refuse to type another stroke. Her breath won't come. Her eyes water. The server only reports the status of the cells. Only a human can open them.

"Lucy?" Carrie asks, but her voice seems so far away. "Lucy, what's wrong?"

"'NSC,'" Lucy responds. "It… doesn't mean 'no status connection.'" Tears roll from her eyes as she looks up.

"It means 'Not Secured.'"

The kennels are open.

1 2

QUARANTINE PROTOCOL

A warm, red light passes over Dorian's closed eyes, then again, and again. His legs ache from sleeping in the stupid chair, and he's about to have a nice stretch when a deafening klaxon fills the air.

He stumbles backward out of his chair and rolls to the ground, banging his forehead on the deck. Lights dance behind his eyes, and he crawls to his hands and knees, shaking off the pain.

A melodic voice booms through the cavernous depths. It's Juno.

"All personnel, evacuate the kennels immediately. Containment failure. Repeat, all personnel, evacuate the kennels immediately."

He repeats the words in his mind.

All fog of sleep vanishes.

Between the howls of the klaxon, he listens. He's disoriented, and in the hours since he was escorted down here, he can't remember the way out. A wrong turn will mean death.

Pounding footsteps approach, the sound of a full-tilt sprint, and Dorian scrambles to his feet. The gait is one of a man, and he's surprised to see the video tech from earlier go tearing past like a star mid-fielder.

"Hey! Was that announcement—" The man doesn't stop. Dorian wanted to confirm, but the man's blind panic is confirmation enough. He sprints after the tech, muscles aching with the lack of limbering up. When a hissing sound fills the gap between klaxons, Dorian gets as limber as he's ever been.

The pair hurtle down the corridors, Dorian glancing behind him into the depths. Red alert light mixes with green paint, tinting everything orange-brown. The familiar becomes unfamiliar, and when Dorian looks again behind him, he finds a black shape rounding the corner, cleanly cut from the light. He misses some of the details, but he catches the important bits: claws, teeth, hateful lips, an elongated gray head glimmering in the warning lamps.

The tech screams, and Dorian redoubles his sprint. With each footfall, he expects to feel knives slicing the skin of his back into ribbons, those long teeth on his neck. It's coming closer, its thunking bony feet rattling the deck with each loping stride.

Dorian closes ranks with the tech, but it's right on him. He can't look back or it'll catch him. His thighs burn and his lungs ache. He hasn't run this fast in years, but it won't be enough.

He shoves the tech hard to one side, sending the man stumbling.

Dorian doesn't bother to watch, but he hears it. The beast falls upon its prey, the tech's scream descending into gurgling begging. Instead of going for the killing blow, it tears at the man, prolonging his suffering.

Sprinting away, Dorian is thankful for his dedicated fitness regimen—except he's still lost, and his guide is dead.

"Juno! Navigate to escape pods!" he pants, and a glowing line appears on the ground. He bursts from the corridor to find a vast, open area, and relief washes over him. He recognizes his surroundings. If he turns right, he'll move past the lab encampment where they were extracting Blue's secret server. He heads that direction, rounds the corner, and stumbles to the ground in shock.

Blood fills the hallway, black against the green paint, massive sprays and washes against every blank wall. Tables lie toppled, wires splaying across the ground in all directions. A severed arm rests upon the floor where it had spun away from the chaos.

Five of the creatures feast upon bodies, reveling in the thrill of the kill. They're a writhing mass of oil, snapping and clawing, pulling chunks of meat away from bone as they yank corpses to and fro.

His feet fight his brain. He wants to run, but the morbid part of his mind urges him to identify the victims. He peers down at them, searching for any sign of who they might have been. One of the snatchers nips at the neck of its prey, severing the head from its shoulders. The head spins in place, and Dorian, in the red-alert light, recognizes Josep's face.

One of the creatures jolts upright, and Dorian scrambles backward into the corridor, hoping he hasn't been seen. In truth, he has no idea how the eyeless beasts locate their prey.

There's an armory station near him, which he'd ignored in his mad dash toward the exit. Dorian creeps over to the rollup door and pulls it upward, cursing every tiny noise that comes from the interlocking steel plates. Inside he finds a tall locker full of various rifles, flares, and handguns. He's about to reach for one when he hears the clacking of claws on metal decking. He presses inside the locker, holding his shaking breath.

The claw noises slowly close in, skittering death in the seconds between the blaring alarms. It's stalking him. He can't pull down the rolled steel shutter without it hearing. Pressed against the racks, he tries to feel his way to a handgun without knocking anything off the shelves.

His fingers touch a rifle, then ammunition cases, then close around the squared-off barrel of a handgun. Without a sound he gingerly pulls it from the shelf, cursing inwardly as his fingers find the hollow of an empty grip and his other hand searches fruitlessly for a magazine.

The creature draws closer. Dorian spots its shadow on the wall with each flash of the emergency lights. Its fingers grasp with deadly intent. It's going to catch him. It's going to pull him apart like bloody dough.

Gunshots echo through the corridor.

"Come on, you motherfuckers!"

The snatcher rockets away in search of new prey. Dorian can't quite make out the provenance of the voice, but it's a man, maybe several men. More gunshots, this time distant. Panicked screaming. Whoever they were, they didn't make it.

Poking his head out of the locker, he finds only bloody tracks dotting their way toward him, then away. It had been within a yard of him.

He turns back to the locker and fetches two magazines and a couple of flares, shoving them into his suit pockets. It's not a comfortable fit, but he hadn't expected to go to fucking war today. He looks down at his shitty little pistol and wonders if it'll have any effect whatsoever on the creatures' armored carapace. Judging from the deaths he hears echoing through the kennels, probably not.

Still, he quietly chambers a round and switches off the safety. There may be other things that need shooting if he wants to get out of there alive. Removing his Italian calfskin dress shoes, he places them inside the locker. If they manage to contain the creatures, he'll be coming back for them.

The waxy concrete floor is cool against his feet, and he's thankful for the silence of movement. He couldn't make a sound if he tried, and he sets off in search of a safer shelter. Maybe he can hide inside one of the labs until he spies an opportunity to make a break for the door.

Or maybe, if he does that, he'll reach the docking area to find all the escape pods missing.

"This is Lucy Biltmore." Her voice comes over the loudspeakers. She has been crying, and Dorian absolutely begrudges her that. "To any crew inside the kennels, quarantine protocol is in effect. We've contained the outbreak by sealing off your area, but… there's no way we can open the doors. If any of you are listening, if any of you can still hear me—" Her voice breaks into sobs.

As she speaks, Dorian stalks from lab to lab, taking stock of his surroundings. Unfortunately, almost every one of them has a viewport for observation from the hallway. While the aliens are trained not to have an affinity for glass, Dorian expects they'll have no trouble breaking into the unprotected spaces.

Lucy finishes her speech. "I'm sorry," she says, and it takes everything in Dorian's self-control not to shout, *"Fuck you, Lucy!"* It isn't the threat to his life that stings so much, it's the fact that the cartoonishly bug-eyed bitch with a fragile ego fucked him over. If he dies here, he's lost, and she's won, and he refuses to let that happen.

The klaxons die out, leaving him with far too much silence. Maybe Lucy thought he should have some peace for his last moments alive.

He finally locates a network maintenance closet and keys the door-open button. It buzzes out an error code, louder than he'd like. He snaps up his gun and glances both ways down the hallway, waiting for the galloping black shape that will destroy him.

This deep into the SCIF, maintenance doors shouldn't be locked.

He places his knuckles to the door and gently raps, "shave and a haircut."

The door rips open and Anne Wexler drags him inside. She shuts it just as quickly and envelops him in a tight embrace.

"Oh, my god," she gasps. "Oh, my god. It's you. I can't believe it's you."

"Are you okay?"

"Yeah… Yeah. I—the crew getting the server, they're… Josep—"

He nods.

She pulls him back in for another embrace, then plants a hard kiss on his lips. When she withdraws, her posture is commanding. She has a shotgun, and through the chamber grating, he sees the bright orange of an incendiary round.

"Don't get any ideas about a farewell fuck," she says with a weak smile. "I just wanted to make sure I got one more kiss."

"I hope it was good."

"It wasn't. We can work that out later, though. We're not going to die down here."

The contents of the closet are anything but helpful: cleaning supplies, a few scrapers, a portable power washer with a little tank. If they were dealing with humans, Dorian could grab the lye and stick it in the sprayer or something. Then again, firearms would be more than enough to handle humans. His grip tenses around the checkered walnut grip in his hand.

"Agreed. What's our play?"

"We've got to get in contact with Lucy. We don't have any wireless allowed in the SCIF, but there's a comm in each of the labs. From there, we go to climate control, which is near the main access point. It's sealed, with no windows, so the bastards won't catch us there."

Dorian nods. "Got to be a few dozen snatchers out there. We won't last five minutes in the open halls."

Anne pushes some of the bottles of chemicals out of the way to reveal an electrical conduit cover, magnetic bolts holding it fast to the station wall.

"These go all through the SCIF," she says. "Man-sized tunnels for the techs to make emergency repairs and pull new cables."

"Okay," he says, pulling off the maintenance cover. It's almost pitch black inside, and it's unnervingly quiet. Dorian has no doubt that the creatures could easily squeeze inside if they chose. He checks the safety on his pistol to make sure he doesn't misfire.

"I'll follow your lead."

1 3

LOCKBOX

ENCRYPTED TRANSMISSION
LISTENING POST AED1413-23
Date: 2179.07.27

(Unspecified A): We're in-system.
(Unspecified B): What about scanners?
(Unspecified A): Our contingency took care of it.
    Indigo flag is flying blind.
(Unspecified B): Good. Time to give these Weyland-
    Yutani fucks a taste of their own medicine.

An alarm wakes her. It's... her medicine alarm? She hasn't heard that in ages. Marcus is supposed to take care of it before it becomes a problem. How long has she been asleep?

Then Blue remembers. Her caretaker is gone.

Getting her own medicine will be almost impossible for

her after being reliant on Marcus for so long. Even though it's just a few feet from her bed, she might accidentally pull out her G-tube or colostomy bag. She worries that she'll administer the wrong dose, in spite of the fact that she has an intellijector for each med, because her eyesight is failing, and she can't read the labels. Everything doubles and drifts, because of her demyelinated optic nerve and atrophied muscles. She wonders how long it will be before she never sees anything again.

Her portable terminal rests across the room from her, where Marcus left it on a work desk. Even though she's spent hours at that desk, with her resting body on the bed, the distance now seems insurmountable.

She scoots her foot toward the edge of her bed, and her leg doesn't want to cooperate. Even if it did, she knows it won't properly hold her weight. Blue remembers the last steps she ever took—six years ago, at her apartment in Boston. She took a shit, washed her hands, made a bowl of cereal and then spilled it all over her couch trying to get back to a seated position. She'd cried when the caretaker arrived to help her into a motorized chair.

What a wimp she'd been.

If only she'd known how bad it was going to get.

If she can just gracefully slide to the floor, she can get across to her meds and the portable terminal. She'll get herself situated in the electric wheelchair, too, in case she needs to get around.

Butt firmly on the bed, she reaches a toe down toward the cold floor, and after a long stretch, touches. She starts to move her other leg when her rump slides free, taking her to the ground in a graceless fall. She cries out as she bloodies her lip on Marcus's chair.

It's been so long since she's felt physical violence against her person. Her life consists of surfing from one wave of ambient pain to the next, and yet the blow from the chair waters her eyes. She loathes herself for her weakness.

Blue claws her way across the floor on her side, careful not to let herself pull out the feeding tube, her catheter, or her bag. She hasn't entirely lost coordination in her legs, and even though the muscles can't keep her upright, they can push her along the ground. She reaches the desk and climbs up the side, eventually coming level with her arrangement of prescriptions.

Sitting down on the desk she grabs the intellijectors, one by one, and does her thigh, her belly, and the back of her arm. Then she silences the medicine alarm.

What the fuck is wrong with Dorian and the crew? It's one thing to take away her surrogate body. It's another for them not to send a doctor around to make sure she survives the goddamned day cycle.

She checks her portable terminal. No messages. She has to get a signal to her benefactors so they can speed up the rescue, and—

—or maybe she shouldn't.

What if they know she's blown? What if they expected her to commit some sabotage to make their rescue happen, and they won't come if she can't accomplish the task? She can't risk telling them the truth about the situation.

Instead, Blue focuses on the one thing she can affect: Marcus. Sudler hasn't come around to gloat about his victory, so she can safely assume he's otherwise occupied. If she can get Marcus back online, maybe she can get out of here and contact her benefactors from the safety of an escape pod.

To make this escape work, however, she'll have to get the portable cipher drive, her meds, the drives with her research, and Marcus—all inside a pod. The cipher is hidden under her mattress. If she can get Marcus back online, she can easily steal her remaining supply of medicine. It's kept in cold storage in the med bay. Kambili is in there, but that piece of shit won't be calling anyone.

Next comes her research. That will be at the center of attention right now, and Director Sudler has made sure nobody trusts Marcus. She can't just go walking around in her android body, yet there's no way to steal her data without it.

When the Company first gave her Marcus, she secretly opened up some of his wireless data ports. It was an act of paranoia—one that no longer seems unrealistic. The ports wouldn't respond to an open scan, but a targeted attack might reactivate him. Blue unfolds her portable terminal and begins typing.

They should've come and searched her room after accusing her of malfeasance. They should've taken her portable terminal, tossed her bed to find the cipher drive, and confiscated any data sources she possessed. But they didn't, so sure were they that she was utterly immobile, and she logs in with ease.

```
>>Weyland-Yutani Systems MARCUS
>>Trademark and Copyright 2169, All Rights Reserved
>>Bootloader v1.6.5 BY DR_HODENT
Basic Motor Functions........OK
Basic Cognitive........OK
Basic Thinking........OK
Higher Thinking........OK
Fine Motor........OK
ISIS........OK
OSIRIS........OK
SET........OK
RA........SUNRISE
>>Marcus Online
>>Last Connected Five Minutes Ago: 0829 2179.07.27
```

She draws up short at the last status message. That can't be right. She's been out of commission for at least a few hours. Has Sudler been ordering Marcus around while she was unconscious?

"Okay," she mumbles, and begins to type. If he really got into Marcus's head, she won't be able to access her pilot programs.

```
//EXECUTE PILOTSTRAPPER.IMT
Searching Local Neural Networks...
...
...
```

The ellipses roll past, her heart beating in time with the appearance of each one. It's taking longer than usual—often a sign that the program is missing. However, she isn't sure how long it's been since she's had to reload her code from scratch. Maybe it's always taken this long.

She gasps aloud.

>>AWAITING BDI CONNECT_

Blue eases to the floor and crawls back to her bed, wishing she had made it to the motorized chair, muscles aching all the while. She reaches across to the brain-direct interface gear and pulls its gelatinous cap over her head, snapping the plastic outer visor tight across her nose. She taps a button at the side of the set, and strength begins to return to her limbs.

She slips into Marcus like a swimming pool, all the discomfort melting away inside his skin. It's cold here. She peers around, expecting to find synth storage, but sees frosty cubic packages lining a hundred shelves. Robots work diligently by the blue lights of their barcode scanners, moving the packages to and from various shelves.

Blue blinks. She's in the cold storage. But why?

She runs her fingers down the bare skin of her arms, and though they're freezing cold, there is no frost on her hair. Marcus couldn't have been here long. She climbs to her feet and gauges the dimensions of the space. She's in the SCIF, on one of the sub-decks.

Blue needs to get out of here, get back to her room, and

start sneaking her necessities onto an escape pod. If she leaves by herself, there'll be a shortage during an evac, but the crew will find a way.

No sooner has she thought this than red light stains the air and klaxons sound out.

"All personnel, evacuate the kennels immediately. Containment failure. Repeat, all personnel, evacuate the kennels immediately."

Blue takes some shortcuts in the run to Juno's cage, slinging herself up pipes and leaping whole floors on the stairwell. She normally keeps Marcus's superhuman abilities in check, since they tend to unnerve the crew— or make them jealous. She hoped she'd never have to field a statement about how lucky she was to have Marcus's body.

Now she eschews modesty in the face of crisis, vaulting across another bundle of pipes, then leaping between two catwalks to sprint for Juno's glass cage. It comes into view, all bright lights and beige walls. She spies eight or nine members of the crew, frantically working at the different terminals. When she arrives, she slaps a palm to the door. Her synth body's biometric access still works.

"What the fuck is she doing here?" Lucy screeches. "She ought to be under arrest! Get out! Commander, get her out of here!"

Blue hadn't noticed Daniel when she came in, but he makes his presence known. He's suited up and armed with a pulse rifle and mag sling. Marcus might have superhuman abilities, but that rifle would punch through his brain case with no trouble at all. Daniel's taut muscles coil.

He looks up at Blue with cautious eyes.

"I don't know how you got Marcus back online, but you can't be here."

"And you can't fire those caseless rounds in here, Commander Cardozo," she replies, "not unless you want to puncture the hull."

"You do your job, and I'll do—"

"I don't have a job," she says, interrupting. "Now just shut up and listen. You have to seal the kennels."

A shadow passes over Daniel's face. "I know that. We're doing it."

Blue takes a quick breath. This is going to hurt her just to speak the words.

"And you can't let anyone out. Those creatures... they'll take advantage of any chance at escape. Through the vents, along the main passageway—they'll get out the second they have the chance, and all of us will be as good as dead."

"Oh, that's convenient," Lucy says. "Director Sudler is down there."

"This isn't about whether or not I keep my job!" Blue shouts. She doesn't hold back, and Lucy recoils, her large eyes traveling to Marcus's deadly arms. "You *know* what those things can do to us!"

Daniel clears his throat. "Anne... is down there, too."

Blue falters, her confidence shaken. She knows what they have to do: destroy the kennels with extreme prejudice, but every time she tries to speak, Anne's disappointed face pops into her mind.

Of all the lovers in Blue's life, Anne had been the cruelest, leaving Blue because she was "depressing." Yet despite their icy professional relationship, Blue can't imagine letting Anne die.

"How many are down there?"

"Eight people," Daniel says. "We have to give them a chance to come up with something."

"It..." Blue swallows. Her whole world has come to the brink of collapse. "It doesn't matter. If Anne is in there, she's already dead. We have to lock it up. And I—I need to initiate the quarantine-all-kill. Lucy, make the announcement."

The protocol will sever the kennels from the station and drop them into the heart of Kaufmann, incinerating everything inside. Millions of dollars and eight human lives. It's a worst-case scenario, one that will damage the orbit of the Cold Forge and necessitate an early evac. The protocol was designed for exactly this situation.

Lucy's rage has boiled away. Blue can see it in her eyes: Lucy knows she's right. No matter what they do, they won't be able to save those inside the kennels—not without jeopardizing the lives of those who remain. They could call for a Marines emergency rescue, and the soldiers would be there in four short weeks. The snatchers will have broken out of their confinement by then.

"We have to do something…" Lucy says.

Blue's gaze drifts to the ground. "Lucy, it's the right—"

"Fuck! That's not what I meant, okay? Like I fucking know they're going to die! I just… like, isn't there something we can do? Like, should we tell them?"

Daniel nods. "I'd want to know. I'd also want to have a few moments of quiet before the end."

"They already know," Blue says. "But maybe you're right—you should say something."

Lucy leans down and clicks the intercom key, then lets off, then clicks it again.

"This is Lucy Biltmore… To any crew inside the kennels, quarantine protocol is in effect. We've contained the outbreak by sealing off your area, but… there's no way we can open the doors. If any of you are listening, if any of you can still hear me—"

Lucy can't contain herself any longer, and she breaks down weeping. Blue wants to join her, but she can't—not while there's a containment threat. She looks over to Daniel, who gives her a pained smile. He's seen this before, hasn't he? There's something in his eyes that tells Blue he hasn't just lost soldiers, he's lost them slowly, impotently.

"Commander Cardozo," Blue says. "We've got to sever the kennels. It's the only way to be sure. If anyone is still alive in there, they'll… they'll be looking for a way out. If they can get out, then…"

He crosses his arms and arches an eyebrow.

"You mean we have to send Anne falling into a star."

Blue shakes her head. "Please don't make this any

harder than it is. You don't even know if she's alive. And if someone opens a passage between the kennels and the SCIF, what are you going to do?"

"It won't work," Lucy says, sniffing. "We haven't rebuilt Juno yet. Someone has to get out there and trigger the explosive bolts manually."

"Then I'm going to suit up in the Turtle," Blue says. "You going to help me, Commander?"

"All right. Suit up. I'll be your operator from control."

1 4

SEVERANCE PACKAGE

Blue mashes the final stage airlock cycle and the door opens to reveal the light of Kaufmann. She knows to look away this time, but the solar load still stings her cheeks and eyes. She spins and eases out in the Turtle, backing toward the star.

As she clears the golden airlock doors, she glances right to see where Silversmile had opened up the heat shields in the kennels. She'll have to range a lot further in the EVA suit to blow the load-bearing bolts. Once the section is severed, she'll have to avoid it, or it will take her into Kaufmann, too.

She shouldn't be incinerating her future. Her research is probably in that module, along with the samples she needs. But this is what she's duty bound to do in a containment failure. So she fires her thrusters in short bursts, moving along the outside of the kennels at more than a yard per second. She has to get this over with quickly, or she'll lose her nerve.

Anne is probably dead. There's no way to get her out. Half the crew are still depending on Blue.

She knows sadness, but physically feels nothing beyond the heat of radiation. A monstrous calm settles over her bones in the weightlessness, and she knows it's because of Marcus. His physicality knows no fear, no pounding heart, no sudden watering of the eyes. He simply is, and through him, Blue will kill her only real friend.

If it was only Sudler down there, she'd *gladly* blow the kennels free. She'd want him to know who'd done him in, too.

Blue reaches the first manual junction. This is her first time atop the station with this view. Her eyes travel down the central strut, past the docked *Athenian*, to the crew quarters where her body lies. Working every day inside the serpentine tunnels of the kennels, it's easy to forget how large they are, but outside, the enormity of the structure is inescapable. It's like a giant wart on the outside of the Cold Forge. There are several dozen murderous specimens beneath her, ready to spread across the station like a plague.

She fires a short burst of her jets and settles onto the hull, attaching a magnetic handhold so she has leverage. Blue grabs a tool from her belt and ratchets open the panel, which bears a written label.

WARNING: MANUAL SEPARATION OVERRIDE

Upon opening it, she finds three banks of backlit buttons. This is one of the six codes every employee of the Cold Forge possesses: docking override, SCIF access, scuttle protocol, Juno reinit, Titus reinit, and kennels severance.

Since it's been a while for her, she checks the instructions on the underside of the panel. Type the code. Pop the lever housing. Pull the lever to confirm. Replace the housing. Get clear in one minute.

In the old firing squad executions on Earth, ten men would line up, and one of them would fire a blank. No one knew who fired the impotent shot. This was supposed to keep the murders from their consciences. In Blue's eyes, all ten of the trigger-pullers are killers.

There are no fake bullets in this execution.

There is no crime, either.

"I'm at the first lock panel."

"Copy," Lucy responds. Nothing else. No words of encouragement. Blue taps each symbol with a gloved finger, keeping her gestures sure and deliberate. She can't miss, or she'll use up one of her three tries. On the fourth miss, she'll be locked out. She completes the sequence, and the panel flashes in acknowledgement.

Grasping the massive grip of the lever housing, she pulls. It takes a surprising amount of Marcus's strength to get it free. A steel cylinder the size of a champagne bottle rises from the heart of the panel, and Blue slides open the latch on the front. The priming lever rests inside, its yellow-and-black striped grip like a venomous snake.

"Priming the bolts now."

"Copy." Lucy's going to cry—Blue can hear the sobs in her voice.

She grasps the lever, but her strength fails her. Every tearful breath Lucy takes weighs down upon her hand, staying it. Anne, beautiful and vibrant, is going to die.

Blue summons her voice and closes her eyes.

"Put Commander Cardozo on. I can't do this if you're going to cry in my fucking ear."

"Bitch," Lucy whispers.

A rustling, then Daniel's voice comes over the line.

"You okay?"

"No." She keeps one hand on the priming lever and the other on her mag hold. "Have you ever lost men under your command?"

"No," Daniel says. "Most Marines never see front-line combat. Thing is, when you've got everything from knives to nukes, most people don't want to fight you."

"You always look so tough."

"My mom was a Gurkha. She killed a lot of Pakistanis before she moved stateside and married my dad. I guess I'm just trying to be like her. Acting like I've got a job to do. Why do *you* always look so tough?"

"My dad managed a hedge fund before he died."

"So a real killer, then," Daniel replies, chuckling. "Blue, I'm going to help you out here."

"How?"

"Pull the fucking lever *now*," he replies, his voice like a slab of granite. "That's an order."

Without another thought, her hand does as it's told.

The lever snaps down under her weight, and when she releases it, it springs back to its initial position. The backlit buttons on the panel pulse blood red. She shuts the housing door and plunges the cylinder back into the panel like an old-timey dynamite detonator.

"Started the detonation sequence."

"Roger that," Daniel says. "Confirmed on our screens. Two more to go, now get moving."

Blue has already landed at the next access point when she feels the peppery staccato of a hundred explosive bolts firing in sequence. It rumbles across the decks and up through her magnetic handhold—a silent saw tearing the station apart. She knows the protocol. Inside the kennels, doors will seal and alarms will sound. The sadness of her physical body creeps over the brain-direct interface, and she begins to hear Marcus cry.

This feels so wrong, but she knows what must be done. Two more lines of bolts, and the kennels can be pushed away with RB-232's retro thrusters.

The heat is beginning to register as greater pain, but she ignores it. Blue looks down at the panel, and her hands don't want to cooperate. It was hard enough to open up the first one, and now she has to do it again. She turns back toward Kaufmann, careful not to look directly at it, its rays hard on her face. She's going to burn up her research to save these assholes.

"I'm at the second panel." Her voice is barely a whisper.

"Let's get this done, Blue." Daniel clears his throat. "You need to be back here."

"Okay, yeah. Copy." She fits her ratchet to the first bolt, and another voice comes over her comm.

"Blue!" Anne says, alarms blaring in the background. "Is that you out there?"

She can't bring herself to pull the trigger on the ratchet. "Anne?"

"Oh, Jesus Christ it's you," she says. "I know—look, I know you're just trying to protect the rest of the SCIF, but we're still alive in here!"

"How many of you?" Like it matters. Is there a number that will change her mind?

There's a long pause.

"At least a few of us. We got separated, but listen—" Panic edges into Anne's voice. "Listen… to me, okay? We can get out. Do you copy that? I know we can get out without them catching us."

The image of Anne's blushing face, sweaty and sated, edges into Blue's mind without permission. The trigger on the ratchet feels like it's made of stone.

"How?"

"I don't know yet, but we'll come up with a plan." Her voice is a rush. "Just don't—"

The comm beeps to indicate a severed connection.

"Anne?" Blue's voice shakes uncontrollably. Her fear has overcome Marcus's body, and she feels her own ailing form, as clear as day. "*Anne!*"

She shouts the name over and over again, but it just

ricochets in her helmet, unable to penetrate the vastness of space. She screams in impotent rage, but Anne's voice doesn't return. Surely the connection wouldn't have terminated if she was killed. Blue would've heard the woman's grisly end.

"I had Lucy cut the comms from the kennels," Daniel says, his voice ice cold. "You still have a job to do, and that wasn't helping."

Blue shakes her head. "Maybe we should hear them out."

"If you don't blow those bolts, everyone on this station is dead. Do I make myself clear? This is a numbers game. Now do your—"

The comm emits a weird squeal, like a hundred high-pitched chimes being struck in random order. Daniel's voice transforms to a low moan, then a breathy whistle, unnatural in its swift alterations, then nothing. Blue recognizes what's happened. It's the loss of comms due to unreliable connections. In the early days of RB-232, the flares of Kaufmann would play havoc on the radios, knocking out swathes of data during wireless transfer. It was almost impossible to speak from one side of the station to the other.

But with modulation and a bit of fancy mathematical footwork, they'd fixed it. Blue couldn't remember the last time someone on the station lost comms.

"Commander?" she says. "Commander, come in."

No response. She keys her suit radio, switching it to an unsecured frequency.

"RB-232 all channels, this is Blue Marsalis, come in." She waits ten seconds and tries again. No one responds, maybe because they didn't hear her—maybe because they can't.

Something is wrong.

She spins her EVA suit to head back to the airlock. They still have some time before they must cut the kennels free. Maybe, while Blue is inside, they can cook up a plan to get Anne out of there.

What felt like a long journey to the second panel compresses under Blue's racing mind, and she's back at the airlock in no time. She keys in her code, and the doors refuse to open. Blue tries the code again, but she notices the pad isn't even active.

"What the fuck?" she mumbles. "RB-232 all personnel, what's going on? Open the SCIF airlock door."

Kaufmann seems to grow even hotter upon her back. Her EVA has already lasted too long. She risks frying herself if she stays out much longer. She can't lose Marcus. Not now. She bangs the airlock, its solid mass quiet against her fist.

"Open the goddamned door!"

The SCIF airlock has access control to stop it from being manually cycled. The other airlocks don't. If Blue's SCIF access code doesn't get her into this one, it stands to reason she could maneuver to another one.

She checks her propellant. She had enough for three stops and a return trip, with room to spare for maneuvering in the middle. She's made two of the stops, but the trips to and from were the longest legs. If she's lucky, she'll have enough to make it to the airlock on the shady side of the SCIF. If not, she'll have to walk the Turtle along the surface, where the solar reflections will roast her legs.

Blue backs away from the hull and fires a short set of bursts to get herself moving. The suit will easily reach forty miles an hour, but she'll need propellant to slow down. She makes a few minor course corrections, then settles in for the drift.

Getting to the opposite side of the Cold Forge's cylinder proves more difficult than she anticipated. Instead of throttling up to speed and waiting for her journey to complete, she has to make six to eight short leaps, each correction draining more of her valuable propellant. Finally, the shadowed side of the station looms in her view, black beside the golden light of the star. A lamp illuminates the entrance of the distant airlock, and Blue nearly sobs with relief. A warning sounds in her ear as she course corrects. She gets a tiny bit of forward momentum, but the nozzles sputter helplessly as the tanks run dry.

"No. Not now."

She clicks the sticks again and reboots the Turtle.

"Come on, you piece of shit."

The tanks give her a tiny burst, but not enough. She can't even be certain if she'll hit the station if she waits it out.

"Fuck!"

She can't call for rescue. There's no backup for her—no one answering anywhere. She can't imagine the reason, and that frightens her so much more. All she has is a dead radio, a dying suit, and the stupid, heavy Turtle shell on her back. Too much of it is taken up by reflective shielding, not enough by fuel, which gives it the worst ratio of any EVA suit she's ever touched.

Maybe I can use that.

The Turtle *is* heavy—far heavier than her body, and it's moving in the right general direction. Even though there's no resistance to stop it, Blue could shove off of it in the direction of the station. It would be pushed away, but inertia dictates that she'll go further because of her lighter mass.

Or, it might spin, and she'd miss entirely, sending Marcus's body into a slowly decaying orbit around a star.

Blue unclips from her five-point harness, careful that her motion doesn't cause much reorientation. She needs the back padding to be a flat surface, perpendicular to the station hull. Then, she can leap outward and try to catch the station. Hanging onto the safety harness, she plants her feet against the flat cushions of the Turtle, then twists to look up at the Cold Forge. The hulk looms before her, cutting night out of the day with its silhouette.

Fixing her eyes on the airlock door, she leaps—

—and strikes the control stick with her foot.

The last bit of propellant charge erupts from the nozzles, and the pack hooks onto her ankle before coming free. She launches, but spins out of control. The station tumbles in her view, and her breath comes in gasps. She has no way of knowing if she's off-course or not. Her tool belt tugs at her waist, and she draws it in closer, which only accelerates her spin, like an ice skater leaping into a triple axel.

"Fuck, fuck, fuck," she mutters, trying to remember how to stop a bad maneuver in zero g. Unbuckling the tool belt she holds it in one hand, splaying her arms and legs as far as they'll go. The stars around her slow down as the tools sling far out from the axis of her spin. The station stops whipping through her view, and she can actually gauge her approach. She's going to hit low, but she'll make it.

Her back connects with metal and her arms go wide. She tries to kick it with one of her mag boots, praying the sole will attach. Her body hit the station all wrong, and she bounces off toward the great darkness beyond. In desperation, she swings the heavy tool belt toward the hull, which spins her along a different axis. To her surprise, the belt hooks into something, and she jerks to a halt, her legs dangling above the stars.

Taking a deep breath, she looks down, the dizzying vertigo of space stretching on forever. Gingerly, she reaches up to get a better grip, but her arm is just a little too short. If the tool belt loses its purchase, she'll never make up the six inches that lie between her and the hull. Gently, she pulls herself closer and wraps her fingers around the lowest safety handhold. With halting motions, she clambers up the shadowy hull toward the airlock.

When she presses the manual cycle and the door opens wide for her, she wants nothing more dearly than to pop a bottle of champagne. She imagines the cold bubbles on her lips, and pressing a sweating flute to her sun-chapped face. But if she did that, she'd have to drain Marcus's digestive system. He's a cheaper model, with a lactic-resistant interior and no real digestion to speak of.

Then it hits her. What a fool she's been.

She never should've used the chimps.

Blue had the perfect *praepotens* sample catcher all along.

As the airlock pressurizes, outside sounds bleed into her suit: alarm bells, muddled warnings, and something that sounds like a sputtering engine, though it's too regular. Her ears take the last sound apart, piece by piece until she finally remembers where she's heard it before.

It's pulse rifle fire, and it's coming from the central strut.

INTERLUDE

DICK

He awakens to splitting pain in his head.

He's... kneeling? That's not quite right. There's something supporting his back, or pressed against it. His shoulders burn. His thighs ache.

Dick tries to open his eyes, only to find that one of them won't open, and the pain is so great that he aborts the attempt. Every time he tries to move his right eye, it's like someone sticks a hot needle into his brain and twists it around. There's a steady drip down his face of something warm, blood, and something cold—he can't quite place his finger on it.

He's missing time. He tries to capture the last moment he remembers, but it's like grasping at smoke. He recalls finding Kambili.

Kambili told them about Blue's server. Then he sat down with... no... they found the server and he was with Dorian Sudler. Dick was feeding the creatures. There was someone skulking around near the cells.

Dick can't pull their face from the ether.

He must have a concussion. He could've fallen, or maybe someone hit him.

Dick tries to move his fingers—maybe he can see what the bloody hell is wrong with his face—but his arms are bound up tight by what feels like coils of steel. His hands throb, almost numb, and he wonders if they're broken. Panic sets in, and he kicks his legs out, trying to stand up. Something shoves him from behind, and a hard steel edge digs into his gut.

He forces open his left eye to find himself pressed over the top of a crate like an arrested man, hands restrained behind his back. He struggles again, and this time his restraints twist, wrenching his shoulders out of joint. Dick screams as loudly as he ever has, though his voice is broken and throat ravaged.

A low hiss drips into his ear, breath hot and rancid, and he freezes, instantly aware of the source.

Blistering pain burns the clouds from Dick's mind, and he forces his left eye open again. He should be dead. He's going to die. For some reason, the creature hasn't killed him yet. As far as he knows, it's only fucked up both his arms, concussed him, mangled his face. He'll never be able to run from it. He tilts his head to get a better look around, and the blinding pain in his right eye is followed by a stringy tug.

When he was a little boy, he remembers reaching into a mailbox, and finding a redback spider on his hand. A lesser boy would've slapped at it and been rewarded with a potentially fatal bite. He'd placed his hand back on the blistering-hot metal mailbox and waited patiently for the spider to leave. When it was off of him, he'd crushed it with a shoe.

He needs to find that patience now.

Blurry words swim into focus on the crate below him.

—NGEROUS SPEC—

He knows the rest of it from heart. *"Dangerous specimen. Do not open without prior authorization."* It's an egg crate. The big fucker wants to impregnate him. Why does it know what an egg crate looks like? He thinks of all the times they hefted one of these past the cells on a power loader. The beasties are always paying attention.

Dick almost laughs when his good eye swivels to the crate's failsafe to find it still blinking active red. It can't be opened outside of the impregnation lab—not without triggering the countermeasures inside.

The snatcher wedges the spade of its chitinous tail into the space between the lid and the lock. Dick's good eye bulges. If it prizes the lock, he's going to get a face full of lye and thermite. The creature crows in frustration as the lock fails to move, and Dick expects a killing blow to fall.

Instead, two sharp tail strikes come down on the hinges, like the blows of an axe, weakening the container. Then again and again the strikes fall, their echoes banging out into the kennels, until the hinges lay twisted and warped from the hits. The long spine wedges back into place and pries the lid, and Dick feels the metal start to fail.

As it cracks, he shoves back hard against the creature, its bony ribs digging into his back. Dick's whole body seizes with pain, but this is his only chance for escape. If he can just knock the beast loose, he might crawl away in the confusion.

There's a flash as the thermite lights inside the crate, filling the air with acrid, flickering orange smoke. One whiff of the flames and acid, and he can no longer smell anything but agony. Blistering heat washes over Dick's exposed face, chapping his skin, and still he pushes back. The blast of lye is coming soon, powerful enough to dissolve his flesh.

The creature loosens its grip and Dick twists free, collapsing to the ground on his side. He lands on his right eye, finishing the job. He knows he won't be able to run, that his internal bleeding is probably going to kill him if he doesn't get to a doctor within the hour. He'll be dead before then when the creature finishes lamenting the fiery crate.

That's when a miracle happens.

It tries to rescue the egg.

Like the anguished parent of an endangered baby, it reaches inside the boiling thermite and catches the splash of distilled lye and molten metal across the front of its body. The egg is doomed, its deadly payload leaking from the sides of the collapsing crate, foaming white. The creature's rage manifests in a bright, piercing shriek, and its tail whips about like a spear, striking anything it can find.

Dick swallows his torment and begins crawling for the

door. If he can just get to a terminal, he can call for help. He knows he'll never be the same again, but he's alive and determined to make that count for something. Lesser men have survived greater wounds, after all.

He's almost at the door when he spies another set of black talons. A blow like a baseball bat comes down in the dead center of his spine. Dick cannot scream because he cannot breathe. Through his one good eye, he watches the gush of blood, knowing it comes from his own lips. His legs are gone, or at least he can't feel them.

And then he is weightless, every last inch of his being in unimaginable pain, the strength of his mangled arms failing. He looks down at his chest to see the glittering black spine of a long tail protruding from his ribcage.

Oh, he thinks, the world growing dim, *the big fucker impaled me.*

Shock spares him the feeling of the creature's tongue digging into the back of his head as if he's an overripe melon.

1 5

ESCAPE CLAUSE

"Oh, my god, they're opening the door! Do you hear it?" Anne whispers in the darkened maintenance bay. "We're going to get rescued."

He hears it as well, the distinct *thunk* of the twelve-pin vault door leading into the kennels. The motors will soon swing it wide, allowing all of the creatures to spill out into the SCIF. The only question that remains in his mind is, "Why?" What's their plan?

As if in answer, the few lights inside the closet flicker, and the most awful grinding sound echoes through the station ventilation shafts.

"Alert," Titus says, his nasal voice echoing through the corridors. "Scrubbers offline. Life support systems critical. All crew to evac stations."

Dorian's eyes lock with Anne's.

"Alert," Titus says, and Dorian thinks it will be a repeat of the same warning. He's wrong. "Orbital dynamics and navigation critical. All crew to evac stations."

The two of them hunker down as the banging of talons sounds through the corridor. The creatures stampede through the hallways like a herd, skittering past the closed door of Dorian and Anne's hiding spot.

"Alert," Juno says, her voice a breathy contrast to Titus's, "Access control systems critical—"

"Alert," Titus interrupts, "Security and quarantine systems offline. Killbox offline. All crew report to evac stations."

"What the everloving fuck?" Anne whispers.

"Silversmile," Dorian replies. "That's the only thing that could pick apart station security like this."

"It couldn't jump the air gap. Those two networks aren't connected."

"That means we've got a saboteur, or an idiot," Dorian says. "My money is on the—"

Deafening pulse rifle fire fills their ears. Anne throws Dorian to the ground, shoving his cheek against the rough deck. Before he can ask why, a shot ricochets through the bulkhead.

"Fucking Christ, Cardozo," she says. "Okay, Dorian, we're going to have to move perpendicular to the swarm. That's caseless, armor-piercing ammo he's firing."

"He's going to breach the hull," Dorian slurs, and she lets him up.

"Not if he fires directly into the guts of the SCIF. Lots of layers between him and the outer hull."

"He could've used the guns from the armory."

Anne looks him over for a moment. "Those are just a

placebo. They'll kill a human just fine, but forget about a snatcher. We put them there so Blue's lab assistants would go inside."

On the one hand Dorian is enraged that no one shared this fact with him. On the other, it makes the creatures all the more perfect. They're gods among men—or perhaps the children of the heavens—patient and cruel, and always capable of escape. He needs to continue where Blue left off. Some people devote their lives to ship design or architecture. He could be the champion of these majestic beasts.

"We have to get those data drives and get to the *Athenian*," he says, and Anne balks.

"Are you stupid? An all-points crew evac means exactly that."

He starts to protest, and she slaps him so hard he tastes blood. Then she puts up a finger, cutting off any response.

"Don't you fuck around with our lives here, Dorian. We evac ASAP."

No one has ever slapped him before, and the urge to retaliate is instantaneous. Heat rises in his breast, and he sucks in a breath. He wants to strike her back, to break her against the bulkhead and wrap his hands around her slender throat. He wants to crush her fucking skull—but then he remembers their wild sex and thinks better of it. He has muscle, but she's so much tougher, with years of combat training. She'd overpower him without any real difficulty. Fighting is her second nature.

The screams of the creatures and the sound of rifle fire

have died down, retreating toward the central strut.

"We're going to discuss this when we get back to the ship," he whispers.

"What, are you going to fire me some more?" She rises to a low crouch and grabs him by the wrist.

He smirks. "Maybe you can get your job back."

She glances back at him, surprised at his pass, but not disgusted. She guides him out into the hallway and toward the kennels vault door, hunkering down as she moves. He follows, his bare feet sticking to the waxy floor. His suit trousers constrict his movements, and he desperately wishes for a set of fatigues like Anne's. He's dressed to impress, not circumnavigate rifle fire while hiding from unstoppable killing machines.

At the last armory, she stops to pick up a couple of smoke grenades and flashbangs. They're surprisingly small, and she fits the bandolier around her waist. Dorian pulls out his pistol, and she touches his hand, shaking her head.

"Put that back. We're only going to get people killed with it, and it's loud." She taps the grenades. "These, however, are useful."

He considers arguing that those "people" might be his targets, and decides against it. He hates the way she talks down to him so confidently, as though he's a child. He'll make her regret hitting him. She's wrong to underestimate him.

"Okay," he says, nodding at the vault door. "You take point, soldier."

Is she disgusted with his ungentlemanly suggestion?

It doesn't matter. She's the one with the training, and chivalry be damned. She rushes from corner to corner and he mimics her movements, sidling up to each one, then glancing out before ducking back to cover. The hissing and rifle fire grow louder again. Dorian and Anne reach the vault door and sneak across the threshold.

What they see is nothing like the polished science center from before. Bullet holes snake through the walls. Warning strobes flash white between pulses of red. The clean light of Juno's glass cage sputters like a dying candle. Broken bits of steel litter the deck, and blood drips from a catwalk onto a gory mess. Dorian hopes it's Lucy—he doesn't know the others well enough to care about their fates.

He smells it before he sees it—a melted hole in the deck plates, about the size of a human. It stinks of rotten eggs, with a piercing sour note as though someone is pushing a needle into his nose. Dorian gives it a wide berth as he tiptoes, barefoot, around it.

"What the fuck is that?" he whispers.

"Commander Cardozo must've gotten one of them. Remember the acid for blood?" She pulls one of the flashbangs from her bandolier. "Just make sure you steer clear when a snatcher goes down."

"Yeah, no problem." He peers over the edge into the hole, which descends two decks down. One of the beasts lies shattered at the bottom. Bilious yellow blood hisses on the floor, spreading from its corpse like drops of water on a hot frying pan. He remembers reading

Mackie's design report, about how the SCIF's exterior decks were super hydrophobic, to stop the acid from breaking through.

When one of the snatchers is killed, it melts into the floor like a hell-bound dragon. Dorian has to admire that. It's almost as if they want to return to the light of Kaufmann, to be consumed as thoroughly as they consume. There's something sad about it, too, knowing they're not immortal. He wonders if this is what humanity felt when it experienced the extinction of the wild lion.

All reverence aside, he hopes Daniel won't shoot any of the beasts on the central strut. He isn't sure the ship can take a flood of acid in the thinner parts.

The pulse rifle fire stops, and Anne rushes ahead. The Commander and crew are drawing close to the escape pods. Dorian is just glad that the crew of the *Athenian* haven't been briefed on the snatcher threat. The classification level is higher than his crew possesses, and that's a good thing. Otherwise, they'd probably leave without him.

He and Anne wind between the various electrical stations and cargo crates. It's clear the crew of the Cold Forge used this open area as a staging ground. While Dorian begrudges them their mess, at least the obstructions provide him with a decent cover. Ahead of them, there's another dark patch, and at first, Dorian thinks it's the next acid crater.

Glancing toward Anne, he finds her frozen in place, eyes locked on the ceiling. Following her gaze, he finds one of the aliens wedged in between two coolant pipes, working with deliberate snaps of its jaw to take apart a corpse. The meal is a man, but describing the gender of the thoroughly mangled remains at all seems generous.

Past Anne, two long, smooth heads emerge from the darkness like a pair of players entering the theater stage. The three snatchers don't react, so they must not yet see Dorian and Anne. He gestures toward the creatures, pointing to his eyes, then behind her. She signals for him to get down.

There's a low worktable within easy reach, and they roll under it. They could try to go back the way they came, but the escape pods will launch without them. Ahead, there's an unknown number of acid-blooded beasts ready to tear their heads open—yet it's the only direction toward freedom.

Anne pops the compression cap on one of her smoke grenades and hurls it into the distance, toward the kennels. It clangs upon the deck before plunging into the melted hole. Only hissing stillness follows the echoing beat. For a moment, Dorian wonders if the creatures heard it.

The corpse bangs to the floor in front of him, yielding a splash of blood and a crunch of bone. Its features give nothing away of its former identity. Skin tone, face, and age are all obscured by the deathly slickness of crimson. It takes all of Dorian's concentration not to cry out in surprise. He peers around the corner, just enough to see the outlines of the two exposed beasts.

Fluorescent illumination dances across their carapaces, like light shining down a blade. Their faces, such as the rows of teeth can be called, jut toward the yawning crater, patiently watching the yellow smoke as it rolls up from below decks. Dorian wonders if they view things in infrared, sonar, or visual light. A chill rolls down his spine as he considers the x-ray spectrum—maybe they can see through walls. Were that the case, however, they would've already been eating him.

Anne nervously eyes him from her shadowed corner in a stack of crates, the dim reflections of her wide sclera the only evidence of her presence. She probably wants to know if they've taken the bait. He looks meaningfully behind her to the open space full of deadly claws and teeth, and shakes his head no.

A heaving thud nearly buckles the table above him, folding its thick steel inward—a hit from another body-sized object. He rolls onto his back and pulls his limbs in tight, tucking all of himself against one side of the workbench. An inky, skeletal tail languidly drips over the side, vertebra by vertebra, until a heavy spine thumps into the deck. There is nothing between the man and the creature save for a thin layer of rolled steel… and hope. In the light of Juno's cage, he can see the thick cord of muscle operating the whip, and he knows it could tear him asunder with a single hit.

This close, the physicality of the thing is intoxicating. In the cages, they looked as though they might be avian-boned, but out here, he senses the heft of its frame. Clawed fingertips wrap around the edges of the table, grasping the edge so the creature can launch itself at a target in the blink of an eye. The beast arranges itself silently on the work surface, passing over it as a ghost.

If Dorian grows to old age, he knows this will be the single greatest moment of his life.

Anne draws another grenade from her belt, and his heart skips a beat. They're going to hear the rustle of her sleeve as she throws it. They're going to see it bounce off the deck and figure out the direction from which it came. If she tosses that little metal cylinder, it will be the last moment they spend alive.

Gingerly removing the compression cap, she looses the grenade. It sails precisely into the acid-cut hole, clinking two decks below before going off with a flash of light and a deafening bang. Dorian's ears ring, and the sound fades into the wild screams of the trio of aliens. They wail with such perfect hatred, such unending rage.

The worktable goes tumbling off of Dorian as the creature uses it for launch. The snatcher bounds away toward the hole, along with its two compatriots, oblivious to Dorian's now exposed presence. Anne wastes no time and rises to bolt for the door that leads to the central strut. He rolls and gets his feet under him, darting clumsily upright. He'd always considered himself graceful, until he saw the biological murder machines.

Together, he and Anne plunge through the malfunctioning station toward the central docking bay and, hopefully, the *Athenian*.

* * *

Blue presses her face to the airlock door, peering into the glass to see if she can make out the reason for the pulse fire. She goes to open the interior door, but a flash of instinct changes her mind. She can't simply rush in—she needs to know what's happening.

Deep down, she already knows—the comms failure, the warning lights, the staccato blasts of gunfire—the snatchers have broken their containment.

She cranes her neck to get a better view of the SCIF door. From the airlock module, she can just barely make it out, and it's wide open. In the shadows of the rafters, Marcus's keen eyes decipher the shape of an alien, crawling along the duct work.

Blue pulls the brain-direct interface helmet from her head, its well-worn straps catching on the stubble of her scalp. Sweat coats every inch of her form, and she's hyperventilating. She has to slow herself down, or she'll choke on her own spit.

If they're loose, then where are the alarms? Why didn't the killbox destroy everyone? Her gut seizes as she hears a beep, followed by Titus's computerized voice.

"Alert. Scrubbers offline. Life support systems critical. All crew to evac stations."

"What?" Blue whispers aloud. *Why the fuck is life support failing?*

"Alert," Titus says, and she steels herself. "Orbital dynamics and navigation critical. All crew to evac stations."

Theoretically, their orbit shouldn't need another injection for another month, but if the calculation systems are down, it might start to degrade immediately.

"Alert," Titus says. "Security and quarantine systems offline. All crew to evac stations."

There's shouting in the halls—it's two of the lab techs, ransacking the next room, and Blue calls out to them, her voice hoarse and dim. She takes a deeper breath and puts everything she has into it.

"Hey! I'm in he—" Then her larynx contracts, sending her into a fit of violent coughing. The banging in the next room stops for a brief moment, then several sets of footfalls take off. They're moving away from Blue, away from the crew quarters—toward the lifeboats. She knows they heard her.

She knows she's been abandoned.

Her eyes, already failing, go blurry and wet. She's never been particularly close with the crew. They either dislike her, or they fear her, but they've felt that way since the day they laid eyes on her frail form. She depresses them, because they're too cowardly to confront their own mortalities.

"God damn you!" she screams, not caring whether or not she chokes.

The shape of her motorized wheelchair resolves through the starbursts of tears. She shouldn't put herself into it without assistance. She could fall. One hit to her chest could kill her. She might tear out her stomas. Her ligaments, weakened from vitamin deficiencies and attacks from her own immune system, might snap under the weight of her upright body. But if she doesn't get the hell out of there, the snatchers are going to make a meal of her.

The sensible thing to do is to end it on her terms. There are enough painkillers in her cabinet for everyone on the station to overdose, but the intellijectors read her blood for potential conflicts and toxicology. The syringes would never administer her the dosage she needs. While the computer chips inside them are stupid, the tamper-resistant housings won't let her in without a fight.

The oxygen canisters, on the other hand, are an old design, and can easily have their valves rigged with a standard-issue pen. Then she remembers Dorian's matches and striker, conveniently tucked away under her mattress.

Her great grandfather burned to death in an oxygen fire on Luna, but before he had the privilege, he lived three days in total agony. They tried to freeze him and get him to a treatment center on Earth, but cold sleep was too much for him to bear. That shouldn't be a risk for Blue, though. No one will come to extinguish her. It would take her about a minute to die, but if she seals up the room, she might knock herself out with the concussive force. She could pass her last agonizing moments in blissful ignorance.

Or she could admit to herself that she didn't drag her bones to the far side of space just to roast them here.

Marcus is still near the egg storage. If she can get to the escape pods, she can instruct him to collect the *praepotens* sample and the drives, then seal herself inside to wait. The creatures may be clever, but they won't get in through an airlock door. She'll have to convince the others not to launch, but she can cross that bridge when she comes to it.

All that matters is getting that sample.

She picks up her portable terminal and unfolds the screen. It still has a charge. She can instruct Marcus via wireless uplink. She doesn't have time to type the painstaking commands just yet. She just needs him to stay alive.

```
Blue: //PRIORITY 1: remain hidden in airlock and
    await orders

>>ERROR: system cannot process the request

Marcus: First priority is rescue and protection of
    RB-232 survivors
```

She scoffs. He's protecting the people who would just as soon leave her behind.

```
Blue: //Can you get me to the escape pods?

Marcus: At present there are more pressing demands.
    Recommend you call out for help. Remain in
    shelter. I'll come for you ASAP.
```

But he won't have time. They'll launch the escape pods without her.

"Well fuck you, too."

Blue reaches down and clamps her G-tube before

disconnecting it. Then, she winces as she gently pulls out her catheter tube. Everything is so raw—those bastards haven't let Marcus come by to replace it and disinfect. She checks the seal on her colostomy bag. It looks nice and tight. Marcus always did a good job locking it down. She swings her legs over the side of her bed, reaching for the ground with her bare toes. Her eyes aren't good enough to perceive depth, so it's like reaching out into a chasm.

The mattress is higher off the ground than a normal bed, ostensibly so she can be close to eye level with visitors. She feels stretched to her limit when her right big toe touches the cold surface. Slowly, she eases her weight forward off the mattress.

"Okay," she says, repeating the word every second to keep the assurances going. "Okay." She hasn't stood in over a year. She won't be able to catch herself if she falls. Slowly she slides down onto her feet and her ankles lock in place, sustaining her swaying frame. She holds fast to the sheets with a white-knuckled grip, her biceps quivering with every small motion.

It's two giant steps to her old chair.

She could try to stumble them, falling into her seat, but that seems too risky. To her left, there's a rolling tray where Marcus usually puts her meds. She reaches out with one hand, pulling it to her, clutching the metal lip to her stomach. To stabilize, Blue throws her other arm across it, leaning her weight onto its wide caster base.

Using it like a walker, she traverses the distance on decaying muscle. When she arrives, shaking, at her chair, she turns to orient her rump to the seat. Pulling the tray with her, she moves cautiously until the backs of her knees touch the edge. She goes to sit, and the tray comes out from under her with a heinous clatter, striking the bony top of her bare foot.

Pain lights up her leg. That hit will leave a green bruise. Her skin is like an old woman's now, mottling over with the slightest provocation. A bruise isn't going to kill her, however, so it isn't worth worrying about. The only thing that matters is getting her ass to the docking area.

The crew quarters module looks like a cyclone went through it. Clothing, gear, and personal effects lie strewn across the deck. Blue wonders what's important enough for people to defy a full evac. Jewelry? Trinkets of another life? Everyone has a fetish, a sentimental object from a time before the Cold Forge, before they became Company property. Maybe the *praepotens* sample is Blue's fetish object, from a time when she was foolish enough to believe in a cure.

Her wheelchair is a stair-climber, so the debris poses little threat to her progress, though she has to make sure when she rolls over an article of clothing that it doesn't get tangled up in the wheels. She'd be stuck. That'd be a horrible way to go—done in by an errant shirt.

Rolling across the threshold of the crew quarters module, she enters the central strut. Several closed doors block the way, and she's thankful for it. If she saw what lay ahead, she might not be able to make herself proceed. She's just meat in a chair, after all—easy pickings for the creatures vomiting forth from the SCIF.

If she hurries, she can barricade herself inside a lifeboat before the creatures spread to the docking area. For the moment, the beasts will be preoccupied with her colleagues. The thought sickens her, but what choice does she have? She must strike while the iron is hot.

The central strut looms around her in the red lights of the evac warnings. How far out have the creatures progressed? Every shadow jumps, dancing just beyond Blue's focal plane. She wishes she had glasses, but every prescription she's tried has failed as her optic nerve continues its sclerotic decline. They could be right in front of her, and she'd barely notice.

As she passes the lights of the medical bay, she glances inside. Dim convalescent lights, like a cool summer's night, invite her into its comfortable interior. It's the only salubrious part of the station, probably because the computer can't override the lighting grid and risk damaging patient care. All of the settings in the med bay are manual, at the discretion of doctors.

Resting quietly atop one of the beds is Kambili Okoro. There's no blood on his sheets, no snatcher dismembering him in rapturous delight. He's alive, and peaceful.

Kambili sold her out. He told Dorian where to find the server. For whatever reason, the station has gone to hell, and Blue is ninety-percent certain that Dorian Sudler's arrival had something to do with it.

But she blackmailed Kambili. He lost half his face doing something he didn't want any part of. It was her fault. As she watches him sleep, chest rising and falling, the sting of her crewmates' abandonment wells inside. If she leaves him to die, she'll have ditched the last shred of her humanity in this godforsaken place. If she tries to help him, it could kill them both.

"Motherfucker," she mumbles, steering her wheelchair toward the door.

The door shuts after she passes inside, and the med bay's soundproofing kicks in, muffling the klaxons. Inside here, there's a chime and a pleasant voice says, "Alert. All personnel please check monitors for urgent messages."

The facility supports ten beds—enough for just under half of the crew. There's a surgical station, but that's rarely been used. The person who needs the most medical attention is Blue, and she gets most of her treatments in her room. Kambili is one of only two crew members who ever needed a bed. Anne was the other, having fractured a vertebra in a fall. Everyone else just used the med bay for the supplies whenever they had a cold or needed contraception.

Anyone still in the SCIF wouldn't need a bed. They'd need a tombstone. Blue tries not to think about it. Since the breakup, she's had a lot of practice shutting Anne out of her thoughts.

She motors over to Kambili and reviews his vitals. He's had a few doses of painkillers in the last hour, but she ought to be able to rouse him. Bandages cover the missing half of his face, and his breathing is heavy. Blue reaches up to jostle his shoulder—this is her first time touching him with her own hand. Kambili is heavier than he ought to be. He stirs, but doesn't open his eyes.

"Kambili," she says, glad it's quiet enough in the med bay for him to hear her.

He blinks at her with his good eye, a fugue over his features. He's not as angry as he usually looks, and she realizes it's because he doesn't immediately recognize her. Almost no one sees her human body on a regular basis, and they tend to react with shock at the sight of her. Being outside of Marcus is like being naked before the world.

"You've got to get up, buddy," she says, trying to keep the panic out of her voice.

"Don't buddy me," he slurs, laying back down. "Go fuck yourself."

"Kambili, wake up." She jostles him again. "You have to wake up, come on, buddy."

He sits up suddenly. "The fuck did I just say to you, bit—"

"Alert," the pleasant voice says. "All critical systems fault. All crew report to docking area."

He squeezes his eye shut, trying to push through the fog of drugs enough to hear what's being said. Blue knows that feeling all too well.

"I know you hate me, but we've got to go," she says. "You're a dead man if you stay here."

"Where are the others?" he asks, bewildered. Moving with some effort, he swings his legs over the side of the bed and goes tumbling off like a sack of potatoes. His ragdoll arms get under him, and he pushes himself upright. Blood spills down the backs of his hands where the IV needles come loose, and he swears. Lurching to his feet, he starts looking through the shelf for bandages, and grabs a package of clotter.

Blue considers her answer. The cruel thing would be to tell him the truth, and he might lose his will to flee. She knows all too well by now that fear can equal death.

"They're waiting for us—in the docking area. Come on, get up."

"They… left us?" Even drugged halfway to oblivion, Kambili is sharper than most. He stops applying the clotter, letting his bloody hands fall to his sides.

"Focus, Kambili, and let's work with what we have." She used that adage with her students a lot, back during her doctoral days. "We can't stay here. We've got to get to an escape pod."

"Okay." He shakes his head, wincing. "Right. Yeah." He stumbles around the bed toward her, obviously unable to walk in a straight line. She backs up her chair so he can pass, but she doubts he'll make it all the way to the door. He's a fall risk, and if he hits his head, it could be lights out.

"Fuck," he says, collapsing to his knees. "Why now?"

"Been asking myself that for a long time." She rolls past him and stops. "Grab onto the back of my chair. I'll keep you steady."

He struggles to his feet, and when he puts all of his weight on the handlebars, Blue fears she'll tip over backward. She leans forward as much as her ailing abdominal muscles will allow, and he eases off a bit.

"You ready?" she asks.

"As ever," he replies, steadying himself.

She rolls toward the door, and Kambili takes toddling steps behind. When the med bay door slides open, the cacophony of the Cold Forge rushes into her ears, momentarily deafening her. Klaxons fill the air, there have to be a dozen different critical alarms sounding, and all systems are under some kind of attack. By their nature, the escape pods must be on their own network, ensuring that a general failure doesn't kill everyone by preventing an escape.

Then again, Titus and Juno were supposed to be airgapped, too. So were the Silversmile servers, and the kennel cells could only be operated by manual control. One system failing is normal. Two systems is unlikely. All systems, and it's sabotage. Will the escape pods even work when they arrive?

There's no time to think about that. She just has to take the next right step, and that's getting to the docking bay. Kambili stumbles along behind her, half pushing so that the motors squeal tiny complaints. If she were alone, she could really open up the throttle, but she made the decision to rescue him, and that's that. Her eyes dart back and forth, searching for the lethal shape of a snatcher, but she finds nothing.

Unlike the walls of the kennels, everything in the central strut is an industrial, gunmetal gray—polished, welded, and installed without paint. She gets a dozen false positives as her failing eyes scan the scene from large conduits to cooling pipes. Too many objects vaguely resemble the slender shaft of a snatcher skull.

"Why are you so jumpy?" Kambili shouts over the alarms. "We just need to get to the—"

"Containment failure," she interrupts, coughing, and Kambili leans in closer.

"What? Like Silversmile got out again?"

"Yeah," she says into his ear. "And the kennels are open."

Her chair speeds up as he lets go. She spins to face him and finds him bewildered, swaying in the hall, hands by his sides.

"We're fucked," he says. "That's it."

"No, Kambili, we can salvage this. You just have to—"

He shakes his head no and points down the central strut. Blue turns her chair around to peer into the blurry distance, but she can't see what he's indicating. She knows what's down there.

He's pointing at the escape pods, toward the screams of the crew.

INTERLUDE

KEN

Nothing interrupts a good time with porno like an all-crew evac. Ken Riley sits in the toilet on board the *Athenian* when the transmission belts over his intercoms. He waits to see if he heard correctly. Maybe it's a drill. Dorian is off looking at a secret project and shagging the hot security officer, and Ken just keeps the ship ready for launch like a glorified errand boy.

Not a lot of pilots would've taken on the posting with Dorian Sudler. It keeps Ken away from home for years at a time, not that he has much of a home. The post was a convenient way offworld, and Weyland-Yutani was willing to be lax in its background checks for qualified star jockeys. Ken owes a lot of people a lot of money, but with a few more missions, those people would all die of old age.

The intercom message repeats. It's not a drill. This kills Ken's wood. He wipes, closes up his portable terminal, then dashes out into the mid-deck toward the bridge.

"Gaia, let's get those engines hot!" he calls, and the

computer acknowledges. "And open up the docking bay doors! Let me know when the rest of the crew are on board."

The next set of alerts come through, and it sounds like RB-232's computer is having a shit fit. Ken races around the mission planning station as it flickers to life, punching in coordinates and knocking out vectors. Without knowing exactly what's happening to the Cold Forge, though, it's tough to plan. If, for example, RB-232 needs orbital correction assistance, then Ken is obligated to help push.

"New arrival: Navigator Lupia," Gaia says, her smooth voice a balm in the stress.

It's going to be okay for Ken, no matter what. They said evac, and he's basically already there. It's hard to get more evaced than being on a fully operational starship with enough supplies to last a hundred years of cold sleep. Sinking into his pilot's chair, he settles his fingers across the controls and chuckles, remembering the old saying at the academy, *"If a pilot doesn't have his hand on one stick, it's on the other."*

"What the fuck is going on out there, man?" Montrell says as he rushes in, panting. He's in his casual gear, and must've been hanging out in the crew lounge. The navigator is way out of shape, and he looks to Ken in that moment like a sweaty brown ham. That ham, however, hauled ass, and Ken is appreciative.

"I don't know but these peckerwoods fucked up something. Like bad."

"Truth," Montrell agrees. "Gonna set up some potential escape vectors."

"Already did that," Ken says, winking. "Didn't know if you were going to make it."

"Thanks, asshole." Montrell mops his brow and plops down at his station by the mission planner. "You know, this better not be a drill, or I swear to god…"

"You swear nothing. Those evac orders mean you do job, drill or not. Commander Cardozo would kick your ass up and down the station. Guy looks like he's seen some shit."

"Engines are up to temperature," Gaia announces. "Maneuvering thrusters at nominal pressure."

Ken nods, a stupid habit when talking to a headless user interface. "Thank you, Gaia. Give me hot sticks and snap that docking tube shut when our last two get aboard."

Gaia chimes an acknowledgement.

Montrell raises an eyebrow. "You're going to do this manually?"

"You've never wanted to do a full-burn maneuver away from a station?" Ken asks. "I bet I can make Dorian's eyes bug out."

"New arrival," Gaia says. "Copilot Spiteri." Within seconds, Susan rounds the corner, her cheeks flushed from the run.

"It's chaos out there. Everyone is panicking, acting like it's the end of the world."

"Suzy, Suzy, Suzy," Ken says, sucking his teeth and spinning his chair to face her. "It's the end of a space station, maybe. The world will still be there."

She narrows her eyes. "Fuck you, Ken."

"Gladly, babe." He folds his hands behind his head, leaning back in his chair.

She starts to protest when the back of Ken's chair taps one of the sticks. The *Athenian* shudders as the maneuvering thrusters fire a short burst. It groans and a half-dozen alarms pierce the bridge. Ken spins back to his console, checking to make sure there's no damage to the docking clamp.

"What the fuck, Ken?" she shouts at him. "You left your shit on manual?" Montrell mirrors her glare.

"It's the plan, goddamn it! As soon as Dorian is on board, we button up and blow this popsicle stand. Now, chill, girl!"

"Fuck you, you chauvinist prick," she says, sitting down beside him. "This isn't over. Dorian is going to hear about this when the time comes, and—"

"New arrival," Gaia says. "Unknown entity."

Ken grimaces, then calls out, "Go to your own escape pods, you fucking dumbasses!"

They wait, listening to the distant sound of RB-232's alarms.

"New arrival: unknown entity."

Ken looks across to Susan, then Montrell, then gives them a *"What the fuck is it with these people"* shrug.

"New arrival: unknown entity."

"Yes, Gaia, we heard you!" Ken says. "Susan, would you please go explain to the jackoffs in our loading bay that we are *not* their ship, so they can kindly get the fuck out?"

Susan unbuckles herself and rises, annoyance flushing her cheeks. It's probably just the evac. As soon as they're coasting in deep space again, she'll be good old Sue.

Montrell looks up, almost like a man praying. "Gaia, was that the same statement three times, or are there three new arrivals?"

"There are three new arrivals," Gaia says.

Ken strokes his mustache. "Well it don't much matter, because they all got to get the hell off the ship. Their escape pods are right next door. Susan, can you do something about that right now?" He exaggerates his mouth movements on the last sentence, as though she's deaf.

"Fuck you, Kenny," she mumbles, headed toward the door. But when she makes it to the threshold, she freezes. A barbed, black spine shoots out of her back, extending a full yard into the bridge. At first, it looks like Susan's spine simply exploded from her torso, dripping with blood, and Ken struggles to process exactly what he's seeing.

The spine is black.

Bones aren't black.

Why would her spine leave her body? What's with the weird, hook thing at the end? It takes him a second to register that, whatever happened to Susan Spiteri, she is most definitely dead.

A darkness fills the portal around her, some looming silhouette Ken can't see. Long black talons wrap around her skull, and with a pop and a spray of blood, a tiny mouth emerges from the back of her head. Her body falls, and with it comes a tangle of thrashing, chitinous limbs. It rips into her, nipping at every loose bit of flesh, pulling her apart with the ease of cooked fish. It's four limbs, a torso and hips, a shaft for a skull and a whipping tail, but this isn't one of God's creatures. It's Satan's vanguard.

Both men sit very still, listening to the sea of alarms and the sickening tearing of Susan's blood-moistened flesh. Then, Ken remembers the gun.

The *Athenian* does a lot of dirty work for the Company, and Ken figured that one of these days, some shithead colonist was going to take offense to getting fired and come looking for revenge. His hand creeps under the console, searching for the pistol strapped underneath. He knows he's going to get one shot, so it has to be perfect. The creature's skull is such a long target, surely a bullet could do enough damage to put it down.

His hand finds the walnut grip, and he slides his fingers over the checks, ready to draw. His other hand unbuckles his seatbelt, and he slowly rises, steeling himself to fire.

Then Montrell interrupts the beast's blood revelry by deciding to scream.

The thing lets out a hiss beyond the malice of any great cat or venomous snake, its lips curling back and body coiling to strike. Ken whips out the pistol and pops off three shots. The bullets hit home, and the beast jumps with each impact, but there's no spray of blood, and it certainly doesn't go down. A glint of silver catches Ken's eye, where one of the bullets pancaked between two of the thing's exposed ribs.

Its scream shatters the air as it drops what's left of Susan. Ken raises the pistol to fire again when two more of the creatures come screeching onto the bridge.

"Fuck—" Ken begins, but the "you" is forever truncated by one of the creatures plunging its claws into his chest, snapping his ribs like a Thanksgiving day wishbone. Pain, unlike any he's ever felt, seizes every inch of his body. He can't scream, cannot raise his arms to protect his face against the raw malice dripping from the creature's toothy maw.

Most importantly, he cannot unwedge himself from the active joystick underneath him.

If Ken's body wasn't failing due to shock, he'd hear the ship crowing with all kinds of alarms. He'd know he was putting the *Athenian* into a full-burn spiral roll. He'd recognize the shuddering hull and the metallic grind of their docking clamp as it sheared off its mountings, taking a good portion of the docking bay wall with it.

Then the ship explosively decompresses to vacuum, silencing everything.

1 6

E X P O S U R E

This is a day of firsts for Blue.

It's the first time she's heard gunfire on the station. It's the first time she's realized how much the rest of the crew truly hate her. It's the first time she's considered self-immolation as a viable plan.

It's the first time she's seen a massive hull breach.

The *Athenian* tears loose from its moorings, exposing an oval of space where the docking tube once was. Blue watches through the viewports, staring in horror as the ship scrapes across the row of docked escape pods, stripping them like grains of wheat from a stalk. The temperature plunges. Her ears pop painfully, and she gasps to force air into her lungs.

Those two unfortunates nearest the severed tube are sucked away instantly, and she can just barely make out Commander Cardozo hanging onto the deck for dear life. The sirens drown beneath the deafening roar of wind coming from the rest of the station, and she knows she has seconds before the bulkheads seal behind her.

The training vids always say go "BACK": Back away, assess your surroundings, close a door, know your escape routes—but when the howling void of the stars gazes directly into Blue's face, it sweeps away all rational thought. The only thing that remains in its place is the primal urge to flee.

She turns her chair to leave, but the swirling gale pulls her over, spilling her out onto the deck. Pain rips through her as she strikes an elbow against the metal grate, and blood oozes forth. Blue locks her fingers into the deck, but the grip is feeble, and she knows she won't last long. Looking toward the ceiling, she sees one of the snatchers scrambling toward her, hurtling along the conduits. Despite the breach, it's still primed for murder.

Every ounce of her strength is focused on her fingers, and she feels them slipping. She can't run. She can only watch in total paralysis as the creature skitters toward her. It pounces down, claws wide, salivating mouth agape, tail poised to strike.

Then the suction grasps it like a small child and carries it toward the tear. Blue watches as it entangles itself in the ripped section of the hull, fighting to come after her.

Her fingers begin to slip on the metal, and her wrist aches with the sustained effort. Her head is going light. Her breath comes in short sips. Soon, she'll have to let go, and the creature will have a go at her before they both die in deep space.

The last finger gives up and she comes free, but jerks to a halt as Kambili's strong hand wraps around her tiny wrist. He strains with all his might, pulling her until she's even with him, the pain clear in the remains of his face. He's fighting to keep her alive, returning the favor she did him.

"Come on!" he screams against the shredding wind. The temperature is almost freezing now. Kambili reaches up to the next handhold, and drags her another foot or so. Her shoulder burns in agony—its damaged tendons can't take much of this. She wants to tell him to drop her, but she can't muster the breath to speak.

Ahead of them, warning lights click on, signaling that the safety period is expiring, and the bulkhead will seal. It's already closed off the crew quarters, and everything further back. They have ten seconds to get inside, then the bulkhead will repressurize. Kambili strains against the failing oxygen, and the wind begins to slow.

They're running out of atmosphere.

Five seconds.

With less air, it's easier for Kambili to struggle to his feet and drag her. It's also easier for the creature to come after them.

Three seconds.

The oxygen is almost completely gone, and Blue's lungs refuse to fill. The partition grinds toward the floor.

One second.

The snatcher is almost on them, its jaws snapping silently in the thin atmosphere, tail whipping like mad.

Kambili shoves her under the partition, falling prone and pushing her as far as he can before it closes.

She wants to scream, but there is no air. Her lungs refuse to fill with even the tiniest amount of oxygen. An oxy station down the corridor blares with alert lights, signaling help for those able-bodied enough to get it, but Blue's strength is already beginning to fade, her vision growing dim. She can't muster the power to roll onto her back, much less the wherewithal to walk to the oxy station and don a mask. She rests her head against the deck. Kambili can take it from here.

But the blackout never comes, and she hears a hiss, gradually increasing in volume as the deck repressurizes. Her eardrums feel like someone has placed the point of a knife on them, ready to rupture at any second. Her skin is chilled to the bone. The only warm spots on her body are where Kambili's hands still touch her back and leg.

"Kambili," she moans. "Are you okay?"

She works up the strength to roll away, and finds only a hard steel door where Kambili should've been. A pair of hands is settled into a pool of cooling blood. She glances down to her leg to find one still gripping her, sheared off at the wrist.

He's suffocating out there while bleeding to death. She hopes it ends quickly. When she remembers the jaws of the snatcher, she knows it will.

She rolls to one side, tucking herself into a safe niche, then passes out.

* * *

When she awakes, she has no idea how long she's been unconscious. Half-focused eyes dart around the room, searching for any alien threats, but finding none. If any of the snatchers was in here with her, she'd already be a pile of ragged flesh. Her breathing gets easier as more atmosphere pours inside. They must not have lost that much pressure—just enough to hurt someone with weak lungs.

With trembling hands, she reaches down and gently peels away Kambili's fingers. She puts the severed appendage beside the other, as though that's what she's supposed to do. It makes more sense than anything else she can think of.

The alerts have stopped. Titus must've been compromised enough to destroy crew updates. She's not sure how much Silversmile understands of their network, but if it figures out that they're barely hanging on from damage to the central strut, it might just open all the doors and vent them into the void.

If she can get back to her room, she can use Marcus to flash Titus back to init state. There's a read-only hard image stored in the server room. She'll kill off Silversmile and re-image the whole thing. That'll be easier if Javier is still alive, but she doubts he is. The man never seemed spry enough to survive something like this.

Then again, neither is she.

Blue probably won't be saving anyone. For all she knows, she's the last person left on the station. She might get Titus stabilized, only to discover there's no way for her to get out to the escape pods without a space suit. Or maybe all the pods are gone. Certainly the *Athenian* was destroyed in the chaos she just witnessed.

Yet every time she thinks it's over, it isn't. Her life has been like that, ever since the diagnosis.

She rolls onto her stomach, and her side of the central strut seems to stretch onward forever into a hazy oblivion. That way lies the med bay, the crew quarters, and her brain-direct interface. She's going to have to crawl on her stomach, further than she's ever gone. It's going to fuck up her digestive appliances, and she'll need surgery within the week.

She has to try.

Blue places one hand in front of her and drags herself forward a few inches. Then another pull moves her a bit more.

Two down, a few hundred to go.

1 7

FLIGHT

Dorian isn't looking the right way when it happens. One minute, he's running through the central strut, a pack of snatchers lurking ahead of them, and the next he's swept from his feet by a blast of wind like he's never felt. It sends him stumbling forward, sprawling across the deck toward Anne. Then he realizes it's not a burst, but a sustained, gale-force wind howling down the central strut toward the *Athenian*.

Fuck.

He looks as far as he can down the hall to find the station missing a chunk of hull where his ship should've been. Then he sees the *Athenian* through the viewport, watching as it bangs along the side of the station, knocking loose most of the escape pods.

And then his ship is gone. Did it take off, or was it destroyed? He couldn't get a good look.

There's a crowd of unfortunates hunkered down close

to the breach, and Dorian thinks he can make out Daniel in the distance, hanging onto a deck plate.

Fury shakes his limbs. They had a plan. This should've worked. It *always* works out for him, and now his ship is missing. He imagines Ken, Susan, and Montrell taking off, writing him off in the Company logs as a loss, making a footnote out of him with their treachery. He imagines them arriving back on Earth.

"We tried everything we could," they'll say, *"but Director Sudler was killed in the accident."* They'll make him a goddamned line item.

"Dorian!" Anne calls. She's made it to one side of the hallway, mooring herself with her muscular arms. "We have to help the others!" He's far enough away from the breach that the suction isn't so bad—worse than an Earth storm, better than a jet-engine intake. He can still find the means to clamber to his feet and rush over.

"Seal the bulkhead!" he shouts back over the din. "Don't worry about the safety protocols, just seal it!"

"What?" It's not the reaction he was expecting.

"They're not going to make it! There are a dozen hungry aliens out there, and a shredding outer hull!"

"Fuck you!" Anne says it with such force that she spits in his face. She maneuvers across the hallway to a fire box, breaking it open. The shards of glass blow down the corridor toward the survivors, sharp pieces glinting as they swirl out of the breach. She pulls out the heavy hose nozzle and throws it into the wind, where it catches a gust. The line whips from the case at breakneck speed before snapping taut. The nozzle wriggles and twists halfway to the embattled crew, tantalizingly out of reach.

Undeterred, she begins rappelling down the line.

"Anne, don't be stupid!" She's just going to be a fish on a hook down there when the creatures spot her. He doesn't see any of the malevolent shadows, but he knows they're out there, ready to strike the second they receive an opportunity.

She doesn't look back at him, focusing instead on getting to those stranded near the breach.

"Goddamn it, Anne!"

He could seal her out right now. If he pressed the emergency closure on the door, it wouldn't reopen until pressure equalized. The heavy steel would chop that fire hose instantly. Anne and the others would suffocate, and though there were bound to be more aliens on board the Cold Forge, at least Dorian wouldn't be stuck in violent decompression.

Then again, the *Athenian* is gone and Dorian doesn't have the crew codes that will grant him access to the escape pods. They may have given them to him in a briefing at some point, but no one ever keeps their safety packets when they come aboard a station. The crew will know the codes because they've drilled once a month.

Anne will have the codes.

If he doesn't help her, he will die.

Working his way over to the hose control panel, he twists the valve, filling the hose with eighty-three bars of fire-retardant chemicals.

"What the fuck are you doing?" she screams as the hose inflates under her grip, but he doesn't reply. His keen eyes scan the rafters, and he spots one of the snatchers creeping toward her, ready to drop down in spite of the howling gale.

"Above you!" He thrusts his finger toward it in an exaggerated gesture, willing her to see the threat. The beast unfolds like lethal origami, all hard angles save for the curve of its domed skull. Anne's attention flicks upward, and she twists the hose to fire a high-powered flush of white chemicals at the creature. It screeches in hatred as they strike, sending it off course, flailing into a pair of Rose Eagle developers.

The thing wastes no time in assaulting its new targets. It flings one toward the breach, correctly intuiting that person will die a more horrible death in the vacuum of space. This surprises Dorian. Prior to this moment, he's always expected their violence to be a food-seeking behavior. It could've easily brained one and impaled the other, keeping them for a snack down the road. Maybe it's more majestic than that.

Perhaps they simply love to kill. Maybe for them, it's their most sincere form of expression. This one locks its jaws around the shoulder of the developer, and Dorian steels himself for a killing blow. Instead, the beast turns toward him and charges up the steel grates, finding purchase in the finger-shaped holes.

Maybe it hasn't seen him yet. Without eyes, who can know what they perceive? Dorian squeezes against one of the support columns, doing everything in his power to hide his presence. Like a fish disappearing beneath the surface of the water with a bug, it bounds into the bowels of the open SCIF, hauling the screaming programmer in tow. Whatever it has planned for the woman, it's probably worse than death.

Dorian squints, and at the far end of the docking area, he can just make out two dark-skinned people, one thin and frail, the other in full head bandages, hanging on for dear life. They're closer to the breach than he is, and must be feeling an incredible strain. A large electric wheelchair slides toward the tear to be sucked out, and he realizes that's Blue Marsalis and Kambili Okoro.

He can't stand the thought of having her die like this. She's treated him like shit, so many times, only to be sucked out of a hole. It's pathetic. It's boring. It fills Dorian's blood with fire just thinking about it.

He should be the one to beat her.

He *has* to be the one.

"Dorian!" Anne's words distract him. She's accrued a few survivors, all latched onto the hose in a cluster. He spots Javier and Lucy among their number, but the rest appear to be low-level techs, custodians and developers. Daniel Cardozo isn't with them.

Pulling them up won't work. Their combined weight is too much. The temperature has plummeted, and his head grows light. The safety protocols will seal this section soon. Dorian wraps his arms around the hose and pulls, but it's like tugging on a boulder.

"Hit the auto-reel, you fucking idiot!" Anne screams at him. If she didn't have the escape pod codes, he'd definitely drop the door on her. Instead he hefts his way to the hose controls, purges the line to slacken it, and hits the auto-reel. The winching system inside whines at the weight, but impossibly, it begins to pull them closer.

The air is unbearably thin, and warning lights erupt from hidden panels, announcing that the partition is going to drop. He looks from the crew to the door, mentally judging the distance. It's going to drop on them either way. He may as well go ahead and shut it.

Using the gratings as a purchase, he climbs across the door controls, keenly watching the progress of the crew as he does. He'll give them ten more seconds, but they're all screwed.

The door begins sliding shut.

As they draw close to the entrance, Dorian peers around them to watch Daniel struggling. The creatures have begun to circle him, looking for the best way to attack without being sucked outside. With each passing second the atmosphere dwindles and the suction lessens. He'll be a meal soon enough.

The airlock next to Dorian beeps, its sound startling him—almost costing him his grip. Marcus comes storming out, tearing off his helmet. Dorian can't recall ever seeing a synthetic move that fast, and his stomach flips at the sight. At first, he believes it's Blue, come to exact some kind of revenge on him—except he locked Blue out, so that can't be the case.

Marcus vaults through the mercurial wind currents, making adjustments to his balance using a series of quick gestures and twists, snatching the grating by Anne's team to make an impressive landing. He then grasps the hose with one hand and drags it forward, using his other to pull himself along the deck.

The air has grown so thin that sounds are dimmed. The lab tech at the back of the hose train faints, and his unconscious body tumbles toward the breach. One of the creatures snatches him out of midair, sinking its teeth deep into the fatty tissue around his thigh.

Dorian searches again for Blue and Kambili, and sees another of the bugs clambering after her. It makes an aborted attempt at a pounce, fails, and sets up to try again. He watches as Kambili grabs her and pulls her toward the door, showing little regard for his own safety. Chivalry is an artifact of his Earth-bound life—it's useless out here.

Earth teaches people that everyone should be treated equally, they are all worth the same. It's a bunch of garbage. Anyone who can't pull his own weight deserves to be dragged down by it, no matter what the reason. To see Kambili risking his own life to save Blue Marsalis, just because she's pathetic, strikes Dorian as a farce.

Kambili shoves Blue under the partition just in time to have his arms sheared off at the elbows. The snatcher is right behind him, about to pounce. Yet Kambili should've been the one who survived, with four limbs and a long life expectancy. He should've cut Blue—with her stink of sickness—out of the herd. That's the truth that animals know, and it's the way of the free market. Kambili has suffered the wages of altruism.

Blue is nowhere to be seen.

The door seals with a *thunk*, and the sound of the gale disappears, leaving only the alarms. Those who can, rush to the flashing oxygen panel. They unspool masks for themselves while Marcus assists those who can't make it on their own.

Dorian is among the first to get sips of oxygen while the bulkhead repressurizes. There are twelve people and eight masks, and the survivors take turns. Marcus apportions the oxygen treatments, taking the mask from Dorian's hand and giving it to Javier. He then guides them one-by-one to the airlock before joining everyone inside. Dorian considers telling Marcus about Blue, then decides against it. Better to keep him focused on their survival.

If Blue isn't dead already, she will be soon enough.

"We have to remain here for the next five hours," Marcus says. He opens a control panel and adjusts the parameters. Dorian's ears pop loudly as the air pressure returns. It feels different somehow—heavier.

"What?"

"No!" Lucy says. "Those things are right outside, Blue!"

"It's Marcus," the synthetic replies.

"Explains all the flipping and shit when you came to the rescue," Javier mutters. "Just glad you were there, man."

"Blue's whereabouts are currently unknown," Marcus says, then he sweeps the group with his gaze. "You are all likely to be suffering from decompression sickness, and you need hyperbaric treatment to prevent an arterial gas embolism."

"Fuck... the bends," Anne says.

"Five hours?" Dorian says.

Marcus nods and gestures to the seats. There are a few space suits hanging on the wall, and some of the survivors pull them down, placing them open on the floor for use as bedding. The airlock is cramped for a dozen people, but they manage to find enough space for everyone to relax. Marcus stands in the corner keeping silent vigil over the tableau.

Dorian chooses a spot closest to the outer hatch, resting his back against it. Every muscle in his body is slackened by exhaustion, and his mind doesn't want to work right as the adrenaline drains from his body. People are crying. Lucy makes an idiotic whimpering noise that sounds like a cross between creaky metal and a sinus infection. He wants to tell her to shut up, but decides another approach will be more to his advantage.

"They're all dead," she says, repeating the phrase as if it wasn't completely obvious. Dorian takes her hand— those frail, slender bones—and squeezes... gently. He looks into her eyes.

"But we're not," he says. *So kindly shut the fuck up.*

Mercifully, she does, until they hear a loud thump on the outside of the airlock. Everyone shrieks except Dorian and Marcus. They calmly peer outside through the porthole. Dorian expects to see a piece of debris, or maybe one of the escape pods, but comes face-to-face with a black skull and knife-sharp teeth, visible through the thick glass. It pulls back and butts the airlock again, to no avail.

More screams.

"Don't worry," Marcus says. "That's twelve inches of unbreakable carbon crystal with a very small diameter. It could withstand a direct hit from a starship.

"Easy for you to say!" Lucy cries, and her distress eases Dorian's heart. It's hard to put a finger on why he hates her so much. Maybe it's her constant overreactions, which seem almost fake.

He places a hand against the porthole and watches as the beast strikes the glass, again and again, to the great distress of the airlock occupants. This close, in the shadow of the station, he can sense the raw strength of the thing, its drool freezing to its face. It's probably dying, but it shows no signs of slowing down.

What majesty, driven to waste.

"It would appear that the freezing point of its blood is far lower than that of a human," Marcus says.

"That's not surprising," Dorian replies. "It's the perfect killing machine."

"Thanks for saving us," Javier says to Anne, then nods at Dorian. "We were fucked out there." His words seem to calm the others, at least somewhat.

"You should all get some rest," Marcus says. "We'll need to move as soon as the time is up." The others look to him as though he's gone mad, but Dorian knows he's right.

Dorian feels no remorse, no pity for those lost to the

violence. They're dead and he isn't. They are useless, and he is paramount. He can't allow sentimentality to deprive him of critical rest.

So Dorian drifts off, lulled by the bass drum of the perfect skull.

Maybe it's been an hour, maybe it's been three, but Blue's muscles feel as though they're going to fall off her bones. She's given up on trying to drag herself without her belly touching the ground, and long ago scraped off her colostomy bag. Not that she knows when she's going to eat again. No G-tube, no shit filling her intestines.

Her stomas itch.

Every yard is agony. Her tender elbows are bruised and swollen, and much of her has been scraped raw by the deck plating. With each push, she swears that it's her last, and yet she always rises, always pulls herself another step closer.

Until her knee catches fire.

It's a tickle for just a moment, in the back of her joint, then a full-blown burning the likes of which she's never felt. It's like a Charlie horse fucking a stab wound. Aliens be damned, she screams out at the top of her lungs. Her cries echo down the halls, and for the second time that day she summons a strength she'd thought long lost.

It won't subside. Blue's eyes drift between the crew quarters and the med bay, and she knows what she must do. There's no time to pause, and yet she can barely think due to the utter anguish spreading through her legs.

She drags herself to the med bay door—closer than she had guessed, thank god—as the fire spreads to her other knee. She repeats every curse word she knows as if it's a solemn prayer and pulls herself toward the nearest operating bed.

Pulling herself up the side, one handhold at a time, she rolls onto the mattress. It might be the softest thing she's ever felt in her life, though she can't enjoy it with her knees about to explode. Blue keeps racking her brain for some explanation, but nothing comes to her, and she can't concentrate. She grabs the control panel wires, pulls the console close enough to see with her failing eyes, and hopes to god the bed isn't on Titus's network.

"Scanning," the bed says in a gentle voice coming through its tinny speakers. Blue lets out a breath in the closest thing she can get to relief. "Please wait." Scanners circle the bed on long arms.

Then she cries out as the pain strikes her again, and she bends her knees, clutching them close. The scanners pull away and go still. Miraculously, the agony reduces slightly, and she can think again.

"Re-initializing scans," the bed says. "Are you able to keep still?"

"Yes," Blue whispers, her throat raw.

The scanners circle the bed again, and Blue wishes she was at a real hospital instead of this pathetic simulation. She wants real doctors, with real gear and real databases containing data for almost every disease known to mankind—though that didn't help her when she was diagnosed with Bishara's Syndrome.

"Were you recently exposed to a vacuum or depressurization?"

"Yes."

"You are suffering from decompression sickness, sometimes called DCS, Diver's Disease, or the Bends. You have bubbles inside your bloodstream composed of soluble gasses which emerged during a decompression event." The bed produces a servo for intravenous feeding. "Recommended treatment: hyperbaric oxygenation and rehydration. Can you get to an airlock?"

"No."

She gasps as cold antiseptic sprays across her hand and the bed slips a needle into her. It shunts aside the first few drops of blood for various test procedures.

"Then the best treatment is rehydration and rest. Elevated heart rate detected. Are you under emotional duress?"

Blue laughs. "Yes."

"Acknowledged. This system will monitor the nitrogen bubbles for potential Type II complications, and you will be administered a sedative."

"Wait, what?" Blue tries to sit up, but her arm is caught in the IV. She can't be unconscious right now. There's too much to do. But the chemicals flow into her arm, sweet and warm, and she knows it's too late. The world swims only briefly before sleep strikes her like a hammer.

1 8

RESET

They've been high on heavy oxygen for hours, taking frequent breathing breaks to avoid toxicity. The air is thick, hot, and foul smelling, and the extreme flammability just makes him want to smoke. In another hour, they'll be close to Earth barometric pressure.

"Eeny, meeny, miney, mo," Dorian whispers, his slender finger pointing toward each person trapped in the airlock with him. "Catch a—"

"You'd better fucking say tiger," Javier says. Dorian smirks, then continues the rhyme in the requested fashion. Javier shakes his head and turns away, curling up next to Lucy on an old spacesuit.

"Do you think the traitor is dead?" Dorian asks.

"What traitor?" Javier asks.

"Someone brought Silversmile across the air gap to Titus. Someone opened the manual-only kennel doors." Dorian picks at his nails. "Maybe that someone is floating outside right now, frosted over."

"That's not appropriate, Director Sudler," Marcus says.

"But my money is on Doctor Marsalis," Dorian continues. "If I had to guess, that is."

"I think so, too," Lucy says. "Marcus, what has she been making you do?"

Marcus shakes his head. "I'm afraid I can't answer that question unless there's a direct threat to your safety. It would be in violation of Doctor Marsalis's privacy. Furthermore, I have no ability to recall actions taken while I've been under her control."

"Screw that," Lucy says, sitting up. "We're not safe. We're stuck in an airlock and there are fucking monsters outside! Tell us anything you know."

"Director," Anne says, putting a warm hand on his forearm. "Do you think now is really the time?"

Dorian quirks an eyebrow. "What, did you have something better to do? Most of us are dead, someone is responsible, and I for one would like to know who it is."

Two of the techs in the corner huddle closer, and one of them yawns. No one besides Dorian has had a wink of sleep. In fact, he's found the airlock to be his most comfortable accommodation to date. There's nothing more bracing than the edge of death, nothing more satisfactory than another moment of survival.

"Blue was in league with someone off-station," Dorian says. "Trying to steal the results of the project and keep them to herself. That's why we had her old boss arrested, so it's not hard to put the pieces together." Just in case Blue isn't dead, he doesn't want any talk of going to rescue her. There are mutterings of assent among the assembly, especially those who knew about Blue's hidden server. It won't take long to herd the sheep toward his way of thinking, and though it gives him great joy to think of turning them against Blue, he also wonders how wise his strategy may be.

What if she's not the saboteur?

At this moment, the Cold Forge could be exporting ridiculous amounts of data, and no one would know. There could be long-range transmitters blasting out secrets to various and sundry parties, and none of the station's countermeasures would stop them. Everything is offline. Everything is compromised.

At some point, this might've been Blue's plan, but he'd interrupted her. There was no point to killing everyone on the station, save for revenge, and that's too petty for such a pretentious woman. Besides, Dorian already had interviewed Kambili Okoro to get the location of her research. Blue was trying to synthesize some super-cure, not murder everyone.

The real saboteur is someone else.

"Are there any escape pods left, Marcus?" he asks.

"Yes. It appears there is one," Marcus replies. "At least, that's what I saw when I rescued you. Though my memory is impeccable, something may have happened to the pod since that time."

"We need to get to it," Dorian says. "Need to get out of here."

Lucy laughs. "Those pods support two people each. Even if you were willing to remain unfrozen for the ten-year journey back to Earth, you'd run out of food."

He does a quick count of the survivors in the airlock. Javier, Lucy, Anne, himself... there are thirteen all told, if he counts Marcus. Blue is somewhere out there, too, if she's still alive, but he'll leave her behind when the time comes. He'd fuck over everyone here for a shot at one of the two remaining pod seats. When he imagines the scenarios for escape, he's always alone.

A sudden rush fills his gut, like he's started a long fall. It takes all his concentration not to vomit in the hot, foul-smelling airlock. Tools rise from the ground. His hands begin to float. They've lost gravity.

"Alert," Titus says. "Gravity drive failure."

No shit, Sherlock. A murmur rises in the crowd as they search for anything to which they can cling.

"We have to reset Titus," Marcus says, looking directly at Dorian. "If the computer has lost control of gravity, Silversmile may find a way to vent us into space."

"Wouldn't *that* be something?" Dorian responds.

"I suggest we cut short our hyperbaric therapy and address the Titus reset." Marcus peers out of the airlock window into the depths of the station. "Someone will need to accompany me, as I do not have administrative access to Titus."

"Why not?" Anne asks.

"Shit," Javier says, his voice falling. "Synthetics never do. They're not allowed to control life support. They're not allowed to use firearms. They can't do anything that would endanger real people."

Dorian looks Javier over. The station sysadmin has grown awfully pale for a brown man. His lips are white where they should be pink, and his eyes are pink where they should be white. His hands shake, and he's only weakly holding onto the seat where he had been comfortably resting.

"I'm going to have to go out there," Javier says. "I'm the best qualified person to do it. Fucking shit." But Javier could be the saboteur. After all, he's the one who introduced Silversmile into Juno. It was his mistake that brought the first round of ruin. If he continues to cripple RB-232's systems, he can run any play he wishes, unopposed. He might just grab a spacesuit and head for the escape pod.

"I'll go, too," Dorian says. "You need someone to watch your back."

Javier eyes him, surprise in his expression, and gives him a smile.

"Thanks, man."

"Marcus, you should act as a distraction," Dorian continues. "Javier and I can handle the reset."

"Very well. I'll go out ahead and see if I can draw some attention away from your egress." Marcus grabs onto the access panel, preparing to open the hatch. Their ears pop as pressure equalizes with the rest of the station. "From what I have observed, the animals will be torpid without targets to hunt."

"Great," Javier says.

"I should go, too," Anne says, but Dorian stops her.

"No way. There are a lot of hurt people here, and as head of security you've got the most medical training. You can't just abandon them."

"While you two are geared for combat ops?" She crosses her arms. "Come on. An out-of-shape sysadmin and an exec in a cheap suit."

"Hey, it used to be a *nice* suit," Dorian counters with a wink. "We're not going into combat. If something happens, we're just going to run—and in zero G, that'll be pretty easy."

Anne shakes her head, but doesn't say anything.

"Look," he says, lowering his voice. "In management, you have to learn how to make these kinds of tough decisions. Decisions by the numbers. I've got essentially no skills, but your group has backup programmers, techs, and you—you're the only remaining soldier on board. I'm comparatively expendable."

"You can't think about things like that."

"That's my job."

It's cute how worried she is for him. When he thinks back to the fierce warrior who subdued him and fucked him senseless, he can't help but grin. She's thinking of these people as her family, and it's clouding her judgment. It's hard to know exactly how he'll exploit that, but he feels certain he can manipulate her when the time comes.

"Okay," she says, "but if you're going out, so are we. We have to get to somewhere better than this airlock—

somewhere we can call for help."

"Our comms are probably fried," Lucy says. "Silversmile will have burned out the alignment motors." She sucks her lower lip. "I, uh, wrote the code to make it do that, so if it's working—"

"What about Rose Eagle?" Dorian asks. "It has all of the equipment to create entangled comms." Some of the techs murmur in agreement. Even if Silversmile has gutted that project beyond all repair, he has offered them a moment of hope. They'll be even more amenable to following his orders.

"There might be some uncorrupted images of the project," Javier says. "I mean, it's not likely, but it's possible."

"Okay," Dorian says. "Marcus will run distractions, Javier and I will reinitialize Titus, and Anne will take her team to Rose Eagle."

Anne claps him on the shoulder and gives him a brief squeeze. It's hard not to retch from her sentimental bullshit.

"Don't die," she says.

Dorian nods. "Count on me, babe."

Their trek through the corridors is silent, both Dorian and Javier steady in their purpose. Dorian can do this because he knows the score, that forward is the only direction— that if death comes, he's on the most sensible course. His head is clear and his eyes are sharp. He doesn't know how Javier has decided to process their journey.

They kick off the walls with bare feet, carefully planning

their landings at each support pylon. It's tempting to simply make a single leap, aimed straight at Titus's server farm, but they might want to change course if they see some hazard—a snatcher, for example. Unlike the crew quarters and the project decks of the SCIF, the central strut is unpolished and industrialized, the sort of place with lots of exposed ducts and conduits. The handholds are easy to find, and controlling their vectors is simple, as long as they don't over-commit.

A sudden hiss erupts to his right, and Dorian slams into the hull, expecting claws to seize his flesh. Instead, he finds one of the atmospheric pumps churning away, trying and failing to keep the ship's gasses balanced. Without help from the centralized climate systems, the survivors will eventually run out of oxygen. The good news is that the number of people still breathing is rapidly diminishing.

He glances back. Javier stares at him, trembling.

Dorian checks to make sure the man isn't looking at something behind him. When there's nothing there, he mouths the words "Let's go," and takes off again.

Even at their slow pace, they reach Titus's server farm within five minutes. When they open the doors, Dorian is shocked by the gust of hot air that greets him. Fans roar ineffectually, drowning out any noises inside. Uneven lights flicker overhead, driving shadows across the open spaces and workstations. The place stinks of hot wiring and melted plastic, and the beginnings of an electrical fire. He scans the scene, searching in corners and under tables for a telltale flicker of oily chitin and bone.

"Shit, shit, shit," Javier mutters, muscling past. "It shut down the thermal controls." The sysadmin swims through the room, bouncing off server racks and pulling up to one of the consoles. Purpose seems to give him new energy. Dorian goes to follow him, but burns his hand on one of the metal racks.

"Don't touch that," Javier says. "It's where most of Titus's heavy lifting is done, so it'll be the hottest."

"How did it get this bad?"

"The virus didn't have to fight its way through the fringe systems. Someone must've installed it with full rights."

Dorian nods, his hand smarting, and wants to slap Javier for failing to warn him. Heat waves radiate through the air around him, making his head swim.

"Where is it safe to stand?"

"Got some empty rack mounts over there by the monitors," Javier says. "Should be good."

Dorian nods. "Anything you need from me?"

"Just keep an eye out."

Dorian pushes off to the front door and pokes his head out. To his left is the long passageway to the SCIF. To his right, the emergency partition to the decompressed docking area and the last remaining escape pod. If he had the code to activate it, he could bump off Javier, don a spacesuit from the airlock, decompress the central strut, and get the fuck out of the Cold Forge.

But he doesn't have the code, and so he must make himself useful. He returns to Javier's side, looking over his progress. A thick binder drifts through the air, a pen hanging from it by a chain. Dorian idly pushes it aside, looking for any good news from his companion. The screen flickers, and the Weyland-Yutani logo animates into life, but the loading progress is slow. It's less responsive than Dorian has ever seen a station computer, and he leans over to speak into Javier's ear.

"How bad is it?"

Javier ignores the question and types his password, which looks like "Rash501!" but it's wrong. Javier types it again, and Dorian gets a better look.

```
Thrash3501!
```

The sysadmin accesses Titus's core functions to get a readout. Only sixteen percent of the servers are still operational. Then, the readout vanishes.

"What happened?"

"Silversmile," Javier says. "Because we pulled up the readouts, it targeted them. The only things it can't touch are the CoreOP and the connection logs. This is going to suck." He points to a junction box in the boiling-hot part of the room. "Kill the power over there."

Dorian complies, pushing off in that direction. Because there's no gravity to pull down the denser gasses, pockets of hot and cold air intermingle randomly, passing over his sweaty face to nauseating effect. The metal of the junction box is scalding hot, and the lever locking the door in place obstinately refuses to be pushed. Dorian wraps his suit jacket around the lever and shoves it until it locks upward. The door opens, revealing a reboot procedure outlined in pictograms and iconography.

"If we're lucky," Javier says, "we're going to get back thermals, power, access control, and maybe life support. Titus is fighting pretty hard. Orbitals are fucked."

Dorian scans the warnings, then engages the master cutoff switch. The server room goes black, becoming a smoldering steel box. Sweat pours from his face, and for a moment he can see nothing. Then an orange star appears in the darkness—an amber LED diffracted through the fresnel lens of a switch housing. Dorian reaches up and presses it.

The room thrums back to life, and once-dim lights overhead click on with full intensity. Squinting, Dorian peers around, half expecting to find the place looking looted, but it's surprisingly clean. External vents blast in frosty air, a balm upon his moist skin.

Monitors all across the room come alive with the olive-drab background of Weyland-Yutani's logos, though half of the server racks still blare warning lights across their housings. Those computers are probably burnt to a crisp.

"Hang on to something," Javier says. "I think I can get gravity back online."

There's a tremendous clatter throughout the bay, as all of the loose objects fall to the ground. Though Dorian believes himself stable, it's like invisible hands tug him from his feet onto the hard steel deck. It's pleasant down there, and Dorian rests his face against the cooling floor plates for a moment as he acclimates to the returned force.

Tense minutes pass as Javier lashes together the remaining computers into a network capable of caring for the station.

"How long does this normally take you?" Dorian asks, glancing at the door.

"Three fucking weeks, man."

"What are you going to do?"

Javier shakes his head. "It ain't going to be a Rolls Royce, but I can get this baby running in a nominal state."

"Enough to keep us alive?"

The sysadmin glares at him before returning to his keyboard. "Back off and go watch for trouble, man. You're distracting me." He points to a monitor on the far wall, which tiles over in a pattern like a chessboard. "Got the security feeds online. Check them."

Dorian's eyes travel to the binder on the ground, with its chained pen. He kicks it closed and picks it up. It's Titus's physical access log, though he doubts the saboteur would've signed in. He pages through it, and finds about eighty signatures, the last one from two weeks ago. Most likely there have been accesses beyond that point, and the organization around here is a shitshow. No wonder the station is compromised.

Dorian can't let this opportunity pass him by. When is he going to be in here again? He needs to know the name of the saboteur. It'll be someone who has the codes for that last escape pod, someone who's gunning for it just as much as him. Everyone is a threat on some level, but the saboteur would do *anything* to leave.

He hunkers down next to the monitors and puzzles through the timeline. Silversmile infected Titus at almost exactly the same time the kennels were opened. According to Dick Mackie, the cell doors were manual operation only. There were no network controls, so someone had to free the beasts by hand.

But infecting Titus required the saboteur to be physically outside of the SCIF, away from Juno control. Those were two exclusive actions, taken simultaneously. Blue could be in two places at once, but that was a best-case scenario. Her frail body would never be able to get to the last escape pod—not with the docking bay exposed to the vacuum of space. He doubted she could even don a suit.

Moreover, Marcus could never open the kennels without her piloting him. A synthetic would do everything it could to prevent harm to humans, and the synths that lacked that programming tended to have spectacular emotional breakdowns. If Marcus had opened the cages, Dorian would've seen some evidence in his behaviors.

There had to be two saboteurs. Were they working together? No one had escaped the Cold Forge to Dorian's knowledge. Yet surely the person who destroyed Titus had a plan to flee. Why let the beasts out of their cages? It couldn't have been Javier. He was helping Dorian decode Blue's research when the attack hit.

"Javier, check the connection logs," Dorian says, creeping back over. "I want to know the last access that wasn't you."

"Buddy, I don't think you heard me. I've got a network

to reconstruct with duct tape and cardboard, and precious little time to do it. I'm trying to get the scrubbers reconnected and—"

Dorian places a gentle hand on Javier's shoulder. "I asked you nicely. I want to know who's fucking us over. Now."

Javier stops and turns to him, eyes wide in disbelief. "Are you seriously questioning my priorities right now?"

Dorian holds the man's gaze, calmly yanking free the ballpoint pen and placing his binder on the nearby workspace. He clutches the pen in his hand, its rubberized grip flexing under his fingers, and draws up to his full height, looming over Javier.

"I'm not questioning your priorities. I heard them, and I gave you an order. There's enough air on this station for us to survive for weeks. There's a traitor who will kill us all—a lot faster. And that's not even your biggest problem."

Dorian waits for the other man to speak, but Javier says nothing.

"Right now," Dorian continues, "you need to worry about what's going to happen the next time you tell me no."

"You're crazy," Javier says.

Dorian takes away his hand, nostrils flaring. It feels good to be able to speak so plainly, all pretenses scrubbed away by necessity.

"My first girlfriend said that," he replies, "but these days, she's in an institution, and I'm pulling down seven figures. I prefer to think of it as focused. Can we get focused up, Javier?"

He's grown accustomed to threatening people's jobs, but that's like playing a video game. There are always extra lives. Dorian's victims will find work, or become wards of the state until some unaffordable disease kills them, but they won't starve. People are scared of him, but they rarely ever commit suicide. Worst of all are the ones near retirement, the folk who know they'll land on their feet, and have run out of fucks to give.

The look on Javier's face is addictive. It's better than the designer drugs passed around at executive retreats. It's better than all of the orgasms at Anne's merciless hands. It's like peeling away a hard shell to get at the quivering meat of the oyster and rake through its flesh for a pearl. Javier has no idea how to react. He's been so focused on the unseen existential threats that he's never even considered battle of wills. One little threat, and Dorian can have anything he wants.

Qui audet adipiscitur—who dares, wins.

"Tell me who the last connection is," Dorian says. "Who could've gotten Silversmile into Titus?"

Javier nods, and begins typing in the commands to bring up the CoreOP. A sudden concern wells within Dorian. What if he's overplayed his hand? What if Javier rallies the other survivors against him, and damages his late plays in this game?

The connection logs pop up, but they're full of junk.

"Fuck," Javier says. "The virus dumped a bunch of shit into here."

All that posturing for nothing.

"So they can't be read?" Dorian asks. "Your cybersecurity is shit."

"I didn't say that." Javier types frantically. "The logs are stored on archival single-write media. The records are still there. I've just got to find the pointers." After another tense minute, he says, "There. That's the beginning of this year's records. There's so much shit in the index, I'm going to have to sort it manually."

For all of his protestations, Javier is quick to comply. Maybe he wants to know the identity of the saboteur, too. Maybe he's more comfortable with someone giving orders. Or maybe, he's going to undermine Dorian the second he gets a chance.

More of the monitors come online. Titus's barebones, bootstrapped image is taking effect, handling the easiest systems first—admin rights, physical access control, basic emergency electrical. A tiling of security monitors flickers to life behind them, but Javier doesn't notice.

Dorian has always wondered what he would do if given the opportunity to hurt someone—to sink his teeth into their raw pathos and look into that dark mirror to find something totally absent in himself. To be secure in the knowledge that a person can be shattered when the reflection is no longer entertaining. But to murder someone—

Would that make Dorian better, or would Javier simply cease to exist? The pain would be so brief that Dorian could scarcely call it reaffirming. Murder is so cheap, the failure to exert the will by any other means. It's intellectually lazy.

"Holy shit," Javier says, interrupting Dorian's train of thought. "What time was the alarm? Do you remember?"

"Had to be about five hours. Maybe six. What have you got?"

"There's a shared setup ID that accessed this workstation right before the records got smeared over with junk from the virus. It's from back during the station's commissioning, when we were setting stuff up for Doctor Marsalis."

"Shared IDs are against Company security policy."

"When we get back to Earth, feel free to fire me."

Dorian crosses his arms, peering over Javier's shoulder. "So that credential is… three years old?"

"Yeah," Javier says. Despite the air conditioning, his face glistens with sweat. "There were only five of us on the Cold Forge when that ID was commissioned. Lucy helped me set everything up. That's why we worked so closely on Silversmile."

"So you're saying…"

"It has to be her, man." Javier gulps once and returns to his scanning of records. "There might be something else we can get from her tracks. Maybe she wasn't trying to kill everyone. What if this is just a cover to do something else?"

Out of the corner of Dorian's eye, a black shape moves across one of the security cameras. At first, he's not sure he saw it, but the shadow moves again, and its skeletal tail uncoils. His heart slams in his chest. Dorian checks the label on the security feed.

CENTRAL 104 A

Four modular spots from the SCIF. It's headed in their direction.

Dorian scans across the server racks for any exits, but the only ways out are through the door to the central strut or into the processor core through a skinny maintenance access. He'd probably fit inside, though Javier never would. That might be why Javier had tiny Lucy helping him with mainframe setup.

"You're feeling me on this, right?" Javier says. "Like, Lucy isn't a bad person, you know."

Dorian makes a quiet, acknowledging grunt.

If it doesn't find anyone, the creature will search the room. It's too obvious that something is happening inside. Javier is clumsy and loud—he might want to share a hiding spot. Dorian quickly calculates the odds, and he doesn't like them. Then, he remembers the empty server racks. Cool and quiet, like standing coffins.

"There's a trail of accesses here that aren't just core functions," Javier continues, leaning in to look more closely. He starts muttering about pointers, and Dorian slowly backs away. He's thankful for the loss of his shoes, and he stays on the balls of his toes so he doesn't make sucking noises with sweaty feet on the metal deck. Taking long, quiet strides, he creeps to one of the empty server racks. It's warm, but not unbearable. There's a small mesh plate on the front through which he can see—and be seen. It doesn't matter—he's going inside or he's going to die.

Dorian hooks a finger into the rack's latch and pulls up as gently as he can, pressing his shoulder into the door to aid the mechanical action. If Javier sees him, he might accidentally draw the creature's attention. But the sysadmin is still nattering away about access pathways and interoperability as Dorian slips into the server rack and quietly closes the door behind him.

A moment later something passes in front of the bright work lights of the central strut, throwing a shadow across the doorway. Javier bolts upright, the change in lighting breaking through to him. Like any prey animal, he immediately looks around for his herd, and discovers that he's been abandoned.

The reaction is instantaneous and marvelous. His cheeks redden, his eyes swell with tears and his hands begin to shake. He's ripening like a strawberry, sweet and juicy.

"Sudler? Not cool, man." He pleads for it to be some kind of prank, but there's dark knowledge on his face.

Through the mesh, Dorian watches Javier duck low to reach the processor maintenance access hatch. They say a rat can get into any space through which it can fit its head. Dorian leans closer to watch this miraculous contortion. Javier isn't fat—there's just a little too much of him to make a comfortable fit. He fiddles with the latches, trying to puzzle out the quietest way to open them.

The creature crests the doorway, and Dorian is thankful for his height. He can stand comfortably back in shadow, almost completely obscured, while the scene plays out through the mesh frame. It's like a movie. It might make a nice painting—the devil looming on the horizon line while the sinner struggles to avoid capture.

Caravaggio would've done it justice.

The thing Dorian likes the most about the Cold Forge is its intense quality construction. So many parts of it result from the finest manufacturing processes. In the now-bright lights of the server room, he recognizes the machined steel that was used for the processor maintenance access latch. Unlike molded or hammered steel, machined steel is precise, strong…

And it makes a musical clink when it unlatches.

Javier freezes in place. The beast snaps its long, gleaming skull toward the source of the sound, and it hisses like an unlit blowtorch, furious malice waiting for a spark. Dorian feels its exhilaration, watches its tightening muscles, and he wishes so desperately to record this moment so that he could watch it again and again in the darkness of his room.

The beast crouches so low as to be supine, stalking the short chasms between the worktables, navigating its way toward its soft, fleshy prey. Dorian's gaze darts back to Javier to find his lips working furiously. He's praying. His finger rests on the catch of the second latch. Maybe he's imagining the story of Daniel and the lion's den. But there is no god here. There is only the devil, the all-consuming fire of a raging star, and the infinite blackness.

The second clink drives a squeal from the creature and it clambers over tables, flowing past them in a deadly ballet. It surges to a perch over Javier, tail poised to strike, lips curling, and it pauses.

Javier lies shivering, curled into a ball, breath coming in heaving sobs. It's waiting for him to look. It wants him to know its glory, to see the exact moment of his transmutation from man into meat. Dorian sidles closer to the front of the locker, trying to peer around the creature for a better view of its prey. Dorian imagines himself within that armored exoskeleton, feeling its steely muscles, and lets out a quiet, hot sigh.

Javier parts his fingers and weeps something in Portuguese.

Then the beast snatches him up and sweeps away through the door, leaving only screams and blood in its wake.

1 9

LINES OF
COMMUNICATION

Blue is so happy to find a backup chair in the med bay that she forgives the vehicle all of its faults. It has no stand for an oxygen tank. She can't hang an IV bag, or run a line for her G-tube. But it has a fully charged motor, and it carries her toward her bedroom at a marvelous rate of speed.

At least the med bay wasn't like the Earth hospitals, where she had to wait an hour for the discharge nurse. The painkillers have worn off, though. The pure oxygen the bed administered helps somewhat, but now that she's away from the salubrious influence of medicine, the bends come back in waves.

She mentally maps what's left of the Cold Forge. The crash of the *Athenian* has effectively divided the station into two long halves, though a few ventilation access tubes may remain unobstructed. As she turns the corner onto her half of the central strut, she hazards a glance back at where the docking bay lies, sealed to the harsh vacuum of space. If her vision were better, she'd see Kambili's hands resting at the door in small puddles of blood.

Blue turns away toward the crew quarters. The alarms have stopped going off, and the lights have stopped strobing, which helps with Blue's visual sensitivity.

She needs to get her meds again. It's been too long without an infusion of the various cocktails that keep the antibodies from stripping her nerves bare. It won't be pretty, but Blue can use the intellijectors instead of her IV. She'd never be able to thread a vein right now. It'll become trickier when she needs to eat. She touches the small cap of her feeding tube appliance to find the site swollen and hot. Dragging her belly across several hundred yards of deck did her no favors.

When she crosses into the crew quarters, she finds one of the doors half open—one she could've sworn was closed when she came this way before. The crew had all fled, though. Kambili was the only survivor, right?

The chair's motor whines softly as she slows, inching toward the open door. She sees boots and blood, and her heart thunders in her chest, making her head swim. What if the snatchers have crossed onto her side of the station? She'll be dead in seconds. It should've already happened, in fact.

With a slight turn of her chair, she nudges the door the rest of the way. She finds Merrimack, one of the station maintenance crew, pistol in hand, brains splattered over the ceiling. It's amazing that in the back-and-forth of the evacuation, they may have missed each other. Or did he not even leave his room?

Blue had a coworker at Johns Hopkins who killed himself—a perfectly healthy, rich white man in the prime of his life, working a prestigious job. This coworker had every kind of privilege: money, power, political connections, and yet one day Blue showed up to work to find everyone crying and learned he'd offed himself. He had some minor debts, and his girlfriend broke up with him, and that was all it took.

Maybe Merrimack never tried to evacuate. Maybe he gave up.

He looks up at her with one eye, the other fixed on some far-off point, his ocular muscles scrambled by a large bullet passing through his brain. His waxy expression strikes Blue as accusatory, with one eye half-lidded. She kind of expects him to ask her if she thinks she's too good for this fate.

Perhaps there are other reasons he didn't want to survive, and the containment failure was just the catalyst. It doesn't matter. Her heart settles at the sight of him. He's proof that there are no snatchers on her side of the station. There are no bite marks on his corpse, no scratches across the walls. She knows she should do something solemn, like close his eyes or feel guilt, but it's the furthest thing from her mind right now.

She has decided to live, and he has decided to die. That's that.

Blue turns her chair to head further into the crew quarters, and she's pleased to find the corridor free of obstructions. Aside from the station's core systems being scrambled by a malevolent, intelligent supervirus, the place appears relatively clean.

The door to her room opens, and she feels a weight upon her that she hadn't expected. The journey from her room to the docking bay and back has been so long, and she's right back where she started. Maybe she's worse off, actually. She wonders if her portable terminal was connected to Titus when Silversmile took over. Being mobility-restricted, Blue is very battery-conscious, and usually turns it off when she's not using it, but she evacuated in such a hurry. If her portable is compromised, Marcus might be, too.

That would be game over.

Seeing her room again, the place where she's spent so many of her closing days, makes her want to weep. She retrieves her portable terminal from the workspace. It's been charging on her induction desk, so the battery looks good, and when she unfolds it, it boots up.

Next comes the hard part. She motors to the bed and prepares to climb back into it. She can't attempt her connection to Marcus while sitting in the chair. She'll lose track of time and suffer spinal compression. With a lot of hoisting and grunting, she's able to get herself onto her sheets.

She thanks her lucky stars that she was so paranoid and kept everything locked down on her terminal. After all, she was misappropriating Company funds, and she couldn't have other machines on the network shuffling through her personal files. Most of the time, her portable was isolated. If she hadn't had something to hide, she would've lost everything to Silversmile.

Blue won't trust Titus to route her signals to Marcus anymore. She'll have to patch into one of the short-range inter-station antennae used to interface with docking ships. Even though the docking area was destroyed, there are plenty of repeaters station-wide, and she should be able to bootstrap a small network together. She used to do that sort of thing all the time, back in school, so she could co-opt data farms for her experiments when IT wasn't looking. There was a time when scientists did more science and less system administration. That went the way of government funding years ago.

Finding herself within radio range of the nearest repeater, she sets up the various alignments to maximize signal blast to the far end of the SCIF. She checks the network traffic. It's all dead, aside from the occasional lighting grid or climate control, checking in.

One of the signal towers jumps with a short spike. Then another. Blue checks the logs. Titus was reset twenty minutes ago, but since then, this tower has repeatedly had something beamed at it. Inspecting the packets, she finds a data stream.

>>WE CAN SEE YOU
DO YOU HAVE SAMPLE

The protocol is primitive and unencrypted, with a short-range transmission, the sort of thing a high-school kid might rig up. It takes her no time to create a response.

//HELP

She watches the screen and waits. The tower pings again.

>>NO SAMPLE NO HELP

"Fuck you!" The words scrape past her lips before she remembers the Cold Forge is crawling with murder bugs. Even though there shouldn't be any in the crew quarters, she still wants to take precautions. She grits her teeth and types a response.

//COME GET THE SAMPLE
NO ONE TO STOP YOU

The reply is quick.

>>60 KMPH OFF AXIS SPIN
CANNOT DOCK
YOU COME TO US
ALONE

That explains why the gravity feels a little strange. She hasn't had time to look out a window, but she knows what she'll find—a nauseating, oscillating starscape. She remembers Titus's alert regarding orbital dynamics. That means two things: the system cannot correct the spin, and the station is likely sinking into Kaufmann's gravity well. An escape pod could get off-station, but the *Athenian* struck the pod cluster. She can't be sure if any of them still exist.

```
//IM BRINGING MY CREW
DO YOU HAVE SUPPLIES
```

The cursor flashes patiently as it awaits their response.

```
>>YOU MAY BRING 1 CREW WITH SAMPLE
DO NOT TEST US
```

If these people are willing to let everyone die, she'll need any reassurance she can find.

```
//HOW CAN I TRUST YOU
```

The response is as swift as a slap.

```
>>TRY OR DIE/YOUR CHOICE
WE WANT YOUR RESEARCH
WE WANT YOU
```

Blue licks her lips. If she could get to the escape pod, maybe she wouldn't have to deal with these people at all.

//WHAT IF I JUST LEAVE

But their intentions are clear.

>>BRING SAMPLE
2 SURVIVORS
NO SAMPLE NO SURVIVORS

Blue swallows and sets her terminal aside. The plan hasn't necessarily changed. Use Marcus to get the sample. Bring it to her in his stomach. Have Marcus crawl through the maintenance shafts connecting the two halves of the Cold Forge—they should still have pressure. Get herself into a space suit and then the escape pod. If she can do that, she can get off the station.

A wave of weariness sweeps over her. She'd love to drift off to sleep, but there's too much to do. Luckily, she's become an expert in staving off rest in the name of research. It's the only part of her disease she's found to be manageable.

Blue connects her brain-direct interface gear to the terminal, then changes a few parameters to use the lashed-together network she's created. She places the helmet over her scalp and folds down the blinders, the familiar cold of the gold contacts settling over her bare skin.

"Let's see what you've been up to, Marcus."

2 0

DISTRACTIONS

There's relief at the rising sensation of Marcus's powerful muscles. After dragging herself across the central strut, she's more than happy to be able to walk ten easy paces, if she wishes. The green walls of the kennels are the only things that stop her from doing a victory lap.

She's hunkered down behind one of the legs of the humanoid power loader. Through shatterproof glass along the far wall she sees a trove of armored crates, each the size of a grown man curled into a fetal position. This is next to the egg-storage facility. How the fuck did Marcus get down here? How did he get past the snatchers?

Peering around the corner, she sees molten shadows dancing in the work lights. She can't tell exactly where the beasts are, but there are more than two, and there will be others nearby. In the experiments, the snatchers exhibited distinct social traits, even if she never discerned the method of communication.

If they see her, they'll rip her to shreds.

Yet synthetics will go places no one else will—underwater, into claustrophobic ducts and tubes, cold storage, airless vacuums. They can crawl for hours in a tiny shaft, making them ideal repair personnel.

There's a grating loose along the wall—that must be how he got in here. He would've wound his way through the circuitous passageways with no trouble, homing in on his destination. She shouldn't have taken Marcus over without messaging him. This environment requires advanced survival techniques, and she's barely coordinated enough to tie her shoes.

It also puts her close to the sample she so desperately needs. If she can get past the snatchers into the egg storage, she can disarm one and infect herself. She works her fingers, and that's when she discovers Marcus was holding something: a portable flash tool and a flare.

The flash tool isn't one of the standard data port interfaces like she might find on the mainframe, or the Silversmile computers. It has a different plug interface; one she doesn't recognize. She racks her brain, trying to conjure the memory of the pin shapes and place them in context, but she can't think of anything, so she jams the tool into one of her cargo pockets. The flare, on the other hand, is something she can use. It's one of the civilian ones, thankfully, not a Colonial Marines striker-type, so she doesn't have to worry about finding a rough surface with which to light it.

The cap is rigid in her hand. All she has to do is yank it off with enough force to get the party started. She glances across to somewhere she might throw it to distract them from the entrance to the warehouse. It'll have to go far, and she thinks she sees a good spot at the landing of a winding stairwell. If she can bounce it just right, it'll tumble down the stairs and lead them on a short chase.

Now or never.

She yanks the cap free. The flare sputters to life with entirely too much noise and light. It's impossible to tell, but she thinks there might be a second hiss lurking under that of the flame. She has to get it out of her hand before she attracts attention.

Her android arm gives it a mighty hurl, mustering so much more force and speed than any human ever could— and it's probably because of this that her flare comes loose early in the arc, sailing high to bounce off the top of the wall and come rolling back toward her in a flurry of sparks, resting two yards away.

One of the creatures screams.

If she didn't have their undivided attention before, she has it now.

Blue launches from her crouched position like a sprinter off the blocks, hurtling toward the open vent shaft. More metallic screams of rage join the first ones, rising in pitch with each of her footfalls. If she'd been going too slow in the central strut, she was going too fast now. Marcus's powerful, limber body is difficult for any mere mortal to control. She's never gone full-tilt inside him before.

Three yards to the open duct. There's a loud bang behind her as one of them hits the floor. Did it leap or drop from the ceiling? She ducks her head as the creature's skeletal tail snaps in the air above her.

Two yards to the open duct. She sinks lower, preparing to leap. They're closing in on her, and they're impossibly fast. She expects to feel their cold claws sink into her back, to rend her asunder.

One yard. She leaps, hoping she's judged Marcus's balance better than his throw.

Blue hits the floor and slides into the open, polished duct like a baseball player into home base. She's astounded by the distance Marcus's body travels with no sweat in his clothes to cause friction, but as soon as he slows down, she begins a frantic crawl into the blackness. The creatures are behind her, trying to negotiate the opening, and she knows they'll follow her. She's seen them fold their bodies in miraculous ways.

Even Marcus's eyes can't make much of the vent shafts—pitch black save for the tiny LEDs of the individual climate sensors and variable airflow valves. Ship designers don't put lights in the ventilation systems, but she wishes to god there was a little more illumination. All the ducts inside the Cold Forge are vacuum-rated and able to be sealed off, and she's looking for one of those controls.

Left turn. She barrels down the shaft as fast as her arms and legs will take her, and the scraping claws along metal tell her pursuit isn't far behind. Right turn, then down two feet, then left again. She's taking any branches she can find while trying to maintain her orientation. She'll need to get back to egg storage, and maybe if all the bugs are combing the ventilation system for her, they'll be too busy to patrol the eggs.

Everything in her mind screams for her to panic, but Marcus's stoic fortitude keeps her from suffering the physical effects. She takes another turn, and another.

Shit. This looks familiar. Has she circled back on herself?

As if in answer to her question, she hears the clicking of chitin across the ductwork ahead. She's facing one of the beasts that was following her. The clicking stops, and she knows it must sense that something is wrong. She can't crawl backward as fast as she can go forward, and she'll make too much noise if she tries. So she flattens her chest to the metal, willing herself to be invisible.

She holds her breath. Even though Marcus doesn't need to breathe, her brain-direct interface transmits the heaving of her chest to him. There's no way to address the problem now, other than to slowly asphyxiate in her physical body while waiting for the creature to move on.

It does.

Blue sucks in her breath as quietly as she can, pleased that she can control Marcus's vocal cords better than her own. She can't wait for the creature to come back around the other side, so she creeps forward, turning left at the junction where it went right. From there she takes her first exit, and is rewarded with the slotted feeling of a vent cover under her palm.

There's no variable airflow valve in the way, so this

must be a main duct output. Another metallic scream echoes through the vent shaft—other snatchers are searching for her, perhaps talking among themselves. Blue runs her hand over the panel, looking for the latches that will let her slide through. She can't see anything below, but that's a good sign. It may be a small, closed-off area, like a closet or something. Finding the latches, she undoes them and pushes through, and everything goes weightless for a second.

The fall was so much further than she anticipated.

Blinding pain erupts across one half of her head, then the neck and shoulders as she goes tumbling down a pile of crates. She curses Marcus's sensitive pain receptors as she goes rolling to the pitch-black deck, skin smarting.

When she was a child she fell out of a high tree. It had been enough to knock her unconscious. When she awoke her head swam, and she couldn't feel her legs. She'd never been so scared in her life, and when her mother found her, they took Blue to the hospital to check for spinal swelling.

The idea of climbing seems so far away now.

The fall she'd just taken makes her tumble from the tree look like hopping out of bed. It would've easily killed a human being, but Marcus is tough, built from the same materials as high-performance vehicles. He bends, but he won't break. At least, not from unfocused, blunt-force trauma.

She rolls onto her back, and thinks she can just make out the outline of the vent thanks to the gentle glow of the LEDs in the shaft. It's far away, but she isn't judging distance—

she's looking for a black, skeletal bug to peel out of it and drop down onto her. Despite the vigorous activity, she isn't winded. All her breath comes from the panic in her physical body, and Blue can tamp that down somewhat.

Surely they heard the fall and the banging around in the darkness. She can't have gotten away. And yet, as she listens for the pursuers, she hears none.

"Help."

Instantly she tenses. It was a gravelly man's voice, and he moans weakly. Without a second thought, she shushes the man and bites her lip. The bugs will *definitely* hear, if he keeps that up.

But there's no sign of pursuit. The voice sobs softly in the darkness. Blue picks herself up, but one of Marcus's legs feels wrong, off-balance somehow. She's surprised to find that they didn't wire him with any "deep pain" receptors, just surface stuff. Weyland-Yutani must have assumed he'd notice if he was missing an arm, or had a knee twisted off. She pats down his leg and finds the ankle out of joint. She can walk on it, but she's not going to be running any marathons.

Pulling the flash tool out of her pocket she powers it on, thankful for the orange light of its tiny readout. Through it, Marcus's sensitive eyes perceive stacks of crates, and shapes in the darkness she can't quite understand— masses of shadow that glitter in the gloom like a blanket of distant stars.

This is the general storage for the kennels, but it's been changed somehow. Her mind can't quite pick out the borders of objects—they're blurry and curved where they should be straight. A black column rises in front of her. She reaches out to touch it.

And it weeps.

Blue stumbles backward, her bad ankle giving out under her. Recovering her balance, she holds the flash tool aloft the same way the ancients must've held their dim torches in caves. Shapes begin to resolve: hands, feet, a mass of inky resin, a slimed and soiled face.

"Blue—" he breathes. His face is beaten and swollen. She wishes she could get a better look at him. He barely even seems human.

"What the fuck?" she whispers. "Oh, my god, Javier! What happened to you?"

He mumbles something, but she can't quite make it out. It sounds like "the tin cans." She tells him she can't understand him, but he just repeats the same slurred phrase. She draws closer, and holding the screen inches away, she sees that he's been encased in hardened resin, suspended and pinned to the column.

Finally, she understands what he was saying.

"They took my hands."

More of the oily resin covers his meaty stumps, and upon closer examination of his wounds, she finds that everything past his wrists has been chewed off. He says something about his legs, and she almost can't bear to look. The creatures have sealed everything up tight. And then she notices the egg crate embedded in the base of the column, its arming panel still closed. Somehow, the creatures knew not to try and force it open.

Javier isn't pregnant, but they're saving him for later.

"Blue…"

Her gaze rises to him, and in the orange glow, she finds the watery eyes she once knew as belonging to a proud man. They both flinch as one of the creatures screams in the distance. They're still hunting her.

"Hurts so bad—"

"I know," she says, shushing him. "I know."

"Dorian… don't trust him," he sputters. "Fucking cow—fucking coward left me to die. And Lucy…" Did Dorian get Lucy killed, too? She doesn't understand, but needs little help hating the director.

"Okay."

Another scream. This time closer. She has precious few minutes before she must hide again. Javier looks down at her with panic in his eyes.

"Please. I want—I want you to…"

He's choking on the words. She knows that look of blinding pain.

"I want you to make this stop," he says, and her heart sinks.

"Javier, I can't."

Tears roll down from his eyes. "Please."

Marcus's hands, so soft and sweet with their gentle ministrations, possess more than enough strength to crush his throat. She isn't ready to put an end to a human life, but she knows the unbearable weight of doom better than anyone. How many times has she wished to slip away in the night?

Blue takes a wobbly step forward, her good foot landing on soft viscera at the base of the column, and places her hand over his throat. "Like this?"

Javier closes his eyes and gives her a frantic nod.

She mouths the words, "I'm so sorry," as his soft Adam's apple collapses under her powerful fingers.

She doesn't expect him to struggle. It's just a jolt at first, but as his face turns blue he surges against his hellish restraints, quivering and thrashing. He tries in vain to raise his stumps. Instinct kicks in, and she can see the human Javier fade from this world long before the animal inside is dead.

When at last he lies still, she steps closer and closes his bulging red eyes. She liked Javier as much as she liked anyone on this godforsaken station. There was a wedge between her and everyone here, because she entered their lives as something other than human. She came from a fringe of existence they couldn't understand, and suffered all of their ignorance, their foolishness. She imagines meeting Javier during her undergraduate days at Wake Forest, before the diagnosis, and wonders if they would've been friends.

Regardless of the tragedy before her, she knows this is her chance to gather a sample. She chides herself for not doing a better job of studying the behavioral characteristics of the *noxhydria* specimens, the facehuggers. Who could be sure if they would attach to a synthetic, much less impregnate her? What if it refused to come out of its egg? Her eyes dart to Javier's rapidly cooling body. His heart might not have stopped. If she moves quickly, maybe something about him—his scent, his brain activity, something—will draw the creature out.

She breaks away some of the dark resin from the surface of the egg crate, sliding aside a protective metal sheet on the control panel. A tiny red LED pulses peacefully within, indicating a locked state. Blue taps one of the buttons, and the Weyland-Yutani logo materializes the card-sized screen. It's the same orange as the flash tool, shitty and hard to read against black glass. It gives her a prompt:

>>DISARM CODE?

If she attempts to force it open, flaming thermite and concentrated lye will fill the container. Blue checks the crate number: thirty-two alpha. There are two codes she can use. One disarms the crate, and the other disarms the entire set of them. Besides Dick, she's the only person in possession of the master unlock. The other crew members would have to look up the individual crate disarm code in the catalogue, located inside the impreg lab.

She tries to recall the codes. She has sixteen passwords for use on the Cold Forge, and she's gotten quite good at dredging them up at a moment's notice. But this crate is one of dozens, and she's not sure she's ever even seen it before. Instead, she takes the first steps of the master unlock protocol.

The procedure is simple and straightforward—slide aside the panel cover, press the arm button, press it again to confirm, and slide the panel closed. The system was designed to lock quickly, without requiring authorization, because its cargo is the most dangerous creature in the galaxy.

Aside from mankind.

The disarm, on the other hand, drives Blue to the brink of madness. The instructions are written in a tiny font, and the light of her screens is dim, even for Marcus's superior vision. Every time she makes an error, the system knocks one of her ten tries off the list, then pauses for five seconds. It takes her six tries to get it right. Finally, there's a tiny clink, and the LED turns from red to green. Up in egg storage, the other crates will have followed suit.

She swallows her nervousness, and knows she's not in mortal danger, but instinct and training tell her to fear an unlocked egg box like an uncaged tiger. Instead, she's going to put her face in it.

Blue has to yank the lid to crack the resin from its hinge. Even disarmed, it's a pain to open with all the caked-on sludge. The lid hisses as compressed nitrogen leaks out the side, cooling the moist egg and off-gassing tiny jets of frigid steam. The pressures equalize and servos engage, swinging the heavy steel plate free of the casing. Cold light emanates from the interior of the egg case, illuminating Javier's corpse and the glossy curvatures of his secreted restraints.

Then there's nothing between her and the fleshy ovoid.

She stares down at the crossed meaty lips, slicked through their opening with viscous goo, and waits. The egg doesn't react to her as it does for the terrified chimpanzees. For the chimps, the eggs open immediately, their deadly payloads springing forth with dark intentions. She's seen it a hundred times, and she knows this egg isn't interested in her. Blue has never tried to force one of these open before, and she hopes there's no procedure built into its biology to stop unwanted impregnation, as there was with the female ducks in her undergrad work.

There's a readout just inside the lid, smudged with grime, but clear enough to see what's happening inside. The ultrasound sensors on the case indicate some small movements, but not enough.

To an untrained person, her synthetic form appears as human as any, right down to the pheromones they incorporate upon creation. The egg should accept her as a viable host. She reaches out and strokes the soft nubs around the top.

The egg grows still, and Blue's heart sinks.

The ultrasound goes dark.

She scowls and, in her disappointment, lets out a long sigh.

The readout lights up.

"Come on, you little fucker," she says, running her hand over it again. Once again, activity diminishes. Is she not supposed to be touching the egg? Blue has to be the only human in existence attempting to lure out a face-hugger, and the little bastard won't come out. It must be something about her synthetic body that stops the embryo's awakening process. Finally, she hooks her android fingers into the crossed lips, and attempts to tug it open.

Underneath the flesh, she finds a stony shell, far too strong for her bare fingers to penetrate. Without a decent purchase, her hands come free and she stumbles backward with a grunt.

The ultrasound readout illuminates once again.

It's her breathing—the sound of healthy lungs and fear.

Blue stares at the egg and tries to conjure what she would feel if she stood before it in her human body. Closing her eyes, she sifts through her memories for something to use. What if it were to choke her out, to force its fleshy appendage between her lips and down her throat? What if she were to lie helpless and used, while some horrific creature metabolized her DNA into raw malice and murder? The thought ripples through her human body, lying back in her quarters. Her chest rises and falls faster, prompted by her fraying nerves.

The ultrasound lights up like a Christmas tree.

The outer lips peel away like the petals of a blossoming orchid. She recognizes the stench that fills the air, like freshly turned earth, mixed with the musky stink of an open abdominal cavity. There's a hint of sulfur, though that could be from the acid—or Javier's recently loosened bowels. She's performed so many extractions that the stink is routine, and yet she tries to recall the fear that came with the first time she smelled it. The synthetic body mimics her reactions.

This is going to hurt—she knows it. She steps closer, her chest heaving in anticipation of the strike, her eyes watering. Then she finds the memory she requires. The first time she died.

It was two years ago. Her esophageal muscles had begun to deteriorate to the point that she could no longer eat, and she'd aspirated a tiny bit of food. That was all it took for her reflexes to close her throat and choke her to the point of unconsciousness. She'd been alone and terrified as darkness closed in on her from all sides. It was the first time she'd awoken intubated, gagging and panicked, in her bed.

The birthing membrane, with a texture like raw chicken, slides out of the top of the egg and down to its base, where it will rot. Blue knows what comes next, her breath huffing quick and fearful. The *noxhydria* preys on the innate curiosity of intelligent beings, and she must commit. She must feel that terrible intubation.

It happens faster than she'd imagined, the palm of the spidery face-hugger smashing into her face, crushing her nose hard enough to make her eyes tear up. All lights wink out as its powerful phalanges lock to her skull. Its tail whips around her neck in the blink of an eye, tightening like a steel cable, trying to make her gasp. The second her lips part even a little, its slithering pharynx shoots between her teeth, painfully wedging her jaws apart.

Conflicting instincts rage within her. One tells her to bite down, the other to gasp for air. Her hands fly to her face, desperate to tear the thing free, everything inside her screaming, *You've made a mistake*. But when she doesn't lose consciousness, Blue remembers that *she* is the predator, and the *noxhydria* is her quarry.

It notices, too.

Its grip around her skull slackens, and the tail unfurls as it tries to get away. She slaps her hands to its back and slams her head to the ground, pinning it underneath Marcus's weight. It tries to retract its pharynx, and she sinks her teeth into its tough skin. It has acid for blood, but its hide could never be cut without a laser scalpel, so she holds onto it with Marcus's inhuman jaws. Its tail whips wildly, trying to break her hold on it, but to no avail.

Then she sucks as hard as she can, drawing on the synthetic's strength, crushing the monster's flaccid glands with her palms. A cold trickle seeps into her stomach, then a flood of bitter oil fills her guts. She rips her head free, the frigid liquid leaking down her chin, and gasps. Blue stares down at her prey, watching it shudder violently. She wipes her chin and glances at the streak of jet-black fluid on her pale skin, like octopus ink. The *noxhydria* weakly flips itself onto the tips of its phalanges, and unsteadily tries to skitter away.

"No you fucking don't," she gurgles, and plants her boot onto its back, flattening it to the deck. It scrabbles madly, but the toll of losing its payload is too great. She reaches down and gathers its long fingers into each hand like a bouquet of flowers. Then, with Marcus's muscles, she snaps them backward. A satisfying crack fills the cavernous space. Releasing her prey, she stands up straight. The face-hugger thrashes upon the metal plates, broken fingers limply bobbing at its side. Then it shivers, and dies.

Blue wants to throw up, but she swallows it down,

forcing the infant *praepotens* sample into her plastic stomach, where it will lie dormant. Marcus has no food for it, no DNA to recombine into nightmarish things. She's a walking biohazard now. Any contact with human tissues could prove fatal, could give the *praepotens* the food it needs to metastasize into a snatcher.

Blue crawls into a small alcove of boxes, then removes her headset, snapping her mind back into her room.

The change is jarring, and her senses swim. From here, it's impossible to tell that the Cold Forge is falling apart, yet she knows the truth. There's no blood on her hands, yet she can still feel the stubble of Javier's throat on her fingertips. There's no sample inside her, yet she knows that she has moved one of her final pieces into play.

Now she needs to get to Anne.

Her console beeps. It's Marcus.

Marcus: What is this?

Blue: //A highly infectious substance. Store it in your stomach until we can rendezvous.

Marcus: I shall go to the laboratory to isolate myself.

Blue: //No Time. Clean your exterior. Do not allow anyone to touch it.

Marcus: What happened to Javier Paz?

Blue frowns, her lip twitching. She will not shed a single tear. Not right now.

Blue: //What had to happen. He was dying.

Marcus: That compromises my programming. You have betrayed me.

She stares at Marcus's words, stunned. She starts to type something, deletes it, starts to type again. A few words of exoneration, maybe, but no good sentences thread together in her mind. Marcus's next message scrolls across.

Marcus: It's irrelevant. I am of no consequence.

What has she done to his mind, by using him to kill someone? Through her actions, she's violated his very reason for existing. Weyland-Yutani makes sure their synthetics are the safest models of all time, but Blue still recalls the stories of lost expeditions, or the rumors of synths who have lost their sanity over the years.

At least they're safer than humans.

Another message…

Marcus: I'll still save you when the time comes. I have to. It's what I am programmed to do.

Blue: //Thank you.

Blue: Do you hate me?

There's a long pause before the next message. Marcus can calculate a thousand answers instantly. Is he pausing for effect, or is this question really baking his processors?

Marcus: I cannot hate anyone, Blue. I trust all of you implicitly, and see the best in everyone. That's why it has such a profound effect that you killed Javier with my hands.

Marcus: I trusted you.

Blue: //Keep trusting me. I did what was right. It was outside your scope of options.

Marcus: Nothing is beyond the abilities of a synthetic.

Was narcissism one of the malfunctions? She tries to remember the warning signs: the acronym they gave her in training. Was it NEST? That sounds right—Narcissism, Erratic Behavior, Solitude... something?

Marcus: You interrupted what I was doing. I was creating a distraction.

Marcus: I was going to request your assistance.

Blue: //You can still ask for my help.

The next message takes a moment to arrive.

Marcus: It is too late, but could be useful for later. I already completed my task.

Blue: //What's too late?

Marcus: I am going to put a second channel on your BDI. CP5000-03. Use in an emergency.

With a burst of clarity Blue knows where she's seen that flash tool port before—on the leg of a Caterpillar P-5000 Power Loader. He must've updated its firmware.

Marcus: I am going to restore Juno. You rest.

She bites her lip.

Blue: //I need to see Anne.

Marcus: You are not fast enough to accomplish this. Stay out of my body until I contact you. I'll inform you when I see her again.

Blue shuts her terminal. Her muscles feel so weak,

her stomach empty. She hasn't taken her meds and she's functioning on adrenaline. She looks across to her desk, where her intellijectors full of anti-spasmodics, SSRIs and beta blockers lie waiting. There are tubes of food, some laced with sedatives—assuming her G-tube still works. She needs them, but they're across the room.

She reminds herself of how strong she's been, and swings one leg from the edge of the bed.

2 1

GOING MISSING

ENCRYPTED TRANSMISSION
LISTENING POST AED1413-23
DATE: 2179.07.28

(Unspecified A): Indigo Flag is crippled. Decaying
  orbit. One escape pod.

(Unspecified B): And the package?

(Unspecified A): Still on board. We've provided a
  nudge in the right direction.

(Unspecified B): Do you think she can do it?

(Unspecified A): Possible, and we have contingencies
  in place.

(Unspecified B): You could execute the
  contingencies. End this.

(Unspecified A): Package's expertise will be useful
  in the future. Suggest we maintain course.

(Unspecified B): Granted. What about other asset?

(Unspecified A): Likely to be liquidated.

(Unspecified B): Good. One less person to silence.

It takes him more than an hour—moving cautiously from room to room, through vent shafts and under gratings—before Dorian lays eyes on the entryway to Rose Eagle. He hasn't seen a single snatcher, but knows they could be anywhere. They crawl along the ceilings and curl up into spaces they never should fit. All he had to do was put one foot wrong, and one of them would find him.

He'd had an invite to last year's Weyland-Yutani Senior Management Summit in Dubai. There, they'd gone into simulated jungles and hunted cloned tigers, all in the name of charity. Each step had to be perfect. Each action synchronized among the hunters for maximum stealth. Dorian's trek through the hallways reminds him of those humid indoor rain forests—except each tiger wore an explosive collar that would cleanly pop off its head if it got within five feet of an executive.

Crouching, he dashes across to the thick door of Rose Eagle on the balls of his feet. He settles into the indention, where he's mostly out of view of the hallway. Pressing against the door, he tries to open it. It's locked, so at least he knows the survivors made it inside.

He's going to have to get their attention somehow. Making noise, however, could prove deadly. Ducking his head out, he surveys the shadowy area around him, looking for any telltale signs of the creatures. He draws in a breath and raps the door with his knuckles. The sound is deafening in the silence of the SCIF, and it travels forever.

No response from inside.

Perhaps one of the creatures slipped in there with the survivors and killed them all. The lab might just be a spray of syrupy blood and gore. That would be regrettable if everyone died before giving him the escape pod codes.

Dorian raises his fist again and holds his breath, glancing around for some sort of shelter or hiding place should this all go sour. He could run back the way he came, but they'd probably find him with little effort.

Still leaning against the door, he raps "shave and a haircut," which seems to have become the ultimate anti-snatcher code. The door shoots open, and he falls awkwardly into Anne's arms. Light floods his vision as she yanks him inside and slams the door behind him.

Unlike the rest of the SCIF, which is pockmarked by small-arms fire and smeared by blood, Rose Eagle's lab is completely clean, though it's still hot like a summer's day. Dorian finds eight grimy, astonished faces staring back at him: Lucy, Anne, and some of the techs and maintenance staff whose names he never bothered to learn. When he arrived, they took the time to introduce themselves, but he only cared to memorize the names of key personnel. The rest were beneath him.

Waving away their barrage of questions, he acts as if he needs to reorient himself, and considers what to reveal. The Cold Forge is spinning off-axis, sinking into Kaufmann's fiery maw, with the vast majority of its systems in failure or backup mode. There can be no saving it. If he tells the crew that, however, he'll have a lot more competition for that escape pod.

Anne props him up. "Where's Javier?"

He glances to see the reactions of the others, finding trepidation.

"I'm sorry."

Lucy starts crying again, and instead of finding her annoying, he finds her weak. He's not sure how or why yet, but she thought she was going to get some benefit from sabotaging the station, and now she can't handle seeing the fruits of her labors.

She makes eye contact with him, and looks away.

Does she know he knows?

Anne interrupts his train of thought. "It's okay," she says, clapping him on the shoulder and pulling him in for an embrace. "I'm sure you did what you could." Dorian stammers out an apology. It has the intended effect, and Anne holds him just a little longer than she should, giving him a light squeeze at the end. He looks away, and she leans into his line of sight.

"You okay?" she asks.

"Yeah," he replies. "Looks like you lost some, too."

"There's no time for that."

"I suppose you're right."

"Good. We've got a plan for getting out of here."

That's surprising news, coming from the people who couldn't handle security on three research projects, but Dorian is keen to listen.

"Rose Eagle was designed to interrupt communications between entangled systems," Anne says, folding her arms. She gestures to the pumps and vacuum chambers that stand behind her. "But more importantly, it's designed to *hack* them."

"So you're thinking…"

"I'm thinking we power this fucker up and transmit a message to the nearest USMC warship."

Dorian cocks an eyebrow. "Except the system was wrecked by Silversmile, along with all of the project data. And Josep got himself eaten."

Some of the crew wince at his statement. Dorian shouldn't be so cavalier with his words.

"I think I can fix it." The person who spoke is in the back of the room, a gawky tech with unruly hair. Dorian knows him as the kid who always wears t-shirts and forgets to take a shower. He waits for the tech to respond.

"Nick," the tech says. "I'm Nick."

"I know," Dorian lies. "I'm waiting to hear your plan, Nick."

"We still need Juno to crunch some numbers, but she's probably pretty fucked up," Nick says. "We could network her to Titus and strap together a decent AI. I can start working on some of the most basic code to run the coolant and laser trapping systems. I mean… this was, you know, like… a solved problem. We're just recreating the software solution."

"How long do you need?" Dorian asks.

"Probably like a week."

The crew won't last a week. There's no food in here, and by the time Nick's solution fetches a rescue, the orbital decay into Kaufmann will be so severe that no vessel would dare approach. Anyone going with that plan would be destined to slowly roast alive, be starved to death, or torn asunder by the creatures haunting the Cold Forge. It's banal groupthink, a failure to employ game theory.

Dorian nods. "Okay. I like it."

Then, he realizes everyone was watching for his reaction. Despite the chaos, these people still cling to their societal norms. They think he's an authority. Dorian thinks back to Commander Cardozo. They would've looked to Daniel, once. Crisis management was the whole reason for putting an ex-marine in charge of the station.

Anne's expectant gaze disappoints him. She should've been an opponent, shouldn't have given two shits about him, should've been angrier that he hadn't returned with their network engineer.

"People, I want you to take stock of what we'll need, because we're going to be here a while," Dorian says. He straightens up, and takes a moment to look each of his charges in the eye. "I'm talking food, medicine, parts, whatever. We're going to have to send out teams to gather supplies, and I'm sure you understand the risks. I don't want to hear we left something outside that we desperately need."

"These could be medical supplies, proprietary tools, chemicals, and coolant, too," Anne says. She assumes she's Dorian's partner now, and he has to restrain a smile. "Think like we're creating a miniature Cold Forge inside of the Rose Eagle project. We've got six rooms. One of them will be sleeping quarters. We can cannibalize some of the work chairs for bedding, but we're all about to get used to sleeping on the floor."

It's a mommy-daddy dynamic, and they eat it up. Everyone snaps into motion—except for Lucy, who sits motionless in the corner, pale as a ghost. She hadn't expected to kill anyone, had no idea someone was going to open up the kennels. While the others set about discussing their project needs in two small groups, Lucy remains alone. Dorian comes to her and puts a hand on her shoulder.

"None of this is your fault, you know."

She jumps as though his touch is an electric shock.

"I invented Silversmile."

"But information security wasn't your job," Dorian says, giving her shoulder a squeeze, driving in the knife of guilt as hard as he can. He needs her off-balance. "Your job was to be a brilliant software developer, and you did that—admirably. When we get back to Earth, I'm going to make sure the Company knows how valuable you are."

He watches with growing pleasure as she wilts. Stupid, doe-eyed Lucy has become devious, sniveling Lucy. An unfamiliar righteousness burns in his chest, long forgotten thanks to years of abusive corporate climbing. Whatever he does to her is okay—acceptable, even—because she is a traitor.

"I'd like to b—be alone," she says.

"Okay," he replies. "I can respect that. You'll tell me if you need anything, right? Even if it's just to talk." He gestures to Nick, diligently working with his small group on supply needs. "That young fellow might think he can get this place online, but he's going to need some of your leadership. We're on a tight deadline, and project management is your specialty. Can I trust you to be there for him?"

Lucy gives him a pained smile. "Yeah." She catches the linen sleeve of his shirt as he turns to go. "I think Anne was really worried about you. I've never seen her like this."

Dorian smiles at her. "Thanks for that."

Crossing the room, he takes Anne by the hand. "Can I talk to you for a minute?" He gently tugs her through the door to the now-defunct data center. The second they cross the threshold, he plants his lips on hers, kissing her fiercely, yanking her body against his. Then he pulls away. "I'm sorry I was gone so long," he mutters, their steamy breaths mixing together in the tiny space between them.

"It's okay." Her eyes sparkle with genuine relief.

He hates her so much in that moment. He's never cared much for the opinions of women, but he thought she'd be different when she held him down and fucked his brains out. He'd hoped to meet someone who could keep up with him, who could compete and make him *feel* something. She's just another disappointment in a galaxy of disappointments.

"When I figured we weren't going to make it back," he

says, "I kept thinking I wanted to see you again. Had to get back to you." Dorian would like to ice the cake with a few stray tears, but he's never been able to cry on command.

He's never cried much at all, in fact. Not when his monster of a father died, not when his slut of a mother died, and not now. The only time he ever remembers crying was when he was a child, and his chess coach decided to "teach him a lesson in humility" and soundly beat him in six moves. Dorian had responded with furious tears, taking up the king in his fist and swinging hard enough to cut the coach's cheek with its crown. His parents had settled the case out of court.

Anne slides her hand up the back of his neck to grasp his thick hair. "It's okay now. You're okay." She pulls his head toward hers. Her muscles are so raw, so potent for a woman, her sexual hunger so great, that Dorian wonders if she could be taught to be smarter. She's not worth it, of course, but then who is? Dorian's ideal mate isn't likely to exist naturally—she needs to be molded, crafted in the same way a great sculptor makes stone into something that can transcend time. Soldiers all go through boot camp, where they're broken down and remade. Anne did it once before. He can make her even greater.

"I wish we had time for this," he whispers, "but there isn't even food in here. We need to provide for these people."

"I know," she replies. "We lost one because he couldn't follow the simplest goddamned instructions. I told them how to move, when to move, and one of the bugs just… scooped him up."

"I'm going to tell you something my chess coach once told me. The weakness of others isn't your fault. When it comes down to it, they have to learn to pull their own weight. If someone dies out here, the only person to blame is the saboteur."

She pulls away. "Do we know who it is yet?"

He shakes his head. "You know the smart money is on Blue."

"She wouldn't do that."

"Anne, there are things you don't know, things I haven't told you," he says. "She was conspiring with what remains of Seegson Corporation to steal Weyland-Yutani secrets. That's who Elise Coto—Blue's boss—was working for."

"That doesn't mean she wanted us all dead!" Anne protests. "You don't know her like I do."

"Really?" Dorian says. "She was about to be fired, lose her insurance, die on a long trip back to Earth just so they could deliver a husk of a body. I listened to some of her voice notes. She was looking for a cure. She'd do *anything* to survive, including defrauding our company to the tune of millions of dollars. And now? She's the only person not actively in danger. So, no, I can't say for a fact that she's the saboteur, but we're all in this together—everyone except her."

Anne grits her teeth. "That's just not—"

"We don't have to talk about it now. We need to make a supply run. Just for basics, food and the like." She nods, but she looks white as a sheet. Dorian hopes that inside that brain of hers, all the feelings for Blue are starting to die. He needs her alone, emotionally and physically, when he strikes. Make a move too early, and his plan won't work.

"These are just techs," he says. "None of them can carry their weight when scavenging. You and I should be the ones to make the first run. We've been alone out there before." He gives her a smirk. "You saw how they looked at me. We're kind of the mommy and daddy now. Got to take care of the kids."

"Okay. You're right…" she says, looking as if she's trying to psych herself up to go outside.

"If we can get to the front of the SCIF, I saw a couple of boxes of ration bars in the break area. There's powdered creamer, too. High-calorie content. That's not going to make everyone happy, but it'll keep us alive." A giddiness rushes through Dorian's veins. A checkmate is about to fall into place. All he has to do is get Anne out the door.

Climate control kicks on, and a familiar thrum fills Rose Eagle's chambers. A sigh of relief rolls through the room, along with cool air. If the pumps inside the SCIF are moving air from the chillers, that means Juno must be back online. Maybe Blue got it back online, or Marcus.

That means Blue is alive, and out there, too, making her moves. Unlike Dorian, she has the escape pod access codes. She doesn't have to achieve checkmate. Blue can just win the game.

"The corridors were clear on my way in," Dorian says. "Never saw a single bug. If we're going to go, you need to be ready now."

"Okay," Anne says. "You're right. Let me just—no…
you're right. Let's go."

"Quick tip, though? Lose the shoes."

2 2

DECISIONS

The others stand back from the door, their eyes wide with fear, though they try to hide it. It's almost cute the way they try to be strong. They must think him so self-sacrificing to volunteer to get them food, and they're all too happy to agree to let him try it.

That will be their demise.

After a moment of waiting, no hissing creatures appear, so Dorian and Anne dart out into the hallway. He lifts up a cable run access grate, and they both slip inside. He used a lot of these on the way from Titus to Rose Eagle. They're small, but not impossible for a human adult, with frequent unsecured openings if they need to pop out. The problem with the SCIF is that all of the rooms must be fully secured, so the cable runs aren't continuous.

They reach a bend in the hallway and Dorian rolls over onto his back, looking through the metal slats to see anything that might lie above. Satisfied that there's nothing lurking in the shadows, he pushes up the grate, careful to catch it so it doesn't make a sound when it swings open all the way.

Anne follows, her movements lithe and silent, and Dorian wonders what she used to do for the Marines. In this combat arena, without all the social constructs that make her weak, she's beautiful. He wants her again, just to remind himself of how great she can be. He imagines what it would be like, grunting and sweaty against a wall while murderous hunters prowl the halls.

It's not worth it. Not this time.

"You okay?" she asks, her voice low.

"Yeah," he says. "The next grating is around there." They pad to the corner, and he watches Anne meticulously check the hallway. Her motion is sure and deliberate.

A clang rings out somewhere deeper in the SCIF. It might be one of the creatures. It might also be Marcus. The synthetic has to be lurking out there creating a distraction in the kennels, working on Juno, or headed toward Rose Eagle.

It'd be nice if they could confirm Blue as dead. Then his work with Anne would be so much easier. She motions him forward, and Dorian quietly jogs to the next grating. He swings it over, dips into the gap, positions himself, gets a couple of yards in—

—and stops dead.

Something obstructs his path. Shafts of light filter through the grating, forming curved blades along a smooth, storm-gray surface. Dorian squints, trying to resolve the details, but it's about five yards away. Then, it stirs slightly, revealing the telling profile of a snatcher skull. Its fingers twitch, and it presses its lips into them, as though in prayer. It's curled up, appearing to be fast asleep.

The creatures have made it into the cable runs, a space scarcely big enough for people. A chill runs up Dorian's spine. He'd thought himself clever for using these. He'd thought they wouldn't burrow down here.

"Dorian!" Anne hisses. "Dorian, you have to let me in!" He can't tell her to shut up. If he wakes the lion sleeping before him, it'll be over in seconds.

"There's one coming down the hall," she whispers.

He's essentially fucked. If he backs out, he's dead. If it wakes up, he's dead. Perhaps he could scoot backward, reach up, and close the gate in Anne's face. It's not like she could argue with him—not with a ravening orgy of teeth and claws coming down the corridor. But then her inevitable scream would wake Dorian's new roommate, and that wouldn't end well.

Dorian Sudler can't die like this. He won't. He's too goddamned important to die on his stomach like some victim, begging for mercy. He deserves to meet his fate on his feet, because he is a fucking fighter and this cannot be the end.

Eyes open and fixed on the shining black death ahead of him, Dorian inches forward. He controls every noise he makes: no banging, no scratching, no loud respiration. It's less like he's breathing, and more like his lungs are open caverns through which oxygen sometimes blows.

Slumber soundly, you beautiful creature.

As soon as there's enough space for her, Anne squeezes into the cable run behind him. She shoves him forward slightly in the action, and his heart seizes with the thrill of it all.

The creature is almost pitch black, but this close, it's like staring into the fires of Kaufmann. Tears stream down Dorian's cheeks and a wide smile spreads across his face. Maybe he was wrong about dying on his belly. Crawling within two yards of a sleeping snatcher is the single greatest thing he's ever done. It's better than his directorship, his massive gains-share bonus, and any thrill his office can provide.

A clank sounds out atop him, and he almost coughs in surprise. He looks up and finds a webbed, chitinous foot— close enough to touch—gripping the grating above him. A charge of electricity shoots through every part of his brain, lighting it up with all sorts of unhelpful suggestions. He feels the presence of the two creatures weighing upon his trapped, prone body. It is excruciating.

It is exquisite.

And then his mind becalms, as if something inside him gave way. He gingerly rolls onto his back and looks up at the animal. To his surprise, he sees no sexual organs. It rapes its way into this life, only to abandon the pursuit of sex in service of something greater—moving from the co-opting of life to the destruction of the unworthy. Indeed, sex and reproduction would be such disappointing drivers for the greatest of creatures.

As he lies still between the two chitinous grips of a black vise, he wants nothing more than to trick them, to beat them, and control them.

He can't see Anne, but if she can see past him, she'll understand that they're well and truly fucked. He wants nothing more than to reach up and touch the long toe claw of the creature. It would be like a magnet, snapping him up into its grasp, turning the lightest caress into a hard lock. The death urge wells inside him, and he feels his hand moving forward of its own accord.

The foot rises as the creature silently scuttles away.

Snapped out of the moment, Dorian still needs to get Anne to back out, so he gently kicks the top of her head with his bare foot, hoping she won't protest. He feels her warmth disappear as she slips out of the grate and into the open air. His broad shoulders brush the cable run's edges as he backs out after her, keeping his eyes locked on the slumbering snatcher the entire time.

When at last he's free of the cable run, he places a finger to his lips and takes the grate, shutting it gently behind him. He feels flushed, his cheeks prickle, his skin beads with sweat. Anne is the opposite—flour white, her face locked in grim damage assessment. Dorian points to the thing asleep inside the cable run and she peers over, swallowing visibly at the sight of it. She makes some soldier gestures he doesn't know, but they end with a finger pointing toward a large fuse box with a shadowed corner.

They sneak across the open floor—the longest twenty yards of Dorian's life—arriving to huddle together. She pulls him close, whispering into his ear.

"You saved my life, you ridiculous son of a bitch."

He would've died if she'd been caught. He knows that. Even so, he doesn't bother to disabuse her of her illusions. Instead of answering, he kisses her hard on the lips, sucking in her exhalation, his long hands wrapping around the base of her spine. He then jerks his head toward the break room.

Moving his last piece into position, he has his regrets. He never got to touch one of the snatchers. Never got to watch a live impregnation. Never really closed down the Cold Forge. Still, if this next play goes well, the game is his.

INTERLUDE

ANNE

They arrive at the break room with their breaths catching, their cheeks flushed. This has to be the highest-risk run for coffee creamer in the history of mankind.

Dorian seals the door behind them, and she checks the vents—all too small for one of the bugs. The walls are as thick as any laboratory wall, since space in the SCIF was designed to be repurposed at a moment's notice. The Cold Forge was supposed to be an example of what Special Projects could do, given the right setup.

Before she can even open her mouth he's all over her, his hands roving her body, searching under her clothes. They both stink. She's fucking hungry, and wondering where those ration bars are. There's very little erotic about the moment, though she suspects Dorian finds eroticism in some strange places. She's seen this shit before in the field, and some grunts swear by a good "combat jack." She's never tried, and doesn't plan to start.

She refuses, and he accedes.

That might be the thing she likes the most about him. He seems to intuit boundaries better than most of her former partners—certainly better than Blue did.

"Sorry… I got carried away," he says. "Just celebrating life."

They'd called Anne a synth fetishist in high school, and at first, Blue had been a dream come true. When she and Blue first started using Marcus's body to sleep together, Blue had been insatiable, as if she'd never touched another person before. The fact that Blue wasn't born a man bothered Anne, but the scientist quickly adapted to the role in admirable fashion, and satisfied Anne's urges in ways others couldn't.

Then, she'd started wanting to see Anne in person, to be close to her in that extremely mortal body of hers. Anne loved Blue for her perfection, and the female body did little to excite her. At least, that's what she'd told herself.

She knew now that it was because she couldn't watch Blue die in close-up. It was too hard, knowing that she'd outlive her lover, and the stronger their bond became, the more painful things would get. Anne broke it off in the one act of cowardice she could remember committing.

"Hey, we need to talk," Dorian says, interrupting her train of thought. She blinks, looking around the break room.

"Sorry, uh, we should probably supply up and get the fuck back to safety."

"Anne, stop," he says, coming to her and touching her shoulders. "You understand that, if we go back with those supplies, we're going to be doing a dozen of these runs for those ingrates."

She looks over his face. Dorian is smiling, as if he's been looking forward to saying whatever it is he's about to say. She doesn't like it.

"Hey," she responds. "Like I said, not now. We need to get those ration bars and get back to the—" She stops, marches over to the cabinets and starts opening them one by one to find mostly empty shelves. There's some plasticware and a coffee service, but no rations. She turns to Dorian.

"This is what we can salvage from the SCIF." He plops down a cardboard box, filled with bottles of powdered, non-dairy creamer packets. He points to the count on the box. "There are two thousand packets in here. So that's... fifteen calories per packet... Thirty thousand calories total."

She stops herself from gaping. This was never about creamer.

"There are other supplies," she says. "You said there were bars in here."

"I needed to talk to you alone, and I think the creamer will prove my point." He pauses, then continues. "A human can subsist on a steady diet of three hundred calories per day, and you have ten humans—so that's ten days of food. Now, I'd like you to imagine how this is going to go." He raises his hands to his face, those slender pianist's fingers that she'd let touch her. "First, we're going to rip open these packets of powdered hydrogenated oils and pour them into our mouths like sand." He mimes doing it with a product model's smile.

"That's... twenty packets a day, take them as you like. But there's no volume, and soon, we're going to get very fucking hungry. Assuming we don't turn on each other, you and I will still be going out for supply runs, getting slower and dumber with each passing day, trying to outwit the most perfect killing machines ever born." ·

Disgust wells inside of her, and she doesn't bother to hide it. He can't be suggesting what she thinks he is.

"So what? That just means we have to get more food from the crew quarters."

"You may have missed the decompressed bulkheads between here and there," Dorian says, his face placid save for a twitch in his cheek.

"You don't know shit about this station, so don't you fucking talk down to me like that," she says, her voice low. "I'm the goddamned head of security. Titus is back online. Juno is online. We can equalize the pressure through the maintenance tubes and crawl."

"Listen, sweetheart," Dorian says, annoyance snarling his perfect smile. "You may be head of security, but I do risk management for entire quadrants. I've seen tens of thousands of these people, these corporate drones, shuffle past. You know what you get when you throw these bullshit, unoriginal losers into crisis? Do you think it's a miracle? No! They turn on each other!"

"Like you're doing right now?" Anne steps toward him. She could take out both of this twerp's kneecaps without breaking a sweat.

He shakes his head. "To turn on someone, you have to

be on their side in the first place. *You're* the only person on my team, Anne. Now you can run back to your suicide mission," he says, smoothing a strand of hair away from her face. "Or we can walk around the corner, step into two spacesuits, EVA through the docking area and just go."

She jerks back from his touch. What a conniving little piece of shit. She clenches her fists, but he gives her that serene smile.

"Think about it," he says. "One week and a nap, and you could be on Gateway Station."

She can't stand to look at him anymore, or she's going to punch his goddamned lights out. Turning away, she massages her temples.

"Or," she says through clenched teeth, "you could go fuck yourself."

Quiet fills the break room. He has no rejoinder. Her breath runs in and out of her lungs in a steady pump as she tries to control the speed and calm herself. Anne massages her eyes. They ache from a lack of sleep. It's not his fault if he's panicking. He's a civvy. Any normal human would start to question things in a situation like this one. She feels badly for the way she's treated him—he doesn't have the training for this.

When she turns to tell him so, he hits her in the face with one of the solid aluminum chairs.

Anne's world rings with the blow and she teeters, desperately grasping for what just happened. Her cheekbone reverberates with pain from the strike, and she's only just put together the pieces when he hits her again, blasting her across the jaw, snapping it cleanly.

She spills to the ground, a spray of spittle and blood whipping across the deck, glossing over a little white something. Her tongue tells her of the broken shards in her mouth, tells her that's one of her teeth. She's about to suck in a breath to scream out when Dorian's bare foot connects with her ribcage.

Her air comes out in a *whoosh*. She's left gasping, and rolls onto her stomach to better protect her face. It can't end like this. She wraps her hands behind her head, and he shatters her fingers with another blow from the chair. She's never felt such pain in her life—not from her military service, not ever. Instinctively she draws her hands under her, crying for him to stop with what breath she has.

This is going to be a killing blow. She braces herself.

Instead, he crushes her knee to the ground with his heel, and she feels something inside her leg give way. He hoists the chair and batters her bare feet, her ankles and shins like he wants to flatten them into nothing.

Surprise turns to fury.

Anne lunges for him with her ruined hands, desperately launching from broken legs. He easily dips backward with the same placid smile he always wears. She'll bite his fucking throat out. He can't win. He can't beat her. Not this fucker. She crawls on her elbows, her broken fingers searing with every motion.

"Too, too late, Anne," he says. "Wish you'd figured it out sooner."

Her mouth and cheeks are too swollen to form words,

but she wants to ask if he'd like to die. She would happily oblige his sorry ass. She's going to sink what's left of her teeth into his fucking ankles.

"How to be an animal," he says. "How to survive. I gave you every chance."

One metal leg comes down straight between her shoulder blades, bringing a blinding flash to her eyes.

"Every—"

The blow falls again, this time harder and sharper, like a corner of the metal strut.

"—fucking—"

It strikes one last time, and a bony crunch travels up her neck and over her skull, rattling her ears with a singular agony.

"—chance."

Anne dips into the blackness.

No. She won't let it end like this. She forces her eyes open. She can't feel her legs. Is her spine broken? No. She'd be out cold. Could be swollen. How much time has passed?

Focus, Anne.

Her spine isn't broken because her whole body flares with agony as Dorian grabs her arm and begins to drag her. Maybe it's just a vertebral chip. She's seen those before. She can't muster the voice to cry out. Her throat feels like it's been smashed. How long did he beat her after she was out?

It doesn't matter. She's not going to die today. She has

a boot knife, and she's going to drive it between Dorian's ribs, crawl back into the fucking break room and cry for help. Exhaustion and shock tug at the corners of her mind, and she rips her brain free.

Stay frosty.

Beneath the sound of her labored breathing, there's an insistent scraping, metallic and long. One of her eyes is swollen shut, but she creaks open the other to catch a glimpse of the aluminum chair flashing in the light between strides of Dorian's long legs. Drops of blood run down one side of it, shimmering across the brushed metal. Her fingers fish for her boot knife, but they've been so shattered; she can't seem to get coordinated. Anne thinks she can make a grip, provided she doesn't go into shock.

If she could just hook her—

A fresh new hell greets her as Dorian drops her and sets the chair in the middle of the hallway, doing so with a ballroom dancer's flourish. He's enjoying this. As soon as she can get her blade, she's going to enjoy it, too.

"You, Anne Wexler," he grunts, hoisting her onto the seat, sending dizzying crackles through her neck, "are the closest I've ever come to loving someone. I want you to know what an honor that is."

She tries to spit on him, but it dribbles down her chin. He's focused on her face. She's focused on that boot knife.

"Of course, I liked you more when you were prettier."

It's going to be tough to swing at him, but she'll manage. She'll put every last ounce of rage into it and sink her blade into the side of his neck. Her right thumb still works. So does her ring finger.

"But nothing ever lasts. You were supposed to go that way," he says, pointing to the exit to the SCIF and the airlock.

She knows better. She never could've lived with herself if she'd done that. Her ring finger hooks into her sheath and unsnaps the guard. She murmurs, beckoning him closer. He leans in to try and decipher her words.

"I bet you think you're somehow superior, don't you?" he asks.

She's going to take his sorry ass out. The knife slips free of its binding, coming snugly into her palm. She's never needed it before, not for a person, but the Marines taught her how to gut a man, how to drive it deep into his femoral artery, and how to slice open his throat. She can really only get the right grip for the throat attack.

He looks into her good eye with the smirk that once charmed away her guard.

"What? There's nothing you can say?"

She *is* better than him, and if she can get him to lean a little closer, she'll prove it. She whimpers something incoherent, and he leans in, putting his ear to her mouth.

He's been inside her. It's her turn to be inside him.

Her left hand sweeps out and smacks against the back of his neck. She fights through the pain to make a hook with the remains of her fingers as her right hand rips the knife from its sheath. She has one shot, and no matter how much it hurts, she's going to make it count.

Dorian easily breaks free of her grip, and her knife impotently bounces off his cheekbone. She drew blood, but not nearly enough. He gasps, clutching his face and staggering backward.

It wasn't enough. Now he's ready, and she'll never get another shot. Still, as her one blurry eye runs across the results of her last attack, it feels nice. Crimson runs down his arm, over his white shirt, and he takes his quivering hand away to stare at it as though he's never seen it before.

Yes, you pretty boy fuck. That should've been your neck. Fuck you. Fuck your executive jawline. Fuck your symmetry.

A tear runs from his eye, slipping into his cut to blister it with his salt. He shakes his head.

"Why do you make me love you so much at the end?"

"If you loved that," she slurs through broken teeth, "come back. I got more for you."

"You were beautiful to the last moment," he says, and then he straightens. "Your ride is here."

He disappears from her vision, leaving her alone in the corridor. The break room door hisses closed out of sight, but the hiss doesn't stop when it hits the floor. She cranes her head to find the silhouette of one of Blue's creatures dripping down out of the rafters to land gracefully on its talons. It takes a careful step toward her, and she shakily raises the knife.

The beast's lips twist and part, obsidian teeth seeming to grow longer and longer with each moment of revelation. It understands when it's been challenged.

It charges.

I wanted to see you again, Blue.

2 3

TRUE COLORS

Blue awakens from dreams of teeth.

Now that she's had her meds and a feeding, her body is marginally more bearable. She needs to reconnect with Anne and put a plan into action. Arms aching, she pulls the BDI headset from her nightstand and drops it into her lap, her breath already quicker than it should be. She misses her android's careful ministrations, his help with setting up their interface. She misses the days when she was simply dying, and not dying on board a doomed space station.

She flips open her portable terminal and logs in, connecting the cipher drive. There's another message.

>>TICK TOCK MARSALIS
CANT WAIT FOREVER

She can't do anything about their demands, but at least she can see what Marcus has been up to while she slept.

Blue: //Marcus, are you there?

The response is almost immediate.

Marcus: I see you are alive and well, Blue. That is
    welcome.

Blue: //Did you get the power loader hooked up?

Marcus: Yes. I told you already, but you forgot
    because you are only human.

Marcus: Also Juno is online, for the survivors that
    are hiding out in Rose Eagle.

Marcus: I've connected her to Titus so they can
    share processing power. Your credentials are
    intact. The safety of the station's occupants
    supersedes classification restrictions.

Blue: //Oddly sentimental.

Marcus: I am a machine, not a monster. Not like
    you.

The wet crunch of Javier's throat comes roaring back
into her ears. She'd done him a favor. No point dwelling
on it now.

Blue: //Go fuck yourself. I'm jacking in.

Marcus: Very well.

She hoists the headset over her scalp and leans back. The feeling of mentally invading a passive-aggressive target sits strangely in her gut, even as shapes resolve around her in the darkness. First, steel panels, then signage. She's near Rose Eagle, in the common part of the SCIF—near Anne.

A few light-footed sprints and she's outside the door to Rose Eagle. She knocks a rhythmic pattern, and the door slides open to let her inside. She ducks in without a second glance, only to find a surprised group of seven survivors emerging from the various side rooms.

"Marcus," Lucy says, large eyes running over her like she should be holding a Christmas goose. "Where are the others?"

Blue looks over every face in turn, making sure she's not missing something. It can't be right.

Anne isn't here.

"Where are the others, Marcus?" Lucy asks, with the sort of tone a parent might take to an errant child. "Did you find them?"

Blue looks at her. "I'm not Marcus."

Tension winds across the faces of the other survivors. They look at her like a criminal, or a murderer... or maybe a wolf. It doesn't help that her synthetic body poses a real threat to anyone Blue doesn't like. She's not sure what conversations have happened in her absence, but she knows they weren't flattering.

It's the first time she's been face-to-face with the rest of the crew since her sequestration. She considers telling them she's sorry, for lying to them for more than a year, but she's not. She stole funds and resources from a weapons development project to try and cure all genetically based diseases. She's only sorry that a piece of shit Company auditor showed up to fuck up her plans.

Lucy's question sticks in Blue's head.

"What do you mean, 'where are the others?'" Blue asks. "Which others?" Marcus's smooth voice fills the roomful of ragged people. It's not Lucy who answers, however, but Nick, one of the techs. Blue doesn't remember much about him, other than the time she caught him sleeping behind some crates in the SCIF commons. The weird guy who likes to work long hours and sleep anywhere he falls.

"Wexler and Director Sudler went on a supply run. We're trying to get Rose Eagle working... so we can call for help." His face is impassive. He's not afraid of her. Blue looks him over and nods. He's one of the few people on the station she doesn't hate.

"Okay. Where would they be? I can back them up."

"They were going to hit a couple of places, starting with the break room," Nick says. "Juno has security cameras, so you could track them if you can find them."

"Blue, maybe you can let Marcus help us," Lucy says, "and sit tight for rescue."

"Maybe you can shut the fuck up, Lucy. You let Anne run outside with that creep."

Lucy's eyes turn into saucers. "Fuck you, bitch! Marcus is Company property, and Director Sudler is trying to get us out of this shithole! You selfish motherfucking—"

Blue turns and opens the door, and everyone shrinks back. Lucy's voice dies in her throat.

"Be back soon," Blue says. "Keep up the good work, Nick." Then she ducks away into the dimly lit hallway, leaving the door to slam in her wake. She rushes to a hiding spot, well aware that the beasts will close in on the sounds. She winds through the hallway on Marcus's silent, strong legs, her thoughts on Anne, alone with Dorian Sudler.

Anne, who left her because she was dying.

Anne, who was the last person to make her feel alive.

She'll kill him if he's done anything to her.

It's the same distance to Juno's cage and the break room. The break room takes her through a lot of open corridor, but the ascension to Juno would be in plain sight, ending in the server's glass cage. It was designed to command a view of the common area, and that means more eyes on her.

So she decides on the break room, and moves as quickly as possible, clinging to the shadows. She hopes the snatchers see in visible light. It had been one of the first questions Weyland-Yutani asked about the beasts' military application, but she never did those experiments. She lied about the results.

She sees it at the end of a long hallway: a toppled aluminum chair, streaked with blood and gore. She can't tell from this distance if the blood is Dorian's or Anne's, but she knows what her heart wants. Blue inches toward it, sharp eyes darting across the ceiling, over the grates of the cable runs. The beasts can hide anywhere, and she'll be damned if she lets one get the drop on her.

When she arrives, she finds bits of bone, and a trail of blood leading off into the darkness, dead-ending at the entrance to one of the cable runs. The snatchers did this, and whichever body they were carrying would've had to be folded or hacked into pieces to be carried away. Worse, there's no reason to have had a chair in the middle of an open area infested with the beasts.

Whatever happened here, this has Dorian's stink all over it.

Blue moves to the grating and peers inside, finding only shadow and gore. Desperation settles into her bones. She needs to know that he gave up, plopped down in a chair and left Anne on her own. Maybe the weight of all the people he'd destroyed finally came crashing down on him. There was a lot of bad shit in his past to regret, just like Blue.

Except Dorian doesn't mind hurting people, so regret isn't his speed. Blue searches for other palatable explanations—maybe he tried to touch Anne and she kicked his ass, leaving him to die in the hallway. That didn't sound like something Anne would do, not unless he hurt her. Then all bets would be off.

Her eyes scan the trail of blood for hairs, but finds none. She should've brought a flashlight, but that'd make her too easy to spot. Finding nothing, she sighs and drops her hands to her knees. She never should've given the okay to separate the SCIF when the kennels were breached. She should've gone in there, rescued Anne, and shoved that Company prick into the waiting maws of the beasts.

A strange swishing in her stomach draws her from her thoughts, back to the oozing jet liquid inside her. It's trying to move—it has locomotion. That, or it's found a way to start the birthing process. She needs to get to one of the med bay scanners to check it out, but she won't do that until she's sure whether Anne is safe... or dead. She can locate Anne from the video feeds in Juno, and stabilize the pressure in the maintenance tubes to get Marcus across. Either way, she'll need to hit the server cage before she can leave.

She knows she's supposed to hate Anne, but Blue can't let it go. Maybe, if Blue rescues her, Anne will come to understand the mistakes she made in casting her off. They could still have something together.

Straightening, Blue slips off the way she came, her heart overflowing with desperation.

Ordered rows of blinking lights extend across the glass, dissolving into foggy spheres where they cross frosted panes.

From the ground, Juno's cage looks like frozen starlight. She'd heard rumors from Dick that the SCIF module was originally intended to be a colonial prison, but the Company purchased it at the last minute. It wouldn't surprise her. It was everything Weyland-Yutani could want: labyrinthine, bureaucratic, gray, repetitive. Most importantly, re-purposing a prison was cheaper than designing a real working environment. The cage would've made a perfect guard shack, looking out over an exercise yard.

She takes her first step toward the catwalks and her nerves crackle. Her Paleolithic mind roars at her to stop, that by moving out of the shadows, predators will see her. Blue swallows her fears and forces herself to climb, taking the stairs two at a time until she reaches the first landing.

There are no hiding spaces from here until she reaches Juno. The catwalks are meshed gratings, and even if she went down on her belly, her silhouette would be clearly visible from the ground. There are elevators, but they're located far from the booth, added as an afterthought. Blue hesitates, puzzling through the best approach, until she realizes that there is no best approach.

So, she runs.

The beautiful thing about an artificial body is that she can sprint up three flights of stairs in near silence, arriving as fresh as a summer rain. Even when she'd been healthy, Blue would've been misted with a fine sweat. Reaching the top, she spins to make sure nothing followed her. Empty rafters soar above her, full of cable trays, plumbing, and ventilation ducts. Every curved water and gas return catches Blue's eye, looking like the domed, phallic skull of one of the beasts.

They're all just tricks, played by a paranoid mind— pattern recognition.

She slips inside the cage and Juno's banks lie waiting, long streams of white lights signaling the synaptic firing of code. Racks upon racks of servers twist into the room like the walls of a labyrinth—except the monsters are outside. She doesn't have a clear view ahead to the terminal, but she hadn't seen anything from the ground, so she hopes she's alone.

The cage stinks of plastic and hot metal. Some of the racks have been destroyed by electrical fire, creating dark gaps like missing teeth. She wonders how much of the server is operational. Maybe Marcus was able to achieve some success.

Taking a tentative step inside, she sticks close to the racks. The place isn't that big, and when she reaches the terminal, she lets out a breath. Given the extensive damage from Silversmile, she'd half expected to find a smoking ruin or a charred husk. Most of its assaults were superficial—code alterations, deletions, corruptions—but it could have overloaded electrical systems, sent turbines out of envelope, or engaged in any number of other hardware-based attacks.

The terminal stands before her like an obelisk, its screen dark. She approaches the keyboard and taps the wake key, its plastic clack like a gunshot against the white noise of cooling pumps and fans. The Weyland-Yutani logo animates onscreen, then data connections interweave as it boots up. She logs in with her old credentials, the ones Marcus reinstated.

```
>>WEYLAND-YUTANI SYSTEMS SERVERS
>>TITUS & JUNO EMERGENCY NETWORK
>>BOOTLOADER v0.0.0.1 BY MARCUS

>>QUERY?
```

Despite the danger, she can't help but smirk at Marcus's formality. Only an android would put a version number on an emergency system. Pressing each key slowly, so the clicks don't resonate in the keyboard's metal housing, she types.

```
//CREW LOCATOR: WEXLER, ANNE

>>NO CREW DESIGNATORS
(ABORT/RETRY/FAIL)?
```

Shit. Anne isn't going to be listed in the Juno database, since the system was wiped. If it was working, Blue could've gotten a public feed, or at least a location. She remembers the chair in the middle of the hall.

```
//VIDEO ANALYTICS

>>WHAT SHOULD I ANALYZE?

//OBJECTS OUT OF PLACE

>>NO HISTORICAL DATA FOR COMPARISON
(ABORT/RETRY/FAIL)?
```

Blue glances back. She doesn't have time to be trading bullshit queries with a brain-drained computer.

//I NEED TO FIND MY FRIEND

The moment she hits "return" she realizes how absurd the query is.

>>IS YOUR FRIEND ALIVE OR DECEASED?

Blue's breath hitches.

//UNKNOWN. DEATH WOULD HAVE OCCURRED WITHIN LAST 2
   HOURS.

The screen flashes and shapes fall into place. Blue recognizes the image as the pixelated feed from the SCIF break room. Anne stands in the dead center of the frame, her back turned. Blue holds her breath, expecting the skeletal black shape of a snatcher to descend upon her. Instead, Anne half-turns as Dorian enters the frame with an aluminum chair, swinging it directly into her face.

"No," Blue breathes, but it's there in stark electronic truth. It won't be denied. He catches her flat-footed and beats her to the ground, savaging her over and over with the chair.

"No," Blue repeats, but she knows how this ends.

Dorian drags Anne and the chair out into the hall, and the camera feed switches to the exterior. Anne gathers her wits long enough to cut him with her boot knife, and Blue dares to hope this is the story of Dorian's death. But the director slinks off-camera, and Anne screams as one of the creatures descends upon her.

Cold fear becomes unassailable reality.

Blue can't bring herself to blink, to move. She knew Dorian was fucking evil, always knew there was something horrifying about him, but this is too much. Why did he do it? She gnashes her teeth and her hands shake, and a raw fury grows inside of her. It's unlike anything she's ever experienced. She wants nothing more than to rip his arms from their sockets. With trembling fingers, she reaches down and types.

```
//GO TO BEGINNING OF INCIDENT
```

The feed jumbles and rewinds to the moment before Anne takes a chair to the face.

```
//TRANSCRIBE WHAT IS BEING SAID
```

Juno plays through the footage several times, running further back with each cycle. When it reaches the point where Dorian tries to get into Anne's pants, Blue stops in disgust, then moves forward to their discussion.

```
//There are two thousand packets in here. So that's
   fifteen calories per packet. Thirty thousand
   calories total.
```

That fits with what the other survivors told her, but at some point the conversation changes.

```
//There are other supplies. You said there were
   bars in here.
```

```
//I needed to talk to you alone…
```

Minutes later, Blue has what she needs to understand. Her head throbs. There's something wrong with her physical body. It's as if she's losing her mind, and it's leaking out through her ears. She wants to tear this place to pieces and burn away everyone inside—everyone who sided with Dorian Sudler.

Everyone who let the monster come here.

She could probably do it, too—kill them all. At the very least she could snap Lucy's little neck for siding with the enemy so many times. She could get access to where they were hiding and turn the creatures loose on them.

Or she could continue with her mission, getting Marcus and her body to the remaining escape pod.

Or she could send Marcus to help the others and wait for rescue.

Or she could take the easy way out.

Before making a decision, though, she needs to beat Dorian to death, wherever he is. The key is to find him. She begins to type.

```
//VIDEO ANALYTICS

>>WHAT SHOULD I ANALYZE?

//LOCATION OF MALE FROM INCIDENT

>>TITUS & JUNO EMERGENCY NETWORK
```

Blue shakes her head. The goddamned thing is going to reboot in the middle of her query. She slams a hand down on the console, before remembering that any noise could bring the creatures down upon her. The screen doesn't go to the next line, either—it's just stuck there.

She checks the connection panel at the base of the system, listening for any arcing or sputtering. Maybe Silversmile took a chunk out of the console when it rampaged through the server farm and burned up some of the boards. As she stands her eye catches on the ready cursor. The system is waiting for input. She types.

```
//LOCATION OF MALE FROM INCIDENT

>>TITUS & JUNO EMERGENCY NETWORK
```

"Marcus."

The voice comes from behind her.

She turns to see him emerging from the stairwell, long-legged and malicious, his face oozing blood from his knife wound. Rage fills her soul, and all she can think about is throwing him through the side of Juno's cage. She's going to pound his body against the bulletproof glass until only miserable broken bits remain.

"Engage override Epsilon."

2 4

EXTINGUISHED

"Override confirmed. Locking out pilot controls."

Dorian's heart soars with glee.

He'd been gambling that things were too hectic for Blue to have perfect control of Marcus, and it'd paid off massive dividends. Because of her negligence, he gets to live. He gets to win. Dorian takes a step closer to the android, passing his hands in front of its face.

"I can still see you, Director Sudler," Marcus says. "I'm simply awaiting orders."

"Terminate all speech and motor functions," Dorian says. Instantly Marcus snaps to the ground in a fetal position, a puppet with his strings cut. Dorian leans down to touch his forehead, running his fingertips over the all-too-perfect skin. He strokes the wavy blond hair, jerking some free at the temple.

"I love this place, Blue," he whispers, sitting down next to Marcus. "I think... I think these might be the greatest hours of my life. You're still logged in, aren't you? I know you're listening to me." He pulls out his cigarette case; he's down to the last three. Dorian has always been a pack-a-day smoker, but ever since arriving on the Cold Forge, he's essentially quit. He only wants one now because he's about to fuck these people harder than he's ever fucked anyone in his life.

"I didn't enjoy killing Anne," he says, "but I couldn't have her talking to everyone about me, telling them I tried to leave them all behind. That might impact how the others think of me, you know? I liked Anne. She was a great lay, and quick with a knife."

He pats his pocket for his matches and draws out the case. Only three left, one per cigarette. Must be fate—but the striker is missing. Rage rumbles inside him like distant thunder, but he tamps it down. He can't show Blue how angry he is.

"You know I can't believe this is the second time I've had to get rid of your body. My father always said, 'If you don't have time to do it right, you must have time to do it twice.'" He claps Marcus on the shoulder. "Guess I better do it right, buddy."

He glances up at Juno's monitor to see that it's blank. "Looks like the system timed you out. You want to see something interesting?"

Dorian drags Marcus and props his curled body against one of the cabinets, so the synthetic has a good view of what's happening. Dorian then flexes his long fingers and types Javier's user name and password into the console.

"First, let's seal the doors," he says, and asks Juno to go into full lockdown. His heart skips a beat as the entrance to the server cage hisses closed, but it's fine. No creatures inside with him. Even if there were monsters lurking outside, they probably couldn't get through the thick glass.

Marcus's eyes remain fixed on the screen. Dorian imagines Blue in her room, frantically trying to regain control of her surrogate. While it's a delicious image, she might actually succeed, and then he would die.

How to stop her from further interference? That's the real question. Dorian spots a cabinet with a fire extinguisher inside, so he opens it and takes the red cylinder into his hands. It has a lovely weight to it, an undeniable density. Then he strides over to Marcus and gently thunks the android on the scalp, eliciting a bass tone from the steel. He swings the pressurized bottle in front of Marcus's eyes, shaking it like he's dangling a treat.

"I like it this way…" Dorian says, hitting Marcus's forehead with the rim of the extinguisher, a little harder this time. "…destroying someone with a device meant to save lives. There's some poetry in that. What do you think, Blue?"

Using it like a battering ram, he smashes the cylinder into the side of Marcus's head, pinning the android's brain case against the edge of a server rack. Marcus makes no response, but Dorian can almost *feel* Blue shrieking for him to stop. Maybe she'll choke on her own spit.

"Tough to answer with no motor functions, eh?" Dorian strikes again, putting his back into it, using the corner of the rack like a splitting wedge. Spasmodically the android's eyes flick left and right, but he sees no visible damage. That won't work. He won't be happy until he's washed his hands in Marcus's milky blood. "What do you think, Blue?"

Dorian presses a foot into Marcus's shoulder, pushing the android's skull up against edge of the rack. Taking the fire extinguisher by the neck, Dorian swings it like a baseball bat, and is rewarded with a loud crack and a clang for his efforts. A small ridge emerges across Marcus's forehead, evidence of a fractured brain case.

"There we go." He strikes the fake plastic head again, and Marcus slumps face up onto the ground. "There we fucking go."

He raises the extinguisher over his head, and with a final shout, smashes Marcus's skull open with a spray of white blood. Dorian drops the bottle and stumbles back, breath rushing in and out. His face prickles with heat, and he touches his clammy neck, sighing away the heavy breathing. He presses his fingers into his neck and checks his pulse, just as he's done a thousand times before while jogging. His heart rate slows as his body reaches rest.

He looks down at his hands, covered in milk. He'd felt Blue's terror, her anger, and her understanding that she'd lost, inexorably, to the greater man. She won't be getting off the Cold Forge. The others won't be able to help her. Dorian has begun to devour her, and killing Marcus was the first, lethal bite.

He should've done this to his father, instead of paying

for the man's nursing home bills. That would've been some justice.

Dorian touches his cheek, and his fingers come away with his own blood. His wound needs stitches, but that's only so he can bring his skin back to an earthly standard of beauty. The cut is the doorway to something underneath—something greater. He imagines pulling back the skin to find black chitin.

Dipping his fingers into the pooling synthetic blood in Marcus's wound, he lifts them to his lips. It has a taste like aspartame, with a breathy undertone of truffle oil.

He shouldn't be wasting this precious time.

He rises and returns to the terminal, tries to remember how Anne said they were going to rescue Blue. Something about the maintenance tubes... It'd been so hard to pay attention to what she actually said in that moment before he killed her. What was the correct phrasing?

```
//EQUALIZE PRESSURE FOR MAINTENANCE TUBES AND
   UNSEAL.

>>DOCKING BAY STRUCTURAL INTEGRITY COMPROMISED.
>>POTENTIAL FOR DECOMPRESSION IN THE EVENT OF
   FURTHER DAMAGE.
>>CONTINUE? (Y/N)
```

Dorian rolls his eyes.

```
//Y
```

Unlike human beings, the computer doesn't protest.

```
>>EQUALIZING MAINTENANCE TUBE PRESSURE... 100%.
>>CONFIRMED 1 ATM PRESSURE MAINT TUBES.
>>WARNING: EXTREME DANGER. CREW USE SHOULD FOLLOW
  EVA PROTOCOLS.
```

That's enough to bridge the gap, but not enough to attract the snatchers. They're naturally precocious—they'll get out there, eventually, but it could take hours. He racks his brain to think of what else he can do in the meantime to smoke Blue out. He wants to open the heat shields on that side of the station, but he's not sure how they work.

And Blue needs to be *eaten*.

```
//SHUT DOWN ALL AIRFLOW IN CREW QUARTERS. DISABLE
  HEAT DISPERSERS.
```

Within minutes, that module will be more than twenty-five degrees Celsius. The air will grow close and muggy. The bitch can die miserable.

He tries to think back to his arrival in this magical place. There were those lights, the ones that showed him the way. What had Cardozo called them?

```
//NAVIGATION SYSTEM STATUS

>>COMMISSIONED AND ONLINE. WOULD YOU LIKE DIRECTIONS?
```

He licks his lips and considers the best way to phrase the request. He's never been much for information technologies, but these servers are supposed to be intuitive. Besides, he's a fast learner.

```
//KENNELS TO CREW QUARTERS ROOM 08.

>>THIS PATH INCLUDES MAINT TUBES.
>>NO NAVIGATION AVAILABLE IN MAINT TUBES.
>>EXTREME DANGER. CONTINUE? (Y/N)

//Y
//MAXIMUM BRIGHTNESS, PLEASE

>>ACKNOWLEDGED
```

He strides to a clear section of window and looks down. A thin green line of light appears across the floor, pulsing toward the central strut. He watches with delight as one of the creatures appears, skittering across the open bay to investigate.

But he doesn't want all of them going to the crew quarters. He still has a use for them inside the SCIF. He needs to track them. Blue had a trick for that.

```
//VIDEO ANALYTICS

>>SUBJECT OF ANALYSIS?
```

```
//NON-HUMAN LIFE FORMS

>>ADVISORY: CANNOT IDENTIFY MICROSCOPIC ORGANISMS
  WITH CURRENT VIDEO LOADOUT
```

Dorian snorts in annoyance.

```
//PLOT LARGE NON-HUMAN LIFE FORMS. PROVIDE ACCESS
  CONTROL.

>>PLOTTING… 100%
```

The terminal changes to a station schematic, with several dozen red dots roving around. They've begun to converge on the green line running to the maintenance tubes. They're curious beasts, quick to react to any changes in their environment—a lot like people, except they aren't useless.

Dorian looks at the name of the nearest screen, printed on a peeling sticker at the bottom.

```
//GIVE ME VIDEO FEEDS ON SCREEN JUNO-2A.

>>ACTIVATING.
```

The monitor flickers to life, filling with tiles upon tiles of labeled security camera feeds. Dorian doesn't recognize all the locations, but he can follow the map from the terminal monitor. Selecting a door in a secluded corner of the SCIF, he toggles it open and closed. Some of the red dots rush over to inspect it. Dorian tries another door somewhere else, opening it up. The beasts follow his cues without a moment's pause.

If only they could sense his hand guiding them. They would follow so much faster. He'll bring them treats.

Watching the security feeds, he spies "Rose Eagle Laboratory Alpha." Peering at the screen, he watches the people inside, scurrying about what remains of their little lives, working in some vain hope of rescue. Even if they could get a message to Earth, nothing would've spared them. Starvation and slow roasting would've been their fates.

Dorian has never experienced a joy like this in his life. Giddy, he thinks of the ancient Prince of Denmark, accused of madness.

"I must be cruel, only to be kind.
Thus bad begins, and worse remains behind."

2 5

NEVER, NEVER

Blue jerks the helmet off her head, her throat stoppered by a laryngeal spasm. The more she fights it, the less she can breathe. Salty tears stream from her eyes, and her teeth chatter with rage. How had she been so stupid?

Anne is dead.

Anne, who never loved her.

Anne, the last to touch her.

She has to force herself to calm down, or she'll aspirate when her throat comes untangled. Blue holds the breath she doesn't have, eyes bulging, head growing light. She feels a trickle of cool air in her throat, and it takes everything to fight her instinct to gasp. If she gasps, she'll close it up again.

Taking the tiniest breaths, she tries to relax, can't pass out. She might need intubation again, and there's no one to help her. That son of a bitch can't kill her like this—

But, in a way, he *has* killed her.

Without Marcus, there is no sample. Without the sample, there's no rescue waiting for her. No one will come and get her from her room, or drag her to an escape pod.

More tears roll down her cheeks. It's all over. Now all she has to do is lie back and wait to die. She wraps her arms around herself and reclines in her bed, too lightheaded to stop the coming sleep, too weak to give a fuck. She tried her best, and that wasn't good enough, and now she's going to fall into a star.

The useless helmet rests upon her hips, its wiring harness running down to the wall terminal like a tail. She wants to take it and throw it across the room, but she doesn't have the strength. She's about to push it off the bed when she remembers that Marcus isn't the only thing to which it can connect.

There's the Caterpillar P-5000 Power Loader.

Her heart thumps with explosive rage. With that exoskeleton, she can tear apart anything that comes between her and Dorian. The loader has all of Marcus's access, so it can move about the station freely. She wonders if he uploaded any of his persona into it. Will it be angry when she uses it to snap Dorian like a twig?

Faced with his own death, will he be glad?

Who gives a fuck?

She's about to put on her helmet when the door to her room opens. The sudden noise jolts her so hard she almost vomits. The corridor outside is dim—it must be the night cycle. Reflected in the shadows is a weak green light, pulsing slowly like a buoy floating on the waves.

She leans forward, trying to make out its source, but can't quite figure it out.

Then, the white noise disappears from her room, ventilation fans spinning down into silence. Blue works her jaw, the sudden lack of sound giving her the distinct impression of having clogged ears.

Perhaps it's a glitch in the failing computer system. Blue considers ignoring the new development and putting on the helmet, but it nags at her. She needs to investigate, but that'll involve some crawling, and she's not sure she's up to it. Peering over the edge of the bed, she tries to ascertain whether her knocking knees will carry her safely to the floor.

The green beckons to her.

Blue slides the helmet to safety, then convinces her legs to leave the bed. The rest of her comes tumbling behind like a sack of potatoes. Her forehead slams into the metal floor, and she cries out in pain. She pushes herself up onto her arms, the only muscles with any strength left, and inspects the spot where she hit. The impact will leave a knot, but she's been through a hell of a lot worse in the past few hours.

Pulling herself across the floor, inch by inch, she reaches her door. Wrapping her fingers around the lip, she pulls herself even with the hallway to the rest of the crew quarters. There's a thin strip of LEDs in the hall with a green light running along them. It's the navigation system, for guiding people around the station. It's been so long for Blue that she barely remembers it—she only had to use it a few times in the very beginning, and even then it wasn't all that helpful.

Who is left, trying to find her room?

A creature's scream echoes in the darkness down the long corridor that leads to the central strut. She knows that tone all too well—it's the noise they make when they call out to one another. Her veins fill with ice.

They're coming.

Blue scrambles back into her room, pulling herself up on a nearby table to slap at the door closure panel. If she can lock it, they might lose interest in her and go back to where there are more humans to eat. Her fingers bounce off the doorframe, and she gets it closed on the second slap. She manages to strike the lock button, and with a chime the door panel turns red.

Then it turns green.

Then the door opens again.

Dorian is controlling it from the server room.

He closes it, then opens it, then shuts it once more, as if to say, *"Yeah, I'm here to watch you die."* She knows he'll toggle it again as a signal, once they get closer.

Blue crawls as fast as she can, frantically scanning the room for some way to hide from them. Her bed is too tall, with no cover underneath. They'd find her in seconds. She spies a ventilation duct, but knows they'll sniff her out. Without Marcus to sponge her, she's grown pungent. No, she must ward them off entirely.

Maybe she could improvise a flamethrower using Dorian's matches. Her room has tubes and oxygen feeds, but the plastic would melt. She crawls to the bed to fetch the matches and striker from between the mattress and frame, fishing her fingers into the crevice. She hadn't ever intended to retrieve them, and only finds three sticks—as many as she'd left him.

Maybe she should just jam her pen into the ball spring valve of one of the oxygen tanks and fill the air with flammable gas. She could spark a match and take out a few of those fuckers with her. But then she imagines Dorian watching from Juno's control center, a wide grin on his face.

Fuck that.

So she can make an explosion, but she has to find a way to survive it. If she had time she'd rig some kind of remote spark using a circuit board, wiring, and a few calls over the network. But that's ridiculous. Even if she hides inside the ventilation duct, it'll send shreds of the vent cover into her face, along with the flames. She needs something solid and flat to place between her and the explosion—something that'll cover the vent completely.

In the corner of the room, sits Marcus's nursing stand, where he keeps the clean implements he needs for minor urgent care: scissors, gauze, and an assortment of other clean, packaged items. They all rest atop a detachable metal tray a little larger than the vent shaft cover.

Blue surveys her course through the room. She's going to have to climb upright twice to make this happen: once at the desk for her pen, and once at the bed for the oxygen valve. Using the drawer handles as a ladder, she pulls herself toward the work surface, kicking her atrophied legs to try and get her knees under her body.

She brings her eyes level with the desktop and spots one of Marcus's pens, arranged to be exactly parallel to the wall. She throws her arm across it and smacks her palm down on the pen before dragging it onto the floor with her. She's panting, so exhausted after what she's done, but she can't stop to rest.

Struggling to the bed she takes hold of the side rail, then scoots her butt to better position herself. Her hand muscles and biceps burn, but she pulls herself up high enough to get a second hand on the side rail. A few weeks ago, she wouldn't have thought she could do this once, and now she's done it a few times in two days.

She folds at the waist over the side of the bed, her legs dangling helplessly over the edge, yanks the medical tubes out of the oxygen valves, and tosses them to the floor. She then unscrews the barrel of the ballpoint pen and pulls out the cartridge, leaving a hollow body with a funneled point. The cap fits almost perfectly within the entrance of the ball spring valve, and Blue shoves until the pen won't go any deeper.

A sharp, whistling hiss fills the air—too sharp, perhaps. The valves weren't meant to be opened this wide.

There's a flammability alarm when there's too much oxygen in the room—it shuts off her tanks when the alarm is triggered. That means, once the alarm sounds she only has a short while before her oxygen dissipates harmlessly.

Her gaze falls upon her portable terminal, resting upon

her nightstand. She needs to bring it with her if she can. It's the last, best way to access Juno and Titus, and maybe the power loader. She hugs it against her chest and falls back to the floor, protecting it with her body. She strikes her shoulder and almost cries out, but stifles it. Every part of her is exhausted, and she feels like she's on the edge of a seizure, like distant rumbles before a storm.

The nursing tray isn't far from her—maybe a yard or so. She must crawl over the caster base of the gurney to get to it. Her hands and arms don't want to cooperate anymore. She's put them through too much already, and she needs to rest. No time. She hauls herself over the bed's base to the nursing tray. She'd originally thought she would pull herself up on it, but her body won't let her. She rocks the nursing stand to see if the tray is detached, and it sways freely. She could knock it over, but that would be like smashing a gong while the snatchers stalk the hallways. She'll have to catch the tray if she wants to live long enough to get into the ventilation duct.

Grasping the stand, she leans it carefully toward her. It's lighter than she expected, and it topples almost immediately. Blue catches the tray, but the tools on it roll and clink to the ground. She flinches hard, certain that the chitinous beasts will come scrabbling at her doorway like hungry cats.

But they don't, and Blue is left staring at the closed portal, shaking. She rolls onto her stomach and crawls toward the maintenance shaft, pushing the tray and portable terminal with her chin. They make a negligible scraping noise, but it sounds like a bullhorn. Reaching her goal, she pushes the tray and computer aside so she can get better access to the ventilation cover and its knurled thumbscrews.

She takes hold of the first one, and it refuses to turn. In her heyday, Blue could open any jar or bottle, but now her pinch-grip strength isn't enough—either that, or some maintenance person threaded the screws too tightly. She eyes the slot that goes across the top of the screw head and glances back to the tools on the ground. Next to the roll of gauze, she finds a pair of surgical scissors.

Her lock beeps, freezing her heart in solid ice. Dorian is locking and unlocking her door to get their attention.

Not dead yet. Just go. With her soft medical slippers, she hooks her big toe through the finger ring of the scissors and drags them up toward her hand. Grabbing them, she slots one of the blades into the screw head and twists with a little more leverage.

The screw clicks free, and she repeats the process on the other screws before shoving the scissors aside. She's gotten the first screw entirely out when a terrifying sound fills her ears.

The oxygen saturation alarm.

It rings out again, and the hiss of her oxygen leak fades. Another hiss comes in its wake—muffled out in the hallway. Dorian hasn't opened the door yet. He's savoring this.

Fuck fuck fuck fuck. Blue mouths the words as her fingers work the second screw, unwilling to utter even the tiniest noise. She takes out the third screw.

The oxygen alarm rings again. How many goddamned warnings do they get? There might've been a footstep outside her door. It doesn't matter—she can't look back. What would it change if she did?

The fourth screw comes free, and she pulls the grate aside before carefully setting it on the floor. With all of her strength, she lifts the portable terminal into the ventilation duct. It's grown so unbelievably heavy.

The door opens, and the sounds of chewing and ripping meat slide into Blue's ears. One of them is eating Merrimack. The dead bastard bought her some time.

She frantically slides inside, but there's no room to turn around, so she has to push back out. Her skin is electric with fear. This isn't her best plan. It's not even a *reasonable* plan. If she isn't eaten, she'll be blown to pieces. Blue turns around on the floor and positions herself to go in feet-first. She pushes herself backward, her robes riding up her thinning body, scraping her stoma-ridden stomach even more.

The lock panel on her open door chimes a few more times in rapid succession—a dinner bell. The creature in the hallway screams.

Blue tucks her shoulders and pushes all the way into the darkness of the shaft. She pulls in her computer, then reaches out and takes hold of the nurse's pan, ready to position it over the opening. As she lifts it into place, Blue swears she can see a snatcher's long talons wrapping around her doorframe. She wants to scream, but she holds it in—years of pain have taught her how.

The nursing tray must be propped at just the right angle—it's big enough to fully cover the opening. Too much, and it might be knocked free during the explosion. Too little, and it might tip forward and give her away. It's solid surgical steel—if it seals against the opening, it should blunt the explosion. Blue sets it into place and scoots further into the ventilation shaft to put even the tiniest distance between herself and her room.

The oxygen alarm has stopped. Does that mean her room is safe? It can't be. It's only been a few seconds.

With shaking hands, Blue draws the trio of matches from her pocket and lines one up with the striker, only to immediately break it in half. She hasn't lit a match since she was a small child, and there aren't a lot of uses for them in modern life.

Tossing it to the side, she raises the next match, aligning it to the striker. She's deep enough into the ventilation duct that her feet come to rest against the deactivated airflow motor. Blue ignites the match, and as she places it against the tiny crack between wall and tray, her own shaking hand extinguishes it.

One match left.

Maybe she can wait for them to clear off. They might not see her. Then comes the click of a talon so close to the opening that Blue can count the toes. It's now or never—light the fire or lose the oxygen. So she edges up to the tray, so close she can almost touch it with her forehead. She holds the last match close to her body, as though it's the last remaining source of heat in the universe. She places it against the striker.

The crack on one side of the tray darkens.

Black lips, a sneer, viscous drool and glassy teeth. It hisses like a flamethrower, and Blue gasps, taking in its fetid breath. It's been eating corpses.

Then she exhales the words "fuck you" as she strikes the match.

The flame catches and zips around the corner of the tray. Fire licks between the openings, scorching her arms in the fraction of a second. Then the explosive pressure snaps the tray against the ventilation duct with a deafening clap, and Blue screams.

The explosion has nowhere to go except out her door—but she could swear she failed to fit the tray right. A roar fills her head and rattles her bones, spinning her world with the concussive blast.

The howl dies to tinny ringing, like a drill on teeth.

She imagines the beast propelled into the hallway.

The creature's cries drown hers out, its anguish palpable, and she remembers the fury of the one she let burn to death over the fires of Kaufmann. She'd been so terrified then. This time, she was close enough to touch it with her flesh-and-blood hands. She backs away as station fire alarms blare, curling further and further into the ventilation duct. The fan unit blocks any further egress.

Steam forces its way inside the duct with her, scorching her exposed face and hands. The pressure in the room diminishes, and the nursing tray falls away, creaking and steaming.

A shadow thrashes in the flames, its scorpion tail striking everything in sight, its mouth and toothy tongue snapping at anything it can find. Her linens have caught fire, belching dark smoke and licking the ceiling in spite of the sprinklers. The creature isn't going to die, though. The systems designed to save the humans on the station are going to extinguish the flames around it, and it will kill her.

Then it knocks over her medicine cabinet, full of all her supplies for the next six months—gallons and gallons of isopropyl alcohol along with emergency oxygen bottles and spare compounding waxes. The resultant fire is like staring into Kaufmann's light.

Heat washes over Blue's face as the flames begin to draw their air from the ventilation duct, sucking at her, beckoning her inside. Cold, fresh air slides across her legs, and she yearns to taste it.

The shadow's thrashing grows more labored, and it slumps against her bed, plunging into the bonfire. Its skull splits like a pustule, acid blood boiling over the side, choking the room with sulfurous smoke. The sprinkler system doubles its output, washing the deadly blood and blue-burning alcohol outward—toward the ventilation duct.

Blue pushes back as far into the vent as she can go, kicking at the deactivated fan blade. The cyan flames creep closer and closer to her face, and she makes herself as small as she can be. Before the roving wave can reach her, it recedes. The flames in the shaft flicker out. She peers down the duct, through the opening, to see her flaming bed sink into the floor, the creature atop it like a devil returning to hell.

Its acid blood has created an impromptu sinkhole. Blue hopes the station's hull will eventually stop it, but it's pointless to worry about now. She cannot escape this vent—her room is scorching hot, and she needs to wait for the acid to neutralize on the metal.

So, she waits in her long coffin, trapped within in the walls of the Cold Forge, clutching her portable terminal and weeping.

INTERLUDE

LUCY

Of all the people in RB-232, Lucy Biltmore doesn't deserve to be there. She's the one who developed a conscience.

She'd written to her mom about the horrific experiments that were going on, and her communications leaked somehow. Maybe her mom's network got hacked. Maybe her mom talked to someone. Either way, it'd been all too easy for her contact to blackmail her.

Do as we say, or this goes out.

Lucy hadn't responded. She'd been too frightened. Weyland-Yutani assigned a COMSEC officer to her, as well as a member of USCM Counterintelligence Command. She was given explicit instructions to report suspicious contact. Before she could answer, however, a second message arrived.

A picture of her mother entering her apartment.

Do as we say. Do not contact Bill Prater or Colonel Weber. Do not discuss this with your crewmates, or anyone else.

Whoever it was, they knew her handlers, and that

was the most credible threat of all.

Then they sent her code to insert into Silversmile, followed by code for Javier's flash tool. It was supposed to export all the security feeds from the Cold Forge to a satellite downlink. That was it.

There was no way the snatchers ever could've gotten out. The cell doors were all manual control—no computer in the loop. Yet the creatures now roam the station, and it has something to do with Lucy's betrayal. She's certain of it.

Watching her crewmates working diligently, taking shifts, aiming for their long-shot rescue, their deserving salvation, her heart sinks more with every passing moment. Every time she looks at her fingers, she imagines all the blood on her hands, and wants to vomit. Kambili's blood mingles with the rest of the dead. He'd comforted her without question when she was falling apart, loved her, and now he was just a corpse.

"...we know of your faults," someone says, and Lucy jumps. No tears come to her eyes—she's cried them sore already. It's Nick.

Is it happening? Have they found her out?

She looks the kid over and swallows. "Excuse me?"

He cocks his head, concerned, verging on cautious. They've all been suspicious of her for weeks—she can tell.

"We know of four faults in the electricals. Do you think you can run some diagnostics?"

"I'm," she stammers. "I'm not really a power grid person."

"And I'm not a project manager," Nick says, smiling at her, "but you know… stuff has to get done. We need someone to review our routing code, and you're the most available person here."

Lucy can't imagine concentrating right now. In truth, she wants nothing more than to slit her fucking wrists and bleed out in a hot bathtub.

"Sure," she says. She imagines herself getting through this, arriving back on Earth, living in happiness for a few months—until she gets the subpoena. The line of inquiry starts out innocently enough. *Can you explain the events that transpired on the Cold Forge, Miss Biltmore?* The deeper they dig, the worse it gets, until they know beyond the shadow of a doubt that it was her.

She killed everyone.

That's probably why Blue hates her. Lucy sees the accusations in Blue's eyes, one traitor to another.

Lucy sits down at one of the Rose Eagle terminals and sighs. The letters on the screen don't want to make sense anymore, and she can't make her fingers type her credentials. It's pointless to try.

Given what she's done, does she owe it to everyone to get them home safely? Can she still have a purpose when she's committed so heinous an act? They don't deserve to be here. Not one of them.

Then there's Dorian, the newcomer, who had nothing to do with the hideous experiments taking place on the Cold Forge. He's the most innocent of them all—brought here by work just days before the containment failure.

The man tracked down Blue's embezzlement, and was probably close to sniffing out Lucy's secrets when everything went to shit.

"When we get back to Earth," he'd said, *"I'm going to make sure the Company knows how valuable you are."* And now, Dorian is out there risking his life for her, with Anne, hunting down supplies. Lucy should be out there, too.

Lucy takes a moment to compose herself, then dredges up her login ID and password. She's sluggish and disorganized, and wonders if she'll be able to code at all. She messes up her password the first two times, frustration building in her gut. She strikes the enter key with a loud *clack*.

The front door to Rose Eagle slides open.

Into the hallway, where the creatures roam free.

Everyone stops working. The room goes silent. They look from the door to Lucy.

She gapes like a fish, trying to understand the connection between what she just did, and why the door could've opened. Stephen, the tech standing closest to the entrance, stares at her with nothing short of wonder, until black talons wrap around him, snatching him into the hall. He disappears with a shriek.

His anguished cries echo through the SCIF, disappearing in a muffled gurgle. The others are slow to react, as though they somehow missed what happened. Then Nick, the newly appointed manager, screams to the rest of them.

"Run!"

Lucy stumbles upright from her station, her movements sluggish as though she's trapped in amber. Another hissing snatcher leaps onto the doorframe, then at a shrieking woman who collapses backward out of the way. Lucy doesn't bother to watch—she can't care in that moment. All she can do is run.

She runs to the door furthest from the snatcher and hurdles through, deeper into project Rose Eagle, as screams grow louder behind her. Maybe she can hide somewhere. She charges for the open door leading into the entanglement lab—it has the most nooks and crannies, cable runs and crawlspaces. Surely there's a place for her there.

The door slams in her face, and she hits it running full-tilt, bouncing off to the ground. Blood runs from her nose into her mouth, filling her tongue with copper. The lock chime sounds—no more access for her, or anyone. She shakes her head, dazed, lips stinging from a split.

Arms wrap around her.

"No!" she cries, throwing elbows, but the hands are soft. It's Nick. He's helping her, but she shouldn't be helped. She needs to die.

"Come on." He wrenches her to her feet, taking her wrist.

Two crewmates rush past Lucy and disappear around the corner, headed for one of the open side rooms. So much hissing, so many screams ring out behind Lucy and Nick, and he jerks her arm as he heads for the next lab door.

It's too late. The other survivors close the hatch. Nick pounds on the door, but they've locked it. Lucy turns to see if the creatures are coming for her. She wants to watch them come, to feel the biting, piercing, and ripping their dark shapes bring.

Nick won't give up on her. Even though she slows him down, he takes her hand once more and sprints for the other exit to Rose Eagle.

It's closed. Locked. She can see the red LED indicating that he's leading her down a blind alley. Yet, as they approach the door, the panel turns green and it opens. Beyond, she sees the lime-green walls of the kennels.

Lights flash and extinguish behind them. There is nothing but screaming and bedlam, and as Nick drags her away, Lucy stares back into the darkness, just as Lot's wife once looked upon Sodom.

But righteous fury never comes to smite her, and they slink away together into the darkness.

2 6

DAEDALUS, WHO BUILT THE LABYRINTH

Juno's cage has become a holy temple.

Dorian opens and closes doors, sounds alarms, silences others, and runs people through the hallways like rodents through a maze. With each passing moment he adds another layer to his map of the SCIF. First the creatures, then the crew, then the doors and access controls, then warnings and alarms.

He guides the snatchers with a loving hand. On his terminal he sees red dots and blue dots, he can quickly switch to the video feeds to watch the beasts skitter through the hallways.

There are six people to kill, and one to save.

The victim is "GRANADE, S," a blue dot near the front door of Rose Eagle. Dorian selects the door and opens it, and a red dot races toward the bait. Dorian watches camera feed, then sees the beast seize and drag poor Stephen away.

The other blue dots remain still, and Dorian rolls his eyes. It's no fun if they just die. They need to play the game, need to try to outsmart him, or at least stretch this out as much as they can. In the end, he'll feed all the fucking rats to his predators—all except Lucy. Her dot blinks near the back of the room, which is convenient. He can't have his creatures tearing into her. Not yet. She's the weak one—the one ready to crack at a moment's notice.

While he's fixated on Lucy, another snatcher bounds into the commons, knocking down "BRYSKI, K." His quick eyes find the best angle to watch on the video, as little Kay stumbles backward and tries to hide under a table. The creature is quick to slide underneath with her, slicing at her with its tail and claws. Dorian isn't quite sure what he's seeing, but he's fairly certain it rips off one of her arms before dragging her away in a wide swath of her own blood. Near to her, "SANDBERG, T" goes down without a fight, as though he was hoping to die.

Then Lucy is running for one of the labs and that's good—he needs her far away from the others. He slams a door in her face and she falls prone in the hallway, the other survivors running around her, all except for "HARMON, N," who comes to her side. Lucy doesn't move, though.

The bitch wants to stay and die.

"Get up," Dorian whispers, but she won't. It isn't until Nicholas Harmon drags her upright that they start running again.

Dorian shuts the front door to Rose Eagle, giving them a

few seconds to get down the hallway. By then, the other two survivors have barricaded themselves into one of the labs, much to Dorian's chagrin. He'd wanted them to spread out. This is the most power he's ever wielded, and he'll be damned if he squanders it all in a single fucking burst.

Nick and Lucy are inseparable, which is obnoxious, but he'll have to let it go. Without Nick, she's guaranteed to be eaten prematurely. They head for the secondary exit of Rose Eagle, into the kennels, and that's where Dorian wants them, at least. He begins slowly, inexorably funneling the pair toward the secure operating theater at the front of the complex.

Then, he notices another set of doors—emergency bulkheads designed to seal off parts of the station during a sudden loss of pressure. They're designed to be automated, and should boast restricted access, but the new Juno has no restrictions. She's like a newborn—completely trusting. Dorian drops segments of impenetrable bulkhead down across Lucy and Nick's path, protecting them from snatchers, keeping them moving.

At long last, he sequesters the two in the operating theater, and helps Nick lock the door. All that remains is to deal with the remaining two survivors trapped inside Rose Eagle: "HOGAN, C" and "DAWN, M." Leaning in closer to the monitor, Dorian struggles to decipher their faces from the blurry feed, and tries to remember their first names. When he'd first come on board the Cold Forge, had they emerged to greet him, or had they stayed in their rooms? He touches the knife wound on his face. The other Dorian had come here a lifetime ago, excited by the prospect of corporate politics and balanced budgets. He'd come here to be a cutting agent, acting in the name of order.

He'd come to trim fat.

As he opens up bulkheads and hatches, Dorian knows his true purpose. Chaos is the only order, and nothing will be right until this entire station is put in its place. He picks at the loose skin on his cheek, stinging and cracking. By the end of this cycle, it'll be covered in pus and scabs.

His red blood feels wrong somehow between his fingertips. He was once a white-blooded drone, but now he's a yellow-blooded killer. When he'd had a mother, she told him, *"You can be anything you want when you grow up."*

It's time to grow up.

Dorian opens the final gate between the pair of random losers and the snatcher population, setting them up for a running of the bulls. He expects it to be a short affair. After all, the things can leap ten yards at a gallop. Yet humans are wily. Maybe these two can keep him entertained for a while. He sets off the alarms in their laboratory, and triggers the halon fire extinguishers.

The blue dots begin to sprint.

A gap forms between them. One of the runners is obviously faster than the other, so Dorian slams down a bulkhead between the two. Trailing behind, Dawn would be so disappointed to know that Hogan didn't miss a single step in running away from his trapped companion. She flees back into a different room, the acceleration lab with its many nooks and crannies. It'll take the devils a while to find her in there, and so Dorian casually routes a trio of red dots, using their curiosity for flashing lights and their disdain for sprinklers.

Once the creatures enter the lab, Dorian shuts the door behind them.

Abruptly there's a frantic banging on the outside of Juno's cage.

Dorian cocks his head slowly, making certain he heard correctly. He moves away from the terminal console and peers around the edge of a server rack. Through the clear stripe in the frosted glass, he sees HOGAN, C. The man's face is the picture of panic, and Dorian is impressed with how quickly he made the journey from Rose Eagle. Or maybe it wasn't quickly at all.

Time flows so strangely when Dorian plays God.

But here is HOGAN, C, who climbed Mount Olympus. He shouldn't be here—the very act of begging for entry is a mortal insurrection. Dorian regards the lock on the door—human-proof, but not guaranteed to keep out the snatchers. He can't have HOGAN, C, bringing the creatures up to meet their master. Not yet.

He opens the lock and the man rushes inside, all apologies and trembling. He hugs Dorian tightly and begs him to shut the door. Dorian strokes HOGAN, C's curly brown hair, shushing him.

"What happened to Dawn?" Dorian whispers into his ear. HOGAN, C, backs away, horrified.

"I didn't," he says. "Something got—somehow the pressurization s-system—"

"Separated the two of you?" Dorian asks, flexing his fingers. His hands itch. He wants to feel what the creatures feel. "Started acting up on its own?" HOGAN, C's eyes dart across the server control room. The dumb mammal has started to put two and two together.

Dorian takes a step forward, spreading his arms wide. "Was it like something was guiding you? Shoving you out of your cowardly little holes?"

"S-stay back," HOGAN, C says. His rearward steps take him out onto the catwalk. There Dorian looms over him, his unusual height coming into play as he loses his humble slouch, like a raptor stretching its wings. He smears away a stringy black tangle of hair from his forehead.

"What was your plan?" he demands. "To run? Did you come to my temple to beg? Where's your offering?"

HOGAN, C's back strikes the railing.

"You're crazy."

"People keep telling me that." Dorian knocks on his forehead with his knuckles. "Except—I'm still alive." He rushes HOGAN, C, pummeling him across the chest and abdomen. Slashing at the man's eyes with his manicured nails, wishing for all the world that he possessed the talons of the devils below. He grabs his prey's love handles, pulling his gut like fresh bread dough. Though Dorian is unable to do any real damage, he can inflict pain. Unhappy with the result, Dorian switches to his teeth, biting HOGAN, C's chest and neck, nose and brow.

Sinking his teeth in as hard as he can, he is rewarded with the taste of warm, wet copper—and shrieking. Dorian grabs a fistful of the man's hair and yanks his head to one side, pressing his teeth into his Adam's apple and biting down with every last newton of force. The neck gives off a soft crunch, and HOGAN, C stops screaming.

With a gurgle, he slowly goes limp.

Dorian pulls, his teeth sunk deeply into the man's throat, but he can't cut through the skin. He redoubles his bite force in anger, shaking his head, trying to tear loose a chunk, but gets nothing. Finally, he lets go, and HOGAN, C slides to the ground. A distant beast cries out as it enters the SCIF commons in search of prey. He leans HOGAN, C onto one side, then pushes him out between the rails of the catwalk.

The body appears to go weightless for a full second, then falls and bounces off the lower deck with a thunderous bang. Two black shapes rush forward to tear it limb from limb, neither bothering to look up.

By the time he can return to the console, DAWN, M is long gone, dragged away toward the depths of egg storage, her worthless frame the foundation of greater things.

The beasts are born of human weakness.

This will be Dorian's birthplace, as well. Once he escapes, no one will ever know what happened here—no one but him.

He sets off in search of Lucy.

27

INVIGORATION

Blue hasn't dared to leave the ventilation duct. According to her computer link, it's been an hour. She's moved neither forward toward her ruined room, nor backward toward the variable airflow valve. She's remained perfectly still, her heart breaking with the knowledge that no rescue will come for her. Marcus isn't coming. Her sample lies dead inside Juno's cage, his synthetic brain split open like a melon.

Her chest rumbles with each breath, as if the sprinklers had begun to flood her lungs. All the smoke and ash constricts her sensitive throat.

As a child, she'd once had a pet parrot. One day her mother had burned something in the oven. Her mother sprayed cleaning solvents on the hot pan, and the parrot dropped dead from the fumes. Blue finally understands that bird—choked as she is by solvent and ash.

She opens her laptop again and checks the connection.

Wireless still registers in here, and she doesn't feel quite so exposed. She connects to Titus and signs in.

```
>>QUERY?

//ESCAPE POD STATUS

>>ONE ESCAPE POD PRESENT. CONDITION UNKNOWN.
```

Blue sighs. The chance of getting out of this place still exists, no matter how slim the hope. She can't give up.

The loading cursor flickers on her screen. Someone is trying to talk to her. Blue struggles through a hard swallow as she waits for info.

```
>>NEW CONNECT. ID: MARCUS014385 / INIT CHAT PROTOCOL
>>SIGNAL COMPENSATE AND BOOST 1534 + QRAT
>>FINE MOTOR.......CRITICAL DAMAGE
>>ISIS.......CRITICAL DAMAGE
>>OSIRIS.......WARNING
>>SET.......WARNING
>>RA.......SUNRISE
>>MARCUS ONLINE
```

She can't believe it when she sees it. She watched Dorian beat Marcus's head in with a fire extinguisher.

```
Marcus: Blue.
```

Blue: //Marcus? How are you alive?

Marcus: My model possesses numerous regenerative functions.

Blue: //Can you walk?

Marcus: I will never walk again.

Blue: //Are you okay?

Marcus: I will never be "okay" again.

She closes her eyes. "Fuck." She begins to type once more.

Blue: //At least I understand how you feel.

Marcus: You could never perceive how I feel. You are a murderer.

"Well screw you, too, buddy," she whispers.

Blue: //Where is Dorian?

Marcus: Unknown. I have only just come online.

Blue: //Is he still in Juno's cage?

Marcus: No. I am alone.

Blue bites her thumbnail. If Dorian isn't overseeing things from Juno, where the hell did he go? Does he already have the escape pod codes?

Marcus: Blue, I have just interfaced with Juno. The only remaining survivors are Lucy Biltmore, Nick Harmon, and you. Director Sudler is en route to the Impregnation Lab. We have to stop him.

Blue: //Yes we fucking do. Thanks for joining the goddamned living, Marcus.

Marcus: No need to be unpleasant. Before you ask, I will not kill him.

Marcus: I am not a bad person, like you.

It's cramped in the vent shaft, and extremely hard to type. There are a billion things she wants to say back to him, but she'll have to be more utilitarian than that.

Blue: //I can handle Dorian better than you. A single command from him stops you in your tracks. Can you get to an escape pod? My survival depends on it.

Marcus: Calculating... 100%

Marcus: At current rate of locomotion, I can reach

the escape pod in two hours. One of my eyes still
retains nominal function.

Blue: //Can you make it if the snatchers spot you?

Marcus: I don't think they care about me. In that,
they are no different from other species.

Blue swallows. Her synth is emotionally falling apart,
and she needs him more than ever. She flexes her fingers.

Blue: //Meet me at the escape pod.

Marcus: Confirmed.

Blue snaps shut the portable terminal to save battery.
She'll need every kilowatt of juice for what she's about to
do. Her eyes rise to the vent shaft exit, and her ruined room.
She drags herself from the shaft and onto her sloping floor.
The place where her bed once stood is a gaping hole, with
stringy bits of melted steel hanging down like Spanish
moss. The running water has cooled the deck, and she
prays the contents of her hardware cabinet are okay.

Slithering across the wet floor, she's unwilling to consider
what she must be doing to her immune system by dragging
her cut belly over corroded metal. She reaches the cabinet
beside her nightstand and tugs on it. The metal must've
warped in the fire, because the door won't come open.

Yanking hard enough to get the door slightly ajar, she

wraps her fingers into the crack and pulls. The rolled steel door cuts her skin, but pops open, almost hitting her face. Blue sweeps the door aside and looks down at her palm to find crimson dripping into the puddle on the floor.

Underneath everything that the others see, the disease, the anger, the pain—she's just red. How many times has she lost sight of her own humanity in pursuit of the sample of *Plagiarus praepotens*?

She's going to get Marcus to the escape pod. Before she dies, she's going to herald in a new era of genetic engineering. Blue pulls out the alpha prototype of her BDI helmet—a stringy mass of tangled wires and sensors, woven into a mesh. It used to take Marcus fifteen minutes to get this thing on her. It's far from sleek, and she'll have to stick down the sensors by hand, but it'll work.

The medical cabinet exploded, burned to a crisp, so there's no chance of supplies. She crawls over to it, and her head begins to spin. Her skin grows sweaty and feverish. Her strength is fading. She wants to lie down and sleep, but when she awakens, will her condition have worsened? She can't take that chance.

She pries open a drawer where Marcus keeps unopened boxes of medical supplies. There are always more down the hall, but that's a hell of a crawl, and she still has work to do. After a moment, she finds some surgical tape and a tube of lubricant.

Blue shuffles through the cables in her hand, searching for the visual cortex and gross motor segments. With great strain, she props herself against the wall and squirts a dot of surgical lube onto each sensor. Then, she hoists the harness over her scalp and presses the sensors down. Taking the surgical tape, she wraps it around her head as tightly as she can, creating a band like a baseball cap. She tries to tear the tape from the roll, but she can't get a good angle, and her fingers don't want to cooperate. She leaves it dangling at her temple.

Then she hefts the portable terminal onto her lap and opens it, and slots her BDI cable into the bus.

```
//EXECUTE PILOTSTRAPPER.IMT
>>SEARCHING LOCAL NEURAL NETWORKS...
>>AWAITING BDI CONNECT_
>>CHOOSE CONNECTION:
>>1) MARCUS014385
>>2) CP5000-03
```

Blue tags the "2" key and closes her eyes, hoping to feel the rush of the BDI washing over her. A queer sensation of separation covers her arms and legs, as though she can move a ghostly form, but not her own body. Blackness covers her eyes, and she struggles to see. For a moment, she fears that something has gone wrong, and she'll be trapped inside this black nothingness. A servo whines as she moves her right arm.

It's working. She recognizes the singing of the loader's joints, but why can't she see? Marcus should've given her access to all the loader's systems. Maybe there are some lights on board.

As she thinks of "light," a pair of headlamps ignites on her shoulders, rendering the scene before her in oozing gray and lime green. She "sees" through a forward camera, and a dizzying drop looms before her. She'd always known the power loaders were enormous, but wasn't prepared for the sense of vertigo.

Her camera swivels back and forth—not like a neck, with smooth articulation, but jerky and lagging. The resolution is poor, but she can decipher the shapes of a nest. The creatures are building something down here—a new home to replace the cells, created in their image.

It's only been a few hours since she crushed Javier's neck in the egg-storage area, but the creatures have covered every pylon and crate in obsidian resin. They've worked so fast that Blue scarcely recognizes the place where she's worked for a year and a half.

She takes a step forward and immediately trips on the sticky floor, landing with an earsplitting *bang* that registers through the built-in communications system. She toggles through the alternate camera feeds until she finds one looking down the power loader's back, and sees that the creatures built a nest around her legs. The material is strong, and the servos whine as she slowly but surely breaks free. After the last strand breaks, she places her forks against the ground, pushing out to rise to her feet.

When she finally gets upright, she switches back to the forward camera and finds two snatchers before her, pacing and spitting with rage. She considers attacking them, but such a hostile act could bring the whole nest down around her. She wonders what they would do—would they sever her hydraulic cables? Would they tear out her empty pilot's seat? Better not to find out.

She swivels her clunky yellow body to look around egg storage. Pale hands protrude from the high walls, clutching and unclutching, and as Blue looks closer, she finds faces. This is where they've been taking the stolen people, cementing them to the walls. When Blue looks to their feet, she wants to vomit.

There are open egg crates at each victim, deadly payloads already delivered.

She laments the lack of eyelids on the power loader's cameras, unable to shut them. These people are hosts now, and have no hope of survival. Soon, they'll add their own fleshy worms to the station's snatcher population, their last moments lived in utter agony.

All because Blue disarmed the egg crates with her universal code.

If she's a good person, she'll kill them. That's what she'd want for herself. She takes a step toward one of the restrained hosts, and three snatchers jump in front of her, screaming and hissing, clanking their tails against her empty cage. She conjures the image of fire in her mind, and the welding torch on her forearm ignites.

One of the creatures rams her leg with its domed skull, and she almost loses her balance. If she attacks the hosts, they'll almost certainly topple her and prevent her from leaving. As it stands, she's not a threat for which they should risk their burgeoning hive.

Her video feed travels over the trapped, half-conscious crew, and Blue doesn't want to recognize any of them. She doesn't want to know who she's leaving behind, and so she turns away, lumbering over to where Javier lies rotting, the egg crate empty before him. Blue needs a crate if she wants her plan to work. They're airtight, damage resistant, and one will fit into the escape pod. She reaches with a pincer and one of the beasts jumps onto the box, snapping its tail across her metal arm. Blue brings the blowtorch close to the snatcher, and it skitters away, less than eager to deal with fire.

She threads her forks into the crate's lift points and tries to pry it free of the hardened resin. Servos protest until the crate finally comes free with a crunch. She turns the crate onto its side and pushes her free pincer into it, extracting the empty egg. Its thick, leathery shell comes out like a used melon rind, tearing in places with shearing force. Blue must be extra careful not to rupture any of the lye bottles or thermite contacts, or she'll have to get a new crate.

"Blue."

The voice comes from the wall, thin and reedy, but enough for the loader's microphones to hear it. She turns to find Charles, one of the Rose Eagle lab techs, sunken into the resin like a syrupy waterfall. His hair is matted with mucous or viscera of some kind—her camera isn't high enough quality to see.

"Charles," she says, her voice croaking and overdriven like an electric guitar. The power loader's speakers were meant for blaring safety warnings, not conversation. "I'm so sorry."

"Knew it had to be you." He smirks. "No, you're not sorry. You're going to get out of here, aren't you?"

She doesn't respond. Doesn't move. Around her the snatchers hiss their displeasure.

"You always were smarter than us," he continues, his raw voice even worse over the ragged connection. "You knew how to get out all along."

"Where are the others? The ones from Rose Eagle."

"Scattered. Gone." Charles shakes his head. "The doors started opening and closing on their own."

Blue knows exactly what happened. In Juno's cage, Dorian had power over all access controls. It's how he led the snatchers to her. He was deliberately killing everyone—but why?

"Listen, smart girl," Charles says, his head sagging, "kill me."

She hesitates, unsure if she can do it again. There's something in his voice, though—a pleading certainty—that reminds her of the alternative. A swift death is far better than the agony a chestburster will bring. So she raises a pincer.

The snatchers descend without hesitation, spitting and screaming. They're like a murder of crows, ready to peck out anything they can pierce. They're already pissed off at her for talking to Charles. He surges up in his restraints, eyes wide with desperation.

"What the fuck are you waiting for? *Do it*, you fucking bitch!"

He jolts with a shocking strength—that was the phenomenon that drew Blue's attention in the first place. No matter how weak, the chimps would always be at their strongest right before death. When she'd first seen a live birth, its subject exhibited remarkable vitality in the moments before demise. In that moment, she'd envisioned an enzyme—one she could inject into herself to regain control of her muscles.

From that moment on, nothing else mattered.

"Fucking kill me!"

But she can't. She turns away from him, and begins tromping toward the door.

"Fuck you!" he calls after her. It will be easier to walk away now. "Fuck you!"

"Goodbye, Charles," she rasps through the loudspeaker before ascending the loading ramp out of egg storage.

2 8

THE FREEZER

Dorian has gotten pretty good at avoiding the creatures. Their patterns are becoming easier to spot, and he's started to intuit their favorite places to hide. His destination isn't far, just the operating theater in the kennels.

A rhythmic rumbling echoes from below. Some giant machinery has started up, uncurling like a metal dragon in the depths. Dorian narrows his eyes. It couldn't be the power loader, could it? Those things aren't intelligent, not like a synthetic.

What if Blue got ahold of it?

Is that something she can do?

A nervous discomfort tickles his stomach, as he realizes power loaders don't have verbal overrides. He'd better get a move on if he wants this plan to work—so he sneaks along the edge of the SCIF commons, hiding behind crates and pipe fittings as he goes. The last he checked, the red dots were headed deeper into the kennels, down around the cells and egg storage. That puts the beasts far away from him and his intended path. Hopefully, the racket downstairs will hold their attention.

Plunging into the dim lime-green hallways, he scans in every direction for any sign of movement. The failing, flickering safety lights in the ceiling trigger dozens of false positives as he creeps, each scare sending his adrenaline higher.

He should be allowed to walk among the snatchers. They should accept him as one of their own—an apex predator. He understands what they do better than anyone: acquire, optimize, exploit. He just wishes he could make them see.

Ducking down one of the side passages, one that's too small for a loader to fit through, he still feels the vibration from below. With any luck, it'll pass, headed to some unknown destination. Finally, he reaches the operating theater and taps the door panel. It's locked, and so he gently knocks out "shave and a haircut." No response. He glances down the hall and knocks louder.

I swear to god, if they've fucking killed themselves…

The door opens, and he rushes inside, planting a broad smile on his face. Lucy and Nick stand before him, terrified, but fear quickly turns to elation. Then they pale when they see his sliced face.

"It's fine," he says to them, patting it down.

"Thank God you found us," Lucy says.

"It's a miracle you did, in all of the confusion," Nick adds.

"I saw you run off in this direction, but I couldn't call out, and I had to hide. Just got lucky, I suppose." He needs to make them more comfortable. "An operating theater, huh? You wouldn't happen to have any gauze here, would you?"

"What's that?" Nick points to Dorian's chest and arms. "Is that… android blood?"

Milky crust covers his upper torso. It was a messy thing, and he'd forgotten all about it. Did that one count as a murder? Marcus was an intelligent being who didn't want to die, but he seemed beneath the notice of the snatchers. Had Dorian profaned himself by stooping to kill the pointless machine?

"I—" Dorian composes himself. "I was sent to get creamer, remember?"

"That's right," Lucy responds. "Where's Wexler?"

"Dead," Dorian says, remembering to approximate remorse. "Taken." He ceremonially clenches his teeth, flexes his jaw muscles. "Like everyone else."

Nick does something Dorian doesn't expect. He picks up the surgical mallet.

"That was you moving the walls and doors, wasn't it?" he asks, stiffening. "You led them right to us!"

Dorian shrugs and rolls his eyes. Poor, sweet, skinny Nick, with his thick-rimmed glasses and spiky black hair. He might've been a good match up for Lucy—the gawky couple complaining about late-stage capitalism while working on a secret weapons station so far from Earth. They seem like the sort to have bleeding hearts.

Gasping, Lucy clutches her hands to her chest. Dorian hates her expression of weakness and femininity as much as he hates Nick's expression of masculinity. She's preying on Nick, looking for protection. Dorian laughs.

"This is like seeing a cow holding a bolt gun," Dorian says, and Lucy takes a step backward. "How do you not understand that she's using you, Nick? She's used you to get to me, and now that I'm here, you're no longer required."

"What the fuck, man?" Nick says, stepping between him and Lucy. "You've gone totally off the deep end." She continues to move away.

"You know, people keep saying that," Dorian replies, cocking his head and widening his stance, "but once I've delivered Miss Biltmore to safety, I'll have completed my mission, and you'll all be dead."

Lucy, who had slipped over to the fire axe case, stops short.

"What?"

Dorian slicks back his hair. Time to lie. Lucy needs to give him the escape pod codes, and Nick needs to die. Lucky for Dorian, this little intrigue between Blue, Elise, and Lucy has given him all the material he'll need.

"Nick. Nick. Nick. This is the part I hate to tell you, Nick. I work for Seegson. Lucy Biltmore over here has been feeding us valuable information, and now I'm here to extract her."

Nick laughs and raises his mallet, but hesitates when he sees Lucy's reaction. She's scared, but she also looks ashamed. Dorian nods to her.

"You wanted to destroy this place, and you got your wish. It's too late to turn back now," he says, then he rushes Nick.

The loser takes a furious swing with the surgical mallet, striking Dorian's shoulder. It'll leave a bruise, but no permanent damage. Dorian reaches out with slender hands and wraps his fingers around the young man's face and neck.

Nick screams, his breaking wail at odds with his heroic posturing. Dorian tangles his feet into his target's and shoves, sending Nick sprawling across a table full of glassware. He pins the nerd down, smashing the back of Nick's head as hard as he can. Shards of equipment fly in all directions, and Nick seizes a broken stem, stabbing for Dorian's neck.

Dorian easily stops the man's limp attack. He's a ten-time decathlon finisher. Nick is a fucking code jockey. Dorian twists the glassware from Nick's hand and pauses. It'd be an easy shot straight into the man's eye, but Dorian isn't ready for this to end—not yet. He could go through the neck, and while it'd be spectacular for a moment, that moment would be altogether too short. In the second of indecision, Nick shoves Dorian's arm down into the table, and the glass shatters in his hand, slicing his palm to ribbons.

Dorian stumbles backward. It doesn't hurt. It's one of those itchy cuts made by a too-sharp blade. There's a lot of blood, and Dorian makes a fist, drawing forth rivulets of red. He slaps Nick with his glass-laden palm, smearing his blood into the man's eyes. Then he kicks Nick as hard as he can in the balls.

Lucy—bug-eyed Lucy—just screams and screams. The screaming is good—it works for Dorian. As long as she doesn't interfere, he's happy. Stepping back, he searches the room for some exciting feature, some climactic finish to this too-easy fight. Nick's life can't go to waste. There's a glass cage in the corner, lined with drab ceramic tile and all sorts of brassy nozzles. It's about the size of a shower, but the glass looks bulletproof. He sees a surgical robot in the ceiling.

"Uh, oh, Nick," Dorian growls, taking his prey by the collar and laying a hard punch across his jaw. Nick retaliates with a few limp slaps, but he's already beaten. Dorian smacks him around some more, just to ensure compliance.

"Uh, oh, Nick!" he repeats, maneuvering the man toward the glass enclosure. What pisses Dorian off is the suspicion that Nick could be fighting back, that he's chosen to comply in the hopes that the predator will leave him alone. The man is wasting the last moments in this life, praying for mercy.

That's why, instead of just throwing Nick into the glass cage, Dorian stops and lands a few body blows. Fuck this little nerd for giving up so easily. Nick coughs up blood, which is funny to someone like Dorian, who's literally stared a snatcher in the face. Men like Nick don't deserve to draw breath. They have no redeeming qualities. They only survive at the fringe. They only mate through pity. They're an evolutionary maladaptation.

"Uh, oh, Nick."

Dorian shoves him into the glass cage and slams the door, engaging the magnetic lock. He looks back at Lucy, his murderous eyes momentarily softening.

"I want you to remember that you chose this," he says. "You chose to betray all of these people, and that's why you're going to get to live today. Do you understand that?"

"Yes," she whimpers.

"Tell me how you're committed to your betrayal."

"Yes."

He bores into her with his eyes. "That's not a question, much less a yes-or-no question. I want to hear you say that you want to get out of here."

She starts crying again—it's always crying or shouting with her. She isn't qualified to be operating at this level, to be running a Seegson operation in a protected Weyland-Yutani lab. She's not like Dorian, who knows everything. He takes a step toward her, dripping with blood like a furious wraith.

"Fucking say it, Biltmore!" he bellows. "Say you want to live, so your little friends have to die."

"I—" she starts, and he slaps her, cutting up her cheek.

"Louder!" he roars in her face. "You killed all these people! The least you can fucking do is be sure about it!"

"I want to live!" she screams. "I want to live! I want to live, you motherfucker. I want to live!"

He turns to watch Nick absorb these new facts, to truly understand that he worked so hard to drag Lucy Biltmore here, so she could betray him. Although they've probably never been close friends, the look on his face says it all. Her betrayal wounds Nick deeply, and Dorian drinks it up.

Dorian spots a flash freeze button with a safety latch. "That's what I'm talking about." He flips up the latch and jams down the button. The glass chamber fills with bright mist and screams as the nozzles flood it with aerosolized liquid nitrogen. When the screams stop, Dorian lets go of the button.

Nick's body rests in the corner, eyes shut, skin covered with a fuzz of fresh winter frost. Little glossy trails run down his cheeks, because of course the white knight was crying when he died. Dorian opens the door and, glancing back at Lucy, steps inside. She could rush up to him, seal him up, freeze him to death, but she won't. She's just like Nick—there to be consumed.

Ice seeps into the skin of his bare feet, and he gazes in wonder at what he's wrought. He raises his hands, as if in prayer, then smashes in Nick's brittle face with a savage kick. The skin cracks apart, but he's only frozen on the surface. His warm, bloody center comes oozing from between the cuts, so Dorian takes him by the hair and smashes his head against the tile a few times. He's getting good at killing people.

Dorian dances out of the enclosure on freezing feet and looks to Lucy.

"That's everyone, you know. We need to go."

"E-everyone?"

"Yeah," he says, acting like it was his plan all along.

"Everyone. I was instructed to leave no survivors, except for our mole. That's you."

She wipes her bug eyes on her sleeve. "You were so cruel."

"You fucking brought me here!" Dorian laughs, then he cackles, spreading his arms wide. Selling himself as a spy is more fun than he'd expected—though not as fun as breaking Nick's face apart. "You summoned me, and here I am! What did you think was going to happen when you started fucking around in the wallets of megacorporations? Stern letters? We're talking about *billions* of dollars here, and thousands of lives." He strides to her and pokes her on the collarbone with a long, bloody finger, shoving her backward. "So why don't you drop the whole doe-eyed babe-in-the-woods act and get to the fucking airlock?"

Now comes the fun part. If she buys it, she'll unlock the pod for him, and he can be done with her.

Her eyes search his, a hint of rebellion in her. She hates him, that much is clear, but she's wondering what she can get away with. For a moment, he considers throttling her—something he's wanted since before he started killing people. He's so much taller than she is, and she's so skinny that he could twist her apart like taffy.

"You get to leave, because you showed the correct loyalty," he says, a little quieter. "Now get a move on."

The halls in the kennels are the worst, with no cover and a lot of blind corners. The creatures shriek deep within egg storage, the sound echoing up through the winding passages. There's something happening down there—something beautiful, Dorian knows, because the beasts no longer prowl the long corridors. He wants to go down there and bear witness. But he can't.

His objective is holding his hand. He leads Lucy out of the labyrinth and into the SCIF commons—

Where he is promptly hit by a car.

2 9

VEHICULAR HOMICIDE

That's the only way his mind can describe what he feels—white-hot pain across his entire form, crushing breathlessness, tumbling, bashing, the complete loss of orientation. He rolls to a stop, and the world swims before him, splitting and congealing into the wide-open area.

White light floods his sight, like searing daggers in his eyes. He rolls onto his back and scrambles away from the source, shielding his vision. Yellow lights flash.

Thunk.

The ground shakes. He shakes his head, trying to get his balance back.

Thunk.

He rises to unsteady feet, stumbling as he does.

Thunk.

His eyes adjust, and he looks up at the yellow metal colossus before him—the Caterpillar P-5000 Power Loader. Caution stripes run up the sides of its arms like a paper wasp's stinger. Yellow lights flash on its limbs. Its scarred pilot's cage hangs open, seatbelts jangling as it lumbers toward him. Its pincers spin and open, whining as they do.

"Hello, Dorian," it rasps at him in a voice so distorted that it is neither masculine nor feminine. "I've been waiting for you."

It takes a wide swipe at him and he jumps backward, landing all wrong on his ankle. His breath comes in huffs, from where the machine smashed it out of him. The loader's reach is longer than he anticipated, and the edge of a pincer catches his shoulder, spinning him to the ground. He scrambles away as the second arm comes down on the deck like a meteorite.

Dorian tries to juke past the behemoth and run toward the SCIF side airlock, but its wide arms halt any forward progress. If he gets pinched, if he gets pinned, Blue is going to smear his guts across the deck. Out of the corner of his eye, he spots Lucy trying to make a break for it.

"Get to the airlock!" he shouts to her, and the loader swivels, searching. He takes advantage of the distraction to try and run along the wall, but the loader kicks a steel crate, sending it sliding into his path, causing him to stumble and fall to one knee.

"No you don't, you little shit," the loader barks, lumbering after him.

Dorian barely avoids being crushed by the charging vehicle. He clambers over the crate to get past, bobbing and weaving to stay out of reach of the pincers. But everything he's experienced is beginning to take a toll on his body. His ankle sears with agony as Blue grabs the crate and rolls it, knocking him loose.

Blue's control of the loader is so much more thorough, so much more natural than anything he's ever seen. Though it's clumsy and slow, she uses it as her own body, often moving in unpredictable ways. Dorian searches for any weakness he can exploit, but find nothing. He's not a licensed operator, but he's pretty sure the electrical controls are housed on the loader's forearm. He'd have to be inside the pilot's cage to stop it.

It raises its arms and slams them at him, and Dorian darts past to get a better look at the back. The working camera on top swivels around and snaps onto him. It bats a transit case at him, and the plastic box hits Dorian harder than a baseball bat. He falls to his hands and knees, trying to shake the concussion from his head.

"Stand still," it shouts. Still between him and the exit, the loader comes jogging backward, before tripping in Dorian's direction, grinding toward him like a semi. He rolls out of the way, but only just.

While it moves to right itself, Dorian gauges the distance to safety. There's too much chance that, with its long legs, the loader could catch him at a jog. He finds a cable run grating and rips it open, then worms his way inside.

"No you don't!" the loader rasps.

Its stomping shakes the deck like a bomb going off. Dorian's ears ring and his head spins, and his hands and knees go numb with the vibration. He can't quite see it, but he can hear it up above him. There's a fork in the conduit in a few yards. If he can reach it, maybe he can lose her.

The loader's foot comes crashing through the grating, collapsing it within a few feet of his face. Then again, and again, working its way backward toward him. It hasn't yet made it back to the fork, and Dorian turns the corner before it bashes through his section. He races down the duct toward an exit grate.

His bloody hands sting. His frozen feet burn. Every muscle aches with exhaustion. He has never been more alive.

"Get back here, you coward!" Blue shouts behind him. "Who's a big, strong man now, huh? You fucking limp dick!"

He pauses for a moment. Did she just call him that? How *dare* she?

Pincers wedge into the cable run behind him, ripping the grating open like a can. He struggles forward, shearing metal and sparking electrical cables in his wake. He just has to get to the end, and—

The pincers smash down in front of him, skewering the grating and shattering it. They close around the twisted steel and rip it free. A piece of conduit becomes tangled up in the mess, and a sudden wind across his beaten body tells Dorian he's trapped, fully exposed, and awaiting death. He rolls onto his back in his trench to see the loader straddling the cable run, poised to deliver a crushing blow.

She's beaten him. This infirm woman, this goddamned

cripple. She can't. It's not possible. Nature favors the fittest, and he's an unstoppable machine. He was first in chess club. He's a card-carrying genius. Dorian is the successor to the inevitable legacy of the snatchers.

So she can't win. It's not allowed.

"This is for Anne, you son of a bitch."

A loud clank fills the hall, and the loader stumbles. Through its flashing yellow lights, Dorian makes out a black shape, snapping at its cameras, at its hydraulic hoses. The loader thrashes, and another beastly shadow leaps onto its caution-taped bulk.

They've come to save him.

They've come to put things right.

Dorian climbs to his feet, struck by the majesty of it all. Her stomping must've brought the hive down upon her. In the battle of the physical, she cheated, and now she's paying the price. Two more beasts join the fray, then three more, bounding up out of the kennels and scampering across her metal body, searching for weaknesses.

He can't stay to watch, though. They'll be on him any second, and he has a lot more fleshy spots than a power loader. So Dorian jogs as best he can around the corner, out of the front of the SCIF, with a limp in his step and a song in his heart.

He finds Lucy cowering outside the airlock, waiting for him, and stops to give her a hand up. She's crying, of course. How is she crying? Did she not see what just happened? He wants to shake her and slam her against the wall and tell her, "*You just saw the greatest sight any human alive has ever seen, and you're just huddling in a corner, trying not to look!"*

Instead, he says, "Come on. It's almost over."

This is why humanity is doomed—because when true art and beauty are thrust upon them, they'd rather look away than face it. Because they're so afraid of dying that they don't do any living.

That's why he's got to find a way to kill this bitch.

3 0

OPERATOR ERROR

He got away. The son of a bitch just took off through the far door while the creatures swarmed her.

No matter where she looks, Blue finds an alien appendage striking at her. They surround her like piranhas, darting across her unfeeling body, knocking her off balance. The power loader's internal sensors aren't like Marcus's. When she starts to fall, she doesn't feel it until it's too late. Blue swings wildly, batting two of the creatures into the far walls, but their hardened carapaces shatter against her pincer. Their intensely acidic blood turns her right forearm into a smoking ruin.

She looks on in horror as crimson hydraulic fluid sprays from ruptured cables in her exoskeleton. Her right pincer slides limply open, unable to grip anything. If her left pincer goes, she won't be able to carry the egg crate. If she can't carry that, she can't live through what's coming.

Blue steps out, seizes a piece of broken steel conduit

with her left pincer, and swings it like a whip, cutting one of the creatures in half. Acid sprays far and wide, coating part of her hip. She doesn't notice any pain, just a slow list to the left. She cracks the conduit against the deck a few more times, trying to get the bastards to back off, but to no avail. They snap and rage at her even harder, as if to prove they'd never let her best them.

She can't wait. If Dorian and Lucy are working together, then they'll commandeer the escape pod, leaving Blue high and dry. She must stop them, and so help her, if Lucy gets in the way, Blue will crush her. Anyone who's thrown her lot in with Dorian can go to hell. Threading her pincer through the lift hold on the egg crate, she drags it toward her.

Then she turns and marches for the SCIF exit, igniting the blow torch on her limp right arm and sweeping it back and forth as she does. It's a short jet of flame, but it annoys the creatures. The aliens hiss and spit at her, but they don't charge.

The dangling hydraulic cable on her right side is obvious, however, as is the damage to her hip. The snatchers knew enough to get the egg crates open, so they might be clever enough to cut her cables. Her fluid is crimson, just like human blood, and the beasts must know to seek blood.

One in the back of the pack bounds toward her and she swings the egg crate at him like a baseball bat. The crate connects and the creature flies across the commons before smashing into a wall, acid spraying from several broken pieces. It was an instinctual move, but her heart stops when she realizes what she's done. She can't afford to jeopardize the airtight seal of the box.

But the crates are all shock-proof, tamper-resistant, and best of all, super-hydrophobic. The acid rolls off, leaving no damage at all.

Blue has a battle mace.

She steps into the pack and catches another of the beasts off-guard, slamming it toward the distant wall like a baseball. She swings again, but they've become wary and quickly leap out of the way. They're so much faster than she can be in her cumbersome body, and have little trouble avoiding her attacks.

As she moves forward again, however, they do back away, retreating into the corners, leaping up to cling to the ceiling, darting toward the shadows. Blue's right leg whines where the metal has fused, and she almost trips. If she follows them, they'll get her eventually. They're at an impasse.

Retreating into the open corridor of the central strut, she switches to the camera behind her as she walks backward, yielding a strange sensation.

There's no sign of Dorian or Lucy. She does, however, find the telltale slug trail of Marcus's blood. He's dragged himself through here on his way to the escape pod, and that means Dorian is bound to find him soon. She stomps down the hall toward the airlock, and stoops down to find it empty, several of its suits missing. Blue can't remember if they were gone before or not.

If Dorian and Lucy reach that escape pod before her, she's dead. It can't end like this. Not after everything she's done.

"Fuck you!" she screams out, her metallic voice filling the corridor. She bangs once with her flaccid right pincer, then backs away. If Dorian and Lucy launch, she'll know it.

She has only one choice—keep going.

Backing out of the brain-direct interface, Blue returns to her own body in her burned and stinking quarters. Her swollen lungs and throat aren't handling the soot well, and she may develop pneumonia out of this. Maybe she'll start coughing, choke and asphyxiate. Or maybe she can do what needs to be done and get out of this shithole.

The loader has all of Marcus's access, which means it can open and close sealed emergency bulkheads. It can move through the vacuum-exposed docking bay, perhaps even build impromptu airlocks using emergency bulkheads. No telling how long it might take, and it might not work at all. She keys in the message code to communicate directly with the loader's memory.

>>HELLO, BLUE.

She blinks. How much of Marcus's personality was he able to cram into that tiny computer?

```
//I'M IN THE CREW QUARTERS. PROCEED TO THIS
    LOCATION.

>>ACKNOWLEDGED.
```

He might encounter Dorian and Lucy along the way. If he's too similar to Marcus, he might try to help them.

```
//IN MORTAL DANGER. HURRY.

>>ACKNOWLEDGED.
```

So maybe not much of Marcus's personality after all. She closes her portable terminal and winds the BDI cord around her wrist. She won't have time to reapply it to her scalp if it comes loose.

Blue then begins her long crawl toward the central strut, and with any luck, freedom.

Unsealing the emergency bulkheads would've taken too long. Once Dorian and Lucy don their suits, the fastest way to the escape pods is out the airlock and through the hole in the docking bay.

Besides, that makes it a lot harder for the maniac in the power loader to follow them.

The bright line of Kaufmann's light seeps across the hull of the Cold Forge in a slow transit along its length. Dorian pokes his helmet-clad head out of the airlock to time its passing and mentally gauge how long he has in shadow. It takes about ten seconds, and then Kaufmann peeks over the far side of the hull, blinding him. Dorian ducks back inside, immediately grateful to have the heat off his face.

Lucy huddles in the corner while they wait for it to pass, hugging herself. The doorway grows unbelievably bright, and they inch around it, seeking cover from the burning sun below.

"I can't do this," Lucy repeats over and over again. "We're never going to get out of here."

"Not with that attitude, you won't," he says, clamping a rope harness to her suit's belt. "Because getting off the station is a vapid goal, Lucy." He manhandles her upright, slamming her against the wall to get her legs under her, then reaches down and activates her mag boots. They clamp to the surface and the green safe light illuminates along the side. "You see, you need smart goals, Lucy. Specific, measurable, achievable, results-focused and time-bound. Smart, you understand?"

He shoves her toward the open door, full of tumbling stars.

"Specific: get to the fucking escape pod."

She steps out, and he can hear her sobbing. How long has she been crying? Who the hell would cry when everything was going so well?

"Measurable: stop when we get to the escape pod."

They step out onto the hull, their bodies no longer shielded by the thick, metallic walls of the Cold Forge.

If they get caught out in the sun, it's going to hurt. He shoves her forward.

"Achievable: we will make it if you move your ass, Lucy."

She cries even harder as he forces her to take step after step toward the docking bay puncture. The gash where the *Athenian* struck RB-232 isn't that large, but it certainly caused more than its share of damage. She pauses, and he shoves her so hard she almost comes unglued from the hull. The soles of her shoes flash a yellow warning light.

"Results-focused. You will keep walking, or I will leave you here to burn to death. No distractions. No more hesitation."

They're not far now, and the gash looms large before them. Dorian inspects the escape pod as they tromp past. It looks like it took a bit of damage in the crash, but nothing more than superficial—there's a long scratch down one of the sides and a small puncture, but he's guessing it'll fly. Control lights are visible inside it.

The edge of the Cold Forge starts to glow with the rising sun. It's about to complete another revolution, and if they don't get inside, they might be roasted.

"And time-bound," he says, pointing to the forming halo and dragging Lucy forward. "Either we get inside in the next few seconds or we burn. Now *go*."

One of Dorian's first assignments had been with Weyland-Yutani's massive steel-smelting operation outside Johannesburg. He'd watched them work before closing the plant. When they'd poured out the contents of the crucible, two thousand gallons of molten steel, it'd tanned his skin, made his hair feel crispy.

When the sun pierces the horizon of the Cold Forge, shining its infernal light upon his suit, Dorian feels as if he might die then and there. The golden tiles of the station become fiery white. He closes his eyes, and his lids begin to burn. Lucy screams, but that seems to be her default state. What shocks Dorian is his own screaming.

He can't see anything. His whole body roasts. The only thing he knows to do is make for the gash, wherever it was. He grabs Lucy's hand and yanks her forward, stomping across the surface until his boot finds only a hole. Dorian forces Lucy down into it, then dives into darkness after her. Blackness fills his vision, and he tumbles before striking his back, hard.

But the shadows are cool and merciful. He's safe.

Gradually, his vision returns, and the world comes into dim focus. He's inside the torn docking bay, and gravity is only a fraction of what it is elsewhere on the Cold Forge. A long scorch mark runs the wall opposite to the tear, where radiation has reached the inside of the station, which lacks the reflective protection of the exterior. Kaufmann has been carving on it like a sundial.

Panicked, Lucy struggles with her helmet, so Dorian braces against the deck and sinks a fist into her gut as hard as he can. She's shielded by the space suit, but his punch drives the point home. Her sobbing becomes uncontrolled.

"You can't take off your helmet in space, Lucy," he

says over the comms. "Now let's get that escape pod opened up." He takes her to the pod hatch, a smaller tube about half the size of a normal docking tube, and finds something curious: white blood.

"Marcus," he says with a smile.

Dorian's eyes travel the scene in search of more blood, and he easily spots it near one of the maintenance tubes. Marcus has been using the emergency seals as an airlock for his android body. It'd never work for an adult in a space suit, but for someone who doesn't need to breathe, it's ideal. He must've crawled from Juno's cage, through the tunnels and into the pod. But why?

Lucy's caterwauling is starting to bother him. Her mind must've gone. He pops open the control console for the escape pod and gestures to it.

"The code, if you please. I'd like to get out of here." But she keeps crying. He shakes her and bangs her against the wall, but her suit stops him from having any real impact.

"I'm going to need that code, Lucy."

Nothing. She's utterly incoherent. Letting out a disgusted grunt, he searches the broken-down docking bay for anything that might be of assistance, and finds his answer in the burned slash across the far wall.

Dorian grabs Lucy by the shoulders, and she tries to bat him away. He spins her to face the scorched trail along the wall and marches her one step toward it. A sliver of brilliant light forms at the top, throwing the whole docking bay into sharp relief.

"Lucy," he says.

She screams and hits him, so he pins her arm behind her back and twists.

"Lucy, please listen," he says firmly. "I'm trying to be reasonable here. If you don't punch in that code, I'm going to put you under the tanning slash so I can see how long your face lasts." He's able to wrap his whole hand around her middle finger, and he bends it backward. "Lucy, are you listening?"

"Yes!" she screeches. "Fuck! Let me go!"

It's annoying behavior of her to make demands like that, so he pulls harder on her finger.

"Would you like to add a magic word?"

She tries to turn to face him, but he has her arm locked up. He imagines he could break it even through her suit, if he tries hard enough.

"Please, Dorian."

He shoves her against the console. "It's Director Sudler, Lucy. Now unlock the goddamned pod."

She taps in her code, one number at a time, and he watches carefully: four-eight-zero-eight-sigma. The pad lights green.

Dorian spins Lucy to face him. She looks so tired, so frightened—mentally demolished from the harrowing ordeal.

"Thank you."

With a quick set of movements, he unclips Lucy's helmet and twists it free. Frosted air shoots from the sides, then vanishes. Her bug eyes go wide for a moment, then roll back in her head as sudden and complete decompression takes its toll. Dorian marches her backward to the gash, then with a hard kick, consigns her body to the brutal rays of Kaufmann's light.

Her skin boils up under the solar load, and she convulses as though something of her consciousness has returned. Her hair smokes, and globules of zero gravity fire emerge from her collar, stoked by her oxygen tank. Then the tank blows, propelling her out of sight.

He's wanted to do that since laying eyes on her.

Besides, what would've happened if she'd gotten home with him? What might she have said? Better that Dorian was the only one to make it out. All he needs to do now is step into the escape pod and he can leave.

He can't hear it, but he feels a tremendous grinding through the deck of the docking bay. Something huge is moving through the SCIF side of the central strut. Maybe it's one of the emergency bulkheads opening up. If it's Blue coming after him, Dorian will have to move quickly.

He rushes to the unlocked escape pod and opens the door, clambering inside. There's no atmosphere, but he can change that when it's time to flee. For now, he simply checks his surroundings for anything he doesn't like.

He finds Marcus, lying on the ground, his white blood frozen to his face. Gone is the synthetic's kind smile, replaced with a malformed look of idle curiosity and evaluation. Maybe it's the closest the android can get to genuine fear, or maybe it's that Dorian fucked up his face so badly Marcus can no longer appear sympathetic.

"How you doing, buddy?" Dorian says.

Marcus replies, but the vacuum steals his words. He wants to ask Marcus what the hell he's doing here, but he'd have to charge the atmosphere if he wanted to do that. Instead he sidles over to the open door and peers out, searching for the source of rising vibrations.

Jets of misty air shoot from the emergency bulkhead on the SCIF side, and yellow warning lights flash. The shield rises up, revealing an ailing power loader, burned and melted in places—it fits with the rest of the ruined docking bay interior. It carries an egg crate in one of its pincers, barely able to hold onto the enormous titanium box. It's not moving like a human anymore—it must be on a sort of autopilot.

Anger burns in Dorian's gut. Why is she still trying? Doesn't she understand that she's lost? Does she know of another way off the station?

Then his heart freezes.

The loader is carrying an egg crate. Blue was able to get back into Marcus after Dorian shut him down. Maybe she's the one that set the creatures free, and now she wants an egg for someone who's coming to pick her up. Those eggs may have cost the Company a modest sum to procure, but they'd be worth untold millions to the competition.

If she'd let the beasts out, if she'd put everyone in this position... then she'd helped Dorian discover himself. She holds some stake in his new identity. Like a poison, this very idea taints all the magic he's experienced, the epiphanies he's experienced.

The bitch is still trying to win.

She's been mouthing off to him since he got here, and

she doesn't have the good sense to lie down and die. She subjugated the snatchers. She *struck* him. Now she may have devised a way to escape—a way that might *work*. Even if she can't get off the station, she can still kill herself peacefully.

She doesn't deserve a peaceful death.

He hides as the loader shambles past, shoving through the detritus of the docking bay. The far emergency bulkhead slowly opens, and the power loader disappears from sight. There's an airlock by the crew quarters. If he took a spiral path along the outside of the central strut, he could outrun the sun and reach her before the power loader.

He could show her such exquisite pain.

3 1

THE HARD WAY

Blue sticks to one side of the corridor as she pulls herself along the central strut. It won't be enough to save her if one of the creatures finds her, but at least it might buy her time. She can always pretend to be a dead body.

A troubling smell wafts up from her stomach, where her tubes should've been—a faint forewarning of something far worse, like sepsis. If she doesn't get some antibiotics soon, she won't be *pretending* to be a dead body at all.

She glimpses the med bay. She's so tired, so beaten. Dorian has almost certainly left without her, and she's indulged in a fool's errand. Yet she carries on, every inch closer to an unknown goal. Her eyes drift to the med bay again. If she's going to die, she may as well have some measure of peace. She can wait there in safety.

Blue misses her wheelchairs. The first one must've fallen into Kaufmann's gravity well by now, becoming a pile of carbon and slag before fusing with one of the most effusive power sources in the universe. The second one burned in her room. There aren't a lot of backups. Maybe she could've gotten someone's office chair? No, her legs would just dangle uselessly over the side.

Her stomach hurts so much. It's been through too many traumas, and when she rests her hot cheek against the cold deck, she can press her fingers into her abdomen. It's hard. That's bad.

Changing course, Blue struggles toward the med bay, ready to scream with each passing foot. If she could only get some painkillers, she might be able to bring herself up to a baseline needed to continue. Or she could drift off into peaceful slumber. There's always the comforting embrace of death…

She never wanted to hurt anyone, she tells herself, but knows it's a lie. She wants to hurt Lucy for helping Dorian. She wants to hurt the corporate penny-pinchers who came after her project when she'd tried to produce a cure instead of a weapon. She wants to hurt the fuckers that are coming to pick her up, who indulged in intrigue and espionage, instead of honestly funding a goddamned cure. They could've rescued her, could've rescued everyone, instead of leaving them scrapping for the remaining escape pod like a bunch of animals.

Most of all, she wants to hurt Dorian, and see him brought to his knees like the unspeakably evil bastard he is. He should die for what he did to Anne, and to everyone else he has hurt. He reveled in his actions, and for that, he needs to feel pain.

Blue doesn't bother going to one of the beds. She knows she's beyond fixing, and the blasted things will try to sedate her. She isn't falling for that again. She just needs a place to set up her terminal so she can see what's happening in the outside world—and maybe get a dose of pain meds to blunt the edge. She feels like she's dying, but she's felt like that every day of the last decade, so it's nothing new.

Inching her way toward the compounder, she croaks out a verbal order for an opiate. She's one of the few crew members with authority to order addictive substances, and so it readily complies. She makes it a super-stiff one, since she might not need to wake up, and the machine spits out a syringe. She places the intellijector to her hip, but waits to deliver the payload. She needs to know how much time she has.

Flipping open her terminal, she connects to Marcus.

```
Blue: //Where are you?

Marcus: I'm in the escape pod.

Marcus: Dorian was here.
```

Blue swallows. She taps the keys, one finger at a time.

```
Blue: //But he's not now?

Marcus: He left. I think he's coming to kill you.
```

Marcus: Don't let him kill you, Blue.
It's not good to die.
You see—I'm helping.
I'm here to save you.

The loud hiss of the crew quarters airlock cycle pierces the air. The rush of wind filtering through steel sounds like the cry of one of the creatures, and Blue shivers uncontrollably—she'd rather have a gut full of *Plagiarus praepotens* than Dorian on her body. The creatures are swift, businesslike. The video of what Dorian did to Anne plays through her mind. Dorian takes pleasure in the kill.

It will take a full minute to cycle the crew airlock. Her quarters will be the first place he looks for her. The med bay will be the second. She needs a plan by then, something like what she did to the alien in her room. But looking around the med bay, her mind is blank. It's been too long since she's had her meds, she's exhausted, and everything hurts. The ventilation ducts are so far away, and even if she could make it, they're smaller than the ones in her room.

She doesn't have a pen, or matches.

Blue regards the portable terminal by her side. Even if she took over the power loader, it's still moving through the emergency bulkheads. It won't be here in time.

A klaxon sounds as the inner hatch of the airlock slides open. Stomping footfalls. The clatter of a helmet being tossed aside. He's coming.

She scrambles back toward the entrance to the med

bay, intellijector clutched tightly in her hand. She needs to get the drop on him somehow, with her clumsy hands and slow muscles. Maybe she can level the playing field with her painkillers.

"*Doctor* Marsalis!" he shouts, headed down deeper into the crew quarters, away from her. It's going to take him less than a minute to realize she isn't there. "I'm here to make a house call!"

Reaching the wall beside the doorway, she sits back against it and pulls her knees in close. She clutches the intellijector in both hands like a gun, or maybe a rosary. Either way, she's praying to kill him.

"Blue!" he calls again, his voice breaking with anger. "Hurry up, I've got a flight to catch, and—"

He stops. He's found her crispy room. She presses her forehead against the cool metal of the syringe, her heart thundering. More footsteps ring out as he marches purposefully toward her. It's not hard to imagine him at the Shinjuku office, striding down those glassy hallways, poised to deliver devastating news. Even though he's wearing a spacesuit, she can almost hear the heel-toe click click of fine Italian leather shoes.

She raises the intellijector, ready to plunge it into his calf muscle, but stops short. He'll be wearing a spacesuit. That needle isn't long enough or strong enough to puncture the thick mesh. She stuffs her weapon behind her back as he rounds the corner.

She blinks. There he is. The details are blurry, but his form is full and bristling with malice. He steps one foot inside the med bay and looks down at her.

"Hello, Blue." The blur wears a sharky grin wide enough for even her failing eyes.

His large palm wraps around the side of her face, and he slams her head into the wall. Lights explode behind her eyes and she cries out. Then, he does it again and again. She recovers quicker than she thought she would and realizes, *he's being gentle*. He doesn't want to knock her unconscious or kill her—he wants her to feel everything.

When she raises her hand to push him away, he bats it away with little trouble. He slaps her so hard that her left eye convulses.

"You were intubated, right?" he asks, grabbing a handful of her gown, and leaning down to get in her face. "I'll avoid the throat, then. I don't want you choking to death." He drags her further into the med bay, no doubt hoping for a more visible reaction, but Blue has grown accustomed to keeping her screams down.

"'I didn't think "director" was an honorific title,'" he mocks in Marcus's haughty voice. "Fuck you. Trying to lord your degree over me like I haven't done big things. Who the fuck did you think you were?" He laughs bitterly. "I'm every bit as smart as you, or Dad, or anyone else out there. And you know? If you were so smart, I guess you wouldn't be so fucked right now, would you?"

"Don't leave your daddy issues at my doorstep," she rasps as he picks her up like a baby, every hard edge of his spacesuit digging into her skin. It's like being hugged by a cliff face. He squeezes even tighter, crushing her.

"What was that?" he demands. "What the fuck did you just say to me?"

"I said," she replies, struggling for breath, "you ain't shit and you never were."

"Some people," he mutters, his face reddening, "just don't know when they're done."

"No, they don't," she says.

With every ounce of strength, every iota of coordination, she jams the intellijector up into his carotid and pulls the trigger.

The tip flashes red, like a gunshot.

Dorian sucks in a breath through his teeth. His eyes widen and his face reddens. But there's no hiss, no thunk, no delivery of a potentially lethal dose of opiates. Blue blinks.

The display on the back of the syringe reads **ERROR // RECIPIENT MISMATCH**.

Fuck you, intellijector.

Dorian raises her aloft, his fingers digging into the loose skin at the back of her neck, her atrophied buttock, and slams her down onto the cold steel table with a force she's never felt. Her shoulder hits first, then her head whip-cracks the table with blinding pain. A whimper seeps from her mouth, and Blue feels as though she will never breathe again.

When she tries to draw breath, she finds out she was right.

"Bitch."

Dorian straightens her onto her back, climbs onto the table and straddles her. Distant klaxons sound—the interior emergency bulkhead is opening. The power loader has almost made it to her, but it will be too late.

He delivers a punishing blow to her diaphragm, drawing out what little air she had left. Blue arches her back, raising her hands to her clogged, spasming throat, but he pins her down. Panic possesses her every muscle. There's no air.

He presses his sweaty forehead to hers, lips drawn back in a snarl.

"Fucking choke."

Her eyes feel like they're going to burst. Her neck muscles are like a tangle of roots. She always thought it would be peaceful to choke out this way, but fear takes hold of her, shaking her, begging her not to leave this mortal coil. Darkness pulls at the edge of her vision. The last thing she's going to see is Dorian's smile.

Her heart slows. Her strength fades. She can't resist him any longer. All sounds blur together and disappear.

Then comes infinity and the queer sensation of falling out of time.

A spark.

A pinprick.

A rising fire in her chest.

A slicing sword in her throat.

Her mind begins to unfurl as she tries to make sense

of it. She just needs to get it—

"Clear," the computer says. A strength returns to Blue that she hasn't felt in ages as her whole body spasms. Her heart bursts into flame.

"Charging," the computer says. She knows what comes next, and she can't cry out to stop it.

"Clear."

The tube suctions her lungs as she struggles to scream into it. Her vocal chords won't make the noise as her eyes flutter open. Dorian stands by, smiling at her, testing a steel scalpel on the back of his hand.

He won't let her die.

"Not until I say so."

The medical bed has shoved a tube down her throat to clear it. A needle threads her arm, and Dorian rips it out, sending a spatter of her blood to the floor.

"No painkillers," he says, breaking the tube's articulator.

The metal stomp of the power loader fills Blue's ears as it travels the hallway. The long windows of the med bay pulse yellow with its caution lights.

"Oh, look," Dorian says, glancing behind him. "Your toy is here." He turns back. "I want to know something from you before you die."

She can barely maintain consciousness through the spiraling world. Her gag reflex goes wild as he slowly yanks out the tube in her throat. She can't fight back. She can only lie limply and wheeze.

"The creatures, they're... poetry. Did you let them loose?"

Her slow blink darkens her vision for a moment, and he gently slaps the side of her face. She musters enough mental acuity to shake her head no.

"I think you did," he says. "I think you made Marcus do it. No one else would've deliberately opened the cages."

She shakes her head no again.

"Stop lying. You're going to die. It's time to be honest."

"Not…" Speaking is like vomiting razor blades. "… lying."

"Who else would've done it?"

Then Blue remembers the ship waiting for her escape pod, waiting for her to flee with the sample. How long had it been there? Wireless connections in the SCIF are forbidden—that exposes the SCIF to hackers.

Someone else had connected to Marcus from outside the station.

"It could only be you." Dorian pats her face. "Just admit it, so we can get this over with."

A deafening crash rolls through the med bay as the power loader shoves its pincer through the window, trying to get inside. It crouches, unable to fit through the hole, and smashes the wall again. Its yellow pincer quests toward Dorian, a few feet too short to reach him. Someone else is piloting it—someone who doesn't mind killing people.

Dorian cackles and steps toward the back wall, amused at the loader's antics. Blue musters her last ounce of strength to roll from the bed, and the hard deck slams into her like a truck. He steps down onto the hem of her shirt, and Blue can't pull away.

"Where the fuck are you going?" he asks. "I'm not done with you, not by a longshot." She rolls onto her back and tries to get loose, but he's got her dead to rights. The power loader's yellow caution lights fill the room with twisting shadows—

—some of which persist between flashes.

"Dorian," she whispers, her voice sucked away from the intubation. He doesn't hear her. He just keeps mumbling what he's going to do to her before she dies.

The snatchers draw closer, like stalking cats, as the power loader pounds away at the med bay wall. Its noise must've drawn them here through the maintenance tubes. Blue smiles. This might be the last thing she ever does.

Chitinous black arms wrap around Dorian's chest, and his eyes go from joy, to shock, to anger as the creature sinks its glassy teeth into his shoulder. Rivulets of his blood spill from the wound, but he never breaks eye contact with Blue. He raises a leg to crush her neck, but the beast snatches him from his feet.

Dorian Sudler disappears in a furious blur, screaming her name all the while.

A rough hand wraps around Blue's ankle, and she looks down to see one of the creatures looming over her, dripping saliva through parting lips. She's not scared anymore, because she knows there is justice in the galaxy, after all.

It yanks her toward the med bay door, the skin of her back rubbing against the deck. It hurts, but the pain no longer overwhelms her. She's at peace. In spite of it all, she finds a deep and abiding sense of well-being as the creature drags her into the hall.

Then a scarred, yellow pincer comes down on the creature, folding it in half with a splatter of yellow acid. A glob of its blood strikes Blue's foot, and like a fool, she tries to scrape it off with her other foot. The snatcher acid burrows into her skin, chewing away at each individual pain nerve. Her feet begin to smoke and her eyes fill with tears. This new agony is unlike any she has ever experienced.

"Get in," the power loader rasps, gesturing to the egg crate and shoving it toward her. She shakes her head, willing herself back into the moment, out of the hellfire. The wounds will cauterize. She just has to get to the box.

Once she's pulled herself up the side of the crate, she punches the button to open it. She isn't prepared for the powerful stench that the egg had left inside—rotten meat and antiseptic. She swallows her bile and, with the loader's assistance, plunges headfirst into the airtight chamber. Then the lid closes over her, sealing her inside with the brimstone sulfur smoke of her own burning flesh.

3 2

MASTERPIECE

Dorian awakens in darkness, his world swimming. He remembers nothing of what has transpired. When he tries to pick himself up, his face sticks to the ground, as do his arms and legs. Pain sears his cheek. With a slurping noise, he attempts to pry himself free, but he's glued down tight.

A warm tickle runs down his face and neck, whispering to him that he's reopened his knife wound. He can move one hand, sliding it along his belly to find the emergency release for his spacesuit. Pulling a few tabs and twisting some seals allows him to get his other hand free. Then, he works his way up and down his body, unlatching everything he can find until he bursts forth from the back of the suit, gasping and covered in viscous gunk. Humid air hits his wet skin. His only modesty is the pair of briefs he wore when he donned the spacesuit.

Eyes adjust. Lime-green walls come marching into

focus. Their iridescence reflects and falls upon the cave of chitinous resin, where Dorian now kneels gasping. He reaches out for something to hoist himself up, and finds a solid metal box. Its LED panel strobes to life, acid green, and he shields the lamp to preserve his night vision.

It's an egg crate, wide open, its lethal contents long since evacuated.

His gaze drifts to the floor, and in the sharp relief of electronic light, he finds a fleshy, withered, arachnid form. It rests flat on its back, long fingers curled inward as though grasping at something precious. Dorian instinctively knows what lies locked within those fingers—his own life.

He's infected, and he's going to die very soon. That thought gives him an immense measure of comfort. From Dorian's barren breast, a life will be born, bearing some genetic semblance of him. It will enter this burning ecosystem as his child, more intelligent than the chimpanzees, more beautiful than all the others.

How could Dorian care about balance sheets, performance appraisals, and quarterly earnings reports when his destiny is to co-mingle his starstuff with that of the greatest race of killers ever to grace the galaxy? He touches his naked sternum, pleased with the knowledge that he's finally part of a joint venture worth pursuing.

He pushes to his feet, and the distention of his gut tells him the time is nigh. Dorian shambles toward the door, but in truth he's physically more fit than he's ever felt in his life. He's taken so many injuries, but they're all ignorable under the circumstances—noise in his model of self. He takes a step toward the egg-storage exit, then another. When he reaches the door, two of the creatures descend before him, hissing and shrieking.

They can't kill him. As much as they might enjoy posturing, they're benign now. He reaches toward one, and it snaps at him, the clack of its jaws echoing into the warehouse. He doesn't flinch. He can't. He's becoming.

Fingertips come to rest upon the smooth skull of the beast, and its steaming breath emerges in angry puffs. It hates him, wants to tear him in half, but Dorian is teaching it something he's known his whole career: the power of leverage.

"I'm not going to hurt anything," he says, though whether or not they believe him is questionable. "Just let me pass."

He pushes the beast's snout, and it moves.

Dorian wanders up, through the kennels, through the SCIF commons, across the central strut and into the maintenance tubes. He wants to leave something to them, a gift to commemorate his evolution. He crawls through the maintenance tubes and marvels at the heat they've acquired. Warmed by some tiny sliver of exposure to Kaufmann, hot wind spirals through their depths, blowing against his face.

All the while, the creatures follow at a distance. Either curious or protective, he cannot say. Dorian emerges beside the med bay and walks toward the crew quarters. The only indication of impending doom is the occasional twitch in his gut, like a muscle spasm, but deeper. Its effects on him are almost euphoric. He can do anything he wants now. He wonders if that's some chemical secreted by his passenger, or if it's the simple relief of being divorced from all expectations of civilization.

When he reaches his room, Dorian understands that he's come to his long journey's end. No one can touch him here, in the furthest reaches of space—not the Company, not those fools from finance, not his father. He can finally witness lonesome perfection with no obligation to appear as a human to all the others around him.

Dorian opens the door to his room to find an ever-changing light slashing across the darkness to the beat of the Cold Forge's spin. Some might find it dizzying, but this is where his oil paints live. This is where he can be the man he was always meant to be.

He walks into the center of his quarters to where his easel stands, absorbing the light and shadow, caught between an angry star and uncaring space. That unforgiving balance is where all of humanity lives, they just don't have the vision to understand it. His paints still rest where he left them.

Dorian picks up the brush and his oil palette.

Gestures form out of the chaos, a shape in transit, condensed into a set of flowing lines and hard angles. He dips his brush and brings the fire to it, then the shadow. He wants to teach his heir what this life means, shortly before it's consumed in the fires of an unforgiving sun.

Yellow ochre for rare evolution. Burnt umber for consumption of all living things. It is to be Dorian's only masterpiece, as fleeting as an ice sculpture. His failing condition gives him a rare focus he wishes he'd had in life.

He never should've joined the Company. He should've brought his myriad worlds to the hearts and minds of any who would've listened. He was cunning. He was beautiful. He could've been an artist, no matter what his father told him.

But here, in the last studio on the edge of a galaxy, Dorian finds all that was missing. He works in the character of the souls he's ushered into the hereafter: Javier, Nick, Lucy and fierce, fierce Anne. They've all made indelible marks upon him, which he transfers onto the canvas. And still, the painting is missing something.

When all cultural, corporate, and human expectation has fallen away, Dorian finds his own perfection. A dull ache, then a sharp pain.

It's coming.

It rocks him harder than any punch he's ever taken. It gnaws against his ribs, pushing between them, parting his chest like a curtain. It strains against his skin, every nerve in his body lighting up in tandem.

And then, with a spray of blood, emergence.

His crimson life sprays across the canvas, gouts here, speckles there, completing the composition. Dorian stares in shock as the wormlike being emerges from his form. Together, they have made a gorgeous collaboration. This is his best work, and it shall descend into the gravity well of a star.

The beast burrows back into him to give suckle at his

arteries, and a great peace floods Dorian's body. Darkness closes in upon him.

He is complete.

He has rendered unto the universe what it will accept.

He is a father.

And he shall pass beyond this veil of tears.

If choking to death was a peaceful exit, the egg crate is the opposite. Blue can't be sure what drugs the bed gave her while she was unconscious, but her throat remains open, allowing every shallow breath of smoky flesh to fully penetrate her lungs. Her feet burn like candle wicks, and Blue wonders if the acid will eat into her forever. She dares not touch the wounds again.

The egg crate sways nauseatingly, left to right, in a pendulum swing. The scrabble and scratch of creatures outside fills her ears. They want her so badly, and they assault the egg crate with deafening claws, teeth, and tails. Then come klaxons and hissing.

Then comes the silence of the vacuum.

Blue remains alone in her tiny, smoky coffin, waiting for whatever deliverance might await her. She'd intended to pilot the power loader herself from the inside, but she'd left her portable terminal in the med bay. So now she's in a submersible, sinking into the blackness of space.

There's a gentle thunk and the swaying stops. She's been put down.

Some time passes, but she can't tell how long. It could

be minutes or days. Her existence has become atemporal. She only knows that she's starving yet sick, dizzy yet aware, cold yet feverish.

The lid clicks and blinding light spills inside with her. Fresh air floods her lungs, a feeling she thought she'd never have again. She shuts her eyes as hard as she can, then reopens them, willing the bright blur to become something. The shape of Marcus's ruined face resolves from the ether, and Blue has to blink again to loosen up the tears that flood her vision.

He doesn't smile like he usually does. She thinks of all the horror stories of synthetics losing their minds, and wonders if she's come so far to die by his hands.

"Marcus," she breathes in the remains of a voice she used to have.

He doesn't reply. He crawls to her on his knees, his feet beaten to milky stumps, and lifts her out of the crate like a baby. With plodding movements, he takes her to one of the two cold sleep beds, raising her up over the lip of it. Arms outstretched, on his knees, he must look as though he's offering her up as a sacrifice.

Gently, he rests her onto the cushions, making sure she has no sudden movements. Her feet still burn, but the pain has grown dull compared to what it was.

"Marcus," she whispers again, and he stops, awaiting her question. "Are you happy that I got out? That... I came back, and not Dorian?"

"My happiness is irrelevant to my duty," he replies, his voice metallic and chorusing out of sync with itself.

He positions her limbs and pulls a cryo cap over her head, then runs his hands over her shoulders, settling her clothes, his crooked eyes traveling over her body in search of any impediments to the sleep process.

"I did the right thing, Marcus."

He smiles, his lips canted. "You have never given up, this entire time. As long as there was a glimmer of hope, you pursued it."

The smile fades.

"But when it was Javier's time to give up, you ended him. You used me to conspire with saboteurs and murderers. Dorian would've come back and terminated my life. You will force me to carry on."

He presses a button, and the lid of Blue's cryo pod hums closed. She reaches up and presses a palm to the glass.

"So, no," he says. "I am not happy."

Then he taps a few controls and sleep overtakes her.

A red light passes over Blue's eyes. Then another, and another. Nausea fills her stomach, and dread. She opens her eyes to see red warning lights bouncing off the escape pod ceiling. A voice repeats the same phrase over and over again, and Blue strains to make out the words.

"Warning: unidentified life form detected."

Her breathing comes faster now, and she shakes the cotton from her brain. Reaching up to touch the glass, she draws back fingers blistered from the cold.

"Hello?" she calls, her voice distant somehow.

"Good morning, Blue." It's Marcus, his voice like wet gravel. "I woke you up because I've changed my mind."

She searches for him. She's so cold. Something has gone wrong with the cryo pod, and now frost creeps up her legs.

Marcus's hand, encrusted with android blood, falls across the glass, and he pulls himself atop her, straddling the pod. His torn right eye leers at her, and his left stares at some faraway object through a crushed orbital socket.

"You were never worthy," he slurs, shining onyx ink dribbling up around the corners of his mouth. He leans back and takes a deep breath, flexing his neck as he does. With a sudden heave, he paints the glass canopy black with the stolen sample.

Blue shrieks and presses back into her bed, drawing her arms close. The sample smears together with Marcus's blood, and she can see it undulating, crawling and curling. He's blinded her as a squid might, plunging her into darkness.

"Marcus, no!" she cries. With each breath, she can smell her burned feet once more. A deafening thump splits her eardrums. Another comes, and she spies the smear of Marcus's fist through the glass. On the third strike, the glass spiderwebs, its vertices meeting directly before her eyes.

"Please!" she begs, her voice shaking. She crosses her arms in front of her face, but he strikes again.

A tiny droplet of *Plagiarus praepotens* forms at the center of the web, hanging down above her. It worms around, stretching for something to touch. Then it falls onto her bare forearm, sinking into her, staining her veins black with its corruption. Its cold rush travels up her body, spreading through her, sprouting thorns and barbs in her veins. The skin of her infected arm begins to writhe, pressing hungrily toward her.

It splits, and there's a flash of chitin.

3 3

RIBBON CUTTING

"You're all right. You're all right," Rook says, pressing his soft hand to her forehead.

Blue opens her eyes to gentle nightlight and a breeze. A low orange glow floods her space as she awakens, falling upon a desk, a nightstand, and a plethora of medical equipment. She can't feel her arms and legs, but that's normal. They put her in a full-body management machine. She rests her head against the lip of her high-tech casket.

It's been two cycles. Rook is the only face she's seen, but he's been kind to her, as all synthetics are. Rook has a different skin tone, bone structure, and eye color from Marcus, but somehow they're exactly the same.

"You were dreaming," he says.

"So I noticed." Her reply comes through the speaker mounted over her chest. She can't speak anymore. They're afraid it'll kill her, so they've opted for direct oxygenation of her organs. "It was about Marcus."

"We already took care of him. He was happy not to suffer."

"I understand." That doesn't make her feel any better.

A short chime sounds, and a blue light flares. Rook turns to look at it.

"You're being summoned," he says, and without asking he slips the net of a much sleeker brain-direct interface over her bare scalp. "Are you ready?"

Blue gives him a short nod: the most motion she can possibly display.

Rook returns to a console and keys something into it. Blue closes her eyes and the world falls away. It's a smoother transition than her bare-bones system on the Cold Forge. They must've spent a pretty penny on it.

She finds herself in a brightly lit laboratory, filled with top-of-the-line equipment. Two people sit in chairs awaiting her—a middle-aged man and a woman, both wearing crisp suits. They're probably the most non-threatening people Blue has ever seen, with a little bit of extra fat on their faces, giving them an appearance somewhere between childlike and everyman. They recognize her presence inside whatever synthetic body she's connected to, and smile cordially.

A third chair sits empty. The woman gestures to it, but Blue remains standing.

"I'm Helen," she says, "and this is Dan. Would you mind stating your full name for us?"

"Blue Grace Marsalis." Her voice is female, though sonorous. She glances down at her body to find an approximation of her hands from so long ago.

Dan gestures to her. "We, uh, thought you might like a body more in line with your own, instead of forcing you to walk around in a Marcus." His cheeks swell like a baby's when he grins.

Blue looks both of them over. They seem so hopeful. "I prefer a male body."

"Of course." Helen nods. "Our mistake. We'll get that rectified. Dan, if you could—"

"Way ahead of you, Helen." Dan types something into his portable terminal. It couldn't have been easy for them to make a body like this for her, but they didn't mind her rejection at all. He looks back to Blue. "What would you like us to call you?"

"Doctor Marsalis."

"We have cookies, Doctor," Helen says, and Rook walks in behind her holding a plate of soft, buttery chocolate chip cookies. The scent is comically enticing, almost a parody of temptation. "Your previous body couldn't really taste correctly, but this one has a few upgrades."

Blue takes a cookie and bites into it, warm tendrils of chocolate pulling away where it breaks.

"Seems like the perfect time to take it for a test drive," Helen continues. "Dan, would you like one?"

Dan pats his gut. "No thanks. The doc is telling me I need to lose a few—"

"Why did you kill everyone on the Cold Forge?" Blue asks, and Dan and Helen stop dead. In the awkward silence, Blue detects a few strains of classical music wafting in through a speaker somewhere.

Dan leans forward, steepling his fingers. "The personnel on board RB-232 were conducting dangerous and unethical experiments."

"Bullshit," says Blue. "I deserve to know."

Helen looks to Dan, and they share a look. Some of her politeness grows brittle and chips away.

"The station," Helen begins, "as well as Glitter Edifice, represented a substantial investment for Weyland-Yutani Corporation. It was a chance to deal them a significant financial blow."

Blue remembers how Kambili rescued her, and her chest hurts.

They didn't deserve to die.

"Every one of the personnel on board the Cold Forge were working on high-value projects," Helen continues. "A loss this large on their books, both in terms of infrastructure and human resources, could substantially alter their share price come quarterly reporting."

"Human resources," Blue echoes. "Is that what you do?"

They both nod, and she wrinkles her nose in disgust.

Blue walks to the chair and sits down. "I think you would've liked the last HR guy I knew. I bet you'd have a lot in common." She glares at them. "So this was all a big play to damage Weyland-Yutani stock price? Why?"

"Come the end of the fiscal year, Seegson Corporation will be a five percent shareholder," Helen says. "That'll get us a spot on the Board. Symbiosis is the best way to survive, don't you think?"

"And think of the power differential when we

approach them with an applied pharmacological usage of the sample you've brought us," Dan adds.

Blue starts to speak, but Dan raises a hand. The prick actually interrupts her.

"We're here to offer you a choice, Doctor Marsalis. We don't believe your research is complete. We want you to continue with us, and we'll sustain you for as long as you need."

"To research a cure?"

"To design a cure is to control the sample," Helen replies. "We want a broad portfolio of applications before we approach the possibility of a merger."

Blue searches their faces. More of the same corporate stooges, just wearing different name tags. The problem with Dorian Sudler was that he wasn't one in a million—he was a promotable opportunist. He contained every trait Weyland-Yutani valued in an executive: quick, cruel, creative, self-starter. He was brutally efficient, the type of man to obey a business model over a moral compass. Those were all skills required to make it in the modern workplace.

Blue played chess with the devil. She knew his tricks, so Helen and Dan had no idea who they were fucking with. She'd design her cure, and they'd double-cross her, but she'd be two steps ahead by then. She couldn't be sure how they'd come at her, or what she'd use to respond, but she knew some things for certain.

She was clever. She was powerful.

She was unbreakable.

After all, she'd been through the forge.

ACKNOWLEDGEMENTS

By trade, I am not a biologist, virologist, entomologist, or physicist. Luckily, I know people who have pushed the boundaries of genetics, experimented on bugs, and shot things into space. Thanks to Dr. Stephenson, Lali DeRosier, Sola, and Dr. Granade for helping me with the science stuff. I'd be screwed without friends to undo my ignorance.

This journey began when my agent, Connor Goldsmith, asked me what my favorite sci-fi properties were. "Alien" was the first on my lips. He brought home this book deal, an incredible gift for me, and I'm so grateful.

Thanks to my editor, Steve Saffel, who worked with me to turn into reality this long dream of writing for Alien. It was nice to prove to my parents that I didn't waste my time by wearing out our VCR on those tapes.

Thanks to the folks at Titan Books, including Nick Landau, Vivian Cheung, Laura Price, Ella Chappell, Joanna Harwood, Jill Sawyer, Paul Gill, Katharine Carroll, Polly Grice, and Cam Cornelius, as well as the team at Fox: Carol Roeder, Nicole Spiegel, and Steve Tzirlin. And, of course, thanks to Lydia Gittins for working tirelessly to promote this book. Lydia was assigned to my debut novel before moving over to Titan, and I am so glad I was able to work with her once more.

ABOUT THE AUTHOR

Alex White was born and raised in the American south. He takes photos, writes music and spends hours on YouTube watching other people blacksmith. He values challenging and subversive writing, but he'll settle for a good time.

In the shadow of rockets in Huntsville, Alabama, Alex lives and works as an experience designer with his wife, son, two dogs and a cat named Grim. Favored past times include Legos and race cars. He takes his whiskey neat and his espresso black.